Listening to Ourselves

More Stories from "The Sound of Writing"

BOOKS BY ALAN CHEUSE

Candace and Other Stories

The Bohemians

The Grandmothers' Club

Fall Out of Heaven

The Tennessee Waltz and Other Stories

The Light Possessed

BOOKS BY CAROLINE MARSHALL

Fugitive Grace

Listening to Ourselves

More Stories from "The Sound of Writing"

Edited by
ALAN CHEUSE
and
CAROLINE MARSHALL

with a foreword by James A. Michener

Anchor Books
DOUBLEDAY
New York London Toronto Sydney Auckland

AN ANCHOR BOOK
PUBLISHED BY DOUBLEDAY
a division of Bantam Doubleday Dell Publishing Group, Inc.
1540 Broadway, New York, New York 10036

ANCHOR BOOKS, DOUBLEDAY, and the portrayal of an anchor
are trademarks of Doubleday, a division of
Bantam Doubleday Dell Publishing Group, Inc.

Book design by Claire Vaccaro

Library of Congress Cataloging-in-Publication Data

Listening to ourselves : more stories from "The sound of writing" /
edited by Alan Cheuse and Caroline Marshall ; with a foreword by
James A. Michener. — 1st Anchor Books ed.
p. cm.
1. Short stories, American. I. Cheuse, Alan. II. Marshall,
Caroline, 1943– . III. Sound of writing.
PS648.S5L57 1994
813′.0108—dc20 93-10828 CIP

ISBN 0-385-46954-3

PRINTED IN THE UNITED STATES OF AMERICA

FIRST ANCHOR BOOKS EDITION: January 1994

1 3 5 7 9 10 8 6 4 2

This book is dedicated to Elizabeth J. Morris,
known to the thousands of writers who
send us manuscripts as "E.,"
and to us, as friend

Contents

Foreword

It was exhilarating to learn that this second volume of stories from "The Sound of Writing" was to be published. When a man or woman has spent a lifetime trying to write works that will instruct, entertain, or illuminate lives, he or she naturally begins to wonder who will step forward to continue the great tradition of storytelling. The older writer looks with approval at publications which bring younger writers to public attention and to schools which dedicate themselves to helping young aspirants learn their trade.

Anthologies are among the agencies which serve our national culture, for, with the demise of the magazines which used to publish short fiction, writers have had to look to them as pathways to a larger audience. The perceived wisdom in earlier days was: "Publish three short stories in the good magazines, and some book publisher will ask you to write a novel." If I were a beginning writer now, I would fight to get broadcast on "The Sound of Writing" and then into a book like this.

But "The Sound of Writing" also provides a home for the proven writer who finds delight in writing shorter tales or in developing telling incidents not suited for development into full-length novels. Some contributors to this volume are established writers, as their stories demonstrate.

So I was honored when the editors asked me to provide a foreword to this second volume. Anthologies like this are a major adornment to America's cultural landscape. They deserve wide circulation, careful readership, and enthusiastic support, for they nurture writing talent and indicate directions in which the books of the next decades will be moving.

In these days of violent change in publishing and turmoil among writers striving for a foothold in our profession, I find myself drawn, as well, to university programs which provide postgraduate courses in writing, especially those giving the Master of Fine Arts as a terminal degree. This degree is the arts equivalent of the Ph.D., except that the M.F.A. requires not a formal thesis but the completion of a substantial writing project, such as a book-length collection of poetry, a body of short stories, a screenplay, a novel, or a book of nonfiction. The student learns a great deal about writing, past and present, in these programs, and then proves his or her capability by bringing to successful conclusion a major writing project. The three-year M.F.A. has an enormous advantage over a two-year course in creative writing, for it not only prepares the young person to write but also certifies him or her as a teacher of writing and the literary arts at the high school, community college, and university level. It is a degree worth having, for it puts many additional arrows in the writer's quiver.

The successful graduate leaves such university programs qualified to follow either of two courses: leaping headlong into a full writing career or taking a position on some faculty to teach creative writing. If the latter sounds like hedging—''If he can't write, maybe he can teach''—I respond from a lifetime of monitoring the writing field as a student, beginner aspirant, university professor, editor in a major publishing company, and practitioner: Nonsense! Neither the M.F.A. nor teaching is in any way an evasion. The overwhelming responsibility of the young writer is to earn enough money to stay alive till she or he reaches the age when one's career may be sufficiently established to permit full-time concentration on writing alone.

I think it wonderful when some teenage brilliant like Truman Capote, Gore Vidal, or Françoise Sagan flames across the heavens like a full-blown meteor. We should all be entitled to display our talents like that, but alas, most of us are not so gifted. We have to struggle, as I did, accomplishing nothing of note till we are in our mid-thirties or forties. I am mindful, too, that talented, all-purpose writers like Thornton Wilder or excellent poets like John Ciardi have had to spend much or all of their lives teaching in order to survive, while other would-be writers like Ernest Hemingway and Ben Hecht served their apprenticeships as cub reporters. I marvel at the survival strategies of young writers. My heart goes out to them; they deserve every encouragement we can give.

I am painfully aware of the difference between today's meager avenues to publishing and the wealth of opportunities that were available to me when I was starting out. Then the aspiring writer could mail off his or her early efforts to any of a dozen prosperous magazines, each of which offered five or six stories a month: popular magazines like *A Woman's Home Companion, The Saturday Evening Post, Collier's,* and the two literary journals, *Harper's* and *The Atlantic Monthly.* In those days, as I've suggested, the traditional route to a writing career was to place three or four worthy short stories in the magazines and wait for book publishers who recognized merit to issue an invitation, often accompanied by the promise of a modest advance if one wished to submit a full-length novel. After I started in the 1940s with two rather good short stories in *The Saturday Evening Post,* I was quickly invited to write for two other magazines and to take an editorial job on a third. I was on my way.

Today the magazines in which so many of my generation started no longer exist, and those which have survived, like *Harper's* and *The Atlantic,* publish little fiction. *The New Yorker* and *Esquire* deserve credit for continuing to provide a medium in which writers can cultivate their reputations. If we subtracted from the American scene all the recent writers who got their starts in these two magazines, our culture would be impoverished.

We older writers who are involved with M.F.A. programs therefore cherish the anthologies and the little magazines which strive to keep alive the literary tradition, for we know that they help to keep American writing vital. We are indebted to them.

"The Sound of Writing," unique in its radio format, is one

such magazine. If I were now just starting out, I would do everything in my power to place one of my stories in its broadcast lineup, and subsequently in a collection like this, or in the little magazines which so often provide entry to anthologies. And if, perchance, my story did appear in this volume or one like it, I would be justified in believing that I had at least caught a foothold in my profession. I would be on my way.

I suspect that in the years ahead you will encounter the names listed here again and again, for the writers who will ultimately replace Saul Bellow and Eudora Welty will come from such beginnings.

—James A. Michener

Introduction

Anyone growing up in the United States between the 1920s and the 1940s had his ears full most of the time. Whether one was sitting at the kitchen table, or in the easiest chair of the living room, listening to the radio was as American as saying "as American as apple pie." In our New Jersey house the evening radio news took precedence over just about everything, including supper-table conversation and occasional family quarrels. On Sunday mornings it was "Uncle Don" reading the comic strips aloud. And then there were the nights when you could scarcely hear yourself breathe with the sounds of "Gangbusters" or "The Green Hornet" or Saturday mornings with the fantasies of "Let's Pretend" or "The Buster Brown Show" trembling in the air. Where was this undersea kingdom, the Land of the Lost, to which all lost articles tended, that we heard about when Froggy plunked his magic twanger? Beneath Raritan Bay just down the road? Somewhere nearby, we believed!

All those stories, all those lost hours. It was a time of the ear; the aural was king. Then television swept through the country like some strange neurological plague and closed our ears even as it—we thought—opened our eyes to the world. Decades passed, TV images metastasized into computer-generated video games, and now, like the oddly shimmering light patterns of an optical migraine, they, too, seem to be running their course, passing off to the edges of our vision.

If you can imagine the years between the end of World War I and the beginning of our serious approach to the millennium as a battle between the attentions of the ear and the distractions of the eye, we now live in a time when the ear has managed some major tactical victories. Twenty years of National Public Radio has won millions of old listeners back to their places at the radio and made many new converts among those born into a world that conventional wisdom had long ago ceded to the tube.

It was in this climate that ''The Sound of Writing'' was launched in 1987 as a showcase for the contemporary American short story. At first hearing, the casual observer might conclude that our weekly half-hour debut of new short fiction by some of America's best—and best-known—writers, and by many newcomers to the short story as well, is yet another important example of the renaissance of American radio programming. I, for one, would be happy to let it rest with that if something else, something perhaps more important, weren't also true about the show. While our production appeals to that same sense of wonder that kept millions of us young listeners fixed in place alongside our radios during the grand years of U.S. broadcasting, ''The Sound of Writing'' belongs as much to the future as to the past.

Let me take a step back to make this leap forward. In the 1930s and 1940s a great many popular (and what today we would call mass-market) magazines came out each month and included, as James Michener has pointed out, much original short fiction between their covers. Faulkner, Fitzgerald, Hemingway, and Katherine Anne Porter, among others, had a regular venue for their best short stories. But it was a forum that by the end of the post-World War II period had begun to disintegrate, the magazines succumbing to changing currents in the marketplace, the rise of television, and, some pessimists would say, the first signs of the current decline in reading as a primary means for connecting to the world.

Seen from a certain perspective, ''The Sound of Writing'' may look like the aural reincarnation of just such mass-market magazines which published fiction for a large middle-class audience, the same audience that drifted away from print to television and is now drifting back to broadcast radio productions. Maybe. One could argue the case: Each program presents the public premiere of two stories, much as *The Saturday Evening Post* did. But since radio at one time also had its theater programs, wonderfully imaginative shows with terrific narratives that caught the attention of large listening audiences, our short story magazine of the air might appear to some people to be radio theater reborn. Again, just maybe.

But the situation is more complicated than this. Although we present stories to a large audience the way the old magazines used to do, and although we broadcast these narratives over the airwaves each week to hundreds of thousands of people who sit within earshot of their FM radios, we're neither strictly a mass-market magazine nor radio theater, but, rather, a hybrid of both. Because of the special potential of our venue—National Public Radio—the show can be more than just another vehicle by which writers publish stories and an audience finds them. It is, unlike any other literary venture of its kind, a *national* project, since the NPR affiliates who pull the show in each week by means of their satellite dishes are located all around the fifty states. Because our stories then move at the speed of sound out from these various FM affiliates in towns and on college campuses across the country, they spread far and wide beyond the limits of these local venues. Consider this: Some may listen to the show in an apartment high above city traffic. Others will hear only birdsong or the yip and whine of coyotes as they turn up the dial—or will soon be driving over a vast desert distance when they next pick up "The Sound of Writing" in their ears. This is *electronic publishing* at its finest, and it reaches an audience that is, I would guess, a lot more diverse than that of most literary magazines and probably more discerning than the readership of most mass-market pulp.

As for radio *theater,* that's not what we do. As many of you already know, we don't present dramatized readings of short stories. We offer good—I might even say great—readings by good actors, but nothing that will detract from the primary experience of allowing a story to reenact itself in your own mind. They're the kind of readings, we hope, that the writers themselves would be pleased in the best of all possible circumstances to deliver in their own voices.

Bringing the best new stories we can find to the largest possible audience by means of state-of-the-art radio broadcasting, stories by the masters of this second half of the century, stories by as yet unfamiliar writers whose names will last beyond the millennium: that's our mission as we see it. So we call "The Sound of Writing" America's "short story magazine of the air" because it's a hybrid for our time—part throwback to the grand old days of broadcasting, part radio that's moving forward toward the next century, not just revived but more vital than ever, charged with the business of making good its part in the national culture. So the show may be a forerunner of all sorts of technological innovations for the serious reader—stories at your fingertips *wherever* you may happen to be—novels in your eye or in your inner ear. But the best of all things may be that it saves the best of the past, those days when we were children sitting around the radio at the kitchen table on a Saturday morning, waiting for the words on the air that would help us travel to the fabled Land of the Lost . . . so that we might find ourselves again someday.

—Alan Cheuse

A friend of mine, friend that she is, has a habit of interrupting me in my headlong telling about some daily woe or wonderment. "*Listen to yourself,*" she'll suggest in the parlance of therapists and self-helpsters so popular these days. "*Do you hear what you're saying?*"

Stopped in my tracks, I realize that I must have just taken a turn, stark naked, in the mirror of my words. But when I think back to what I've described, my chagrin always dissolves. Offered an occasion to pause and pay attention, I invariably see the shape of who I really am—or someone I love is—moving through something I or they have just done or are about to do. Without exception, my small tale's revelations let me see clearly, too, how whatever it is we're up to is utterly, eloquently human.

This is the way it is with words: They can work for you, and they can work against you. But in stories, it seems to me, *words always work for us,* whether that story is conveyed in conversation or as a formal piece of short fiction. Like my friend, they give us occasion to reveal ourselves, then urge reflection. And like a friend, they introduce us to each other. Indeed, I would argue that stories are among our *best friends.* How else to account for the fact that storytelling, no matter the medium, has been with us since the first utterance of an intelligible grunt? Best friends, despite our passing, *remember us.* Stories do no less, and theirs is arguably the most generous testament to our humanity.

No stories seem to me better able to prove the point than those we have gathered to introduce you to here. As Alan often says on "The Sound of Writing," stories "tell us who we really are." Those you will find here do just that. Like good friends, they offer us a glimpse of the complex, evolving creatures we are beneath emotions and attitudes made fashionable, instantly classic, by the media—attitudes we too quickly imagine others wearing, in which we dress our own public selves. They are the kind of story we need now as a nation, these days when we are so various, sometimes judgmental, a people. They offer us the kind of honesty that forces understanding, but gently, with subtlety, goodwill.

I think of Julia Alvarez's story "Snow," for example, the exquisite epiphany you will meet as the volume opens. With breathtaking brevity, it divulges a simple, if startling truth, a truth that John Edgar Wideman also makes manifest in wrenching detail later in his story "Newborn Thrown in Trash and Dies." The truth: That if we were only able to see from another perspective what to us is familiar, hence acceptable, we would realize how strange and arbitrary it really is. Indeed, how *unacceptable.* Conversely, the shifting world that Gerald Vizenor's tribal trickster offers us in "Almost Browne" is a strange place, but through "his" wonderful wordplay it gradually begins to seem all too familiar. That the whys and wherefores of the world he gives us remain, at the same time, wholly incomprehensible is its bitterly ironic truth, a truth at once amusing and sad.

Each of these stories and many more to be found herein ask us to consider how relative our individual reality really is. Like Rick Bass's lyrical offering, they take us to "The Valley," then demonstrate how the weather and terrain of a time and place work to create a state of mind. They show us how easily that state can be entered, how easily it can be left.

If these stories "noodge" us to pay attention, to listen to ourselves, to what we're really saying, as my friend is wont to do, there are others here, again like friends, which call upon our empathy even as they explore the rigors and the limits of that most congenial impulse.

There is Faye Moskowitz's "Spring Break," a *cri de coeur* saturated with a passion to understand, for one, and her good friend Richard McCann's "Fugitive Light, Old Photos," for another. For all their yearning, their protagonists, like Ken Chowder's narrator in "We're in Sally's House," still "can't know what Rich knows, exactly." Nor can they find the dignity and peace that the actor Simon Fantara so hopes to find by assuming another man's character—the ultimate empathetic act—in William Kittredge's luminous "Looking Glass." Like those soul-bearing moments one has with a confidant, even a newly minted one, these stories pull us out of ourselves.

But if some of the stories you meet here remind you of the intensity, even the effort, of fellowship, most will put you in mind of the kind of brief, engaging meeting you're likely to have on a train or on a plane, where your seatmate, a complete stranger, begins gradually to describe his or her life, one both akin to and utterly unlike your own, and soon you are sitting, chin cupped in hand, utterly rapt. The characters in Robert Olen Butler's "Crickets," David Shields's "Audrey," and Elizabeth Winthrop's "The Golden Darters" grip one that way, it seems to me. But that is to name only three, rather capriciously, of the several dozen included here who do no less.

Unlike those strangers from whose unexpected companionship and newfound warmth you must depart on leaving planes and trains, however, you can return to all the good folk whom you meet here. And whenever you please, once you have made their acquaintance! We hope that you will indeed find them good company, and that you'll seek them out, as we do, again and again, as one does the old friends *who know us best.*

—Caroline Marshall

Listening to Ourselves

More Stories from "The Sound of Writing"

Snow

JULIA ALVAREZ

In the summer of 1960 my family immigrated to the United States, fleeing the tyrant Trujillo. In New York we found a small apartment with a Catholic school nearby, taught by the Sisters of Charity, hefty women in long black gowns and bonnets that made them look peculiar, like dolls in mourning. I liked them a lot, especially my grandmotherly fourth-grade teacher, Sister Zoe. I had a lovely name, she said, and she had me teach the whole class how to pronounce it: "Yo-lan-da." As the only immigrant in my class, I was put in a special seat in the first row by the window, apart from the other children so that Sister Zoe could tutor me without disturbing them.

Soon I picked up enough English to understand holocaust was in the air. Sister Zoe explained to a wide-eyed classroom what was happening in Cuba. Russian missiles were being assembled, trained supposedly on New York City. President Kennedy, looking worried too, was on the television at home, explaining we might have to go to war against the Communists. At school, we had air-raid drills: an ominous bell would go off and we'd file into the hall, fall to the floor, cover our heads with our coats, and imagine our hair falling out, the bones in our arms going soft. At home, my mother and my sisters and I said a rosary for world peace. I heard new vocabulary: "nuclear bomb," "radioactive fallout," "bomb shelter." Sister Zoe explained how it would happen. She drew a picture of a mushroom on the blackboard and dotted a flurry of chalk marks for the dusty fallout that would kill us all.

The months grew cold, November, December. It was dark when I got up in the morning, frosty when I followed my breath to school. One morning as I sat at my desk daydreaming out the window, I saw dots in the air like the ones Sister Zoe had drawn—random at first, then lots and lots. I shrieked, ''Bomb! Bomb!'' Sister Zoe jerked around, her full black skirt ballooning as she hurried to my side. A few girls began to cry.

But then Sister Zoe's shocked look faded. ''Why, Yolanda dear, that's snow!'' She laughed. ''Snow.''

''Snow,'' I repeated. I looked out the window warily. All my life I had heard about the white crystals that fell out of American skies in the winter. From my desk I watched the fine powder dust the sidewalk and parked cars below. Each flake was different, Sister Zoe had said, like a person, irreplaceable and beautiful.

The Valley

RICK BASS

One day I fled the South, fled my job, and ran to the heart of snow, the Far Northwest. I live in a cabin with no electricity, and I'm never—never—leaving.

There aren't many people up here, in this valley—thirty-three—and rather than disliking almost everyone, as I found it so easy to do in the city, I can now take time to love practically everyone, all thirty-three of them. I have to start small; I have to get it right.

Wendy Michaels is sixty years old, lives up in the woods, takes in stray dogs as they come her way. There are more than you'd think: they jump out of the backs of trucks, or they just run away from home, and strike out for the north.

Wendy's is the last cabin they come to, before going over into Canada. She keeps a large team of sled dogs—huskies and malamutes, blue-eyed creatures that have so much wolf in them that they do not know how to bark and can only howl.

When the moon comes up over the mountains that ring our small bowl of a valley like a high fence, all of Wendy's dogs begin to howl, a sound that echoes all around the valley. Perhaps the wild, strong, sled dogs attract the strays. Whatever the reason, dogs always show up at Wendy's.

Often we'll see one running down the road, dragging a broken leash, a broken chain—they're big dogs—and it will be heading north, for Wendy's.

She's got a holding pen, and she keeps them for one week—puts an ad on the blackboard out in front of the Mercantile and uses her radio to call the vet down in Libby, sixty miles away, up across the windy, snowdrift-covered (even in August) pass. Then, if no one claims the dog after that week, she does a very odd thing.

She hikes up to the top of Hensley Mountain with the dog and sits down with it up there and watches it for a while.

You can see all of the valley from the top of Hensley. It's above the tree line, just barely, and the wind whips and gusts, blows your hair in your eyes. Wendy must feel a little like God, sitting up there watching everything.

She watches that dog—watches the way it pants, the way it looks out at the valley below and out at Canada—and Wendy knows dogs so well that she can tell, up in that blowing wind, if the dog can survive on its own or not. If it can, she'll unclip the dog's leash, take the collar off, and let it run off down the mountain, down into the deep woods that cross over into Canada—she'll let the dog keep going the direction it was headed, will let it have its wish. But if Wendy doesn't see what she's looking for, sitting up there with the dog, she'll lead it back down the mountain, back to her cabin, and later in the day she will drive it down to the pound, where, almost always, it will be the end of the line for that runaway dog. There is a man in the valley, never mind his name, who for a dollar will take unwanted dogs up the road a ways and gas them or shoot them; but Wendy, needless to say, does not employ his services.

I am like those stray dogs, and I think Wendy is, too. Those dogs have run a long way to get to this valley.

No one has money in the valley up here—no one has money even in the little town sixty miles away—and some of the people who have sled teams up here rely on road kills, occasionally, to feed all their dogs—such large, hungry dogs—and for a fact, you never see a road-killed deer or elk up here. But that may also be because whenever one of us does strike a deer, instead of leaving it, we load it into the truck (if the truck is still driveable) and head into the Dirty Shame Saloon.

The Dirty Shame Saloon sits at the base of Rausch Mountain,

which, back in the forties, had a radar dish on top of it, one of a whole chain of dishes the Air Force had set up along the northwest peaks, along the Canadian border, to detect bombers coming over from Russia—they'd just have a zip across Alaska, across the Yukon, British Columbia, and they'd be here, dive-bombing and strafing the valley, riddling the Dirty Shame (which has been here forever) with bullets, bombing the Mercantile—but nothing ever appeared, though the radar dish still sits up there, abandoned, and the lonely dirt road to the top, the dirt road leading up into the clouds, has long been grown over, crisscrossed with wind-fallen timber and young aspen trees. But something that did not get grown over, did not fall into disrepair, is the warning siren that was supposed to sound whenever a Russian plane was detected. The owner of the Dirty Shame is good with tools, good with electronics, and he hiked up there one day and disassembled the siren, brought it down to the bar, and mounted it out on the front porch; and now, every time someone strikes a deer and brings it in for barbecue, Joe, the owner, shorts the siren's wires with the blade of his pocketknife and the wail goes up. All the dogs in the valley, and all the wolves and the coyotes living up in the woods, go crazy—and people as far away as Idaho and Washington State can hear it, though the roads are too bad, it would be a long day's drive for any of them to get here in time for the barbecue—and we all know, everyone knows, that something has been freshly killed and that there is going to be a barbecue in the evening.

If it's summertime—and though this place is perhaps best defined in winter, it's the summer that I want to write about—then we'll bring lettuce from our gardens and some of the families will bake bread; Doug, who is not a veterinarian but who is good with animals, who sews them up (as well as people sometimes), will bring jars of honey from his beehives—all of these things are possible during the summer and we do not take them for granted—and we'll all meet down at the saloon around six or six-thirty. Dave Blackburn brings his banjo, Sue Weller her fiddle. Terjaney has an electric accordion that used to belong to his father. The sky stays light until almost midnight. We dance. Wendy has a little go-cart that her dogs pull down the road in summer, and she shows up on that. There are twenty-six registered voters in the valley, and almost that many children.

I want to tell you what happened to Terjaney's father.

He was playing the accordion, which he'd brought over with him from Hungary, and we'd never seen anything like it before.

It had all these rows and rows of colored lights, like a jukebox, flashing in the night, and the sound was magnificent.

Old Mr. Terjaney would drink a lot—we all did, the beer was free and cold (not Joe's store-bought brew but the beer we all made in our cellars during the slow winters and brought to the barbecue in mayonnaise jars, boxes and boxes of those jars, which we kept chilled in the river)—and old Mr. Terjaney would get out in the road and dance as he played his accordion; he'd dance around and around, big one-footed polkas and waltzes, hopping and singing, playing that accordion, and he usually kept one of those big jars of beer perched on top of the accordion.

The accordion was strapped to his chest so that he didn't have to hold it—it was a huge sucker—but it was also electrical.

There's no electricity in our valley, no phones either—and never will be. It's just too remote, too inaccessible, but we sometimes run things off portable generators (again, left over from the Air Force days), and that's what Terjaney—old Terjaney—was doing with his accordion.

He spilled his beer, the whole jar of it, while he was dancing. The accordion was hot anyway from all the use he had been giving it, and it exploded like fireworks: electrocuted old Mr. Terjaney right out there on the street, in front of us. We thought it was something he'd done on purpose, some special function the instrument was capable of when he pressed a certain button, perhaps, and we thought he was still dancing, too, and we were cheering for him at first, while all this was going on.

It's a hard country. It's amazing that Joe was able to repair the accordion.

• • •

Winter—I must speak of it, even if only briefly. When you go out to get wood for your fireplace, if it is snowing, tie one end of a rope around your waist and tie the other end to the cabin door. The snow can start coming down so much harder, in the short time it takes you to get to the woodshed, that you can get lost on your way back. It doesn't sound like it's possible. But it happened to me, once when I went out—a light snow turned into a heavy snow in just seconds, and then into a blizzard in minutes—and so I didn't risk returning because I had heard all those stories, the things that panic can do to you; and I stayed in the woodshed all night and waited for daylight. I felt ridiculous, but not as ridiculous as dying a mile from my cabin, or farther, when all I had wanted to do was get a stick of wood.

There is some compass in all of us that does not want us to walk a straight line. I respect this, and do not try to challenge it, in blizzards. If I don't have the rope tied to me and the snow kicks up, then I sit down in the woodshed and make myself as warm as possible and wait.

Sometimes people run out of gas—visitors, not locals—up on the pass, where traffic only goes by every second or third day during the winter, and some of them freeze in their cars, traveling without heavy clothes, without sleeping bags in the back, and others freeze in the woods when they get out of their cars and try to walk for help. All the people up here have CB and shortwave radios in their trucks. You can live in a dangerous place quite easily. But to visit it is another thing.

We've got a nice cemetery. There are two cemeteries, actually—one that no one seems to know about, up in the hills above the river, that this kid just found while out walking one day. But the other cemetery, which originally catered mostly to loggers (since they were the ones who used it the most, what with trees falling on them and saws back-bucking and trucks and skidders rolling off cliffs and the like) is now used by everybody, is majestic.

It's up on Boyd Hill—Boyd Hill Cemetery—and you can see the river through the trees, even that far up on the mountain.

They're larch trees up there, centuries old—two hundred feet tall, like redwoods, trees that withstood even the big fires of 1911 and 1931—trees so large that eight, sometimes ten people holding hands can't encircle them. The larch trees line all sides of the cemetery's wrought-iron fence, and the air beneath the canopy so high above is a different kind of air, motionless, even when the rest of the woods are windy; and different, too, is the thin light that's able to filter through. Moss grows on the headstones. The shade is cool and smells good. There's a spring nearby, up higher on the mountain.

These trees around the cemetery are ancient. Loggers would love to cut them—each tree is worth several thousand dollars by itself—but no one starts a chain saw within a mile of the cemetery; it's an unwritten rule.

"Give them a rest, for once," says Mack, the little man who takes care of the cemetery—emptying out old flowers, bringing in new ones—and it's not the trees he's talking about.

The names of some of the people in the cemetery, if you can believe the headstones, are Piss-Fir Jim, Windy Joe Griff, and Solo Dog Thompson. There was a hermit, in the sixties, an old man who even by valley standards was an outsider—he lived as far back and as high up in the mountains as you could get, so high that there weren't even any deer or elk up there, so no hunters ever even visited him—and no one knew his name, so they only called him "The Hermit" on his gravestone.

The hermit used to come in about twice a year with his mules to buy groceries—flour and beans mostly—and one spring he didn't show up, so Kenny Breitenstein (more on him later) and some others went on up to check on him, and, sure enough, he'd died.

It was windy up there, windier than you could imagine, says Breitenstein, and they found the old hermit about a mile down the trail leading away from his cabin and down toward the valley, almost as if he'd known he was sick and had been trying to get to town for help.

"Probably a bellyache," Breitenstein will say if you ask him—he knows everything about anything that ever happened, anywhere. The mules were gone ("Grizzly," says Breitenstein), but inside the cabin

(Kenny says) there were the old man's cats, living on mice and melting snow that dripped in through the cracks in the roof on warm afternoons before freezing again in the night (this in May), and when the men opened the cabin door all the cats ran out, except for a large, placid orange one, which Kenny took home to his wife, Edith. All Kenny calls it now, still (the cat's over twenty-four years old; they live a long time up here; dogs live to be twenty or even twenty-five), is "the hermit's cat." "Hey, hermit's cat," he'll say, "get down off that table."

The hermit's grave has an old, rough piece of granite, just like everybody else's, pulled off a talus slope, and John Skabellund, the blacksmith, chiseled the old man's name on it—"The Hermit"—but he's buried off in one corner of the cemetery, as far away from everyone as is possible. It was a joke at first, I think, but I can tell now that a few people feel badly about it.

"You can bury us next to him," says Betsy, speaking, as always, for herself as well as for her whole family. She and Derek run the Mercantile. Their son Trigger (his Christian name; I've no idea why), who is seventeen and the only one in the valley who will dive off the bridge into the river, is going into the Navy this year. Betsy will say anything, and Trigger will do anything. Derek is kind of mild.

"Yep, he was trying to get to town," says Breitenstein. "He either had a bellyache or he was lonely."

About that other cemetery: there's nothing but women in it. It's way over on Yodkin Creek, up in the mountains—no roads, no nothing; just deep woods and grizzlies and elk—and there's no history, no knowledge; it's a mystery to everyone.

Breitenstein says it's being run by outsiders, and he's got to be right. Not many people know how to find it. Kenny took me up there on skis one winter. Somehow, it feels safer in winter.

The women's pictures are on the headstones—pictures of them when they were young—framed in glass, inset in stone.

How're you going to get a marble slab that far back into the woods?

Listen: Some of these gravestones are ancient—from the 1910s, the 1920s—but some of them are new; the newest one is from just two years ago.

We look at the pictures of those women, even in the winter, standing there with snow coming down all around us, and none of the women—not a one—ever smiling.

It's got their names on the gravestones and their birth and death dates, but that's all.

''It's weird,'' says Breitenstein. He takes a puff on his cigarette, finishes it, flicks it into the cemetery, toward the nearest tombstone. ''It's got to be Easterners of some kind.'' He does not mean Hindus, but rather New York, New Jersey, Philadelphia. He's right; all of the women are well dressed, fashionable—not any of them are from out here, we can tell.

Whenever a car drives into the valley—almost always lost—and stops at the Mercantile for gas and directions, Derek and Betsy go out and pretend to be all interested in checking the oil, the windshield wipers. But if that car's got eastern license plates, what they're really checking for is where they've got the body hidden.

''Packhorses,'' says Kenny. ''If the women die in the winter they freeze 'em, then bring 'em out here in the spring, at night, and take 'em up there on packhorses.''

But we never ever see hoofprints, and it's muddy, in the spring.

Kenny shrugs, finishes another cigarette. He knows he's right. ''Got to be packhorses,'' he says. ''That's all there is to it.''

But what I think is that they do it during a thunderstorm, so the rain washes all their tracks away. I would like to see them do it, if I could be sure they would not know I was watching. I'd like to see them all standing there in the rain, digging: the rain beating down on their backs.

The body wrapped in black, tied over the back of a mule, waiting.

Enough!

This is a beautiful valley. The wildflowers that grow in the meadows along the river in the spring are every color imaginable—more wildflowers than I've ever seen, and more stars at night. The other night I saw a cougar run across the road in front of me, flashing across the sweep of my headlights, chasing something.

Edith—Kenny's wife—holds a cigarette in her mouth the dangling way, pointed down, like a man. I remember that I'm trying only to speak of the summer, but one cannot describe Edith without at least mentioning the winter.

The first time I saw Edith, she was running down the road (cigarette drooping from her mouth) leading a colt with a halter. The colt had evidently fallen through some ice into the river, because it was wet up to its neck, and it was a cold day in February, about twenty below. Edith was wet, too—she must have gone in after that colt and somehow lassoed it and pulled it out—and both she and the colt were running down the road. I was driving my truck and I stopped and asked if I could help, if I could give her a ride, but all Edith said (not even shifting the cigarette in the least) was "Can't stop running or the horse'll freeze," and on down the hill they went, so I passed them, waving, and neither Edith nor the horse froze; both are alive and healthy, in the valley.

I have all my days left to live in this place, and I wake up smiling, sometimes, because I am so young. I hike up into the hills to a rock back in the trees, and I just sit there and watch. On the road far below, a friend drives past in his truck, moving so slowly it seems that a man on foot could run alongside. I watch until the truck disappears around the bend. It's dusk: that purple light sliding in, from all directions. In the valley, the lights in my friends' cabins begin to come on; glowing, warm yellow patches in the dark. It's safe.

The Knoll

RICHARD BAUSCH

The two men did not know each other, particularly. There had been several meetings where they had both been present, and they had spoken once near the coffee machine during a break in the planning. A simple nod and hello. The planning sessions had gone on and on, through every possible contingency, the session leaders always shifting, different ones each time, from the first briefings to the field exercises—each one seeming more nervous than the one who preceded him, trying to anticipate everything, to reduce it all to a perfectly understood series of procedural steps; and always in possession of further dark information concerning the nation's peril.

Even so, it was all somehow just games, the younger of the two men thought—like the first scary hours of training in the panhandle. Except that now he was standing here in the broken sunlight, under the shade of the live oak tree, with this other, who was easily in his late forties. A World War II veteran, then. They hadn't spoken yet, had only traded silent recognition of each other.

The older man now checked his watch, knelt, and set his suede case down at the base of the fence under the shrubs there, looking around. There were railroad cars a few feet away, just as in the drawings. The sun was too bright at the edges of the shaded places in the yard.

"So," the older man said. "Nice bright day."

No answer seemed necessary.

"I said, 'Nice bright day.' "

"Okay," said the younger man. "Didn't think you required an answer."

"You a college boy?"

"No."

"Sound like a college boy."

"I read a lot."

"What sort of stuff you read?"

"Newspapers. History."

"Yeah," the older man said. "Figures."

Beyond the fence, down the small, partly shaded embankment, people were gathering. All along either side of the street—men and women and babies. Secretaries and office people; people with welcoming signs, and carrying cameras.

"Were you in the war?" the younger man asked.

The other stared at him.

"Hey, man. Just making conversation. I don't mean anything by it."

"Just talking, right?"

"Passing the time, right."

"It passes quick."

Presently, the younger man said, "So were you in the war?"

"Was I in the war?"

"That's my question, yes."

"All right. Let's say I was in the war."

"You're a patriot."

"I guess that's what we are, id'n it?"

"Figures," the younger man said.

"Sure."

"Where were you in the war?"

Again, the other stared.

"Conversation," the younger man said, and smiled.

"Okay. I fought the Japs."

"The Pacific."

''Korea, too.'' There was a pocked, eroded look to the older man's cheeks, and his eyes were faintly yellow around the irises. It was the younger man's guess that he was a drinker.

''I haven't fought in any wars,'' he told him.

''No, you're a young fella.''

''Not that young.''

''A college kid.''

''No.''

''Hell, boy. It's all over you.''

''Didn't go to college,'' the younger man said.

''Could've fooled me.''

The younger man now took his own small leather case out of his coat and knelt down too. The grass here was burned by the sun, which came in under the shade, through the spaces between branches. The ground all around them was littered with bright fallen leaves. The older man opened his case and removed the rifle from it. The barrel was oiled, and it shone in the sunlight. He sighted along the barrel, then put it on its stock and got slowly to his feet. ''Damn knees. Give me that case, will you?''

The younger man handed it to him, and he shouldered it and tied the strap to his waist. ''Good. Well, reason I thought you were a college boy is you got that college boy haircut. You got that look, you know.''

''Don't let the look fool you.''

''Hey, I like college boys. I wish my own damn son would've gone to college. College is good for you. I couldn't get him to see that.''

''Yeah. What's he do?''

''You college boys are just full of questions.''

''I didn't go to college, and your son didn't either. That's all. I wondered what he did instead.''

''Well, he's not in the battle to save Democracy, I'll tell you that much.''

The younger man said nothing.

''He works in a goddamn grocery store when he works at all.''

''A grocery store? One of these new chain stores?''

"I guess—when he works at all. Most of the time he just hangs around the house and gets in the way."

"So, you don't get along."

"You writing a book, college boy?"

"Yeah. History."

"No kidding."

"The most awful realization of all is that you live in history."

"Is that in your book?"

"What do you think," the younger man said.

"I think you got a sense of humor."

"Finely honed," the younger man said.

"Uh-huh. Conversation is important to you."

"Talk is, yeah. I basically like people."

"Well, see, talk gets people in trouble, too," the older man said.

"Maybe so."

"I guess it depends on what you're used to."

The younger man had removed the clips from his bag and put one in his belt. Then he stood and gave the other to the older man, and handed over the little oblong box with the scope inside it. The older man put the clip in, then took the scope out and attached it to the rifle. His movements were very quick and efficient, and when he was through he sighted through the scope. "Good," he said. Then: "How about you? You get along with your old man?"

"Not anymore."

"Too bad. I guess that's the way these days."

"Well, he died."

"Sorry to hear that, son."

"He was a nice man, my father."

"Yeah, what did he do?"

"He was a grocer. He ran a grocery store."

The older man left a pause.

"It's the truth. Appleton, Wisconsin. A decent man. Good to his family. Worked his ass off and never asked for a thing from anybody. Voted Democratic all his life, too. He believed in the Democratic way. He read everything Lincoln ever said or wrote."

''Did he vote for our mutual friend here?''

''Dad died five years ago.''

''That's what?—'58. So, he lived to vote for Stevenson one more time.''

''It's not a joke,'' the younger man said.

''I didn't mean it that way. A man's vote is sacred. My own father voted for Roosevelt four separate times and was elected to the city council twice himself.''

''What did *he* do?''

''Delivered milk. He did a little drinking in the evenings, though. Also he did some work selling houses for a lousy real estate company. They dealt mostly with foreclosures through the banks.''

''My father's store got closed down, really, by a bank. Couple of years before he passed away. Nobody appreciates the small stores anymore. Since the chains started coming in.''

''Well,'' said the older man, ''and think of it: if time and circumstances were just right, my good-for-nothing son might've worked for your father. We'd have got to know each other.''

The younger man said nothing.

''Right?''

''I don't have any qualms about what I'm doing,'' the young man said.

''I'm talking about time and circumstances,'' said the older man.

''Cross hairs,'' said the other.

The older man looked at him with his yellow eyes. ''Whatever you say.'' He sighted through the scope again. The crowds along either side of the street were getting thicker now. It was past noon now. ''So your daddy died and then what?''

''Nothing.''

''No college?''

''I told you, no.''

''No Army or Navy? That sort of thing?''

''No. I worked some jobs. I got good with certain kinds of lenses and photographic stuff. I fell in with some folks, you know how it is. They brought me in.''

"They helped you decide to be a foot soldier in the fight for true Democracy."

"Maybe. Or maybe I'm a patsy."

The older man smiled. "Maybe. I think we know who *they* are, though."

"Do you know who we're doing *this* for?"

"Sure I do."

"I mean specifically."

"Specifically, we're providing a context. Right?"

"I don't understand."

"Years from now there'll be theories about it all. Who did what and when. Nobody will be able to believe anybody else. Not really. And so everything anybody says about it will be true."

"You're not making sense."

"Well, I don't get paid to think."

Presently, the older man said, "Hey, boy. You nervous or something? This getting to you a little?"

"Right," said the other. "Look at me shake."

"Well, you know."

"Jesus. Nervous. Right. Christ."

"Nerves are healthy, you know."

"Yeah, well, I'm fine."

"No need to get worked up, son."

They were quiet. A few yards away, another man stood with a walkie-talkie. He listened to it and then spoke into it. Then he looked at the older man and held up five fingers, closed his hand, opened it again, closed it and opened it.

"Fifteen minutes."

"You think it'll be Go?" the younger man asked.

"Hard to say." The older man was sighting through the scope again.

"I think it'll be Go."

"You're a thinker."

"Don't you?"

"Don't I what?"

"You heard me."

"Boy, you think too much, maybe."

"I just want to know if you think it'll really be Go."

"I guess we'll find out, won't we?"

"I don't think it actually will."

Behind them, the railroad cars clanked and creaked, metal on metal. They were being moved a few feet on the tracks, and now they stopped. It was one of those inexplicable shiftings of cars in a railroad yard. The sound startled the younger man.

"Kid, you *are* jumpy."

"I wish I knew specifically who we were working for," said the younger man. "I don't like all this smoke-screen stuff."

"You want something to calm you down?"

The younger man didn't answer.

"I got a little something'll calm you down."

"I'm calm."

"Yeah, you don't want to call attention to yourself."

"I'm cold as ice," the younger man said.

"Nothing but frozen tundra inside," said the other, smiling broadly now. The younger man saw that he had a tooth missing on the left side of his mouth. "Right?"

"Right."

"Nothing but the target and whether or not we're Go."

"Right."

A moment later, the younger man said, "Do you hope we're Go?"

"I don't have any opinion on the subject."

"What do you think of him yourself?"

"Who?"

"You know," the younger man said with impatience. "Our friend."

"No opinion," the older man said. "Except maybe that he's a pretty boy. And the chances are better than even that in about thirteen minutes he'll be a dead pretty boy."

"It doesn't bother you who he is?"

The older man shook his head. "I figure there's always going to be somebody. Bothers you, though."

"No."

"What'd you bring it up for, then?"

"Just curious. Just making conversation."

"I'll tell you what, kid. I think maybe you're in the wrong business."

"What business is that?" the younger man said, with an edge of menace.

"Just making conversation," the older man said, smiling again. "Just keeping it light."

"When this is Go, you better be perfect."

"*If* it's Go."

"Absolute perfection. Absolute focus."

"And what're we doing? We're stopping the Communists and saving Democracy as we know it," the older man said. "Right? We're making history."

"Yeah," said the younger man. "Think about it."

"I don't need bullshit like that to help me focus on my job. This is my job, son. This is what I do. I don't give a shit about Cuba, or the Communists, or any of that. Like they always used to say, you know, whatever you choose to do in life, be the best at it. Well? I'm focused, right? I work for it. Because it's all a damn competition. I believe that. Strange as it might sound, I believe it. I couldn't get my son to believe it, but I believe it."

The younger man stared at him, and could say nothing.

"If the kid wanted to be a goddamn ditch digger I'd want him to try and be the best one there is, and that's the truth."

"What do you do when you're not doing . . . this?" the younger man asked.

"I'm a Studebaker dealer."

"Seriously?"

"What do *you* think."

"I just asked."

"College boys. Jesus," the older man said, stepping up to the fence. "They all want everything handed down to them on a platter."

"I wasn't asking for anything."

''Well, remember. Studebaker. I sell Studebakers, anybody asks you.''

''You think I'd tell anybody anything?''

''Hey, I'm not a gambler. But I'll tell you what, you could pass me on any street corner in this country and you wouldn't even remember my face, what I was wearing. I look just like everybody, kid. And what I do, well, it's very, very ordinary and everyday.''

They waited quietly. In the distance, they could hear the sound of a band, but then the wind picked up, shook through the top of the tree, and blotted everything else out. Police were stopping traffic on the overpass, nearby. It would be soon now. On the sidewalk next to the street, a man was holding his little girl on his shoulders, and bouncing her.

''That just might get in the way of a clear shot,'' said the older man.

''Shoot through it.''

''Tough kid.''

''I know history,'' the younger man said.

''And it's made you tough.''

''Can't you do what's called for?''

''Sure I can. I just told you that. I'm just as sharp as any college boy.''

''You can cut the college boy stuff.''

''Okay.''

A moment later, the older man said, ''Listen, are you trying to prove something to me, now?''

''I don't have anything to prove.''

''A minute ago you were telling me you had all these doubts.''

''I don't know what you think you heard,'' the younger man said. ''Maybe you're hung over or something.''

''No, I was thinking maybe if you had doubts, I had some, too.''

''Doubts about what?''

''What if I *was* thinking that?''

''I said, 'Doubts about what?' ''

The older man paused a moment. ''I don't know,'' he said.

"Because I don't have any doubts at all. I told you, I don't have any qualms at all."

"Well, that's good, then. Whatever you say, kid. Remember what *I* said. I have no opinion about anything. I just do what I'm told."

"Okay, well—that's me, too."

"No, but you've got opinions. You're a kid who thinks about history, I can tell. You're an idealist."

"Just make sure you're ready when the time comes," said the younger man.

"Hey," the older man said. "And isn't this really too bad? We might've been friends."

"You can say that sort of thing," the younger man said. "But I'm just as focused as you are."

"I was serious, boy. You think I'd joke about a thing like that?"

"If it's Go, I'm ready."

"Nobody said you weren't."

The music had come to them again, flying on the air, and there was activity in the crowd now, cheers beginning at the far end of the street. The two men waited. "Well, they better decide quick," the older one said.

At this moment, standing a few yards away, the man who held the walkie-talkie lifted it to his ear, then raised his other hand and held up two fingers. The younger man saw this, and his heart shook. "Go," he said with a kind of startlement. A second later, and more evenly, he repeated it. "Go."

Oddly, and only for an instant, he felt as though he had somehow goaded the other into everything; and now that it was all really going to happen, the exhilaration of being involved in it was drained away. His older companion took one look around himself, and moved closer to the fence, in among the branches of the shrubs growing along the base of it. "Get ready," he said. "This is gonna be over a lot quicker than it got started."

The younger man remembered the training, and the strong sense of unreality surrounding the training; the importance all of it had made him feel; but it was just going to be procedure now. Dismantle and pack the article of utility—as it had been called—collect all discharged shells, and move off. Dismantle and pack the article of utility, collect all discharged shells, and move off. He had practiced with several other men, never the same one twice, and he knew what to expect. The utilizer would utilize, then hand him the article of utility and head for the end of the fence, to intercept any curious bystanders with his Secret Service badge and his air of authority. Dismantle and pack the article of utility, collect all discharged shells, and move off.

Behind him, the railroad cars had begun rolling again, clattering, sending up a hollow metallic shriek. From the other side of the fence he heard the crowd, the cheering. Everything was louder now, and the sun was far too bright. It got in all over. The whole, hot light of it. Sounds, colors, odors were intensified; the ends of his fingers hurt. He could feel the cilia moving in his throat.

''Here we go, sports fans,'' said the older man. ''Sic semper fideles or whatever the hell they say when this happens.'' His voice seemed closer, as if he had suddenly got down to whisper the words. It almost made the younger man cover his ears. But somehow he kept control of himself, and no shock came. It seemed to him that the first shock was the longest time coming, and he thought perhaps the whole thing had been aborted. The thought filled his mind like light, and then was gone. And when he had the courage to look he saw that the older man hadn't moved at all. The older man was standing with his arms resting on the fence top, cradling the rifle, keeping perfectly still, cool and ready, seeming now almost serene—peering through the sight at the approaching motorcade, waiting, focused, history about to happen, standing there with the pure, quiet concentration of a hunter after deer.

The Longest Day of the Year

ANN BEATTIE

Toward the end of my third marriage, when my husband and I had enough problems on our hands, the Welcome Wagon lady began to call on us. It was just a rented house—more than we could afford, too, so we were going to have to give it up before summer was over. The first time she came I told her it was an inconvenient time to talk, and that we were going to be moving, anyway. Still, she came back the next day, saying that she hoped I had a minute. That day had been hell: my husband arguing about who should get the dog (*he* brought it home, but I was the one who wanted to keep it in spite of how much shots cost), the dog running and cowering when we raised our voices, the upstairs john backed up. My husband had no idea where the plunger was, although a plunger is a pretty big thing to lose. I had to tell her that it wasn't a good time. Not to be put off, she asked when it would be. I'm not good at putting people off. I start to feel guilty, which I know is unnecessary, but still I do. "Friday," I told her, and made it a point to be out when she came. My husband cooked soil at the greenhouse on Fridays and Saturdays. He wasn't there, either: just the dog, who had looked from the moment we got him like he could use a friend. He would have been happy to hear her rap and be let outside for a few minutes, but all that happened was that she went away.

The next week she came back. She was a tall woman, quite heavy, wearing a white poncho with black stars woven into the wool and ratty-looking fur tails. She had on a black skirt that I knew the dog would get hairs all over, and a ring on her wedding finger that looked like something Richard Burton would have bought Elizabeth Taylor. It was so large that the diamond had fallen sideways, and rested against her baby finger. She was trying to flick it straight when I opened the door.

''Come in,'' I said. It had to be done sometime.

She came in and the dog dashed to greet her. He'd just had two teeth pulled, and we owed the vet for one of them. He seemed fine, though, in spite of what he'd been through the day before.

I thought I should be polite and offer her coffee, although since I stopped drinking it, the aroma wasn't too pleasant to me. Naturally, she said she'd have some, if it wouldn't be too much trouble. ''What's boiling water?'' I said. Something like that.

She eyed the pictures in the side room, where I meant for us to sit. They were hand-colored engravings of trout. My husband was a fisherman. He bought them for a dollar each, from people who didn't know any better. They were the nicest things we had.

She took off the rat-tail poncho and draped it over one of the chairs. I had to force the dog to back off from sniffing it. The sniffing would have been all right, but he was a licker, too.

''As you can probably tell, I love this community and want to serve it,'' she said. She told me she had lived down the road—she pointed, as if I didn't know where the road was—for almost twenty years. ''I came here as a bride,'' she said. ''You know those happy days. Everything looks good to you. But this community kept on looking good.'' She laughed. ''Now I'm almost a dowager,'' she said. She fiddled with the poncho, tapping her fingers over the stars as if they were checkers, and she was debating her move.

''Things aren't going so well with my husband and me,'' I said. ''As I meant to indicate, I don't think we're going to be here much longer.''

She looked like a child who'd dropped its toy off a bridge. She frowned and her eyes made a long sweep along the floor, seeming to focus on the corner. She probably saw the dust balls. It was no more my problem to clean than my husband's. If it was going to be a childless marriage and I wasn't going to be a traditional wife, then he could clean as well as I could.

I got her the coffee and had a 7-Up myself, to be polite and drink along with her. Doing that with alcohol had led to the collapse of my first marriage. My second husband no one could have been married to. He went to Vietnam and came back loony. He thought trucks on the highway would blow up if we passed them. He was given three tickets for driving too slow on an interstate. He lied, telling them that he had rheumatism in his foot and that sometimes he just couldn't push too hard on the accelerator. Actually, he thought everything was going to burst into flames.

"I'm very sorry to hear that you're having problems," Betty said. Her name was Betty. She'd told me that outside, before she came in. Betty what, she didn't say.

I lowered my eyes.

"Don't abandon hope!" she said so loudly she startled me. I wondered if she was a Christian. A lot of those, and Jehovah's Witnesses, came around to the apartment my second husband and I occupied.

"What I mean is, our community needs you," she said. "Our community needs younger people to restore life to it. There used to be children on bicycles, but no more. Maybe a grandchild, or two, on the weekends."

"On the highway?" I said. She was pointing to the road again. Actually, the road was a highway.

"We had rabbits and turtles and squirrels running everywhere. The telephone company came out and put squirrel-proof lines up, and the squirrels were doing acrobatics while the men were packing up their tool kits." She had a wide smile that showed her fillings. She seemed to be warming up to something.

"This used to be a regular stop for a traveling carnival. To this day, I've got stuffed bears and alligators my husband won me at the carnival. He knocked those monkeys off the shelf with that hard-ball—" She held her thumb and first two fingers in the air, curled and spread as far as they could go, so that they looked like a meat hook. "And he was so good at it the man said that he didn't think he'd ever come back to town with the carnival again. Of course, that wasn't the reason why the carnival disappeared.''

I nodded. I was coming to understand that she was suffering, too.

''There used to be two trash pickups a week,'' she said. ''Now it's just Monday morning, like we don't eat and throw things out except after the weekends. I take it to the dump. You can hire a service to come get it, but they want everything wrapped just so. They act like they're the local post office. Have you tried to mail a package from our local post office? If they sold the supplies, I'd think all that harassment was because they wanted to make a profit selling their own goods, but all they've got is manila envelopes.''

I had never been in the local post office. Our mail was delivered —what there was of it. Except for Christmas, we didn't get much mail. At Christmas, various people remembered me.

''I suppose the greenhouse where my husband works had a heyday too?'' I said. I was curious. It looked like it had been built at the turn of the century. It certainly didn't look like it had ever been anything else.

''It offered a landscaping service the year I moved in,'' Betty said. ''There was always a dance on the longest day of the year, out on the big lawn leading up to the greenhouse. All the almond bushes and weeping cherry trees were in flower. It was an amazing sight.'' She took a sip of coffee. ''You know, there are handicapped people in town,'' she said. ''I'm supposed to say 'physically challenged.' They're not on the streets now. I think that ageing made it worse. It was some spine deformity, along with funny speech and a few marbles missing.'' She tapped the side of her head. ''They came to the dance, a few of them,'' she said. ''Everyone looked out for them.'' She had another sip of coffee. ''They were physically challenged because their mothers slept with their own brothers, and so forth,'' she said.

I had a sip of 7-Up. I knew before she said so that the world could be a terrible place.

"Why don't you move, then?" I said. "If it's not the way it used to be, why don't you and your husband move?"

She said, "Ha!" and threw back her head. She had a mole under her chin I hadn't seen before. "Because of my husband," she said. "Now you're going to think I'm trying to sell something, the way I was telling you I suspected the post office of doing. The thing is, my husband is a marriage counselor, and he works out of our home. It's very centrally located, and he's very much in demand. The patients don't want to drive all over kingdom come to find him." She took another sip of coffee. "My husband would never move," she said. Then, as if struck by sudden inspiration, she picked up the bag she'd brought with her and put it on her lap. "If you and your husband did want his services, he's the only marriage counselor in the book," she said. "I'm not here to advocate his services, but since it came up in conversation, I thought I'd be forthcoming. When he and I have troubles, he irons them right out. But that's not why I'm here. I'm your Welcome Wagon lady, and I have some things for you. We'll just be optimistic and say that you're staying in our fine community," she said.

She was a different person when she next started to talk. Her voice rose an octave higher, and her chin strained as if lifting to meet it. First she gave me a trowel. It was green metal, quite nice, with a wooden handle. Narrower than most trowels. It was from the greenhouse where my husband worked. A special trowel to plant bulbs.

She kept eye contact with me, reaching into the bag without looking down. She probably had the things in a particular order, because as she was speaking she produced each thing she began to talk about.

First I got the trowel, then a wide-tooth comb from the local hairstylist. Then Betty took out a golf ball and held it close to my face. "Tell me where that came from," she said.

I moved my head back about a foot so I could focus. It was a white golf ball. I craned my neck to look around to the other side.

"It doesn't say anything," I said.

She yanked it back as fast as a child when another child shows interest in its toy. She examined it, held close to her chest.

"Imagine that!" she hooted. "All these years of giving away Willy Wyler Putt-Putt balls, and this one doesn't bear the name!"

She put it on the table and continued. I reached out and played with it like a worry stone as she continued.

"A box of bonbons is yours from the local market," she said, feeling in the bag. "It can be claimed when you purchase groceries in the amount of ten dollars." She continued to feel around in the bag. "I mean, the bonbons aren't here, but there's a coupon—a coupon that's rather thick, like cardboard." She gave up feeling around and looked into the bag. "Oh no!" she said, pulling out a slip of pink paper. "Look at that!" she said. "I know just what happened. I told my husband about the parking ticket I got, and I said that it was in my bag, and he must have reached in and left the ticket there and removed the coupon for bonbons!" She shook her head from side to side. Tears had started to well up in her eyes. "Imagine taking the wrong piece of paper! *That'll* show you how helpful men are when they mean to help you out!"

Wiping a tear away with the crook of her arm, she continued to shake her head as she spoke. Then she gave me a map of the community, provided by the local hardware store. There was a smudge of blue eye shadow on her arm. It looked like a dangerously bulging vein.

As she unrolled the map, I saw that it was a blank piece of paper. She had a huge smile on her face as she peered over the top of it. From my face, though, she could tell that something was wrong. She looked down and saw that there was nothing on the map. She jumped out of the chair, she was so surprised.

"It can only be one thing," she said. "When they mail me the tube, there's a protective wrapper around the maps. I can't blame this one on my husband. I have to say that in all my years of doing this, this is the stupidest mistake I've ever made."

I heard the chair crack. Just a small sound, but it meant that the glue my husband used hadn't worked. I held my breath. As she started to stand, one of the legs bent under, and the chair went down. She staggered, but caught her balance on the chest between the windows. The chest had come with the house. Never in my life had I had money for a cherry-wood chest. The dog had run into the room when the commotion started, and he was nosing the fur on her poncho when I grabbed it off the floor.

"It's certainly not our day," I said. I started to say how sorry I was about the chair, but suddenly she was crying, carrying on about how the community would never again be the wonderful place it once had been. She had smeared the makeup above one eye earlier, and then she rubbed the other one, so that she looked like a clown peering out through rings of soot. She was trying to get herself together, but for a few seconds it looked like a losing battle. I saw as she patted her hair that she was wearing a fall. It had come partially unfastened as she stumbled across the room.

God, it brought back memories of the days when I drank. Of that awful apartment above the grocery store with the gas leak.

Then, if you could believe it, Betty was taking me to task. She was saying that she had been unnerved by having to stop by so many times. That it was her *job* to drop off the items, and that she hoped I was happy that I had finally found time in my busy schedule to receive them. She grabbed up her poncho and moved her foot in such an odd way that I thought she might be about to kick the dog, then thought better of it.

When my husband got back from cooking soil, I told him about Betty's visit, starting at the beginning: the information about the carnival; the outdoor dances at the greenhouse. I left out the part about the retarded people, or whatever they were, because he always accused me of telling him depressing things. I skipped that and went right to the golf ball, the parking ticket, and the map. It was one of the last times my husband and I ever embraced. We had to, or we both would have fallen over laughing.

During the afternoon, the golf ball had dropped off the edge of the table and rolled off to join a dust ball of similar size in the corner of the room. There was space in that house, and some lovely furniture, and sitting in the sunlight at the table that day with Betty, I had known that I was going to miss the place. We knew when we took it that we were going out on a limb financially. We just thought that a nice place might bring us luck—that it might cheer us up, and that then things might start to go our way. Betty's visit and the chair's collapse certainly would have become our family story if we'd stayed together, but that didn't happen, so it became instead a story that I often remember, going over the details silently, by myself.

The map was useful for wrapping glasses—the one piece of white paper in among the newspaper.

When we left, we took nothing that wasn't ours.

Buckeyes

PINCKNEY BENEDICT

My friends and I head over to the salvage yard to see this crowd of dead Ohioans. My dad drives a wrecker for the yard and he's told me about these people and their car. It's like a curiosity or something to him. He sees a lot, accidents and all. He sometimes brings home items from the wreckage, odds and ends, and he tells me about the really terrible ones, and the ones where there's something funny, like the couple that piled up their car because they were screwing out on the turnpike. When the guys brought up the saws and equipment to cut them out of the wreck, there they were, twisted together in the front seat, and the man's pants were down around his ankles and the woman hadn't got a single stitch on, stark naked in there on top of that guy.

So he tells me about these Buckeyes he brought in, tells me it's something I ought to see. I get some friends together and we walk over there. It's a bunch of kids from my sixth-grade class, like it's a field trip or something. When we get to the yard, the guy that owns the place—Mr. Legg is his name—is sitting in a chair at the gate, and he's got a stick laid across his lap, like a walking stick. When I go up to him to tell him hey, tell him what we want, he pokes the stick in my chest. Gives it a pretty good shove. He's chewing tobacco, got a sizable plug of it hung up in one cheek.

I tell him who I am, I say, "I'm Goody Pettus," and he just looks at me like I'm crazy.

''You go in there, I got a big black dog like to eat up your ass,'' he says to me. I'm standing in front of my friends. I've told them I know this guy, my dad works here, I'll get them in. So I tell him again who I am, thinking maybe he didn't understand me when I said it the first time. I tell him who my dad is. He just looks at me. I tell him what we're all there to see.

He says, ''Little fuckers want to go in there and rip me off.''

I tell him we don't.

He says, ''Each one of you swipes something, you walk out of here with a whole car just about. Jesus Christ.''

The kids behind me are starting to talk like they're going home, but I'm not finished yet. There's a sheet-metal fence all around the place. It's ten, twelve feet high, and no gate but the one that old man Legg has got blocked, so it seems like we aren't getting in any other way. Also I know the dog he's talking about. It's a huge bastard, a bull mastiff that has got to weigh seventy or eighty pounds. My dad has told me the old man beats it pretty regularly with that stick to keep it mean. It hates everybody, even my dad, who is a guy that gets along with most animals.

I say, ''We've got fifty cents.'' I don't actually have that much on me at the moment but I figure we can scrape it up among us. The old man looks at me, spits into the dirt beside his chair.

''Fifty cent apiece?'' he says.

''No,'' I say. ''Just fifty cents.''

He looks the group over. There are about ten of us. He says, ''That makes it a nickel each. Not very damn much.''

I say, ''It's what we've got. We might could go a little higher.''

He says, ''What do you think this is? A goddamn carnival? Pay somebody and you can go in and look at the sideshow freaks?''

A couple of the other kids have coasted off by now but I want to get past this fellow Legg. I say to him that my dad told me it was worth it, something you should definitely see because things like this don't come along so often. My dad said it was something like a piece of history. He said it was practically art, those people in that car.

He peers at me. "Who's your father, telling you something like that?" he says. "Do I know him?"

I say yeah. I tell him, "My dad's Conrad Pettus. He drives a wrecker for you."

Legg laughs. "Conrad?" he says. "That sounds like old Conrad. He says some pretty damn strange things from time to time. I guess I could let you in a minute then. Cost you a buck and a half, though, for all of you."

Those of us that are left huddle together, and with all of us pitching in we've got a dollar and thirty cents, something like that. We're a little short. I give it to the old man, a handful of change, and he doesn't even count it, just jams it in his pocket. He says, "You got ten minutes to look. Don't touch nothing back there, because the troopers are going to be coming by in the morning to look it all over. They say it might be foul play involved. They say that might be the scene of the crime." He pauses to cough a time or two, takes a couple of shallow breaths. "And you got to turn out your pockets when you leave. Nobody gets out with nothing he didn't bring in, hear?"

Then he points into the yard, where there are cars lying on top of one another, sitting on their sides, covered in vines, creeper that goes in at the windows and crawls up the radio aerials. I'm thinking about snakes, and how this looks to be a pretty good place for them to live, to hide in. Some of those cars look like they have sat there for twenty years, and they're all accordioned, got something wrong with them somewhere. Every now and again, a car will look all right as you come up on it, like a car anybody'd have, but then you see that the other side is mashed where a truck or something barreled into it, and you know nobody walked away from that one. So on into the yard we go.

It's evening, and the sun has gone down behind the line of hills to the west. In the half-light in the valleys between the stacked cars, it takes us a while to find the one we're looking for. All I know from my father is we're hunting a Packard with Ohio plates. He told me the Ohioans were still in it when he dropped it off at the yard, and

I'm hoping they're there yet. I keep checking around for the dog, but then I hear it, locked in the little shed the old man's got for an office. It's scraping on the door, whining and screeching to get out and get at us. It gives me the shivers to hear its nails on the metal door of that shed, to watch the tin wall panels shiver when it throws itself against them, and I imagine the others feel the same way.

One of the guys gives a yell when we've been looking about five minutes or so, says he found the car. It's just an old Hudson Hornet, though, that's burned out and empty, nobody in it at all. There is melted blackened windshield glass on the hood, so the fire must've burned pretty hot. I yell at him for wasting our time.

One of the other guys says well, it's been a while, maybe we ought to go before the old man gets tired of waiting and turns the mastiff loose on us. Maybe our time that we paid for is up, he thinks.

I say, "He gave us ten minutes *to look.* We got to find the car before we can look at it." They don't seem convinced, but nobody leaves, and we keep poking around among all these piled-up wrecks, and some of the piles reach up thirty feet or so. They're like little mountains of smashed cars, nothing you would want to climb on. You could put a foot wrong and go through a windshield, break a leg, cut yourself on a jagged edge of sheared steel, bleed to death, catch tetanus. You could slip between the cars, slide down into the dark spaces among the exhaust pipes and the differentials and the cast-off wheels, the rotting tires with the canvas belts showing through. Who knows how far you could fall?

I wonder where all these cars have come from. It seems like more than the people around here could drive, let alone wreck, even in a hundred years. I make up my mind I'll ask my dad about that, when I get home.

I'm beginning to have doubts about the tolerance of Legg and the dog myself, beginning to get itchy like we need to go, and I wish I'd asked my old man a little more about where the car was placed, exactly. Then the same guy, the one who located the Hudson, sings out. He's really found it this time, he says. He's the littlest one of us, and his voice is high, like a woman's echoing off the smashed cars. We all razz him a minute, *oh yeah, what did you find this time, Lou?* but it turns out he has. He's found the Packard full of flatlanders.

The car sits off by itself, right up against the metal fence. It's a bulbous thing with a great long hood, looking as much like an upside-down boat as it does a car. Its finish is completely gone, the bare metal eaten through with rust in any number of places. The tires have vanished, and the Packard rests on its rims now. There is no glass to be seen anywhere on it. The interior looks like it is full of jumbled garbage. I can't bring myself to approach it. No one else goes near it either.

Until yesterday, the Packard sat at the base of a limestone cliff on a mountain to the east of us. No telling how it got there. The cliff is called the Eagle's Nest because they say golden eagles used to live in openings in the rock face. They would cruise the river when they hunted; fold their wings and drop a thousand feet like a rock; hit the water and come up flying, with a speckled trout in their claws. Now it is just noisy black rooks that make their nests in the crevices.

The cliff faces a wide bend in the Allegheny River, with a patch of national forest behind it, and people picnic there all the time, make out on the cliff top at night. The rocks along the edge are covered with graffiti, people's names in bright colors of spray paint, hearts with arrows, little slogans. Sometimes you get a short poem. The crevices up there are stuffed full of old used rubbers, and oftentimes a brassiere or a pair of panties is caught in the branches of a scrubby tree, waving with the breeze like some kind of racy flag. Sometimes but not as often, it's a man's Fruit of the Loom.

All those people coming and going for all that time, and nobody ever saw the car from Ohio down below, sitting at the cliff base like it was parked there. It was in the same place for thirty years or better, from the look of it.

A couple of rock climbers found the car. They had scaled their way down the face, and they were eating lunch at the bottom, sandwiches in plastic bags, drinking from a thermos of hot coffee, getting ready to go back up. They thought it was a boulder that had come loose from the cliff face. There are lots of boulders down there, everything from the size of your head to the size of a trailer house, is what I've heard, and the car was covered in vines and mounds of bird guano, surrounded by trees and bushes. There were trees growing up inside it, right through the floorboards and out through the windows and even through the roof. It was only when they went to climb on it, to start back up the cliff, that they found out it was made of metal, that it was a car and not a natural formation.

It took a crane brought over from a highway contractor in the next county and a team of a dozen men, my father among them, to get the car up the cliff. They lowered the men and their axes and hacksaws and chain saws down to the river bottom in a big basket. I would like to have seen that operation, the car lifting up, riding on the hook of the crane, and a couple of the men scrambling underneath with the chattering saws, cutting away the last few roots that held it. And the car cranking slowly toward the sky, banging now and then against the rock wall, sending stone chips and bits of rust and metal and who knows what else in a shower down on the men who sliced it loose. The stuff probably got in their eyes, them not able to resist watching as it rose into the air and away.

The engine block broke free of its mountings about halfway to the cliff top and dropped out of the bottom of the Packard, trailing the transmission, the metal parts pinwheeling back down the stone wall. The lightened chassis rocketed upward, fouling the crane's steel hawser against a rock outcropping. The men scattered, shouting and pushing each other out of the way, stumbling to get clear. Nobody was really sure which way the falling motor would bounce when it got to the bottom, and the team ended up scattered in a rough semicircle, crouching behind bushes and saplings that could not possibly stop a heavy object falling from that height. The heavy V-8 mill hit a spot of soft ground and didn't bounce at all, just sank deep into the dirt like it had been planted there.

My dad told me they managed to haul the car the rest of the way up in one piece, even with the snarled cable, swung it over the edge with the huge crane, and dropped it onto the back of the flatbed wrecker that he drives, neat as you please, and he chained it down and brought it on to the yard. He said a couple of sparrows burst from the windows when he was winding the chain tight. They were frightened by the rattle of the links against what was left of the car body. He jumped, thinking it was maybe the spirits of the people who had died in the car finally escaping in the form of those birds.

Why weren't there more? I asked him. *Four people in the car but only a couple birds.*

I don't know, he said. *Maybe there were more birds, and I just thought it was a couple.*

You could still see them in there, he said, dark shapes among the limbs of the trees that had grown up, and the sticks and the trash that the birds had brought, the dried skeleton of the driver propped behind the wheel, the others still in their seats. They were the driver's family that had died along with him, or maybe they were his friends, or business associates. Nobody knew.

A bird flies from the empty windshield now, bursting out with its wings fluttering, a sound like the shuffling of a deck of cards. I'm ready for it, but the others fall back a couple of steps and Lou, the little one, gives a squeak. This is stupid, I think, standing five yards from the thing when we come a pretty good way to see it up close and have spent time searching. We don't have much longer to look. The shadows are getting long and deep, and Legg won't wait on us forever. I go to the car and peer in the driver's window.

At first it just looks like a hedge has grown up in the car, some kind of a thicket, bracken that is green and leafed out. I take a sniff, and the only smell on the air is honeysuckle, and the faint scent of metal. The leaves move in a breeze that has sprung up. Lou stands beside me. He's embarrassed that he yelled at the bird, and he's showing off. He calls back to the others, "Hey, it's a car full of brush." He turns to me and he says, "You brought us out here to see this? This old piece of junk?" He kicks at the fender nearest him, and his boot on the metal makes a hollow clang.

"My old man told me," is all I can think of to say.

''Your old man's screwed up,'' he tells me. The others have come up close too, and they're standing around the car. Their voices are loud, like they're glad to have found out that the car's got no dead Buckeyes inside it, even though that's what they came to see, what they paid the old man to see. Lou tells me to hand over some money. ''You owe me thirty cents,'' he says, ''because that's what I give to get in here, and now it's nothing like what you said.'' He's leaning against the trunk of the car, pushing against it with his little legs, rocking the whole thing. The car's rotted suspension is giving out these little cries every time he pushes.

''I owe you nothing,'' I say to Lou, and I take a step toward him, figuring to shake him a little to shut him up. The others are watching us, and I know it is my dad has brought me here, where my friends are mocking me. His jokes. His idea of a joke. An empty car. Lou's still pushing at it, looking at me with this expression on his face, like he thinks I won't hit him, which is an error on his part because I will, I surely will. Somebody else, one of the bigger kids, is shoving at the other side of the car, and they've got a pretty good rhythm going, like they plan to rock the gutted Packard over on its side.

Inside the car, a big mess of sticks, a squirrel's nest or a bird's, gives way with the car's heaving, collapses onto the floor. The screen of brush parts as though a hand is passed through it, and something is gazing out of the back of the car at us. Skin like yellow leather, long lank brittle hair that looks as though the birds have been using it to add to their houses, and dark eye sockets which seem to stare even though there are no eyes in them. It's like an illusion, a magic trick, where at first I couldn't see this thing sitting in the back seat of the car. Now that I know what I'm looking for, I see it perfectly, and I wonder how it could be that I missed it, that we all missed it, before.

It's small, like a child, a girl child, and its hands are folded in its lap. Its clothes have melted away over the years, or been taken away by animals, and it is that same yellow color all over, and wrinkled. It's peering out the window nearest it. At its side is another like it, but this one is even smaller, and its head is missing, maybe rolled off and gone under the seat. Two others, larger, sit in front. They are slumped together, like tired people after a long day of driving. It is a family in there—mother, father, sister, brother—and it must seem to them like they are somehow on the road again after all those years, a rough road that makes the car bounce, and bounce, and bounce.

The others have spotted them, and they back away one by one, until it is just Lou and the larger kid shoving. Then the large kid sees them too, catches them out of the corner of his eye, and it is just Lou. He stops what he's doing, but he thinks we're joking with him. When he looks into the car, he sees nothing. Even when I point things out to him, the bones twined among the tough scrub—"Look, there's the hands, the fingers, lying on the knee. There's the *skull* for God's sake"—he claims it's nothing at all but just weeds and garbage. I don't believe him, that he can't see this family, and I take hold of him. I'm going to shove him in there close where he can feel them, if he won't see.

I'm dragging him to the driver's side door of the Packard when the old man comes into sight around a big pile of loose bumpers. He's got his dog on a rope lead, and the mastiff is straining against him, giving the rope short little jerks. The old man's hand, the one holding the rope, flies out from his body every time the dog leaps forward, and I wonder how strong a grip he has on the thing. It's strangling itself against the knot in the leash, and strings of milky drool hang down off its jowls.

"What the hell?" he says. He seems surprised to see us. "You're still here?" he says. He must be making a last patrol of the place before locking up. "Christ, I said ten minutes, not ten days. Get the hell on out of here."

The others are already making for the gate, Lou at the head of the pack, but I stay where I am for a little longer. It's dark in the yard, dusk getting on to night, and when I look into the car it takes me a minute to make out the little girl, the daughter, in the back seat. Suddenly I'm not sure anymore which is her and which is her brother. I'm not sure what is a bare stick, and what is the bone of her forearm. It's black inside the Packard, no colors showing at all now.

"I said get out," the old man says. His voice is shaking, and he lets his grip on the dog slip just a bit more.

"I heard," I say, and I walk past him. I keep my pace steady.

"I know you heard me," he says. "I know your daddy. He works for me. You better not be stealing nothing. Nothing better be gone from here." I'm out of his sight, but his voice carries to me as I go. "I can check up. I can tell your daddy to smack fire out of you!" He goes on for a while, but it is hard to make out his words, the farther away I get from him.

I walk out of the gate of the salvage yard, and nobody is there. All of them are gone, running to get home, I guess. I wonder what they saw that made them back off from the car. They must have seen the same thing that I did. Or maybe they just saw me seeing it, and that was enough to scare them off. Remembering, I can't tell which way it is, and I know they won't be able to recall either, if I ask them about it at school tomorrow.

All the way home, I make a list in my head of the things my father has brought home from the yard, items that nobody wanted or thought to claim. He's brought home bracelets; two full sets of dentures and an upper plate; a Fuller Brush salesman's sample kit; some tiny atomizers full of cologne that he gave to me, and some miniature bottles of liquor that he kept; a suitcase with a busted handle, full of women's party clothes; several car jacks, with and without handles; spare tires, full of air and flat; packets of bobby pins; a .45 caliber pistol with a broken slide; a crushed box of chocolates; the waxy white hand of a manikin; a barrel full of greasy chain; eyeglasses; sunglasses; empty artillery shells; and a hundred other things that it's impossible for me to remember or that he probably never even showed me.

He keeps these things stacked around the house, or gives them away to people who can't use them either. Our neighbors used to laugh when he gave them stuff, but now they just take the items that he hands over and then carry them away, God knows where to. He never asks about the fate of what he gives. As I walk, the air grows cool and I wish for a jacket, wondering what prize he figures to bear home from this latest find, what terrible next thing will make its way into our house.

Crickets

ROBERT OLEN BUTLER

They call me Ted where I work and they've called me that for over a decade now and it still bothers me, though I'm not very happy about my real name being the same as the former President of the former Republic of Vietnam. Thieu is not an uncommon name in my homeland and my mother had nothing more in mind than a long-dead uncle when she gave it to me. But in Lake Charles, Louisiana, I am Ted. I guess the other Mr. Thieu has enough of my former country's former gold bullion tucked away so that in London, where he probably wears a bowler and carries a rolled umbrella, nobody's calling him anything but Mr. Thieu.

I hear myself sometimes and I sound pretty bitter, I guess. But I don't let that out at the refinery, where I'm the best chemical engineer they've got and they even admit it once in a while. They're good-hearted people, really. I've done enough fighting in my life. I was eighteen when Saigon fell and I was only recently mustered into the Army, and when my unit dissolved and everybody ran, I stripped off my uniform and put on my civilian clothes again and I threw rocks at the North's tanks when they rolled through the streets. Very few of my people did likewise. I stayed in the mouths of alleys so I could run and then return and throw more rocks, but because what I did seemed so isolated and so pathetic a gesture, the gunners in the tanks didn't even take notice. But I didn't care about their scorn. At least my right arm had said no to them.

And then there were Thai pirates in the South China Sea and idiots running the refugee centers and more idiots running the agencies in the U.S. to find a place for me and my new bride, who braved with me the midnight escape by boat and the terrible sea and all the rest. We ended up here in the flat bayou land of Louisiana where there are rice paddies and where the water and the land are in the most delicate balance with each other, very much like the Mekong delta where I grew up. These people who work around me are good people and maybe they call me Ted because they want to think of me as one of them, though sometimes it bothers me that these men are so much bigger than me. I am the size of a woman in this country and these American men are all massive and they speak so slowly, even to each other, even though English is their native language. I've heard New Yorkers on television and I speak as fast as they do.

My son is beginning to speak like the others here in Louisiana. He is ten, the product of the first night my wife and I spent in Lake Charles, in a cheap motel with the sky outside red from the refineries. He is proud to have been born in America, and when he leaves us in the morning to walk to the Catholic school he says, "Have a good day, y'all." Sometimes I say goodbye to him in Vietnamese and he wrinkles his nose at me and says, "Aw, Pop," like I'd just cracked a corny joke. He doesn't speak Vietnamese at all and my wife says not to worry about that. He's an American.

But I do worry about that, though I understand why I should be content. I even understood ten years ago, so much so that I agreed with my wife and gave my son an American name. Bill. Bill and his father Ted. But this past summer I found my son hanging around the house bored in the middle of vacation and I was suddenly his father Thieu with a wonderful idea for him. It was an idea that had come to me in the first week of every February we'd been in Lake Charles, because that's when the crickets always begin to crow here. This place is rich in crickets, which always make me think of my own childhood in Vietnam. But I never said anything to my son until last summer.

I came to him after watching him slouch around the yard one

Sunday pulling the Spanish moss off the lowest branches of our big oak tree and then throwing rocks against the stop sign on our corner. "Do you want to do something fun?" I said to him.

"Sure, Pop," he said, though there was a certain suspicion in his voice, like he didn't trust me on the subject of fun. He threw all the rocks at once that were left in his hand and the stop sign shivered at their impact.

I said, "If you keep that up, they will arrest me for the destruction of city property and then they will deport us all."

My son laughed at this. I of course knew that he would know I was bluffing. I didn't want to be too hard on him for the boyish impulses that I myself had found to be so satisfying when I was young, especially since I was about to share something of my own childhood with him.

"So what've you got, Pop?" my son asked me.

"Fighting crickets," I said.

"What?"

Now, my son was like any of his fellow ten-year-olds, devoted to superheroes and the mighty clash of good and evil in all of its high-tech forms in the Saturday-morning cartoons. Just to make sure he was in the right frame of mind, I explained it to him with one word, "Cricketmen," and I thought this was a pretty good ploy. He cocked his head in interest at this and I took him to the side porch and sat him down and I explained.

I told him how, when I was a boy, my friends and I would prowl the undergrowth and capture crickets and keep them in matchboxes. We would feed them leaves and bits of watermelon and bean sprouts, and we'd train them to fight by keeping them in a constant state of agitation by blowing on them and gently flicking the ends of their antennas with a sliver of wood. So each of us would have a stable of fighting crickets, and there were two kinds.

At this point my son was squirming a little bit and his eyes were shifting away into the yard and I knew that my Cricketman trick had run its course. I fought back the urge to challenge his set of interests. Why should the stiff and foolish fights of his cartoon characters absorb him and the real clash—real life and death—that went on in the natural world bore him? But I realized that I hadn't cut to the chase yet, as they say on the TV. "They fight to the death," I said with as much gravity as I could put into my voice, like I was James Earl Jones.

The announcement won me a glance and a brief lift of his eyebrows. This gave me a little scrabble of panic, because I still hadn't told him about the two types of crickets and I suddenly knew that was a real important part for me. I tried not to despair at his understanding and I put my hands on his shoulders and turned him around to face me. "Listen," I said. "You need to understand this if you are to have fighting crickets. There are two types, and all of us had some of each. One type we called the charcoal crickets. These were very large and strong but they were slow and they could become confused. The other type was small and brown and we called them fire crickets. They weren't as strong, but they were very smart and quick."

"So who would win?" my son said.

"Sometimes one and sometimes the other. The fights were very long and full of hard struggle. We'd have a little tunnel made of paper and we'd slip a sliver of wood under the cowling of our cricket's head to make him mad and we'd twirl him by his antenna, and then we'd each put our cricket into the tunnel at opposite ends. Inside, they'd approach each other and begin to fight and then we'd lift the paper tunnel and watch."

"Sounds neat," my son said, though his enthusiasm was at best moderate, and I knew I had to act quickly.

So we got a shoe box and we started looking for crickets. It's better at night, but I knew for sure his interest wouldn't last that long. Our house is up on blocks because of the high water table in town and we crawled along the edge, pulling back the bigger tufts of grass and turning over rocks. It was one of the rocks that gave us our first crickets, and my son saw them and cried in my ear, "There, there," but he waited for me to grab them. I cupped first one and then the other and dropped them into the shoe box and I felt a vague disappointment, not so much because it was clear that my boy did not want to touch the insects, but because they were both the big black ones, the charcoal crickets. We crawled on and we found another one in the grass and another sitting in the muddy shadow of the house behind the hose faucet and then we caught two more under an azalea bush.

"Isn't that enough?" my son demanded. "How many do we need?"

I sat with my back against the house and put the shoe box in my lap and my boy sat beside me, his head stretching this way so he could look into the box. There was no more vagueness to my feeling. I was actually weak with disappointment because all six of these were charcoal crickets, big and inert and just looking around like they didn't even know anything was wrong.

"Oh no," my son said with real force, and for a second I thought he had read my mind and shared my feeling, but I looked at him and he was pointing at the toes of his white sneakers. "My Reeboks are ruined!" he cried, and on the toe of each sneaker was a smudge of grass.

I glanced back into the box and the crickets had not moved and I looked at my son and he was still staring at his sneakers. "Listen," I said, "this was a big mistake. You can go on and do something else."

He jumped up at once. "Do you think Mom can clean these?" he said.

"Sure," I said. "Sure."

He was gone at once and the side door slammed and I put the box on the grass. But I didn't go in. I got back on my hands and knees and I circled the entire house and then I turned over every stone in the yard and dug around all the trees. I found probably two dozen more crickets, but they were all the same. In Louisiana there are rice paddies and some of the bayous look like the delta, but many of the birds are different and why shouldn't the insects be different, too? This is another country, after all. It was just funny about the fire crickets. All of us kids rooted for them, even if we were fighting with one of our own charcoal crickets. A fire cricket was a very precious and admirable thing.

The next morning my son stood before me as I finished my

breakfast, and once he had my attention, he looked down at his feet, drawing my eyes down as well. "See?" he said. "Mom got them clean."

Then he was out the door and I called after him, "See you later, Bill."

The New Boy

JOSEPHINE CARSON

Once after a party at the Instituto, Felipe and I staggered back to my place carrying a big tapestry of mine that had won second prize. I didn't want to leave it in the gallery because there were no guards and things had been stolen from the school lately.

Felipe taught Anatomy for Artists there, supplementing his medical practice because a long time ago, having been condemned by the priests as a Communist, he had learned to content himself with patients from among the poor, the Americans, and mainly the Indians, who often paid him in live chickens or sacks of corn.

We dragged the tapestry into the studio and, after a glass of tea, we collapsed into bed. It was a Saturday night. The upper part of town where I lived was quiet but no doubt the area down by the market still rocked with life. The phone woke us at about 2 A.M., a call from the police station, the town operators having closed down at 9 P.M. I had one of the thirty phones in town, Felipe another. I was amused that they knew they'd find him at my house but they had probably tried his first. A woman he had treated recently on a ranch in the country off the Guanajuato road was still in labor after twenty-four hours and the two country midwives were busy elsewhere. And there were other unnamed medical problems at the ranch, besides. The respectable doctor across town was not available for this kind of emergency, of course.

''This is a berry bad ranch, *chula,*'' he said when I insisted on going along. But I was already splashing my face in the bathroom. I'd never been to one of the ranches; nor had I seen him in an emergency. The idea of Felipe as a professional dazzled me. No doubt I'd been subtly tainted by his bad reputation—decadent Spaniard, Communist, etc.

We woke Julio down next door to the Bougainvillea Cafe in his little room with the barred windows and he took us in his taxi. They talked through the dark bumpy ride about Julio's having to take the crazy priest all the way to Celaya in the middle of the night last week to catch a bus for Durango. I leaned into Felipe's side and dozed. Sometimes when we were near others but in the dark, perhaps in a movie or in the *tourismo,* he would keep me deadlocked in a grip around my shoulders. Once a long time ago, he had been tortured by Franco's guards in a prison camp and this fierce claim on me in the dark was related to that torture, I knew. It was like a thing said between mutes.

By the time we sighted the ranch, the road had become so rough that Julio feared for his axle, so we got out and walked the last half mile. The moony whiteness over everything made me ecstatic. The low wall and the dark, squat, silent buildings, bled of their color in the moonlight, looked ominous. A dog sniffed at us and limped away. Then a boy came out of the dark and said "Doctor" softly.

"Why is it so quiet here?" Felipe asked him. By now, if Felipe's stories were right, the men would have come home after the cantinas had closed in town and continued their drinking all night here in the courtyard.

The boy was very still, his mouth open. He had been awake all night, one could tell.

"Where are the men?" Felipe asked.

"All behind the big house, Doctor."

"So quiet. What are they doing?"

"They are dead, señor."

I started to laugh compulsively but caught myself.

Felipe leaned toward him in the dark. "Dead? What do you mean, dead?"

The boy stood very straight there in the moonlight, stiff and honorable, as if having brought a message to the general from the front. ''All the men are dead, señor. They had a fight when they came back tonight and they killed each other. Nobody is alive but the boys and the girls and the women. The woman with baby is dying, too. They say you must take out the baby fast. You must come now.''

''Where the hell are these *borrachos?* Take me to these stinking *borrachos* first. Who said they were dead?''

''But the woman is dying. They said she needs you fast.''

''My God!'' I whispered. I was beginning to believe him.

Felipe hissed at him. ''She is not dying! I saw her before. Did the children see the fight? Where are they?''

''They are sleeping, señor. They didn't see it. Only the older boys. And I saw, too . . . everything.''

''Cristo!'' Felipe whispered. And I started to shake.

The boy was pulling Felipe toward a small hut now at the far side of the yard by some stunted little trees. I ran along behind them, wondering if Felipe believed it now about the men. All dead? Why didn't he go look at them first? He must not believe it.

The room was lit by candles. They made these thick white tapers that looked very solemn and holy to me just now. The bed was low, a pile of corn-husk mattresses, maybe, and four or five women squatted around it, one on her knees on a rolled-up serape. The young woman on the bed must have fainted. She hadn't delivered but lay totally still like a huge gourd under the sheet. Felipe pushed the others away and knelt beside her. The sight of him there gave me a queer pain. He lightly touched her belly where the baby was stuck and maybe had died.

I found one of the women clutching my hand fiercely. The mother of the little mother, maybe. I put an arm around her. She moaned and prayed. The others muttered. Someone told Felipe, who had a stethoscope on the mound now, that there was water ready, everything had been ready a long time, they said in whispers. Everyone repeated everything.

Felipe threw off the muslin sheet and began to rock the woman back and forth. He gently slapped her cheek. A leg spasmed out suddenly, straight and long, beautiful. A hand caught at his sleeve and then I heard the rasp that had once been her voice. It sounded old. She had yelled herself mute! Felipe was half on the bed with her. He growled at the old women nearby and two of them pulled the legs up and out, holding on to them. The woman with me vaguely rocked against me and away, babbling some incantation.

Felipe began to push at the mother's chest, to get a good breathing going. Then he gave a few orders and the women brought him a cloth. I gaped there in the dark, the scene—hardly visible—like an old film, foxed, antiqued. The women clustered around the bed and all began to rock and heave against it. Felipe snarled like a dog at them and waved them away. He turned back, groping for his bag, which I grabbed and thrust at him. Our eyes met. He'd forgotten I was there. Then he leaned in on the mother with forceps in his hands, the warm yellow light glowing on them. He began to work very carefully with all of us hovering around silent as moons.

And then the young mother let out a shriek. Suddenly there was blood all over the bed, staining down onto the mat. She writhed and pitched till Felipe yelled at her. The women rushed to dab at the blood with towels. There was a sucking sound and Felipe very carefully slid the baby out as if pulling a goose from an oven. One of the women seized it. He dropped the forceps as if disgusted, turning to stanch the mother's bleeding. He plunged a hand into his bag, poured something on a gauze, and mopped at her. Her moaning was like wind among the big rocks on the flats outside.

The woman near me now had the baby. She started methodically to wrap it, head and all. I couldn't see its sex. Suddenly Felipe grabbed it from her and held it up by the heels, smacking the tiny withered behind. Nothing. He smacked again. Nothing. Then he laid it on the foot of the bed, leaned over it, and in a second there was a whimper, a frail cry, an answer from all the women, and from me, and he handed it over again to be wrapped and dropped on the breast of the exhausted, indifferent girl—I could see now that she was only a girl—on the torn bed.

She would live. Nothing kills Indian women, Felipe had once told me. They die down very low so they can come back when they need to. They go unconscious easily. They spare themselves. They are very good animals, he had said, satisfied, as if he'd made them that way himself.

The young mother looked ravaged, though. The women whisked away the bloody sheet and brought another. They bathed her, rubbed her arms. I loved them all for this, and her for having lived and for being a very good animal. The baby was a boy.

Felipe wandered outside still wiping vaguely at his arms with a cloth the women had given him. I felt for his back and found him trembling. He had wanted her to live, more than the baby. The baby, he muttered now in English, was killing her, becoming her enemy. It didn't need to live; Mexico choked on babies. But he didn't let them hear him.

The boy stood by the dead tree in the courtyard, waiting.

''It's a weak baby. Bad nourishment,'' Felipe told him indifferently. ''Maybe it will live.''

''A girl or a boy?''

''A boy. What about these men now?''

''The women don't want him,'' the boy said coolly. ''They'll smother him. After you go, señor, they'll smother him. They don't want any more boys that make men and kill each other. You'll see.''

Felipe grunted. ''Where are these *borrachos* now?''

The boy led us around to the back of the main house, where we saw in the ghostly light the neat stacks of bodies against the wall.

''How many?'' Felipe whispered, shocked.

I moved a little closer, incredulous. Their feet, bare or still sandaled, jutted out from the three piles as the only distinctly human feature left of them. Their dark heads disappeared into the dried blackened blood that was like a great spill of tar, sealing them together. I leaned against the stone wall thinking I would faint or be sick in a minute. All eighteen of the men, the boy told him, were dead. The boys left alive were all under sixteen. And where were they? The women had given them something to drink after they had stacked the bodies, and then made them go to bed. He had watched everything from the roof, but the other children had all slept through the fight.

"How do you know they were dead? Who said they were dead?" Felipe scowled at him.

"The women said. They felt them all and said they were dead. They said when the big boys are men they will be sent away from here so they won't drink and kill everyone. No more men here. The women said so. The new baby hasn't even got a father now." The boy stood as before, as if at attention. Later, I thought, you will fall apart.

"Where is your father?" Felipe asked him.

"He went away when I was a baby."

Felipe took him by the arm and led him to the women, who had come out. I followed like a donkey.

"It is a boy," one of the women told the boy.

He nodded and to Felipe he said again, "Ask them now. They'll smother him. After you go. They did it once, last year. Take him with you if you want him to live."

I gasped. They killed a baby last year? Why did he think the young mother would give up her baby? I imagined our taking it, Felipe and I, and fiercely keeping it alive.

The women stood like statues in the courtyard. Then a tiny girl, naked, slipped out of a hut and began to yowl. A woman picked her up, soothed her with long strokes on the arm, and then shoved a finger into her mouth. I heard a match struck somewhere.

"Tomorrow," Felipe announced, "someone will come from the police to verify. Don't bury the men till someone comes."

"The baby won't live. It's weak," an old woman said.

Two older boys came out, bare-chested, in *calzoncillos,* one carrying a lamp to which hundreds of fluttering moths swarmed.

"I don't want to hear about smothering this baby!" Felipe shouted all at once. Then he lowered his voice. "That will be murder. If I hear this, I will get the police to take you to jail." He let that sink in a moment and then he said, "There will be no more fighting and killing here. I am telling you. Keep this baby alive. Nobody will kill here again. Never."

Julio had waited for us. Felipe was in an almost catatonic state by the time we fell into the back seat. Julio wanted to know what had happened, but all Felipe could say was that murder had happened and that we had to stop at the police station first. Julio drove like a maniac, the ride so rough we held on to each other with our eyes shut.

In the long dark passage leading to the police desk, which was a card table where a policeman sat with a phone, a notebook, a few pens, and a burrito wrapped in a tear of newspaper, Felipe stopped to smooth his hair and straighten his clothes. I could have wept. He looked ghostly.

He made his report in the coolest style, muttering it at the crude-looking, half-toothless policeman as if the man were a flunky. This worked. In the abstract they had no respect for Felipe, treating him like an incurable foreign disease that had settled on the village long ago; but in the flesh they found him intimidating. I wanted to cheer. The policeman asked if I was a second witness, to which Felipe replied that no witness but himself was necessary and that if they didn't get out there fast they'd have a truckload of rotten flesh on their hands and the priest on their necks. He signed his report and simply turned away.

We walked to my place, the town around us like a graveyard, under the same cool moon that had turned everything at the ranch to ash. "I told you not to come," he whispered. I didn't answer. He had become strange to me because of the queer way in which, in spite of everything, he belonged here and I didn't and never would. Never. I hadn't seen this before. It chilled me. I imagined him without me and that was worse. And what about me? I had only a flash of that picture—a rear view of myself alone in a wood somewhere back home, staring at nothing, in a pause that could last my whole life.

He lay on his back, quiet, his slightly hooked nose silhouetted against the white wall of my room. I moved against him, to find his warmth and to rouse him. I still felt sick. I imagined I could still smell blood.

"Why'd you say that, about there being no more killing?" I waited and he waited. "Was it so they'd . . . make it come true or something? As a sort of hypnosis?"

He turned to look at me. Before he could answer, the roof door of the convent groaned open. Four A.M.! I held my breath, counting the nun's steps across the parapet to the tower, where she struck the old bell. The lingering sound shimmered across the sky like a rattled sheet of tin.

"Tell me."

"Is true," he said softly. Then he reached for me, his body relaxing as if it had made a decision.

"What you are afraid? Hm? They will not have more killing. That is the way it will be now."

The White Bedspread

ELENA CASTEDO

Approaching the closet, Audolina meets María in the mirror. María is her name in the Anglo houses. They are all Marías here, nobody can remember Audolina, Filomena, Mirella, such simple names. Audolina places her ear against the door one more time, then takes from the closet the carefully folded Garfinkel's bag *la Señora* gave her. This is the most delicate operation of the whole week, the most dangerous and eventually the most satisfying. It requires speed and precision.

Someone's coming up the stairs! María drops the bag and looks in the mirror; she takes a hairpin from her chignon and then puts it back. Even with her face all flushed from the scare, her image looks so dignified in front of the attic room, like the pictures of saints with landscapes behind them. *La Virgen Dolorosa* be praised; a bed white as a dove, with her own bedspread, in a room with a door that stays closed all night long.

The sound of steps is interrupted. They go down. Audolina takes a deep breath, opens the Garfinkel's bag, and carefully places a pork chop, wrapped in double tin foil, to keep the cursed dog's nose out of it.

Steps come up the stairs again. Audolina drops the bag nervously. She observes María in the mirror remove her apron. When the lines of the chest and the rump go flat, and hair shows gray, and the months are put to rest, it's the way the body shows what goes on in the soul. Then a woman can become pure again.

The steps are almost at her door. She walks around the bed, caressing out every nonexistent wrinkle. How beautiful. How lovely. Finally, her own bedspread, a dream for more than four times as many years as she has fingers.

The girl opens the door without knocking and walks in, wearing a slip and teen bra.

For the Sacred Virgin, still flat as a tortilla, wearing a bra . . .

"María, hook this bra tighter for me, will you?"

Audolina joins the two ends of the satin cloth; it feels dry compared to the live satin of the girl's back. Rougher patches announce her skin's imminent changes.

"María, you can stay this Sunday and tell me stories. Like that one about that deliveryman. Did he really leave you a red rose? You didn't make it all up? You can tell it to me again." The girl's lips stretch an unsteady smile over braces.

"Why you ask me to stay, Missy Jenny? You know I go and see the friends in La Mamplesa."

"Give me a break, María! It's not Mamplesa, how can you be so ignorant! It's Mount Pleasant."

"Is what I say, Missy Jenny, Mamplesa. I get ready now; in a minute *la Señora,* your mama, she take me to the bus stop. I got to fix my hair now, I got to change now." She lifts her arms to take the same hairpin and puts it back.

"You're so vain, María, always smoothing your hair to the back of your neck, and always putting cream in your hands. Don't tell me old women have boyfriends in Mount Pleasant! Wouldn't that be a riot!"

"Vain no, Missy Jenny. A woman have to be neat and clean, and, when the woman is young, she . . . well, she got to have no choice, but all the bad time have the end, then a woman is not so young, then a woman can be neat, a woman can be . . . clean again. Missy Jenny, you eat more, you put some meat up front, not a good-for-nothing bra you have. Next week we are together, and I fix you the most best *sopaipillas.* Delicious. Okay, child?"

''Child! Have you gone nuts? I'm not a child! You know very well I'm not! It's been five months now; I'm a woman! And I'm almost taller than you. Look. See? And what makes you think I need you around all the time? I have friends. I have a friend called Megan. She'd be right here with me if her parents hadn't forced her to go to the Greenbriar with them, right here. And other friends too. And I'd rather not have you around. You can leave, just leave!'' The girl slams the door as she walks out.

Audolina listens at the door. She must work fast. From the wastepaper basket she retrieves the small packages and tiny jars. Who'd look there, even if they should get suspicious? The rich have a fear of trash. She's so clever it makes her smile. She places the banana—also wrapped in tin foil, so the child won't pick up the aroma. Then the scissors that appeared—a joyous miracle—inside the family room's old couch while she was vacuuming it. She'll admire them later. Maybe she'll trade them for Corina's canned artichokes, or a scarf, or a belt; Corina's very bold; she'll take anything from her *Señora.* Now some of the little jars; Audolina's very conscientious about collecting small containers ahead of time; never leave things for the last minute, her grandfather used to tell them. Actually, nowadays she could buy some of these things if she wanted to, but it's for prevention and why not; she's very good at it. Empty prescription jars are the best; light, small, easy to pack, and ideal for a Sunday's supply. Plus some left over, to go on filling the larger containers in the room she rents from her country woman, Doña Rosa.

Ave María! Steps up the stairs again! Audolina dumps in the bag the small jars with lilac bath salts, lemon-scented Joy, butter, Mazola cooking oil, and vinegar—well wrapped in paper towels inside a sandwich baggie. There's no peace to be had. The steps go down the stairs. *Virgen Santa,* out with the bag again. The little jar with face cream fits snugly. Yes, she's still vain in some ways, Up Above forgive her. Then the whiskey. She'll invite Doña Rosa and Corina, and they'll go to La Latina to buy the best *empanaditas* and *croquetas* and olives in all of La Mamplesa, and come back to listen to Radio Borinquén, and Celia Cruz sing those Ayayay! merengues and salsa, and drink on the rocks, and laugh until their cheeks hurt. The Tide laundry soap fits well in a corner, also the bicarbonate of soda. She brings no perfume; none of that rich woman's perfume; the smell still tugs at her stomach. In the houses of diplomats from her own country, every time she heard those faint male steps come into her room at night, instead of asking aloud, "Who is it?" or turning on the light, she would dab *la Señora*'s perfume—kept in a Kaopectate bottle—in the dark . . .

Steps run up the stairs and the girl bursts in with shiny eyes. "Look what I brought you, María! The jewel box my father gave me when I was little; it's for you." The girl puts the box on the night table and opens it. "Isn't it beautiful music? It says here, 'Rachmaninoff's Prelude in C.' You're going to stay, aren't you, María? We can do fun things. If you want to, we can watch *telenovelas* on Telemundo, or Univisión, the Spanish channels; nobody'll be home but us."

"*Gracias, gracias,* Missy Jenny, but this is not for me, it is for you. I come back Monday and now I get ready."

"Well, I don't care if you go away for all of Sunday, or the whole weekend for all I care! You think I'm going to be begging you to stay? No way! You really think you're the cat's meow, don't you? Well, there're lots of things you don't know. I bet you don't know I don't have a thing under my slip; no panties. Sexy, huh?" The girl lifts her slip playfully above her bony knees. "Ayyy! Shame, shame!"

"Missy Jenny, you go, please; and take the pretty music box; your mama, *la Señora;* she very busy and she go to her office, and she call me in a minute . . ."

"C'mon, María. Pretty soon you'll be telling me your sob stories about no father, and 'thees vallee of teears' and working in houses where your soul split and all that crap. I know it's nothing but lies, because you won't tell me why your soul 'split.' What nonsense. And you won't stay and tell me. And your stupid stories; a red rose, give me a break! . . . María, María . . . I didn't mean it, I like your stories; I want you to stay, and you can tell me whatever you want. Okay?"

''Please, Missy, you go now, please, I get ready now . . .''

''Listen, why don't we pretend that my mom and stepdad are going on a trip today, instead of just going to their offices to work all weekend. That way we can walk to the bus, and we can go to the space museum and get ice cream, like we did when they went on trips. Hey! We can go to the river again, and walk there, and sit on the rocks under the bridge, and watch the water, and you can tell me things. Okay?''

''Missy Jenny, now I pack to go; things I need for the Sunday. Your mama; ask *la Señora* . . . ask *el Señor* to take you . . .''

''C'mon, María, you know perfectly well that my mother can't; she has all that law work to do. And my father lives in Chicago, of course, he can't take me to the river. And my stepdad; he's always got work to do; in the yard, on the computer, all that work to do.''

''Well, your Señora Mama, she is a lawyer very important. You call some friend from school, Missy, to come play.''

''Play! Play! Listen, María, why don't you get it through your thick head; I'm not a little kid! I'm a woman! And kids from school, they are busy; they have to go shopping with their parents, and they have to go eat out, and all that. And also, they can't fix food, or tell me things like you do . . .''

The girl observes María. María's standing firm. The girl goes to the bed doing dance steps that follow the music. With a grand ballet gesture she picks at the bedspread, leaving a big wrinkle.

''Missy Jenny, please, the bedspread is very good, very good bedspread, you know I paid the money for a new white bedspread, is not for play.''

Another ballet gesture, another tug, another big wrinkle on the bedspread.

Audolina freezes.

''Do you want me to leave you a red rose on your bedspread, María?''

''Missy Jenny, the bedspread is very important . . . like the bra for you. Please, for Santa Catalina, *protectora* of young girls . . .''

''Maríaaaaa! Why aren't you downstairs! I'm in a big hurry!''

''*Ay! Virgen Santísima! La Señora,* see? I said to you . . . now you make me very mad.'' Audolina attempts to bring the girl to the door. They push and pull.

''Let me go! Let me go! You're scratching my arms! You horrible old woman! You're the worst maid I ever had!'' The girl wiggles free and runs to the bed. She lifts her slip daintily from the back and sits in the middle of the bedspread. ''Guess what, María, guess what time of the month it is for me-e.'' The braces shine as she forces a smile.

''Missy, please, Missy, I not can buy another bedspread, please . . . go, go now . . .''

''Maríaaa! Are you coming or not? Jenny! Where's everybody?''

The girl gets up and leaves the room with dignity.

In the middle of the white bedspread there is a red spot. Audolina forcefully pushes back a savage assault of unending trampled territories. Where, where are the territories that can't be trampled on? The music stops. With a flushed face, Audolina quickly rearranges the ham piece and the sandwich Baggie with oatmeal. She drops a sweater on top of the bag. This sloppy work is against her principles, but she has no choice.

María closes the door and rushes downstairs, taking care not to jiggle the bag, holding it so it appears very light, saying loudly, ''*Sí, señora! Sí, señora!*''

We're in Sally's House

KEN CHOWDER

Rich is doing well; he's doing fine; he's really doing very well. "Richard is doing phenomenally well," Isabel, the morning day-care person, says. She's just come by to drop off some Desitin and bottle liners for Buggsy. "Because he's not repressing it," Isabel says. "He's letting himself feel the grief."

We're in the kitchen; her black sweatpants seem to flow into one of the black parquet squares. It could happen: the physical world is oddly unsteady in this house just now. The motion of molecules seems obvious; tables can float here, chairs buzz and resonate, people turn into photographs.

Isabel leans against the kitchen counter, her back touching a Nike shoe box with Rich's new basketball shoes in it. The shoes have been there for two months now. Rich has big feet; he's way tall, six-six, and a few years ago he could jump too. I envied him for that, and even more for the comfort he took in his surroundings—his ease in the world, the surety that life seemed to offer him. I keep wondering how much of that will change now.

"Why is that good?" I ask Isabel. "I mean, I know you're supposed to do it. But why is it actually good to grieve?"

"The more pain Rich processes now, the less he'll feel later," Isabel says. I wonder how she knows that; she's thirty-one, her parents are alive, what great grief has she processed, and shed, so far? Besides Sally, of course. Isabel too loved Sally. We all loved Sally.

Even I am processing pain—filtering it, I would say, or maybe the opposite, trying to change strong black coffee into water. And I'm probably repressing some pain, too; I'm from New England.

Isabel puts her Gore-Tex jacket back on—still dripping wet, of course, because this is Oregon—when the phone rings.

It's MJ, Sally's old college friend, calling from Berkeley. Two months later, the phone calls still come from all over. It's as if this house is a sunspot, its radiation felt on distant planets.

I met MJ when I lived in Rich's old house, thirteen years ago. Rich and Sally had just gotten together; MJ came visiting, and it wasn't easy for her. She kept calling Rich "Newboy" or "Nouveau Riche." MJ is gay, and she loved Sally. I don't mean that pejoratively, of course.

But even MJ has changed. "How's Richie doing?" she asks me now. She sounds awkward, and anxious; this is a combination of feelings I already recognize as standard, though I've only been here a few days.

But I don't really know how Rich is doing. Phenomenally well, maybe. Rich has always been good at things; but this is one thing I don't want to think of him as being good at. So I repeat what he said, when I asked him. "He's functioning," I tell MJ. "He's getting through every day."

"Yes?" MJ says.

"That's what he's doing," I say.

I consider telling her the things I've seen. Every night I've seen Rich go out on the front porch, after putting Buggsy to bed, to smoke one of those awful little cigars. It's always raining. Rich studies the rain; from inside the house, he seems to be in it. Usually Rich sobs out there. Or I guess he always does, so far.

A couple nights ago I asked if I could come out and keep him company on the porch. "Only if you don't mind seeing me blow my nose into my T-shirt," he said.

"I don't think I've ever seen a grown man blow his nose into his T-shirt," I said.

''Well, this is your chance,'' Rich said. ''Come on.''

He was holding on to the cigar, not smoking it; so he was out there to not smoke a cigar. ''No noise from Buggsy, I assume,'' he said. Rich has a Fisher-Price monitor in the kitchen; he keeps it turned up, and you can hear the baby breathe. Buggsy breathes deeply, easily, with a beautiful solidity; his sleep is one of the few things in this house that can never change. We like to watch Buggsy sleep, Rich and I; we like to listen to him breathe.

''Buggsy's okay,'' I said. Buggsy is more than okay; a few days after I got to Portland, I had the lunatic idea that what I could do was write Sally a letter to tell her what a terrific guy Buggsy was: *a letter,* I thought. The thought was not in my brain for very long, but even so.

''I want to tell you how great you are with Buggsy,'' I said to Rich. ''I'm proud of you.'' He got out of his chair and stood by the railing, closer to the rain. I'm proud of Rich for a number of things: how much he loves Buggsy, how much he loves Sally, how he gets through each day, how he doesn't blame himself (very often) for Sally—he blames himself for Sally, of course, but he doesn't *always* blame himself for Sally.

Rich leaned against the porch railing with both arms, drew in breath, and sobbed. I've gotten used to Rich sobbing, or almost. He sobbed in the car on the way to Tom's wedding; he sobbed when we looked at Buggsy's baby calendar (Rich had written, ''What does Buggsy mean when he waves to us? Is he waving goodbye or hello? Are we just imagining everything Buggsy knows?''; Sally had written, ''Right now you're cooing on the nursery floor, Buggsy!''). There's always a reason for Rich to sob, and there's almost never a reason for Rich not to sob. I could describe Rich's sobbing—which sometimes sounds like long braying, and sometimes is so deep it makes him, like a hurt child, unable to breathe—but mostly I don't really listen. Rich's sobbing no longer makes me want to sob as well. I don't want him to sob; I don't want him not to sob; it is something constant and steady, like the passing of time, that can't always be truly considered, or even recognized—or else we'd all go crazy in short order, thinking the unthinkable over and over.

Rich stopped sobbing. He looked out at the swarming rain. "I keep feeling she's on the other side of a silent river," he said. The edges of the dark street, Southeast Elliott, were filled with black water running toward the drain. If it rained a little more, the house too would liquefy, then slide down into the city sewers; there would be a gap on Southeast Elliott, a place where something had happened.

"I can see her, and I can feel her," Rich said. "But I just can't hear her voice." He sobbed, pulled up what we used to call a hawker, spat over the railing, and blew his nose.

"That's good, Rich," I said. "I've finally witnessed a grown man blowing his nose into a T-shirt. Thanks for broadening my horizons."

"I always forget Kleenex," Rich said.

"Use mine," I said. I pulled the tail of my T-shirt out of my pants. Rich looked at me just then; we were looking at each other, as if trying to see what the other might feel. And then this happened: Rich took the offered tail of my T-shirt in his hands, and out of his body and onto my shirt came this terrible mess of love.

We're all a mess here. I guess that's obvious.

So I think to tell MJ: Rich is okay: he blew his nose into my T-shirt. But Isabel is still here, leaning against the kitchen counter, eating Buggsy's Cheez-Its from the box, and I can't quite tell MJ what I know: this is what you could call a social situation. "I think Rich will be okay someday, MJ," I say, and I wonder, as always, whether this is what she wants to hear.

Buggsy is doing phenomenally well. He's just learning to talk. He points at something, and Rich tells him its name, and Buggsy says "Vshoo Avushja," approximately, and Rich says "That's *right,* Buggs!" though Buggsy has just pointed at a doggie. He can say a couple of words clearly, and he clearly knows which ones they are: he likes to drop things on the floor just so he can say "Uh-oh." He has this perfect "Uh-oh."

Yesterday I took Buggsy for a walk. "He'll cry a while," Rich said, dropping Buggsy down into my backpack. "Probably until I'm out of sight."

Buggsy didn't cry. "Car," he said, leaning excitedly in the backpack, pointing. There was indeed a car parked on the street. "Car," he said again. Sure enough, another car. "*Car,*" Buggsy said. "*Car.*"

Rich backpedaled toward the front door, going very slowly; he seemed . . . no, I can't say I know what that expression was on his face. I started to walk us down Southeast Elliott, toward the central circle of Ladd's Addition, where roses bloom in another, very different season.

Buggsy was trying to stand up in my backpack. "Car."

"That's right, Buggs. That's a car. Another car, Buggman."

"*Car.*"

"Exactly right. But exactly."

Buggsy was struggling wildly back there. Finally he managed to get on his feet. He pointed at the world again. "Uh-oh," he said, though nothing, apparently, had been dropped, or fallen of its own weight.

"That's a car, Buggsy," I said. I sounded curiously like a stewardess, crazily cheerful: *No, we're not going down, at least not yet; chicken or beef?*

I said, "That's another *car,* Buggsy."

"Uh-oh," Buggsy said.

Bad news over the phone. It seems an American institution, like Time in Airports or Clicking the Remote Control: this is how we live.

This happened two months ago. I guess I already said that. I was in Oakland, where I live, when Kate called. I used to live with Kate; we lived together in Rich and Sally's house.

"It's Kate," she said, and I knew immediately, the way you always do: it announces itself before the words come out. "I have bad news," she said.

I have bad news. Of course: the words are always the same, exactly. Death is always infuriatingly itself, exacting in its repetition, like school figures by a cheerless skater who is at one with the ice.

I said, "What is it, Kate?"

"Sally," Kate said. "It's Sally."

The reaction is almost generic: you say small words, the same words, useless words like "No," or "Oh," or "God," and then of course you cry . . . no, I think I'm wrong. The reactions are completely different, but the words that come out are the same, because the feelings are more than the words, not contained in them. Words don't work; they don't say things. "Sally," Kate said, "it's Sally"; and then I said, absurdly, "Sally *Tollef*son?"—as if I had ever known any other Sally, as if I could escape the terrible fact by letting someone else, some stranger, die on the highway between Missoula and Portland.

I wanted to hang up. I didn't. I listened to details, growing more pained over the growing set of facts, as if the more I heard, the more it became true, and I knew Kate would eventually use the word "seatbelt," the last word in the world I wanted to hear, in the last conversation in the world I wanted to have. At the end I even said, "Thanks for calling, Kate."

Two months later, I'm in Kate's living room. "Rich is getting through every day," I tell Kate now, because she's asked. "He's functioning."

"Of course he's functioning," Kate says. "He has to. There's Buggsy."

Her living room is a mix: elegant rosewood and black-cherry furniture her husband, Greg, makes, and a huge goggle-eyed plastic duck Callie pushes ad infinitum around the couch, and badly beaten pastel plastic letters scattered around the wall-to-wall, and copies of *Goodnight Moon* and *Pat the Bunny* left for dead on the floor. Callie is too old for *Pat the Bunny,* but she still loves it; Kate is concerned.

"It's good, in a way," Kate says. "Rich doesn't have a choice. He *has* to function."

"It doesn't matter whether he has to or not," I say. "Not everybody could do it."

Kate smiles at me a little sadly. Or maybe a lot sadly, who knows. "You don't have kids," she says, in explanation.

I know she feels sorry for me. Do I feel sorry for her? Sure I do. We were lovers once, we know each other; there's always something to feel sorry for.

"No," I say. "I don't have children, Kate."

The guy who towed away Rich and Sally's Volvo said, "Anything but a Volvo, all of em woulda been killed." So Kate and Greg are selling their car now, buying a Volvo. In this way, maybe, they will never die.

I don't have to buy a Volvo. For people like me, nobody dies; or, if they do, we don't happen to be around.

"Want to buy a Toyota Camry?" Kate asks me. "It runs really really well."

"I'm sure it does," I say.

I wasn't there for the funeral; I've never been there for a funeral. I missed the funeral because, in theory, I got the day wrong: I thought it was the *next* Friday, not *that* Friday. Apparently I couldn't believe it would be that soon; didn't everyone need time to collect themselves?

That's what I'm doing today: viewing the vid with Mitzi and Kevin. Mitzi and Kevin are going to buy a house, get married, have kids—so they're charmed, surrounded by that beautiful bubble, the implacable fiction that sometimes works. They were in Florida when Sally died, and they too want to see the vid.

The church videotapes all its funerals; when I heard that, I remembered hearing about a hospital that takes photos of all its stillborn babies. Maybe all hospitals do, for all I know. So a filing cabinet must exist, probably on the hushed bottom floor of every hospital, under winking, indecent fluorescent lights, a deep file that no one in their right mind ever goes through.

Mitzi and Kevin and I are sitting side by side by side on their sofa. Mitzi has placed a box of Kleenex on the sofa's arm; Kevin has stoked the wood stove. We're ready; we brace ourselves; Kevin, the man of the house, clicks the remote.

Church policy must be to set the camera on a tripod in back of the balcony and just let it run. So we watch the church slowly filling up with people, listen to the organ drone. It goes on and on. You can't recognize anyone: you just see the dim backs of heads, a long way away. For a long time we watch a few people sitting.

"This could use a good editor," Kevin says.

"We could fast-forward," I say—tentatively, because this is a sacred object of a kind, though it's just a vid. It doesn't feel good to want to fast-forward a funeral.

Kevin clicks the remote: this is how we live.

Fast-forward works. Bodies begin to fill the pews. They stir and rustle, still in only a slight hurry. "It looks like a wedding," I say.

"Different clothes," Mitzi says.

But I've only got one suit. I wear it to weddings, and I would have worn it to this too. People like me don't even know the difference between a funeral and a wedding.

Eventually the organ stops; Kevin clicks the remote back to real time. A woman comes out and plays the bassoon (Sally played the bassoon); another woman comes out and sings a Norwegian song (Sally didn't speak Norwegian). A priest comes out and talks for a long time: he says that God can help us through times like these, that we should look to God. It doesn't sound like he knew Sally; it sounds like a paid political advertisement.

I don't know what I expected. I was thinking, somehow, that Sally had been there, that a funeral gives you one last chance to see the person, a farewell appearance; I was thinking of Sally going around shaking hands with the audience. Let's make a deal, Sally.

But then people get up and speak. They're far away, indistinct, broken into dots on the screen; but they knew her. Her family gets up, one by one. Her brother Steve says he has six things to say about Sally. The first thing: when they were little, Sally and he used to share a room. Steve was afraid of the dark. He would wake up terrified in the middle of the night; he'd wake Sally up and make her get their mother, who would sit with them until they went back to sleep. It wasn't until many years later, when Steve was in college, that Sally's mother found out: it was Steve and not Sally who was afraid of the dark.

I think this is what gets me: that Sally was not afraid of the dark. I sob, both hands over my face, trying to hold this interior corruption in, trying not to let the noise come out, trying to still the wracking wrenching that's like some child being born within me. What am I *do*ing, for Christ's sake? Sitting on someone's sofa watching TV, looking through tears at a pale fuzz of video dots my eyes have decided represent Steve Tollefson, desolate—someone I love has died, and I'm watching TV, and she will always be dead, and I'm watching TV. I want to stop this: and then I see for the first time that it must be the same for Rich, that he never wants to sob on his porch, that every day he too tries, and fails, to stop himself, and tries again, and fails again.

I pull the tail of my T-shirt out from beneath my shirt and give it all I've got: I blow.

Rich is out on the porch. "The other day MJ asked me if I missed Sally," he says, wonderingly. "And you know what? I almost said no. 'Miss' is the wrong word. It's not . . . basic enough. But what is? What's the word for this, anyway?"

It's raining, of course. And, of course, I don't know the word Rich is looking for. It must be something small and simple, and beyond me. "So what did you say to MJ?" I ask.

He shrugs. "I said yes. I said yes, I miss her."

"I wonder why she asked," I say.

Rich doesn't answer me. He puts his little awful cigar into his mouth and doesn't light it. He says, "When we had the accident, the first thing I did was get Buggsy out. Then I went and found Sally. As soon as I saw her, I knew she was dead. I knew everything, actually. In that one second, I knew everything. I knew she was dead, and I knew I wasn't, and I already saw how it would be, bringing up Buggsy. I knew how it would be. I saw the past and I knew about the future. I even knew things that weren't true, because they're part of it. I knew everything. And I still know. I still know.''

This house is about to disintegrate, from the rain; this house is about to disappear. I can feel myself sliding down the street in the rainwater, buoyed up by the current, on my back, legs first, down the stairs, along the sidewalk, into the street, carried by the black water like a leaf among the leaves, gliding easily along toward the drain, my head up, watching all the dark trees as they reach their branches up toward the sky above me.

But I still can't know what Rich knows, exactly. What do I know? I know that I don't want to know. There are still so many things I don't ever want to know—things we seem to learn, here, under rain, on earth.

Divine Providence

SANDRA CISNEROS

Why is Alma Alvarado crying? Until today she could wake to her mama calling *Alma, Alma,* very gently, the way her mama does—*so as to give the soul time to fly back from the dreams.* The sky was blue and smelled of fresh bread and oatmeal. The navy-blue uniform with the detachable collar and cuffs waited patiently on its hanger same as always. She would save a spear of the breakfast papaya for the parrot in the garden of la Señora Cuca, walk to school with her leather school satchel on her back, sing the Himno Nacional in a loud patriotic voice, color a map of the república, eat a ham and cheese torta for lunch, and on the way home buy a bag of Japanese peanuts from the man with one fat foot and the other skinny, throw her satchel in the air and catch it, play in the courtyard—*but not beyond!*—climb the spiral staircase to the rooftop—clink, clang, clang—peer into the rooftop room that once belonged to la Luz María before the abuela ran her off for stealing a half kilo of butter, tease the mean dog el Lobo who likes to bark from the roof at anyone who walks down their street, eat a tangerine and toss the peels over the wall to the neighbor's chickens, guess how many shards of glass were cemented on the wall ledge to keep out the thieves, stare at the volcanoes that once were people but are now simply volcanoes, read a Familia Burrón comic book and be read to, wash her feet before going to sleep, have her mama sing—*Sleep, my little girl, sleep, rrruuu*-rrruuu, *rrruuu*-rrruuu, *rrruuu*-rrruuu—all in Spanish which sounds sweet.

But this afternoon her mama was busy washing clothes by hand on the scrubboard sink with a tin bowl of water and a coffee can of detergent, wedding ring sitting plainly beside the straw brush, a ring pretty to look through with its rainbow stone and gold band thick and heavy, the kind of ring a girl like Alma likes to wear on her own hand to pretend *she* is the mother, because today her mama had said yes, finally yes, while wiping a strand of hair from her face, *yes,* without looking up, *just leave me be,* pretending she didn't hear the parrot cries of the papa's mama, *Just go see what it is your abuela wants this time,* the mama will say, and Alma will have to go up to the abuela's room with its scent of candles and mothballs and overripe fruit, because the abuela has fallen into the habit of hiding food under her pillow—*In this house they never feed me!*—forgetting she already ate an hour before, will hide hard knobs of bread, or a half tortilla, or a black banana, or those cookies called fatties that crumble into a paste and taste like smoke, the ones they fry on griddles in front of the church and wrap in papel de china, all under the embroidered pillow thinking no one the wiser when all along a string of brown ants always gives her away, because the mama can no longer climb up and down the stairs anymore in her condition since the baby they will name Reynaldo is asleep inside her mama's belly, the child her mama hopes will anchor her papa home nights and mend the marriage like the neighbor lady Doña Eufemia Delgado Ruiz advised.

But now the ring is gone, gone, *I swear I don't know how, Mama, I swear it was on my hand when I reached to flush the toilet like so,* and if Señor Meléndez the plumber can't bring it back, Mama will have her baby right now from so much nerves and crying, while the abuela is screaming in her mad parrot voice for her supper, the papa on the telephone and the mama lying down with a cold washcloth on her forehead, *and the water swirled, Mama, swirled without a nose or tail* when the mama's ring leapt from her hand and disappeared with two little sausages of caca, and now there is no way to bring the ring back except by pumping furiously this useless plunger, though perhaps the ring is floating through the sewers of Mexico City by now, and into the muddy canals of Xochimilco where a plump woman in a green satin cocktail dress is trailing a pink hand from a flowered chalupa named *Perlita,* beyond the floating gardens and beneath the ruins of an abandoned city where an eagle once perched on a cactus and bit a serpent, and has swooped and tumbled and somersaulted into the eddies and spirals of the Gulf of Mexico waters that are as warm and salty as tears, while, no doubt, little and big sharks are nibbling on a ragged piece of seaweed the moment the ring settles finally on the sea bottom with a soundless poof of sand.

And it will be just as his mother predicted long ago for going against her better judgment and marrying a girl beneath his station in life. Unless the ring comes back like the neighbor lady Doña Eufemia Delgado Ruiz advised, the marriage will be finished regardless how many candles are lit, or promises made, or supplications to St. Anthony recited, Ave Maria, Padre Nuestro, world without end, amen. Why is Alma Alvarado crying?

Truck

DAGOBERTO GILB

In the center of the carpenter's shop was the table saw. As always, or almost, Martínez was holding a piece of wood against the fence, his straw cowboy hat a little low on his forehead, a cigarette slanted out the right side of his mouth, his eyes slit onto a bevel cut he was guiding through. A few of the men, carpenters and laborers, had hopped up and sat on the worktable which L'ed two walls. Others stood near the radial arm saw, a couple leaned against the drill press. Two more men hovered near Martínez, so full of admiration their expression verged on love. Since Martínez had once been employed in a cabinet shop, he was the star of the show, the man called on for the fine jobs, when patience and delicacy were more important than speed and strength. These two men near him were especially impressed by his skill.

The table saw was loud, even louder when it was cutting, and nobody bothered much about talking with it engaged. But when the power was shut off and the motor wound down, the contrasting silence was dramatic. Modesty being another of Martínez's virtues, he liked to take the hushed moment at the center of the shop to remark on his just-finished product with self-deprecation.

"It'll have to do," he pronounced, the cigarette between his lips waving up and down with each syllable. He held the cut piece there, eyeballing the length as he savored a drag off the unfiltered butt.

Blondie, the foreman, known jokingly as el mero güero, was at his wooden desk at another corner of the shop. In fact his blond hair was mostly gray. ''Moya,'' he called, waving Alex over. Carlos Davis followed a step behind.

''You wanna buy it?'' Blondie asked. He liked Alex. ''It's almost new.''

''It's a .357 magnum?'' Alex asked. Carlos was big-eyed over Alex's shoulder.

''Forty-four magnum. If you don't know the difference, you don't know.''

''Can I see it?'' Carlos asked.

Blondie's head went back and his eyebrows lifted, meaning ''no way.'' He didn't need to respond with words, and he seldom used them, a result, probably, of his not knowing any Spanish and working with so many men that knew so little English. He'd worked for the city over twenty years, and this was his last week. He handed the pistol to Alex. He liked Alex, liked his work, but he didn't trust Carlos. A few of the other men wandered over, including Martínez.

''I guess not,'' Alex told him as he babied it in his hands. ''Sure wouldn't want it aimed at me.''

Martínez—nobody used his first name—reached for the gun, and Alex passed it on. ''Goes right through two or three walls, I hear,'' he said. ''Puts a hole in the man the size of a football, I hear.''

Blondie nodded, indifferent to the information. ''Good protection,'' he said. ''I just wanna sell it.''

''Not today,'' Alex apologized.

''I own a Remington shotgun,'' Martínez said. ''It'll put a hole in the right places too.''

''Yeah, well . . .'' Blondie stared back at his desk, at a pile of work requests. ''This one's for you,'' he told Alex. ''A partition at the Armijo Center.''

''Just me and Carlos?''

Blondie nodded. Then he shook some keys off the desk. ''I'm going ahead and giving you this truck.'' It was the truck the shop had been promised a year earlier but had just got the week before. If

Blondie hadn't retired, it'd been his to drive home. The new foreman didn't need one because he already had one.

Alex could feel Martínez's sigh of disapproval. He'd spend the rest of the day talking about what a mistake this was, how one of the other carpenters deserved it more.

"One thing," Blondie said, pulling the hand with the keys back to keep Alex's attention. He glanced over at Martínez, who was listening closer than he pretended, before he spoke. "Well, you know, or you should by now."

After he and Carlos slid plywood and two-by-fours onto the bed of the truck, Alex picked up a Skilsaw and a cord and some nails, then loaded them and his toolbox. It was a long drive from the city's yard in the rural Lower Valley to the Segundo Barrio. Alex, who was always in a hurry, was about to get on I-10. "N'hombre!" Carlos told him. "Go the long ways, make it happen slow." He dragged out the last word like he was talking about sex. Alex grinned and nodded and cruised North Loop, whiffing the damp smell of horses.

Carlos was excited about being in the truck—maybe the newest auto he'd ever been in, besides a police car, and it was close to two years old. "You see how I told you?" he said. "I told you about Blondie, how he'd listen. He knows how you're the best carpenter. He knows. He knows about that metiche Martínez too, how he talks pedo behind your back. . . ."

"Forget about it, man," Alex said, cutting him short. "Let's forget about that dude."

Carlos had a habit of going too far, making fights. Not that he wasn't right about Martínez. And Blondie did honor him with one of the trucks—Urquidi drove the one-ton for the large jobs which most of the men went to, but now he and Martínez would be treated as equals for the smaller, two-men jobs. Still, Carlos exaggerated, just like he did about what a great carpenter Alex was. His exaggerations confused Alex as much as his confessions, like the one about stealing from the shop. A block plane, a Phillips screwdriver, some needle-nose pliers. Things did get lost, and probably other men had taken a tool or two. Carlos wasn't exactly wrong about this. But if Alex wasn't sure it wasn't exactly right either, he didn't say so. He couldn't resist the admiration, seeming smart, or skilled, or whatever it was Carlos saw in him, and he didn't want to be a disappointment. And then, even though he was eight years older than Carlos, who was twenty, Alex carried a private respect for him. Alex might stand up and say he could hold his own, but Carlos had been raised real tough and done real bad, and that, like someone who'd been in a war, was a strength which was always veiled and mysterious, envied by those who grew up on the easier side of the highway. All Alex had done to be this great carpenter was work for his cousin's construction company. He wanted this city job because it was steady—he was married and the father of two daughters, one not even a year old. It was Carlos's first job ever.

Carlos had grown up on Seventh Street. He came up behind one of the turquoise-framed screen doors, with only one light bulb, in that gray brick building, its seventy-year-old lintels and thresholds tilted and sagging, the building across the street from the one painted sapphire, next to the ruby one, a block away from the one whose each apartment was a swath of brilliant Mexican color—the whole street woven with shades as bold and ornate and warm as an Indian blanket. Across the street from the Armijo Center, at the Boys' Club, Carlos stabbed a dude when he was eleven. Across from there, under the mural of Che Guevara, where all those gang placazos are sprayed in black, he soaked red bandannas, shut his eyes, and sniffed until his mind floated away like in a light wind.

"That's some stupid shit," Alex told him. "Make your brains turn to hamburger."

"Already I know now," Carlos said, serious, "but I didn't then." His lips bent sarcastically. "If they turned into tacos, that'd be something else, eh?"

Alex had been driving real slow down the street listening to Carlos, even went past the Armijo by a couple of blocks before he U-turned around.

"Park in the front, güey," Carlos said. "You got the city sign on the side. I wanna show off for my bro's."

''It's a loading zone.'' Alex parked in the lot beside the building. He didn't want to mess up. That's what Blondie had meant: Martínez was behind the scenes saying how Alex was no better a carpenter than Carlos was his helper. ''My grandma could do as well, and she's got cataracts,'' was how he'd say it. That the two got along was evidence of even worse things, since Martínez especially didn't like Carlos. The truck was Blondie's way of backing Alex.

Carlos shook his head displeased, pissed off that he didn't get his way. ''It'd be *bad* parking out in the front like we own the place.''

''We ain't rock stars driving a limousine,'' Alex said, at these moments wondering why he ever tried to work with the guy.

While Alex went through the glass front doors, Carlos hung back, doing a slow, unhappy strut outside in his chinos and white T-shirt. But once he did push the doors too and saw nobody else was around, he quickened his pace and dropped the attitude. They unloaded the material and tools and even flirted with the secretary while they worked—she was married, but she was all right. They built a partition to close and lock up a small room for basketballs and pool sticks, Ping-Pong paddles and the like. They didn't hang the door because it wouldn't be available until next week, but framed and plumbed and anchored and sheeted it with plywood, even fixed a couple of other things the secretary pointed out. All of it was done in three hours. Alex *was* fast, especially compared to the other city carpenters. It was all they were expected to do that day.

''Fucking Martínez,'' Carlos said out on the hardwood basketball courts. ''That old dude would still be chopping the tree or some shit. His camaradas would be right at his culo. Oh, Mr. Mar-*tí*-nez, you do it so *good.* Maybe he'd still be hitting on a nail. Tac. Tac. Tac. Fucking put a dude to sleep, like to dead.''

Alex had borrowed one of the basketballs. He'd played on his high school basketball team, once in a while on the asphalt courts on the grounds of Austin High School with some old friends—he was shooting better now than he did back then, and he'd been good in high school.

''Andale, güey!'' Carlos was shaking his head under the hoop. ''What don't you do good?''

Alex was feeling fine because of his play, and of course the compliment helped. So fine it made him think of those things he didn't do anymore, that he'd left behind. He'd been doing right and that wasn't wrong. But he'd missed out too. He didn't get to shoot hoops often enough, and he'd forgotten how much fun it was messing around for no reason when—maybe even *because*—he knew he should be doing something better. All his girlfriends were because he made baskets. His wife, who was the best-looking, sweetest girl he met in high school, first smiled at him because the ball swung in the net.

"Let's go to lunch," he said.

"Let's get some beer," Carlos suggested.

"Let's go to lunch and get beer too," Alex said.

They went down the street to the Jalisco Cafe and ordered the special and two beers each. It was still real early, and Alex didn't think it was a good idea to go back to the Armijo with nothing to do.

"Maybe we should just go back to the shop," Alex said.

"N'hombre! We ain't got nothing *there.* Better we do nothing *here.* How am I not right?"

It was one of those subjects that Alex didn't feel like arguing about. And Carlos was right—if they went back, they'd have to sit around bored, look for Blondie, who probably wouldn't be around, even chance having to explain themselves if someone bigger came by.

Carlos told Alex about a shade tree they could park under, but first he made him stop at Peña's Bakery. Alex assumed it was for some cigarettes. Instead, Carlos came out with two quarts of beer.

"Are you crazy?!" Alex said.

"Yessir, I am the crazy dude, at your service." Carlos unscrewed the cap from one and passed it to Alex. He was already having fun.

"We can't do this," Alex said.

Carlos put on his cholo slouch, his head drooping sideways and back. ''It's not chiva, not even mota. It's not nothing, güey, just some *beer.*''

Alex shook off his worry. He even felt ashamed for being afraid to do something as harmless as this. What kind of man was he becoming? It was no big deal. Who couldn't handle a little beer? And once he settled down and relaxed, he even liked it.

They kicked back under the shade tree for over an hour, then agreed to drive a long route back.

''Over there,'' Carlos said. Alex stopped the truck by a small grocery on Alameda. Carlos took a five from Alex for the peanuts that would disguise their breath.

He came back with a cocky smile and two more quarts of beer.

''No way, man,'' said Alex. ''We're just going back. We can't walk in there after we drank these.''

''I got the peanuts. And these were on sale.'' Carlos opened his. ''Those dudes won't see nothing different in this dude.''

Alex fought off his first impulses, even criticized himself again. Then Alex went ahead and opened his and drank and started enjoying himself—not quite like Carlos, who was chugging the bottle in a hurry. But Alex slipped into such a calm about it he drove with his mind on all kinds of things he'd wanted to do which he'd forgotten about, and he drove not thinking of much else other than this until he realized he'd driven too far, way east of the city complex. He both laughed and got mad at this lapse, looked both in front and in the rearview mirror. No cars were coming, and he turned left into the empty field on the other side of the street to turn around.

''What a stupid move, güey,'' Carlos said, irritated. He was more drunk than Alex. He was a sure bust—everybody would see him and know. ''That pinche Martínez is gonna be out here to get us and be laughing in our face. What the fuck you do this for?''

They'd tried everything to get it out but half the tire had dug itself into the sand. They'd tried putting rocks under it, chunks of wood. The tire spun, spraying sandy dirt.

"We ain't gonna get this truck no more," Carlos complained. "You lost us this truck."

Alex didn't disagree, or argue, or offer a word in defense. Like Martínez, Carlos was far away. Alex felt himself quietly in the air, his arms cocking, the ball rolling off his fingers. It stretched the net, and the net held it there—a long time, or short, depending on how it would be remembered, just like a first kiss.

The Theft

RON HANSEN

While he was waiting in the kitchen, the police sergeant got out a cigarette and hunted a match. His name was Dunne. He was mustached and gray and thirty-six years old, dressed in a hard navy-blue uniform that he'd ironed until the creases and pleats seemed sharp as paring knives. Dunne opened a dessert service drawer and then a drawer with torn coupons and hand tools and batteries in it. Dunne stared at the hand tools for a good while before closing the drawer again. At last he went to the stovetop and held his cigarette inside a puttering ring of green-and-blue flame. He turned off the gas flame and took a hard drag on the cigarette as he looked at the fresh pumpkin-orange paint on the kitchen walls. Talk was loud on the radio handpack attached to his belt, so he tuned it down. He exhaled gray tobacco smoke. She'd put wineglasses in the kitchen sink, the four rims all stained with pink lipsticks.

She finished her shower and hurried in, holding shut a white terry-cloth robe as she considered the policeman. Her blond hair was wetly brown and the tracks of the comb were still in it. She seemed surprised to see him there though she'd heard his voice and invited him inside when he called to her from the kitchen porch. "Took a while," she said.

"Wasn't an emergency, just a burglary. You weren't in danger, were you?"

''Skip it,'' she said. She tilted away from his too interested attention and sat down on a kitchen chair.

''Just tell me how it happened,'' the police sergeant said.

Linda sighed. ''Like I told the flake on theft detail, I was just coming back from the grocery store. I parked the car in the alley and carried the stuff up the back porch steps and inside and he must have followed me.''

''Was the door unlocked?''

''Sure. I mean, I unlocked it. With my house keys.''

''You have them?''

She tried to remember what she'd done with them and then turned to check the ajar kitchen door. She stood up and frantically peered at the kitchen table, the white pantry countertop, and the child's kneehole desk that she usually put her mail on.

''Are the house keys gone too?''

She looked at him with panic.

''You opened the door with your house keys,'' the police sergeant said. ''Your hands were full. You may have left the house keys in the door and carried the groceries inside.''

''Yes; I suppose so.'' She gazed at the door. ''That's really terrifying.''

''You could change the locks again,'' Dunne said. He tapped the jagged ash from his cigarette into his palm, then carried the ash to a wrinkled grocery sack on the floor.

She asked him, ''Aren't you supposed to be writing this down?''

''Sergeants get rookies to do their paperwork, that's one of the good parts of the job.''

''Congratulations,'' she said.

''About time,'' Dunne said, and looked at the furniture in the front room and hallway, then leaned against the kitchen doorway and crossed his forearms and ankles. ''What else?''

A flock of sparrows flushed up in the yard and she followed their flight until they'd completely disappeared in the east. She said, ''You'd think you'd have a feeling that an unfamiliar person was in the house with you, but I didn't. Everything seemed so normal until I heard the spring on the back door."

Dunne walked over and pushed open the screen door to hear the noise. The iron spring was orange with rust and rang slightly as it dragged against the wood.

"Like that, but not so much," Linda said.

"You could hardly hear it."

"Right."

"You looked behind you, though."

"And nobody was there," Linda said.

"And?"

"And I put away the groceries. Wind, I thought."

"You heard the door. Was that him sneaking in or him sneaking out?"

"I have no way of knowing."

"When did you notice your purse had been stolen?"

"Exactly?"

"You reported a theft at a quarter past three."

"Well, I suppose I hunted around for fifteen minutes or so before I was positive that I hadn't simply mislaid it."

"Any idea of the contents?"

"My checkbook. Wallet and credit cards. Lipstick. Kleenex. Hand cream. Junk mostly, except for the wallet. And there was just a few dollars in that."

The policeman took his cigarette to the kitchen faucet and killed it with a jolt of water. "Was it expensive, that purse?"

She perused him and said, "Extremely."

"Was my picture still in it?"

She shook her head.

Dunne peered out through the four-paned window just above the kitchen sink. A fat, aproned woman was kneeling in her garden next door and putting in flower bulbs with a trowel. She sat back on her haunches and shaded her face from the sunshine. "I'm trying to imagine how you must have felt," Dunne said. "You must have felt like there was a ghost in the house. Haunting you. Watching every move you made. Stealing your purse and your keys. And you didn't even know it."

"You're enjoying this, aren't you?" Linda asked, but from the hard intensity of his frown she could tell he was not.

A half minute of silence passed between them, and he said, "You've painted."

"Yes."

"Looks nice."

"And then the rent went up."

"Much?"

"Fifty bucks."

"Still a good deal," he said.

Linda stood up and got a diet cola from the Hotpoint refrigerator. She snapped it open and sipped from it. She asked, "Was it a coincidence that you came?"

"I heard the address on the radio."

"And you decided to give it your personal attention."

He turned up his handpack and heard a rookie patrolman reading information from motor vehicle registration papers, and then he lowered the volume again. "Shall I figure it for you?"

She sipped her cola. "You're the cop."

"You got a guy thinks you're hot stuff," he said. "You knew him once maybe, but he isn't getting anywhere with you now. Wants to, though. Would like to let you know he's still around. Looking out for you. And then he sees you getting your groceries. Wonders about talking to you, but doesn't. Hangs out, just waiting for you to get into your car. Still doesn't make his move. And so he follows you here. You surprise him. You stun him, probably. Here he's been on your tail for an hour and you haven't seen a hint of him. And you've been the only thing beside himself that he's looked at or thought about. So he steals your purse like a kid writes his name on the sidewalk, just to say he exists."

"And he takes my house keys to tell me he'll be back."

She could have counted to one hundred in the silence, and then Dunne asked, "So how are things?"

"Getting better."

"Yeah?"

"Yeah."

"You happy?"

"Up and down. You know."

"Having fun?"

"Off and on."

"Seeing anybody?"

She shrugged.

"Any chance?"

"Who knows," Linda said.

"Okay," he said. "Your purse is in the milk box outside." He put his hand in his pocket and took out her house keys and handed them to her. "You watch it," he said.

"You," she said.

A Family Resemblance

JAMES D. HOUSTON

It wasn't a bad-looking car, a 1984 Citation with AM/FM, air conditioning, automatic transmission. Baby blue. Not my first choice for getting around, but my mother had enjoyed it. I started out thinking I could get thirty-three or thirty-four hundred, which seemed to be a fair price at the time, according to the classifieds. I was prepared to take less. I had to get rid of it. I wasn't planning to drive it, and storing it was not an option.

After the ad came out half a dozen people called. Three stopped by the house to look at the car, among them Harold Wang, a medical student from Shanghai. He drove it around the block and haggled in a preliminary way, then said he wanted his cousin's opinion. For reasons too trivial to go into—let's say it was mutually convenient—we agreed to meet a second time in a parking lot on the outskirts of San Jose, a Safeway lot on a long boulevard of malls and discount stores.

I had decided I would let Harold have the car for thirty-two, or even a bit less, if he could come up with the money right away and not keep me waiting. I liked the way he had presented himself. He was twenty-six or twenty-seven, a clean-cut fellow—dark slacks, sport shirt—in his second year at Stanford and obviously under a lot of pressure, as graduate students always are. He had brought along his young wife and their new baby and a couple of people who stayed in another car while we talked. One of them was his father.

They were all from mainland China. Though the father did not open his mouth the whole time, I could tell he had coached the son on how to shop for a car in the United States. The son was in a way performing for the father, trying to be shrewd and manly in these negotiations.

I liked the family unity, since this was the way I had grown up, among relatives who had come West during the 1930s, new to this coast and sticking together while they made their way.

I also figured Harold had access to the necessary cash. I had only seen the father from a distance, but he had a prosperous look about him. At our second meeting, as a matter of fact, I was certain Harold carried an envelope full of bills in his coat pocket. He was as ready to buy as I was to sell. Or almost as ready.

The cousin he brought along was younger by four or five years, a small and careful fellow, also from mainland China. He wore running shoes and sunglasses and an acid-washed jacket, blue denim streaked with white. He could not speak much English but he knew something about cars. He tapped around on the doors and fenders searching for Bondo patches underneath the paint. He examined the spare tire and the muffler and the door latches and the seals around the windows. He opened the hood and listened to the engine and held his hand at the end of the exhaust pipe to feel the engine's pulse. He tried the brakes and the horn and the lights and the radio. Finally the hood was shut, the engine was silent. It was just a matter of reaching an understanding.

Harold had offered me twenty-nine hundred. I told him my absolute bottom price was thirty-one. Anything lower and I would be losing money, I said. We both knew he wanted the car and we knew what the final price would be. Yet Harold was procrastinating. It wasn't the money, really. I didn't feel that. It was a matter of trust. We had not yet crossed some final threshold of trust.

I had the feeling that he needed to be reassured about my opinion of the car, or about my loyalty to this transaction. Or perhaps he needed to be reassured about me. I was after all an unknown quantity, not simply a fellow with a car for sale, but a foreigner, the mysterious other. If I were in Shanghai trying to bargain in Chinese with someone I did not know, for something in this price range, I would surely feel the same. I wondered if they had classified ads in China, and I wondered if it would be the first time Harold had thought of handing over this much cold cash to an American.

Standing in the Safeway lot at three o'clock on a sunny, blue-sky afternoon, we had reached this curious impasse when a woman came toward us, pushing a shopping cart between the diagonal rows of cars. She looked to be in her late fifties, and she wore a neck brace that made her back too erect. She had short red hair and the kind of white skin that turns to flame when anything unexpected occurs.

Between the rows she stopped, with a tight and cautious smile.

"That's my car," she said.

A Dodge two-door was parked in the next slot, eight or ten years old. We had all inadvertently gathered next to it.

"We just happen to be standing here," I said. "They're looking at my mother's Chevrolet."

"Your mother's?"

"By chance," I said.

"What are you talking about?"

Her hand held the cart as if its push bar were the guardrail at a drop-off cliff.

"I mean, it's by chance I'm parked next to you."

"I just don't know what to expect anymore."

She was speaking to me but looking hard at Harold, whose sallow and scholarly face had turned severe, as he pondered his cash flow.

"Sorry," I said, for the three of us.

"It's been broken into so many times I've lost count. They chip the glass, they ruin the doors. My life has been threatened. I'm a teacher. But do you think that makes any difference? Right outside the classroom I have had things happen."

"I know the feeling," I said.

We moved well away from the Dodge, giving her plenty of room. Harold was now consulting in Chinese with the cousin, who kept looking at his watch. Harold explained to me that a brother had dropped them off and would soon return. Time was becoming a factor. His jaw muscles were pumping. He had to make a decision. He stared at me, then he stared at his cousin's wrist, as if the watch held the answer to the riddle of this moment.

We had forgotten about the woman. But she had not forgotten us. Our tense reverie was broken by a long, grinding scrape, then the clunk of thick metal. About thirty feet from where we stood she had jumped a circular divider. Her Dodge now straddled it. Inside the car she twisted and turned, as if pursued. She lurched into reverse, scraping the underside again. When the front tires met the divider, she shifted into low. The car lurched forward, and the rear tires hit the island, which was the height of sidewalk curbing. She was stuck.

She opened the door and called out to anyone within earshot. "What did I do? What did I do?"

This was a huge parking lot that merged with other huge lots, all filled with diagonal rows of empty vehicles. There was no one else around.

"You went over that divider," I said.

"Oh my God! Did I ruin the car?"

"Just a scrape," I said. "When your wheels fell, the body hit."

"I didn't see it! I didn't see it! With the three of you so close I thought I ought to get out of here."

She was outside the car, next to the open door, her face red with accusation and alarm.

When Harold asked if the Dodge had front- or rear-wheel drive, her brimming eyes went wide.

He held his hands low in front of him to make a lifting motion. "Then we will know where to lift," he said.

She did not seem to hear this. Or perhaps she did not believe he would understand her reply. She spoke to me. Her eyes were aimed at me, as if I were Harold's interpreter.

"It's too heavy to lift," she said. "It's a very heavy car. Can't you see that?"

The cousin had his hands on an invisible steering wheel, telling her with sign language and broken English to cramp it tightly, then inch the car back and forth. He was moving toward her grille, while Harold approached the trunk, ready to organize a lift. They were both talking, signaling. The woman's eyes leaped wildly from one to the other, then looked at me across the roof, asking me to translate their cryptic messages. These eyes said she was prepared for the worst.

I guess I wanted to put her mind at ease. I dropped down on all fours to peer at black tire scuffs on the concrete curbing and at her car's crusted underbelly, searching for dents and hanging parts. I thought about my Levi's, which were recently washed. I thought about my life and the ludicrous indignity of this scene: all I wanted to do was get rid of a car for a reasonable price and there I was on the asphalt squinting at this unknown woman's oil pan and tie rods and grimy axle.

"Is it ruined?" she cried. "What if it won't drive? I can't take this car back to the shop. I couldn't face taking it back."

"It's okay," I said. "I really don't see anything here. Just get in and do what that fellow says."

She looked at the cousin, who pantomimed another tight turn of the wheel. Above the brace her neck and cheeks seemed to fill with blood that could not escape.

Still on my hands and knees, I said, "Cramp it hard to the right, then back up as far as you can."

"This car has been trashed so many ways. It's been to the shop for everything. I never find out who does it. The police aren't any help."

I ducked again to examine the muffler, the rusty tubing. "I don't think anything has happened. Really. Just get in and give the wheel a try."

By the time she slid onto the front seat I was around on her side of the car, standing at an angle that happened to block the sun. I must have looked ominous to her. She froze, staring straight ahead. By a freak of timing, Harold's brother appeared just then. He pulled his Honda pickup into the slot she had vacated, hopped out and looked around, but said nothing, evidently grasping the situation.

Unfortunately, he too wore sunglasses and an acid-washed

denim jacket streaked with white. As he moved toward the front of her car, joining the cousin, the glasses and the jackets had the look of a uniform they both shared.

In all three of these fellows you could see the family resemblance now, narrow faces with black hair angled across high foreheads, and all equally somber as they waited to see what the woman would do—while she waited to see what we were going to do. I could imagine what was running through her mind: we were some kind of transpacific shopping-mall gang working our way down the California coast, and now we had her surrounded, the cousin and the brother in front, Harold behind, me looming on the driver's side. She was trapped, and outnumbered. She was babbling.

"I hear something in the steering wheel. Do you hear it? When I turn the wheel like this? My God! It *is* something. What did I do?"

"You didn't do anything," I said. "It's going to be okay. Try cranking it hard to the right."

With the car in reverse she gripped the wheel and tried a tight turn. The effort squeezed her face with pain. She could not make the move. Her eyes, when she turned to me, were full of terror and defeat.

I hunkered next to the window. "Is it your arm? Your neck?"

Her shoulders slumped. Her tears began to fall.

"What happened?" I said.

"It was whiplash," she said. "Somebody braked in front of me. I never saw who. I didn't hit them but I got thrown around. It's the second time it happened. Do you know what it's like to be completely out of control? And to realize that nothing you have ever planned for yourself is going to work out? I think I am having a nervous breakdown. I don't even know what I'm doing here. I never come to this part of town."

The way color rose into her face had been reminding me of someone. Now I saw that her sense of the pointless anarchy of this moment reminded me of me, while in coloring she resembled my mother. I felt my own tears welling. I almost reached through the open window to touch her arm. Perhaps I should have. I had seen my mother in a similar state of mind, after she'd been sideswiped in heavy traffic. For weeks she had the highway jitters and the late-life jitters, and being a widow had not helped matters much. From where I hunkered I could see this woman was on her own. Her manner told me that, and the single sack of groceries and something about the interior of the Dodge, the way the seats were strewn with paperwork, bits of clothing and Kleenex and receipts, the back seat as well as the passenger side. This was how my mother's car had looked before I cleaned it up to sell, a car no one rode in but her.

"Would you like me to try it?" I said.

She couldn't answer.

"Scoot over," I said.

"Oh no. No. Please. I'll get out."

As if she had to choose between the car and her life, she surrendered the wheel. I slid in. With my eyes on Harold hand-signaling in the rearview, I cramped it and inched backward until the tires touched concrete. In low I cramped it the other way and watched the cousin and the brother in their matching jackets waving and winding their hands in the air, with their eyes on the front tires, calling out one-word instructions.

"More! More! Stop! Stop! Okay! Okay!"

It took five moves in each direction, and for those couple of minutes we were allies, liberating the Dodge. When the front wheels finally cleared the divider, their three faces opened in sudden grins.

The woman was grinning too, a wild grin. She was giddy, on the edge of crazy laughter. She had been prepared, I think, to see me disappear with her car. In the driver's seat again she only wanted to flee. She shifted fast and the car lurched again.

"What am I doing here?" she called out the window. "None of this makes any sense. I never shop at Safeway!"

We watched her swing a wide U-turn into the next aisle, speeding for the exit lane. Harold said nothing about this episode. Neither did I. It was hard to know what to say. Yet there was no doubt that she had brought us closer together. Her panic had cleared the way. I knew he was ready now to make another offer.

His father came to mind. I was thinking Harold would be getting the car for a decent price, one to make his father proud. And I was thinking again about my mother, who had started life in rural Alabama and in some ways never left. She would have panicked at the sight of any three or four men standing around in a parking lot for no apparent reason. If she had come upon an Anglo in Levi's and three young men from China outside Safeway, well, it would have made her dizzy; the foreign faces would have been enough to push her sense of peril to the limit.

''I can pay three thousand,'' Harold said at last. ''But no more. I do not have more than that.''

I waited a moment, as if weighing this proposal. ''To sell the car for that amount, I would have to have it all in cash.''

He nodded and reached inside his coat for the bulging envelope.

While the cousin and the brother observed from the back seat, we sat in front, where I filled out a notice of sale and passed it to him along with the pink slip and a tire warranty from Sears and a battery warranty. He counted out thirty one-hundred-dollar bills and asked me to count them. Then we shook hands.

The brother and the cousin left first in the pickup, followed by Harold in the Citation, hunched forward, nervous with responsibility. I had expected the money to bring more satisfaction than it did. Watching him leave I felt abandoned. I stood there on the asphalt while the car turned right at the intersection and the flow of traffic carried it away.

The boulevard sounds receded with that car, as if an invisible screen had closed behind it. In this strange stillness, as the taillight winked its final wink and the baby-blue trunk disappeared, I wondered why I had kept to myself the collision that once mangled her rear fender. I wondered why the cousin had not noticed the repair, and if he had, why he didn't mention it, thinking then of the many things we never mention. My mother's passing, for example. I had not mentioned that to Harold either. She had lived a long life, so it came as no surprise, but it wasn't something I was ready to talk to anyone about.

The afternoon breeze fell away. Alone among the rows I found myself inside a tent of silence. An awful yearning gripped me, and then the fear that can stop you in your tracks, the fear of what is not yet known, which will sometimes take in everything imaginable. I couldn't tell you how long it held me there, how long I stood watching the long parade of silent cars.

Rock Garden

JEANNE WAKATSUKI HOUSTON

Early morning was Reiko's favorite time. Above white-peaked Mount Whitney, the cloudless sky sparkled and crisp air cooled the desert flatland. Alone, she could sit on the tree stump outside the barracks door and watch people begin their day.

Her family's cubicle faced the latrines, giving her a grandstand view of neighbors clattering past in homemade wooden *geta* slippers as they formed lines outside the two buildings—one for men, another for women. Like colored rags of a kite's tail, the queue of robes and kimonos snaked through the block's center. Yawning and clutching tin basins that held their toiletries, the neighbors seemed not to notice the lone spectator.

Since coming to the internment camp a year earlier, Reiko had learned to entertain herself. The elders had talked about starting a school, but so far the only classes were those run by Miss Honda and Myrtle Fujino, old maids from Block 22. Shy and soft-spoken, the thirtyish spinsters volunteered their services, which actually amounted to caretaking, since neither was a teacher. They taught the girls sewing. Not knowing what to do with boys, they made them saw wood, or sent them out to the firebreaks, which were open, sandy acres between the barrack block compounds. For hours the boys roamed in the sand, looking for arrowheads left from the days when Paiute Indians flourished in these high desert valleys.

Reiko hated sewing. She never had handled needles and thread, and kept pricking her fingers while stitching rag dolls made out of old clothes. What was supposed to be Raggedy Ann's white shirt face looked more like a mangled fist, lumps and bloody smears disfiguring it.

People watching in the morning was much more interesting than sewing. It was Reiko's new game. She imagined herself a queen, seated on a throne while the throngs passed in review. A wise and dignified queen. When Potato ran by in his Boy Scout uniform, twirling a dead rattlesnake like a lasso, she remained unruffled. Nor did she flinch when he came back and dangled the limp snake in front of her face.

Potato was the block idiot. Fat and tall, he always wore his Boy Scout uniform, swollen torso and haunches bursting at the khaki seams. He was twenty, but had the mind of someone Reiko's age. She was ten. He was her court jester, and when she grew tired of the sinewy rope swaying in her face, she waved him away imperiously. With a final flick of the snake, he stuck out his tongue at her and lumbered out of sight.

One morning someone joined her. Old man Morita, who lived two barracks away, was sitting outside his door, whittling wood. She figured he was people watching too. In the year they had been neighbors she never had spoken with him. Morita-san was deaf. The block people said the din of his wife's nagging had caused him to lose his hearing. Reiko believed it. She had heard Lady Morita's high-pitched rumbling while waiting in line at the mess hall. It was no wonder they called her Thunder-mouth. Her loud words crashed and gushed like white water storming over river rocks.

After a week of sitting, Reiko finally caught Morita-san looking her way. She waved. He smiled, creasing his walnut brown face into tiny folds. Even from a distance, she could see his eyes were merry, and those eyes filled her with sadness. Both her grandfathers were dead, and she hadn't seen her father for more than a year, ever since the FBI took him away to prison in North Dakota. The only male in the family was Ivan, who was fourteen. Seeing Morita-san's smiling eyes reminded Reiko how much she missed her father.

The next morning she waved at the old man and called cheerfully, "Good morning, Morita-san." Showing off how she knew some Japanese, she added, *"O-hai-yo-gozai-mas.* Good morning." Then she remembered he probably couldn't read lips from a distance.

Morita-san beckoned. She scampered over to his perching place, which was a large square boulder, probably retrieved from one of the creeks. Sitting on the rock and framed by closed double wooden doors, he looked like pictures she had seen of her ancestors in Japan. He wore a dark blue kimono, belted low on his belly, and was barefoot.

"You like meditate in morning?"

It was the first time Reiko had heard his voice. She had wondered if deaf people could speak, and it surprised her that he spoke pidgin English, just like Ba-chan, her grandmother.

"What's meditate?" She spoke the new word slowly.

"Like pray," he said. His warm eyes crinkled. He dropped the long limb he was carving and bowed his forehead against his clasped hands. She'd seen Ba-chan doing the same thing before the Buddha statue in their room.

"Oh, to Buddha, you mean?"

"So, so," he answered. "I pray Indian spirit too."

This fascinated Reiko. People said the internment camp was built over old Indian burial grounds. That's why there were so many arrowheads. The countless stories of Indian ghost sightings terrified her and she never walked in the firebreaks alone or went to the latrine at night except with Mama. In a way, she wished she wasn't afraid, because she would like to see a ghost.

"Have you ever seen an Indian spirit?" she asked.

"All time. I see many. They talk me."

"Really? What do they say?" She wondered if he read their lips.

"They happy Japanese people here in desert. Say we come from same tribe across ocean."

He stood up, leaning on the cane he was whittling, and motioned for her to follow. Standing next to him, she was startled to see he was her height. They rounded the barrack corner past tall bamboo plants that extended in a row to the next barrack, screening from view the space between. She had often wondered what was behind that feathery wall.

Reiko knew she was entering a special place, maybe even a holy place. In her view, Morita-san already had changed from a deaf old henpecked man to a wizard.

Hidden behind the bamboo was a brilliant white lake of tiny pebbles. Kidney-shaped and smoothly raked, it was about four feet wide and seven long. At one end, five huge stones formed an altar-like platform. One flat stone held dried bones, rocks, feathers, and gnarled driftwood. Two covered urns stood in the middle.

She watched while the old man knelt before the altar, eyes closed, lips moving. He stood up and shuffled over to a moss-covered rock. With a tin cup, he drew water from a bucket and ladled it over the green velvet mound, chanting strange sounds.

''I teach you meditate,'' he said.

''*Arigato.* Thank you.'' She spoke another one of the few Japanese words she knew. She still didn't know what ''meditate'' was, but if it meant getting to know Morita-san, she would try it.

''Tomorrow morning. Same time,'' he said, and patted the top of her head.

For some reason she decided not to tell anyone. Not that anyone would be interested. Since coming to camp, her brother and sister went their own way, making friends and eating in another block's mess hall away from the family. Ba-chan was suspicious of everything and probably would claim that Morita-san's deafness was a punishment from the gods.

''Bad karma,'' she could hear her grandmother say. ''He do something bad in past life.''

The first few days he never spoke a word. He sat cross-legged, ignoring her. But she guessed that was the way he began things, remembering how he didn't acknowledge her when they people-watched earlier.

On the sixth morning, just as she was about to decide not to come anymore, things changed. He had set up a low table, a smooth flat slab of driftwood, and motioned for her to sit down across from him.

"Close eyes," he said.

She obeyed. Her eyelids quivered, eager to lift so she could see what he was doing, but she kept them closed. A breeze blew above her head, like someone had waved a fan.

"*Namu-amida-butsu* . . . Crazee Horse-su . . . Geroneee-mo. *Namu-amida-butsu* . . . Crazee Horse-su . . . Geroneee-mo," he chanted. Over and over he singsonged the Buddhist mantra and Indian names until Reiko was lulled into a dreamy state.

She imagined braves on horses galloping across the open firebreak. She heard drumming—sharp, staccato beats that cracked like firecrackers. As they raced back and forth across the desert, the horses' manes fluttered like torn flags and orange smoke trailed from dilated nostrils. They flew to the desert's edge but stopped suddenly, rearing up and neighing. Something prevented them from passing over to green pastureland. It was barbed wire!

Her eyes snapped open. The old man was beating two smooth stones together. Clack-clack-clack.

"So, so. You see something?"

"Am I supposed to?"

"What you see?"

Reiko liked this game. "I saw Indians. They were riding horses with smoke coming out of their noses. They were trying to get out of camp."

"Hah! Hah!" Morita-san laughed loudly. "Very good. You good meditate."

"Is that all I do? Just imagine things?" It wasn't much different from making up stories about people, except she had never seen these Indians before.

He brought one of the urns to the table and from it retrieved a large obsidian arrowhead. It was glittering, black and perfectly shaped.

"For you," he said.

She gasped, too pleased to speak.

"This magic. Make wish come true."

"Thank you, Morita-san. *Arigato.*" She couldn't wait to show it to Ivan.

From that day on, Reiko practically lived at the old man's sanctuary. After breakfast, instead of going to recreation classes, she sat with him before the shrine, "meditating," and helped garden his rocks. She learned to chant while pouring water over the moss stone, which looked to her like a turtle, asleep with head drawn inside its shell. Once she thought she saw it move.

He taught her to rake the white pebbles with rusty prongs, to carve flowing lines that undulated through the frozen sea.

"Rock, water, plant, wood all same. You, me, rock same." He pointed at Reiko and then some stones. "Everything same, same."

It amazed Reiko how his garden reflected this. He had watered a boulder until it became alive with moss. It wouldn't surprise her if it did turn into a turtle someday and crawl away. And the lake of pebbles seemed to surge and roll, making her seasick if she stared too long.

Sometimes he performed rituals. After burning orange peels in a tin can, he sprinkled ashes on the altar and drew symbols . . . circles, diamonds, squares, calligraphy. They rarely talked, mostly meditating, which she saw as another form of people watching, except she made up the people too. When she told him what she saw in her mind, he would cackle and laugh very hard, slapping a hand against his sinewy thigh.

One day he took her outside the camp. People had begun to venture beyond the barbed-wire fence since the soldiers in the guard towers had left. Reiko was glad they were gone. She was afraid of guns. One of the soldiers had shot Daryl Izumi, who was only fifteen and just looking for arrowheads. She stayed far away from the high wooden towers, thinking of them as castle turrets bordering a wide desert moat.

About a half mile out, a clump of elder trees rose from the barren landscape. Inside the oasis, a creek gurgled over shiny white pebbles, the same as Morita-san's rock lake.

"We walk on path," he said, and splashed into the creek.

Reiko was baffled, but followed anyway, having learned to accept his strange way of seeing things.

As they waded in the creek/path, he picked up pebbles and

driftwood, depositing them in a sack tied around his waist. It was almost as if he were plucking fruit from a watery garden.

Then one morning she found Morita-san dressed in shirt and baggy trousers and boots. He was tinkering with a bamboo fishing pole. She wondered if he planned on fishing in the pebbled lake, not doubting for one moment he could pull up a wriggling trout from its raked depths.

"I go fishing up mountain." He pointed west to the sheer wall of the high Sierra Nevadas.

"But that's so far away. Are we allowed to go that far?"

Reiko knew it was at least ten miles to the base of the mountain.

"Me old man. I go fishing."

Just then, Lady Morita flung open the door and began jabbering. Morita-san continued working on his pole, as if she weren't there. Thunder rolled from her mouth. Finally she stomped back into the cubicle.

Reiko walked with him to the edge of camp.

"Can I go with you, Morita-san?" She felt nervous about his going alone.

"No," he said bluntly, then patted the top of her head, smiling. "I come back tonight."

He shuffled past the barbed wire. "I catch many fish," he shouted, waving to her as he trudged through the sagebrush. She watched him weave around tumbleweed and boulders until he became a small spider, the bamboo pole an antenna scanning the desert. She imagined his path turning into a creek, glittering with brilliant stones that led up to Mount Whitney.

He didn't return that night or the next day. By the third day, Mr. Kato, the block manager, called a meeting, and the men voted to form a search party. Lady Morita was screaming and hysterical, afraid the administration would find out her husband had violated the boundary. It was a mess . . . with neighbors arguing about ways to keep her from having a nervous breakdown.

Reiko wasn't worried. She knew Morita-san could take care of himself. The gossip made her angry, though. Someone said he had committed suicide, driven to it by his thunder-mouth wife. Someone else said he drove himself crazy meditating. She even heard he had hiked over the mountains to Fresno, where he was passing as Chinese.

After a week, she too became anxious. Very early in the morning, when the sky was gray and still sprinkled with stars, she stole over to the sanctuary. She sat in front of the shrine, cross-legged, the large arrowhead in her hand, and began to chant. She tried to emulate Morita-san.

"*Namu-amida-butsu* . . . Crazee Horse-su . . . Geroneee-mo. *Namu-amida-butsu* . . . Crazee Horse-su . . . Geroneee-mo." She made her voice quiver, sucking in her belly, surprising herself with strange guttural sounds. She lost track of time.

The urgent swishing of leaves . . . and then a horse's neigh broke her reverie. Across the rock lake, several warriors approached leading horses. When they arrived at the pool's edge, the pebbles turned to water. As the horses drank, their frothy flanks heaved. They had been riding hard. Suddenly a figure materialized. It was Morita-san! Standing with the braves as if he belonged there! Her heart raced. She wanted to open her eyes, to shout and swim across the pool!

But a whirlwind suddenly spun up from the center. It grew wider and wider, churning waves and shaking leaves, whirling through the garden. Encircling Morita-san and the Indians, it lifted them high over the barracks. Morita-san was smiling, waving to her with his bamboo pole. She stood up to wave back, and was just about to open her eyes when the figures became iridescent, enveloped in golden light.

"Morita-san!" she cried.

The search for the old man continued. After another week, it was called off. By then, Reiko had resigned herself to his permanent disappearance, even to the thought of death.

She returned to people watching, no longer caring to meditate. And soon the much-talked-about school finally began, a real school like the one she had attended in Santa Monica before the war. Her life became full—with studies and new friends. Ivan began lessons at the judo pavilion, where Reiko spent many warm hours at dusk watching him flip and fall, grunting unintelligible commands.

Years later, in the last month before the camp closed, some Caucasian hunters hiking in the mountains reported sighting human bones at the bottom of a narrow ravine. It was assumed the remains were those of Morita-san. Reiko didn't feel too sad. Her old mentor had taught all things were one—flesh, rocks, plants, water. "Same, same," he had said. And so his bones, strewn about in the deep crevice, were resting comfortably, slowly returning to mountain granite and, later, desert sand, while his ghost would roam the barbed-wire firebreaks forever with the Indians, his tribesmen, chanting and laughing as they galloped in the clear black night.

Keeping Company

CLAIRE KEMP

William wakes me with water. He sprays me through the window screen and I am introduced to morning under tangled sheets, sprinkled damp and rolled like laundry ready for the iron. He's whistling. When he sings, "Lazy Mary, will you get up?" I do and go outside in my nightdress to stand barefoot on the cool wet cement close to William. "Hello, wife," he says.

Two men walking to the beach smile and wave a hand in greeting. I raise my hand to wave to them but William checks me with a look. He aims the hose at the street but the pressure is down and the water falls short. "Missed by a mile," he says. "I'm losing my touch."

"They're not bothering anyone. What do you care?"

"They're bothering me and I care." A small muscle in his cheek keeps an angry beat.

"You'll be late for work," I tell him, and run inside to make his eggs, soft-boiled on white toast.

"Never happen," he says. The hose, a fat green snake, uncoils and follows obediently wherever he walks.

Mornings I go to the beach. I go alone because William won't. Certain young men come to stroll on this beach. Their walk is a slow dance, graceful and sure. They glide on pewter sand like skaters do on ice. In their brief suits, satin bands of azure blue, magenta, yellow, emerald green, they appear as exotic flowers blooming in the desert. I am taken with their beauty and don't mind sitting in their shade. Not unkindly they dismiss me with their eyes, unencumbered souls walking free at water's edge with perhaps a scarlet towel over one tanned shoulder or a small cloth bag worn round the neck to hold the treasures of the moment. They have smiles for each other but not for me. I'm a cabbage in their garden, a woman large with child, a different species altogether. Next year, I'll have someone to keep me company. I'll teach her how to make castles with turrets from paper cups and wet sand. Swizzle sticks will make a fine bridge to span the moat. Perhaps we'll place cocktail parasols for color in the sand-palace courtyard. And I'll take her home before the tide comes in to take it down. She's with me now, tumbling and turning in her water bed and dancing on my ribs with tiny heels and toes. She's coming to term and letting me know. It won't be long.

Afternoons I tend my flowers. Today, I see an open truck parked next door. And a piano on the porch. Two men are discussing how to get it through the door. One goes inside to pull, the other stays out to push. I think of the piano as a stubborn horse, its mahogany rump splendid in the sun. "Perhaps if you offer it sugar," I suggest. The outside man grins. "Hello," he says, and vaults over his porch rail. I brush potting soil from my hands and reach to shake his hand.

"I'm James," he says. His eyes are gray-blue and direct. When he smiles his features merge brightly like a photograph in focus. He has a good face. He says, "Dennis is inside. He might come out or he might not. He's shy." Behind him, someone parts the lace curtain at one window and lets it fall.

I tell James my name and he says, "It's nice to meet you, Nora. Your flowers are lovely." But he's not looking at my flowers. Just at me. He nods in affirmation of some private thought and says, "Moving's more work than I bargained for. I'd better get back to it."

"Yes, see you again," I reply, and bend to the task of breaking off the blooms gone by. The aroma of geranium is so strong it seems to leave a taste on my tongue. When I go inside to make myself a cup of tea, the piano has made it through the door and there is no one in sight.

After dinner, I tell William we have neighbors and he tells me he's not blind. He uncaps a beer and tilts the bottle to his lips. He wipes foam from his beard with the back of his hand and gives me a long look I'm meant to pay attention to. "Don't bother with them, Nora. They're not our kind." From next door I hear a tentative chord or two. I listen for more but the night air is still, not another note. I listen for sounds from their house over the sounds of our house all evening long. I don't know why I would. After a while the heat leaves the house and it's cool enough for sleep and still I listen.

James brings me a croissant sprinkled with cinnamon and sugar. I put down my watering can and take it from his hand. Dennis is practicing scales and I remember how it felt to play, my eyes on the page, not on the keys.

"What are you hoping for?" James asks shyly.

"It's a girl. We already know. Doctors can tell in advance now. We've named her Sara."

"Imagine," he says, but his eyes are worried as if he marvels at giving credibility to someone who can't yet breathe on her own. "She's like a present, as yet unwrapped," he says. Abruptly the music stops. I picture Dennis closing the piano, covering the keys, and going to another part of his house.

"Dennis is tired," James explains. He has already turned from me toward the silence and I am left holding the still warm pastry in one hand and nothing in the other.

I hang the wash, William's work shirts, dishcloths and towels, heavy sheets that pull on my arms. Next door, James and Dennis are talking, always talking. Their voices rise and fall and blend together. They have so much to say. They never seem to tire of talk. Their screen door opens and shuts throughout the day as they come and go. When they are out of each other's sight, one calls out and the other answers.

Late in the day, I take in the dry clothes, stripping the line and folding as I go along, leaving the clothespins to bob like small wooden birds. Dennis and James head for the beach. Dennis wears a light jacket zipped to the neck as if he is cold. His short sandy hair curls up around his cap, leaving the back of his neck bare, like a young boy's. I can tell James would walk faster if he was alone. Perhaps he would run. As it is, he holds back to keep the pace that Dennis sets but his energy shows itself in the enthusiastic swing of his arms and the quick, attentive way he inclines his head to catch the words that Dennis speaks. When they're out of sight beyond the dunes, I go inside to wait for William.

James is teaching me backgammon. We sit on his patio under the Cinzano umbrella and drink iced tea with lemon slices on the rim of tall oddly shaped amber glasses, no two alike. Dennis will not play but once he points out a move for me and seems quietly pleased when I take that game from James. I do not tell William where I spend my summer afternoons. I'm where I belong when he gets home. He slides his arms around me and rubs my face with his beard and says proudly, "Nora, I swear, you're as big as a house." "I am," I agree, laughing. "I'm Sara's house." He does not ask me what I do all day and I would not tell him if he did. I know something about myself that I didn't know before. I'm successful at sins of omission, never really lying, never telling truth. I hoard secrets like a dog who buries bones to relish at some future time. I wonder if when that time comes, I will remember why or where I dug the holes.

William comes home early, tires spinning in the sand on the lane between our house and theirs. I'm caught and stand up fast from James's table and hurry home, leaving James in the middle of a play.

"I don't want you over there," William tells me. "Is that clear?"

"But why? They're good company."

"They can keep each other company. Not you. I'm your good company. The only good company you'll ever need."

William sighs when he looks at me as though I'm a chore he must complete.

Dennis gives a concert in my honor, all my favorite pieces played perfectly, without flaw or fault. I sit on my front step as evening falls to dark and listen till he's done.

William is building a wall. To make certain he's within his rights, he engages a surveyor to determine the exact boundaries of our land. After supper and on Saturdays he works on his wall. There are guidelines he must follow as to height. I know if permitted he would make it six feet high, five inches taller than the top of my head, but the law won't allow it. Its purpose is to keep me in my place. When he's done, he calls me out to admire his work and I do. I tell him it's a fine wall, which is what he wants to hear. James, on his porch, raises his glass in a silent toast. I send him my best smile, an apology big enough for both William and myself.

William has gone south to deliver a boat and won't be home before midnight at least. James invites me for dinner. I'm invited, so I go. Their kitchen is yellow and blue, quaint, like a woman's sitting room. There are many plants I can't begin to name in clay pots and hanging baskets. I sit on paisley cushions in a wicker chair by the window watching James make stew from scratch. While James chops vegetables, his hand on the knife making quick, precise cuts, Dennis copies the recipe in his spidery script on a card for me to take home. I set the table, lace cloth from Ireland, tall rose-colored candles in crystal, linen napkins in shell rings, and sterling silver by the plates. James holds my chair and seats me as if I am a lady and not a country girl in faded shorts and one of William's shirts. Dennis searches the yard for hibiscus blooms. He floats them in a shallow blue bowl for a centerpiece. I have gone over the wall.

Unlike Cinderella, I'm home well before midnight in my own

kitchen, with a bowl of stew for William over a low flame on my stove. He eats out of the pan. "What are these yellow things?" he asks, poking with his fork.

"Parsnips."

"Okay," he says. "Next time peas. Otherwise, not bad at all."

I let him think I made the stew myself, which of course I could have done. And maybe will someday. The recipe is out of sight in the bottom of my sewing box.

We are in a tropical depression. Hot steady rain for a week and thick humid air that leaves me worn out and sleepy. I stay inside, an idle woman, changing in spite of myself like a mushroom growing at a furious rate in this damp and fertile season. We lose our power and Dennis brings candles. He hands the bag to William and runs off without a proper thank-you. William hands it quickly to me as if its contents are not candles but sticks of dynamite that could go off at any minute. He follows me like the tail of a kite as I place lighted candles on waxed saucers in each room of our house. "The wall is holding," he says. "Can you believe it?" I say, "Yes, I believe it."

In September, Sara will be born.

When the storms give in to sun, I'm glad, but it reigns in the sky like a lion. Its heat is fierce. I have not seen Dennis or James. The piano does not play. I knock on their door and finally James is there behind the screen. He doesn't lift the latch. I say, "How are you? I miss you two." "Not to worry," he assures me without meeting my eyes. When I ask for Dennis, James shrugs as if Dennis is someone he's lost track of somehow and can't be bothered getting back, which I know for sure is not the truth. He laughs then, a short harsh sound like a bark. "Sorry," he says. "Dennis is in the hospital. I don't know that he'll be coming home." He says this like he's asking a question, like he's asking me for an answer. I put my hand on my side of the screen and James touches it briefly with his. We stand for a moment, like visitors in prison, before he closes the inside door and shuts me out. I wish I could take back the days.

I go home where I belong. There is laundry to fold, chores to do, an entire house to put to order. I do a proper job of every task, a proper penance. Before bed, I tell William. I know as I begin to speak that it will not go well, but I'm bound to tell it, to lay it out like a soiled cloth on our clean table.

"Dennis is sick," I say, and at just that moment I know that this truth is another bone I buried.

William says, "Yes, he is. Very sick. Have you been over there again? I told you to stay away from them. I warned you. But, knowing you . . ."

"You don't."

"Don't what?"

"Know me." I stand up. There is a knot of sorrow that drops in me like a sinker in a tidal pool. I walk out the door and away from William. At the jetty, I climb the slick black rocks, heedless of the cruel pockets of stone that could snap a limb as easy as not. I find a smooth stone that makes a good seat. I'm surprised to know I'm crying. Our porch light comes on and there is William, his pale hair like a halo under its glow. He calls me, "Nora, come home," but the tide takes his voice and swallows my name. When I'm thoroughly chilled and empty of anger, I leave my perch and travel north on the wet sand, close to the cool fingers of incoming tide. I'm a small but competent ship sailing the coastline. I set my own course. I hear someone running in my wake and it's William, breathless from the chase. He passes me on fast feet, then turns, dancing backward like a boxer until I stop just shy of the circle of his arms. He carries my sweater, which he puts around my shoulders with great care, as if it is a precious fur he wraps me in and I too am precious. He buttons one button under my chin with clumsy fingers. "Let's go back," he says, so we do. We do not talk about anything, simply walk forward in silence, which is the way it is between husbands and wives, with married people.

Looking Glass

WILLIAM KITTREDGE

Simon Fantara imagines standing on a sandy bar at the edge of the Clearwater River, which was known as Kookooskia. He is attempting to imagine Looking Glass, warrior chieftain for the Nez Percé, people who thought of Canada as Grandmother's Land in those days when they believed Queen Victoria owned it all and was grandmother to the world.

When the U.S. cavalry began winning the battles, and there was nothing left but escape, Joseph aimed the people for Grandmother's Land on their way to that final battle in the Bear Paw Mountains of Montana, where Looking Glass died and Joseph gave up because the children wailed in the cold.

There could be no fires and no light. All they had suffered for was lost. The wind was filled with snow and Looking Glass died on the cutbank above Snake Creek. Simon Fantara tries to become Looking Glass, imagining losses and lies.

The mists lift away into the great forests beyond the green twists of water and the black boulders. The people thought there was no sin in telling a lie the first time, and that there was little sin in telling the lie a second time. But the third time was unpardonable. So many lies and you become someone else. Simon Fantara imagines dying in the Bear Paw Mountains.

''So leave,'' Corrie said, and her eyes were golden and solemn behind her huge amber-colored glasses.

Simon Fantara had his nights of driving the freeway up to Santa Barbara or out to some honky-tonk tavern on the edge of the Mojave, anywhere so long as it took the night: the great rows of sprinklers whirling over the desert alfalfa fields in the early morning; Corrie sleeping beside him.

On the sloping lawn above the swimming pool they played badminton after coming out of the sauna their first morning together. She gave him the uphill side.

''Don't want to pick on a cripple,'' she said, and he wondered if she thought of him as an old man because his right leg had been broken so many times and so badly he had to wear a chrome-plated brace buckled to his thigh and curved under the sole of his boot. It was the kind of thing she kept on saying, which didn't bother him at first, because anybody knew it took a certain amount of smart-ass to survive.

Simon was barefoot and his leg hadn't hurt enough to bother, the sunlight was discolored by haze from a fire in the mountains north of Ojai, and Corrie was a pleasure to watch as she beat him, until she fielded his serve and stopped. ''That's enough,'' she said. ''I'm sorry.

''I'm always beating people,'' she said, looking up at him with her head turned so the morning was red in her hair. She said she had never been able to cure herself.

''Makes my kidneys ache,'' he said, as if that meant anything. That evening on the hillside above Malibu the world seemed green beside the imitation Moorish house her father bought her the first time she was married, vines climbing to the ironwork balconies, and they went back in the sauna and that second night got drunk on mescal again and slept wrapped in blankets on the lawn. At daybreak the edge of sunlight came sparkling toward them from the ocean toward Catalina, and four days later she had him downtown trying out for a Chrysler commercial. He was, after all, a Champion of the World.

. . .

Corrie had been gone three days without saying she was going anywhere when Burton Davis called, saying there was this number in Montana, playing Indian, and Simon hitched his four-horse aluminum trailer to rattle along empty behind his yellow Continental and crossed from Malibu into San Fernando and then over to Bakersfield and north, not thinking in the hot wind of the valley with the windows open and the air conditioning off until he checked into a motel on the outskirts of Lodi, a line of woodframe shacks painted orange and only six blocks from the Holiday Inn, where he could have stayed. Back to it now, he thought, and he knew this was foolishness, his old life in motels being the last thing he was after. He cut the plastic around the cap of a pint of Johnnie Walker Red and when it was gone he wasn't sleepy.

So with morning just beginning to show he crossed Donner and curved down into Reno and a one-hundred-and-fifty-eight dollar hour of losing at a crap table on the second floor of Harold's Club. Walking out, he won a hundred back on a dime slot as four stars spun into a row.

Simon slept in the Lincoln just south of Pyramid Lake, stopped in the twilight outside Winnemucca to puke while traffic thundered on toward night in the east, his head aching after five shots of Johnnie Walker in a glaring Lovelock barroom, nothing to puke but the whiskey and three pickled sausages from a half-empty plastic jar. Simon wiped his mouth and at last had a sense of having got away. The desert was empty under the smoky light, and he thought of turning north to find a ranch in the unknown country around the Black Rock Desert and asking for a job.

North of Wells he was off the freeway and onto narrow pitted asphalt rising and falling through scrub-brush sand hills, a dark line in the beginning of morning. The highlands were soft and undulating like the palms of the first buckskin gloves Simon had ever owned, bought with wages earned starting colts the summer he was fourteen.

Corrie said he had too much imagination. She said that was why they liked him. "You're willing to be anybody," she said, "so they love you. Why wouldn't they?"

But it was easy enough. Those gloves had been chewed and stitched by the women in their camp alongside the Bitterroot River, a willow ramada and three tin-roofed, rotting houses built of cottonwood logs that had been bulldozed into a heap and burned on a fall day in the late fifties, after that one-eyed and crazy old man named Daddy Clock-Stocking was carted off to die with relatives on the reservation near Browning. It was easy enough to imagine being the color of that light. Simon slept through the day in Twin Falls, Idaho, while the air conditioner hummed and the television picture revolved.

The blond girl from Salmon shook her bracelets and talked about a man she loved, she thought, she said, laughing, who had gone north to roughneck in the oil fields around Calgary, and stayed. She said she was going to find that man.

Simon wondered if he should tell her about the old days in Calgary, parties every night and wild cow milking with Oscar Dodson the year they started out, driving to the perfect snowy mountains off west in the morning with two Blackfeet girls from Shelby, and going back to the mountains with Jackie Belle Deer the summer Simon won bareback and the bull riding and the all-round money, and dust hanging above the willow corral at Boulder Cabin before sunrise as he stood by the juniper center post with seventy head of geldings circling counterclockwise around him and then reversing when he flipped the sea-grass riata underhanded and dropped the loop over the head of a long-legged bay with scabbed withers, somebody's traveling horse: catching the horses one by one, the men behind him trailing bridles and hackamores and then going down the taut rope toward the trembling animal to touch the flaring muzzle and slipping the cold steel snaffle bit into the mouth of whatever horse it was they wanted for that day.

The blue '61 Ford pickup and the camper and Jackie Belle Deer and the flush days of going from one show to another with Jackie Belle, and Jackie Belle taking off with better than $2,500 and a calf roper named Verlon Perkins, and who could blame her after the summer his leg was smashed against a bucking chute in Jacksonville, Oregon.

"You'll never marry me," Jackie Belle said. "I got to take care of myself." Who could blame her for that. Only a fool would go into life imagining a talent for staying on horseback would get you through, even if you owned a buckle, heavy silver and gold, the size of a man's hand, engraved with your name: Simon Fantara, Champion of the World.

Out on the northern plains just short of Canada, Simon parked under the trees by the Bell Tree Hotel in Havre, and stood at the bar feeling the silence was for him. The bartending woman seemed like someone he knew. One of the old men turned and said, "Hell, been a long time."

An hour or so later Simon was drunk and a black-haired girl named Mary Ann was watching him drink. The Miller's clock, yellow-edged and plastic, a rotating sphere with the time on one side and an imitation glass of beer on the other, was something to think about as Simon tried to tell the girl named Mary Ann that the color of whiskey and water was a color he could live in, a color for remembering the fishing. "That's pretty," she said, and she drifted away.

The summer he was thirty, completely down, crutches under his arms after Jackie Belle left, Simon hocked the buckle in Reno and bought a bed and some food and then called Benny Jackson in Elk River, Idaho. "You're doing all right otherwise," Benny said, "so you might as well come on if you're crippled."

Benny wired money for bus fare and Simon got the buckle out of the hock shop and hitchhiked, waving his crutches until some car stopped, and wore away the summer scuffing around and limping to serve tap beer in Benny Jackson's bar in Elk River, shacking up with Benny's wife while Benny was off team-roping in California with his roping horse.

Things to do in Elk River, Benny's hometown. Screw Benny's pride and joy behind his back and feel sorry for Benny because he'd married such a woman to get his hands on her father's bar.

Simon stood before his mirror and contemplated the lead slug that would strike him center in the forehead, take after take, until it was right, suitable to print. Simon imagined the blow being no more forceful than that of a hummingbird strike before death. The dry brown stain over his chest and shoulders was another skin ending at the whiteness of his neck. The makeup people out at Bear Paw would do his face. It had to be right as the bullet struck and Looking Glass died.

"What it is, see, is simple. You stare off like you were watching something, supposed to be the cavalry, and then you're shot and you fall forward. It's against the rules of physics, but who gives a shit?"

Swallows were nesting in the bluff above Snake Creek, and off west there was dust curving up behind a yellow Buick convertible. Simon stood with his face painted and did not fall, and Looking Glass lived until the dust fell away.

The sixth take was perfect, the camera eye widening in leaping jump cuts. Behind Looking Glass there was the enormous eastern sky as the camera slowed and Simon fell, until nothing moved, that last image of the falling man enlarging and becoming fainter and grainy while the jagged alpine Bitterroot Mountains under first snow were imposed over it, the black endless forests of the Selway beyond, the Clearwater, Kookooskia, where Looking Glass was chief.

The Difference Between Women and Men

BRET LOTT

Later, she piled everything up in the corner of the room. The armoire she'd had to leave in its place, the huge piece of furniture centered against the far wall of the bedroom. But she'd managed to move their bed across the room, inching it one end at a time across the hardwood floor until it was nestled in the corner, her side of the bed and the headboard touching the walls. She picked up the small table she used as a writing desk, set it upside down on the bed, pushed it to the wall, then set the cane-seat chair on the bed too.

Next came the dresser drawers, each pulled out and set one on top of another next to the table on the bed, four drawers filled with her clothes stacked on the bedspread. Then she pulled the empty dresser itself across the floor, the dresser top littered with barrettes, bracelets, bottles of perfume on her side, on his side a comb, an ashtray, three AA batteries, and a small red rock from somewhere she could not recall. She pushed the dresser up along the footboard until it too touched the wall.

Finally there were only the odd items left on the floor: the clock-radio from on top of the desk, still plugged in, *9:42* blinking in red; the black three-legged nightstand, more a stool than anything else, and the lamp that sat on it; the assortment of clothes she'd intended to drop off at the dry cleaners someday: two rayon skirts, a silk blouse, three sweaters that'd been ready to go since October.

There were some of his things mixed in too: a blue cardigan, a pair of gray wool slacks, a sweater vest.

She gathered up the clothes, made her way across the room to the bed, her footsteps on the floor strange and loud now that the room seemed empty, everything in the corner.

Except the armoire, centered there at the far wall, inside it all of his things, and now, suddenly, it seemed fine that she hadn't been able to move it. Nothing in it was hers. Only his.

This was when he came into the room, stopped just inside the threshold. Already she could smell him, felt on the air in the room the cold he'd brought with him from outside.

She smiled at him, let the clothes drop to the bed.

He said, "What are you doing?" and his words, like her footsteps across the room, were strange and loud to her. He still had his jacket on, still had on the muffler and his gloves. And he smelled of the eight or ten cigarettes she knew he must have smoked out in the car, where she'd left him before coming up here to move furniture.

It came to her, the answer to his question. She'd known for the last half hour, ever since she'd slammed the car door shut in the garage, then slammed behind her the door into the laundry room, that at some point he'd pose the question he had, *What are you doing?* Until that moment she'd had no answer ready, no reason she could see for doing what she'd done. She was simply moving furniture, what seemed to her the only logical thing to do after what he'd told her on the way home.

Or what he'd tried to tell her: the difference between women and men.

She looked at him, and it occurred to her that this man, her husband of twenty-seven years, was a strange and loud man, stranger and louder than any man she'd ever known.

Moving furniture is what I'm doing, she thought to tell him, but the words came out: "You are a strange and loud man."

"What?" he said, and left his mouth open. He took a step closer to her, then stopped. "What did you say?"

"I said," she said, "I'm moving furniture."

She went to the clock-radio, unplugged it, carried it to the bed while wrapping the cord around it. She said, "What did you think I said?" She set the clock-radio on top of the clothes in the top dresser drawer.

He took another step into the room. "I—" he began, and stopped. From the corner of her eye she could see him working off first one glove, then another. "I'm—" he began again.

"No need," she said. "Apologies not accepted," and she reached inside the lampshade, twisted off the black knob. The room was dark then, the only light that from the hall, what fell through the open door behind her husband. He was only a silhouette now, big and vague.

She stooped, unplugged the lamp, brought it to the bed. Fifteen cigarettes, she thought then, smelling him in the darkness, that smell growing louder and stranger, his silhouette growing bigger and more vague the longer he was in here with her. He'd smoked a whole pack out there, she thought, and set the lamp on the cane seat of the chair.

"I believe I'd rather we discuss the matter," he said, and she heard the rustle of the muffler as he pulled it from around his neck, heard the first buttons on the jacket unsnap. "As your husband—"

"You are a big and vague, loud and strange man," she heard her own voice give out, words she'd had no idea were leaving her.

The buttons stopped unsnapping, and she saw his silhouette, frozen against the light from the hall.

She picked up the nightstand, carried it to the bed, laid it atop the clothes for the dry cleaners.

He said, "What did you say?"

"I said," she said, "I believe I'd rather move furniture."

But now she was done. In the light from the hall she could see that she'd piled everything up in the corner of the room, that everything she could move had been moved. Except his armoire.

She looked from the armoire to him, put her hands on her hips. What words would come from her now? she wondered.

She said, "Please move the armoire." They were words she'd planned herself, words she'd made on her own.

He turned from her, looked to the armoire. She could see his profile in silhouette now, and he seemed to grow even more vague, even bigger.

He looked back at her. He said, ''But my back.'' He paused. ''You know my back. My back.''

She watched him reach a hand behind him, touch his back.

''Move the armoire,'' she said, her own words again.

''But—'' he said, and he took a step back, toward the light from the hall, toward the open door behind him.

She walked across the room to the armoire then, her steps suddenly quiet and sensible, him so big and vague and strange and loud. He'd smoked a carton of cigarettes out there, she knew.

Then she knelt next to one end of the armoire, centered there against the far wall.

She looked back to his silhouette one last time, saw him stopped in the doorway.

Her arms holding tight to the huge piece of furniture, she then lifted the armoire with a miraculous ease, lifted it and lifted it, the armoire no heavier than a blue cardigan, a rayon skirt. All his things, just like that.

The top of the armoire bumped the ceiling, made a quiet and sensible sound in the darkness. She brought the piece of furniture down a bit, then brought it up to bump the ceiling again.

She looked at him. He was out in the hall now, and she could see his face in the light out there, his mouth still open. The gloves were on the floor next to him, his muffler hanging loose in one hand, the jacket still half unbuttoned.

''A quiet and sensible sound,'' she said, and they were still her own words. She bumped the armoire against the ceiling again. ''Wouldn't you agree?''

He said nothing.

She said, ''Where would you like this?'' and started toward him with the armoire containing all his things, then lowered it so as not to scrape the top of the doorway on her way out of the bedroom.

She would sort out the dry-cleaning things later, she knew, then clear off his side of the dresser. But right now there was this business of the armoire, and where to put it.

Scat

CLARENCE MAJOR

"Just take us to the city. I'll tell you where to stop," I said to the taxi driver.

Now we were spurting in fumes of gas and metal from JFK through the complex night. Colored objects dashing zooming by. This ground-level entrance was so sensuous and ritual-like. Up ahead, through the windshield, I could see the comforting persistent lights of the great city.

But how about this driver? Could we trust him? I kept looking at his audacious name: *Gunman.* A warped scheme in his mind? Is he simply a man of routine, simply doing his job?

And Baby, from the very beginning, injured like a lonely ovary in a vacant woman, simply refused to think, to make decisions, which left me with the colossal load of not only my mismanaged self, but slightly cringing, restless, and pummeled under the load of her spirit. Though I wasn't fully aware of it yet, I was desperately, wildly, happy.

I watched the back of the driver's head. Then he gave a quick boorish laugh and called over his shoulder, "Popular impulses at special human rates?"

"What'd he say?"

"Baby, listen—" I began, slightly weary, showing my ill-breeding already. And we had been together only since October 28, and this was like the day after the Plot, I mean the Sacrifice, December 26; but I decided to control my usually unveiled but mystifying tongue, which, in any case, was tired.

"What were you going to say?"

But the cabby thought Cathy was addressing him and retorted: "I only was trying to remind you folks that I haven't the slightest idea where I should take you. How about Brooklyn?"

I thought of asking several questions at once but all of them jammed up in me and nothing came out for a moment anyway. "You see," I began, "the problem, mac"—and I threw my weight forward, elbows on my knees so that he could catch the body of each word in at least the ear on *this* side of his head, over the roar of the expressway traffic, the heavy groaning of trucks and buses and the swift oozing metal-sounds of the glittering modern buggy-wagons that still had horsepower for some mysterious reason—"the problem is *this*—" Suddenly, while still focusing his cumbersome head forward like any good driver, he shamelessly cut into my sentence. "The only reason I suggested Brooklyn is there's a lot of superstitious people in other parts of the city. I live in Brooklyn myself; you'd never know it, though, because I don't have a Brooklyn accent—did you notice? Well, you folks are obviously from outta town, so you didn't notice. Even grew up there, and I don't talk like your ordinary taxi-cab driver—if you know what I mean—"

Cathy, in a furiously cheerful voice, broke his dialogue, announcing: "Didn't you use the word 'superstition'?"

"Yeah, lady, that's what I said, but I'll explain to you what I mean by that, if you give me a moment—*can you both hear me?*" A little too loudly we assured him, but he cranked up his voice anyway and pumped on: "Like the gentleman called me *mac*—" and now, directly to me: "I know you didn't mean nothing by doing that, but it just proves a point; the same thing I'm talking about, the way I talk. I mean, I never call people mac, you know what I mean?" I could feel his passionate desire to turn around to witness my reaction to his clouded question; but he didn't, and because he was obviously such an excellent driver, I never saw his face. After a while it was like his voice was coming out of the back side of his head and it seemed so natural for him. "That's the way cabdrivers talk, you know—hey, mac, mac this and mac that." His pause was very stingy. "Well, the young lady asked me about superstitions. Now, I ain't—I mean *am not*—no expert on the real nature of these kinds of things, and I don't know anything about you people. I mean whether or not you two are married or just friends or what have you, but I know this, that—except for in Brooklyn—a mixed couple, and as I say, I don't know if you are a mixed couple, I mean if you two are—you know what I mean, married or going together—for all I know, you could be a couple of civil rights workers. Right? Right! And I really don't care, I mean I don't even care to know, but in case youse in some way romantic—" For the quickest and most tense moment of his speech he suddenly and automatically took his fat, reddened hands from the wheel to form the beautiful word "romantic"; he just threw his palms up, facing each other, as though he were holding something round and invisible. "Then I'd suggest Brooklyn, because there's less hard feelings there against . . . Well, you know what I mean. In Brooklyn, you'll never find people going around using bedbugs, for example, as a cure for sore eyes. But in Manhattan—oh Christ! There are folks who do this kind of thing—they actually mix bedbugs, all crushed up, with salt and the human milk of a pregnant woman, if they can find one, and not only for sore eyes, but the poorer people, in the ghetto, you know, they're even dumber than just the average guy, they even take it internally, they claim it cures urban hysteria. It's witchcraft, is what it is . . ."

O merciful wrathful gods. I was too tired to laugh, but this was about to get to me. And to make matters worse, Cathy in her usual innocent manner flatly stated, "Are you saying that this is generally true of *everybody* who lives in Manhattan?"

And the driver, really excited now, defensively snapped, "Do you know what 'literal' means, young lady? Yeah, you do, huh. Well, that's the way I mean it. I wouldn't tell you anything that isn't true." He hunched his shoulders.

I was still leaning forward to hear better. Cathy now anxiously joined me. I was looking straight ahead, fearful suddenly at his lack of concentration on his driving but trying to keep my composure. I must have been peering for some indication of our destiny—signs to Manhattan?—or at least my own, as I listened to the sovereign voice of our volunteer tour guide.

"There certainly ain't nothing in it for me, I mean for me to lie to you, deliberately," he said. "Ask yourself. What could I get out of it? Just trying to be a decent fellow and tell you how it is in Manhattan since you both are obviously from no parts of New York. It's the worst part of the city. But I can tell you everything you want to know about the Bronx, Queens, and Staten Island too. Now, you find some kind of superstitious practices, but to a lesser degree, because, well, those people out there they've had a little more education, but Manhattan is the worst of all."

I could feel Cathy's excitement and frustration and confusion; she obviously wanted to argue with the man but didn't know how to begin. His voice was so coolly antiseptic, so sure: "My son-in-law, he's a lawyer, told me just the other day, believe it or not, that a Manhattan lady came to him to file for a divorce from her husband. Want to hear the reason she wanted a divorce?" By all means, I smoothly assured him. "This husband of hers, the poor guy, he dropped a black ace of spades—*accidentally*—while just playing a normal game of cards"—he pronounced the word *cads*—"in their living room. You know, just sitting around with the fellas. *That's why* she wanted a divorce. And before you call me a liar, I'll tell you this, my son-in-law is, first, a good Catholic, a Harvard man, a responsible gentleman who maintains his ethics, and a decent husband to my daughter. They're even buying a home in Brooklyn Heights. And if you knew anything about the city here at all, you would know what *that* means."

"Mr. Lawman," Cathy shot, "you *must* be putting us on—"

This, of course, steamed him up again. *I* wanted to hear what he had to say; I was ready to believe anything. And everything he said, so far, sounded perfectly logical to me.

"Look," he snapped ambitiously, "do you know anybody, in

your hometown, wherever you come from, who hangs garlic around in their home? I mean to keep evil spirits away?''

''No,'' Cathy admitted.

''Do you know or have you ever heard of people who go around rubbing bald-headed old helpless men on their heads just to try to improve *their own* memory? Or how about this theory that water is fattening? Have you ever known anybody to stop drinking water because it's fattening? Well, there're a lot of Manhattaners who are right now, I mean this very minute, on a *water* diet. I mean a lot of them don't drink the stuff at all, and nothing that contains it, not even liquor. And furthermore, all over Manhattan there are like thousands and thousands of voodoo rites. And I don't mean concealed in some basement. Right out in the open. Certain people are put under spells by certain other people for certain reasons, and they're actually held like that, as victims. They use everything from rotten apple roots to certain kinds of perfumes to get certain effects, cause people to go insane or walk around crazy-like, you know, restless, can't sit down or nothing, just going on and on until they drop dead. You've heard of the hippies, haven't you? Sure you have. That's what's happened to those poor kids. They're all under a spell. They've been hexed. And, believe me, I'm not trying to scare you folks. I'm just trying to inform you. Actually, there're a lot of cabdrivers who won't even go into Manhattan, especially way uptown, the farther you get uptown the worse it is—'' He coughed, and now speaking directly to me: ''Nothing personal to you, sir—but the colored peoples are the worst of all. But it's not just *them*. I don't want to give you that impression. It's all of New York City. Like I say, except for Brooklyn. It's really funny sometimes. You can be driving around in Manhattan and see people strutting and just, ah, strolling along and everybody, I mean *everybody* is carrying an umbrella—''

Cathy cut in: ''But why?''

''Well, you see, they have this belief, it's like part of Manhattan culture, you know. They believe that if you carry an umbrella *that* will forestall rain.''

"But what have they got against rain?" Cathy was about to lose her temper.

"Search me!" His shoulders lifted and fell again. "All I can tell you is what I see!"

I cut in: "But you *are* still taking us to Manhattan?"

He pondered the hugely serious and complex question for several moments. "You see, it's a long drive in, and right now you still got a chance to choose. Like they say on television, when they're talking politics, you know, an *alternative*—" He chuckled, his shoulders rocking. "That's a nice big word, huh?" He stopped laughing, then said, "I don't mean to dwell on this subject. If I hate anything it's somebody who dwells on a subject. But while you're making up your minds, let me ask you a question. You sir, *or* the lady. Have either one of you heard of the art of capnomancy?

"The art of what?" I cleared my throat, hoping my mind would also defog.

"It's an evil art that's practiced, very commonly practiced, in Manhattan; some people call it pollution—"

Cathy cut in: "But how about the Village, certainly the Village—"

He cut her off: "The Village is no different. Of course you may find some strange people there, you know, they're all weird down there. Really weird people. And as I say, some of them might call it pollution, but the true name of it is capnomancy. It's an art. It's done with smoke. And it's very deadly. So, if you decide on Manhattan *anyway,* remember that. Because you're going to come up against it."

"But if it's smoke, certainly it would drift to Brooklyn too," Cathy pleaded.

He answered her swiftly, very curtly: "Nope. We don't have that sort of thing in Brooklyn." His tone was absolutely self-righteous.

After a moment of silence, I said, "I won't ask you what *do* you have in Brooklyn." This statement obviously bewildered and confused him.

He said, "But why not?"

I said, "Because I've heard that, aside from other, more private reasons, they haven't started body snatching yet, in Brooklyn.'' We were shooting straight ahead eighty-six miles per hour on the expressway and for the first time he turned completely around. He was so perplexed he looked like the Ambassador of Confusion. He also looked like Jackie Gleason.

''What're you talking about?''

Well, I was a little surprised that he hadn't heard, but I faked more astonishment than I felt. ''You *mean* you haven't heard?''

''No, but I'm all cars—''

I relaxed and quickly cleared up his confusion. ''Don't go around talking about this to anybody you don't know, because you could easily get into trouble. But already in certain parts of the world—I'm not saying where—people are being *snatched* off the streets under the shadowy cover of night and taken to certain places, usually hospitals, where very rich or important people who have heart trouble are in critical condition, about to die. They call these captured people—who're always poor and defenseless—*donors.* They're especially interested in pregnant women because their hearts are in better shape.''

''No!'' said the cabby. He chuckled, obviously not taking me very seriously.

Cathy, by the way, was listening intently. She should have been, because I had never before told her this secret information that had come my way, quite by accident (and even now I'm not at liberty to reveal the source). He now was truly puzzled and seemingly more seriously intent on what I was saying.

''You see, the only way the operation can succeed is if you catch a person who is healthy, walking around with good blood circulation—and you have to *act* swiftly, like they say where I come from. And they use very sharp instruments, have everything all ready. Then *shuph!* cut out the donor's ticker and get it into the other person's chest pronto.''

''Holy Christ! In heaven! What *are* you talking about?'' The man was truly alarmed.

For the first time since we'd left Wayne at the airport in Chicago, Cathy laughed, though it wasn't a happy laugh.

As an afterthought I thought it only fair to add: ''Of course, they use antiseptics and all kinds of—''

He cut me off: ''Just hold on a second, will you? Answer me this. What has this got to do with Manhattan?''

''Nothing—'' I said, so thrilled that he had finally gotten the point. ''That's *why* I've decided we're going to Manhattan. Just head for the Village and I'll decide where you can let us out when we get there.''

''Look!'' the driver said in an offended tone. ''If you're talking about what I *think* you're talking about, which is murder, *and* if you think for one minute that we have that sort of stuff going on in Brooklyn, then you're dead wrong. You got another thought coming.''

It always makes me feel joyful to know what I'm going to do next. So, by now, I was quite overjoyed when I reached up and gave our friend the driver a friendly slap on the shoulder. ''Well, pal, I certainly wasn't referring to Brooklyn and I'm mighty happy to have your word that Brooklyn is still safe, at least to that degree.''

At the same time I could see the huge black mouth of the Midtown Tunnel up ahead, specked with yellow lights. I had the distinct feeling that we were making an exit rather than an entrance.

Fugitive Light, Old Photos

RICHARD McCANN

At the morgue, the attendant showed us two Polaroids.

In one, my brother Davis was prone. In the other, he'd been turned face up on a steel examining table. *Who combed his hair so neatly?* I wondered. *Who gave him that bright blue T-shirt?* But in the flashbulb's glare, his face looked mottled, the way a sleeper's face is sometimes marked by the imprint of his blanket, so that he seems to be bearing a harsh dream's souvenir.

"That's not my son," my mother said, putting the Polaroids down on the counter. She said she would have to see the body.

But the attendant returned to his desk—green metal, like government issue. He read from his clipboard: we couldn't see the body unless we had prior written permission, he said, since actual viewing was no longer the standard procedure. Then he resumed his work, watching "Soul Train" on a miniature TV.

I know I should have argued with him, as my mother wanted. I know I should have insisted.

But I wanted to see nothing further: not the tiled corridors, nor the refrigerated units, those rows of identical steel doors. After all, wasn't it enough to have cleared Davis's garbage-strewn apartment, to have disposed of the urine-soaked mattress on which he died, dragging it down three flights of stairs to his building's alleyway Dumpster? And afterward, when the police came to search his apartment for evidence, wasn't it enough to have hidden his used syringes at the bottom of a grocery bag, beneath old newspapers, like ordinary garbage? Davis was thirty-six. He had died of a drug overdose.

I signed the papers.

All the way home, I tried to reassure my mother. I told her, "That was really Davis whose picture we saw."

We had his body cremated. There is no body anymore.

Here is Davis at six, shrill with laughter, embracing our father's cocker spaniel, who is lying feet up on the lawn. Here is Davis at eight, conspicuous in the back row of his fourth-grade photo, burdened by the brown patch the doctor has affixed to his eyeglasses. And here is Davis at twelve, standing at the swim club, awkwardly shielding his pubescent body with a towel.

"You don't know this," my mother tells me. "But Davis was a blue baby. When he was born, there were critical seconds when he didn't get air."

We are sitting at her dining-room table, beneath a bright ceiling light, sorting old black-and-white photos with scalloped borders. We are making a scrapbook of Davis's life. "Look," my mother says, handing me a photo of Davis as an infant, toddling across a lawn of cut grass, holding an Easter basket.

"That's why he cried too much," my mother says. "The doctor came to my room after the delivery. He told me that because Davis was a blue baby, he could have serious trouble later on."

What does she want me to tell her? That Davis could not be comforted because something terrible had happened to him in the abrupt moment between being taken from her body and delivered crying into her arms?

I could just as well remind her how Davis laughed with pleasure whenever our father called him "Davy Crockett."

He was thin and graceless. His teachers labeled him a "slow learner."

When I was angry at him, she made me recite: "Let me be a little meeker / With the brother who is weaker."

But I know what she wants. She is seventy-five. She tells me that I am her best friend, now that most of her friends have died.

She wants me to say, "He was a blue baby. A long time ago, there were critical seconds when he didn't get air." She wants me to caption these flimsy Kodaks—these proofs of happy impetuosities, of sudden Saturday outings, of picnics and festive hats fashioned from aluminum foil—so that she can mount them onto the huge black pages of the scrapbook she has bought.

Instead, I hand her the photo of Davis toddling across the lawn.

None of this—not even this snapshot, with its streaks of light—is the past I now recall. I see how Davis stares dazedly at the camera, as if he were drowsy and fretful in the noonday heat. And suddenly I want to draw him close, to offer him my protection.

"Look," I tell her. "By 'trouble,' I don't think the doctor meant that Davis was going to die of a heroin overdose."

She is silent, as if to tell me I have hurt her. We have not discussed the autopsy report she has received: *"Needle punctures involving right forearm . . . ," "Kidneys, 300 gms., no gross focal lesions, sections not remarkable . . . ," "Lividity. . . ."* Then she busies herself. "That isn't what I meant," she says. "I was just trying to explain a theory."

She holds a photograph beneath the table lamp and examines it. Then she chooses another. "I remember every detail," she says.

Don't, I tell myself. After all, it is only a snapshot of Davis in cutoff jeans, lying on our porch glider. It's only a snapshot of Davis washing our old two-tone Chevy.

But I am furious.

And suddenly, in a long drop, before I can stop myself, I am falling, weightless and unconstrained, through all the unphotographed moments of her rages and her terrors, toward memories that rise beneath me like hard earth. She comes to our room at night, searching the house for her cigarettes, whispering accusations . . . *"Why can't you ever . . . ," "I shouldn't have hoped . . . ," "If you would only . . ."* By morning, she is sprawled in her beige slip on the basement daybed, her silver bracelets—her "lucky bangles," as she calls them—discarded in a crystal ashtray. She murmurs in her sleep . . . *"Don't let . . . ," "I never hated . . . ," "Not harmed. . . ."*

Sometimes, after school, we find her waiting in her Impala at the edge of the parking lot, her face obscured by the sun visor's deliberate black slash. When we open the car door and get in, sliding across the wide vinyl seat, we find her strangely girlish and tearfully apologetic. Other times, when she is not there, we walk home slowly, past a power station and across a divided highway, and then on through acres of identical subdivisions, afraid to say we think we'll find her drinking.

Listen, do you really want a theory so badly? Then here is my theory: You were supposed to be the mother, but you let your child die.

And again I am returned to those long, fatherless nights of our adolescence, when Davis and I sat on the back porch, beside a black iron railing, still waiting for the appearance of late-blooming constellations, as if our father's impassive face might appear to us among them.

Our mother sat in her bedroom, listening to a radio call-in show. "Dear hearts," the deejay whispered. "It's late. I know you're lonely."

Go to her, Davis and I would argue.

For a moment, when I look up, I am not sure who she is—this woman who sits beside me, sorting old photos; this woman who has hung a stained-glass Serenity Prayer in her kitchen window. *She is an old woman,* I tell myself. *She lives in an old woman's house.* There are her floe-blue plates, displayed on shelves along the wall. There are her tiered end tables, neatly arranged with bric-a-brac. There are her cut-glass dishes, filled with sugarless candies.

"I have to go," I tell her. It is late. Soon she will need to check her blood sugar.

I know she is disappointed. I know these photographs have awakened in her a story she has no one else to tell. But tonight, I cannot hear how as an infant Davis cried when anyone approached him. How he feared crowds so badly she could not take him on the streetcar.

Tonight, I want no stories. Tonight, I want only the singular, precise moments of these snapshots—these snapshots reversed from negatives, these sensitive emulsions dependent upon even the briefest, most fugitive light. Tonight, I want only the singular, precise moments of everything that remains unfixed, unsorted, not yet pasted to its final page.

"All right," my mother says. "We can finish our scrapbook later." She starts to gather loose photographs from the table. "You haven't told me why you think he died," she says.

"Drugs," I tell her. "He died of a drug overdose."

"I know," she says. "But that isn't what I'm asking."

I tell her I will straighten the table. I cap the bottle of white ink we have used for writing captions; I wipe it with a paper towel. Then I set it inside an old shoe box, alongside the loose photos she has gathered. She carries the shoe box to her bedroom, to store in what she calls her "memory drawer."

When she comes back, she is carrying a large manila envelope. She says she has filled it with photos she thinks I'll want to have.

Then she sees me to the door.

For a moment, we pause beneath the yellow porch light. From there, the boxwoods that border the garage seem almost blue, dense with luminescence. "Good night," she says.

"Good night," I say. I walk to the car. But when I turn to wave goodbye, I see she has already closed the front door.

I get in the car. I switch on the dome light. I open the manila envelope.

It is not filled with photos of Davis, as I expected. Instead, it is filled with old photos I studied as a child for hours, drifting through them—long rainy Saturdays, sitting on the screened-in porch; whole summer afternoons, lying on the cool tiles of the basement floor—until I grew so mesmerized I could scarcely recall my own name. Here is my mother at six, nervously stroking a spotted pony, her bangs cut short across her forehead. And here she is at fifteen, standing on the broad lawn of her parents' summer house, smiling at the suitor who has filled her arms with cut hydrangeas, in order to take her picture just this way. And here she is, in the photo I loved best, taken during her first marriage, when she was barely twenty. The photo is torn. But within it, she calmly regards herself in her dresser mirror, so that one sees her as she sees herself, reflected, a Stargazer lily pinned to her dark hair. On its back, she has written, "I looked like Merle Oberon."

But where is a photo of the night Davis was first arrested? I was there.

Two policemen had brought him back to the house. They said they'd caught him in a park having sex with a man for money. He was eighteen.

From where I stood in the living-room threshold, everyone seemed so still and silent I thought they would turn into a photo. *Click,* I thought. *Click.*

Then my mother leaned forward. "Get out of my sight," she told Davis.

What could I have said to him the last time we spoke, the night he phoned from jail—"Don't tell Mom," he made me promise—because his headaches had grown so fierce he thought he would pluck out his eyes?

Once, she was beautiful.

Once, a man gave her cut flowers.

We are all of us blue babies. At critical seconds, we all lack necessary air.

My mother shuts off the porch light. The lawn falls into darkness.

I put the key in the ignition and start the car.

But when I look up, I see my mother framed in her picture window, walking back through her living room, carrying the shoe box of old photos. She has changed into her housecoat. For a moment, she disappears into the darkened doorway of her kitchen. Then she returns with a glass of water and seats herself at the dining-room table.

She turns on the lamp. She leans forward. She opens the shoe box. She chooses a photo and lifts it into the sharp white light.

No, I warn her. *What you are doing is too difficult. Too difficult and wrong.*

But she works on. She studies the photo closely, as if the steady effort of her attention will force it to yield the mystery she imagines it holds. She examines it beneath a magnifying glass. What year is it for her, as she sits at her dining-room table? What does she see now, outside that photo's glossy white border?

Watching her, I imagine her standing on the front lawn in a flowered sundress, holding a box camera, as years ago she must have done. She wants to take a picture of her son.

Her sundress flutters in the spring wind. With one hand, she balances the box camera. Then she extends her free hand toward Davis, who sits before her on the lawn.

"Davis," she coaxes. "Davis, come."

And when he stands at last and takes a toddling step toward her, she presses the shutter, and, through the viewfinder, she sees her own life walking precariously toward her, with his arms outstretched.

Don't die, I whisper.

But she can't hear me. She pastes the photograph onto the black page. She reaches into the shoe box. She chooses another. When she finishes the page, she turns it slowly; slowly, as if turning the page were the last thing she wanted to do.

Slice of Life

MARY MORRIS

Bennie's Leaning Tower of Pizza—the original one in the Westfield Mall, and not the five chains Bennie's now got all over Orange County—is where I work five nights a week and Saturday afternoon. I've worked here for a long time and what began as a part-time kind of thing is starting to turn into my life. Of course, I've got other plans. When I get out of high school, which should be in another few years at the rate I'm going, I want to open a small retail store. Maybe video rentals off the Coast Highway.

For now I toss. My girlfriend, Sue, does the toppings. We've been going out since our surfboards collided on Huntington Beach two summers ago and I got her her job here. I toss and she chops. We didn't plan it this way, but it just kind of happened. Sue is good with the clean, swift strokes. She raises a knife in her suntanned hand and brings it down hard. Her wide hips and her long dishwater-blond hair sway like she's dancing. She can get rid of a mushroom or a green pepper the way a magician gets rid of a white rabbit. I'm better with dough. I know how to pound to make it pliable, how to get it spinning on the tips of my fingers until it's going like a top. And then I toss, higher and higher. I am not good at everything I do, but I'm proud of the few things I do well, and tossing pizza is one of them.

We make all kinds of pizzas here and some that even seem kind of strange, like pizzas with broccoli or melted goat cheese. And then we've got your average sausage and cheese, mushroom and anchovy. Some of them have names like the Sophia Loren with its big dark circles of pepperoni and the Al Capone with lots of anchovy, and the Joe DiMaggio, which is all veggie. Bennie gave them their names, don't ask me why.

I know most of the people who come here. Mr. Schultz comes in on Tuesday nights. He was my math teacher for umpteen years until he gave up on me. Mr. Schultz always orders a small Joe DiMaggio and always tells me how this is his wife's night to play cards with the girls. He seems sad when he tells me this and my mom says it's because everyone in town knows that there's no card game on Tuesday nights and his wife's having an affair with the soccer coach.

The O'Sullivans come in every Wednesday when we've got giants for the price of mediums and they always order the same thing, the Slice of Life. They've got three boys—Buddy, Oscar, and Scott. Oscar can't move his arms or legs. That is, they kind of just flop around and his head bobs in a funny way too. I can't quite describe it, but it's like Oscar's made of Play-Doh. I always bring the pizza to them myself because I like the way Oscar's mouth shapes itself into words that his mother translates for me as thank you. I give Oscar a free Coke when he says thank you because I know what a difficult thing it is for a kid like him to say.

I don't really know what's in the Slice of Life, but I know that it's got everything, plus something else. It's the something else I can't describe. Bennie says with a snicker it's a family secret, an ingredient handed down by the ancestors from the old country. I always ask if it's some kind of hash, but Bennie just laughs. He says it's a combination of things.

My mom comes in sometimes and she always wants a small plain cheese, which I tell her is the dumbest thing, but she says a haircut that looks like the tributaries of the Amazon with little rivers and canals running through it is also pretty dumb, so to each his own. I don't argue with that. Mom comes in more now since Dad stopped coming. He used to come a lot, but it dwindled to less and less, like those letters I used to get from a pen pal overseas.

My dad's got this funny way of doing things. He always has to know where we are, but we can't know where he is. He says he's not a gunrunner or involved with the CIA. He's just a very private person and needs his space. Before they split, my mom didn't complain much about this in front of us. But now, especially when his payments are late, she says he's involved with the mob and they're going to cement and deep-six him one of these days.

One night Sue and I are in the back and I've got her pressed against the butcher block. She's a big woman, strong as a horse, and I'm drawn to her the way I was to Amazons as a boy. I'm running my flour-coated hands up and down her arms until I can see the tattoo of a unicorn on her shoulder. When I first fell in love with Sue, it was for her tough walk and her unicorn tattoo. She starts moaning. "Let's close up and get out of here," she says just as my dad walks in. I pull away from Sue fast as if someone's come to rob the store and she says, "Hey, what's wrong?" He was never one to show up at good times and this is another instance. Where are you when I got expelled? I want to shout. When I fell off my motorcycle last year? Instead I say, "What'll it be?" I keep my hands under the counter so he can't see them trembling. It takes a moment for me to notice that he's got a girl with him, a small blond number who looks like his stenographer, if he ever needed a stenographer. They both have tans and some of her skin is peeling off her face. My dad's got his Hawaiian shirt unbuttoned and a few gold chains around his neck. "A medium cheese with half sausage, half mushroom, right, Marlene?"

Marlene just nods and smiles dumbly at me as if I really only am a pizza chef to this man. "So, Dad," I say emphatically, "how about a Coke or a nice root beer?"

"You've got a new haircut, I see."

"It's the latest," I tell him, turning so he can see the lines zigzagging, made by the tiniest razor in the world. "The California special, it's called."

I take longer than I need with their pizza. I make sure the dough is perfect, the edge just fluted in the right way. I arrange the sausage in a special swirl. Put the chopped mushrooms in a nice moon-shaped arrangement. I put it in on a slow bake and watch as my dad holds Marlene's hands as they sit by the window. He says things to her and she laughs, each time putting her hand across her face to cover her mouth until I realize she's wearing braces, wired teeth. This, I tell myself, from the man who spawned me.

I don't really hate him, but I can't say that I like him much either. I never did. The thing about my dad was you never knew what he'd do next. One minute we'd be washing salad in the kitchen. Next moment he'd slam me into a wall. One night at dinner we were all sitting around laughing. Next minute he throws a Coke in my face.

He used to take me out to learn things like golf. He'd put down a ball and say, "Look, kid, here's a ball. Now you hit it." Then I'd hack at it and miss until he'd take the club out of my hand and hit a long smooth drive. "See, kid," he'd say. "Any idiot can hit a nice drive." My mom said that one day when I was just a little kid and we were at a swimming pool, he said, "Well, time you learn how to swim." And he tossed me in. I don't remember any of this, but she said she had to dive in after me and I gagged for an hour.

My mom told me this just after she threw him out. She'd had a tough time with men, my mom. The guy before my dad was an actor who on his way to the wedding drove past the church and just kept going. At least my dad made it to the ceremony. She said she could have lived with him being unfaithful and not paying bills. What she couldn't live with was the things he did to me.

My girlfriend, Sue, tries to understand. Sue actually comes from a happy home where everyone gives each other presents for no reason at all and the hallway is filled with pictures of smiling relatives. She had an easy life until one day her twin choked to death at the dinner table. He was fraternal, so she never felt as if half of her had died, but she's never felt quite right after that either.

It's the O'Sullivans' night to show up, but so far they haven't. They weren't here the week before either, which I found strange since they've been every Wednesday since I started. I am beginning to think something is wrong, when I realize my dad's pizza is ready and it's smelling very done. The crust is a little burnt and I say to myself without him saying a word to me, can't you do anything right? If there's a wrong way to do it, do you have to find it?

I'm about to take the pizza to them when Sue grabs me by the arm. "Relax," she says. "He can't do a thing to you now." Wanta bet, I think of saying.

I give them their cheese with half sausage, half mushroom, and Marlene asks for a fork. I watch as she picks off every mushroom, one by one, moving them into a little pile by the side of her plate, like a squirrel hoarding its nuts. "Is something wrong?" I ask. "Would you rather have plain cheese?"

Marlene just smiles and shakes her head. "I like to save the best for last," she says, winking at my father. I understand that this is some joke between them, something I don't want to know about.

My dad chews carefully on his sausage. "Sit down, son," he says. "Looks like business is slow. Sit down. I want to talk to you." I don't want to sit down and I'm not sure I want to talk to him, but Sue nods for me to go ahead. "I can handle anything that comes in," she says. I'm hesitating, but just then Mr. Platsburg comes in. I can't stand Mr. Platsburg, because he always comes in and asks for a giant with everything, then he says just hold the anchovies, the sausage, the extra garlic, and the peppers. And I always say, Mr. Platsburg, why don't you just order an extra cheese and veggie, no peppers, but not Mr. Platsburg. It's always the giant everything and what to hold for him.

"Marlene and I are involved in a small business venture."

"Oh, yeah?" I say, giving the diamond in my ear a twirl.

"We were thinking of opening a small beauty parlor and thought maybe you'd like to come in on it. You've got a stable income, some money saved."

"Oh, yeah?" I run my hands through my hair. Then I don't say anything for a while. I just look at him, then at her, then back at him. My dad is waiting, poised, and I am pleased that I am keeping him waiting. Once he kept me waiting. I'd done something wrong at school and the principal called my dad. I don't know why he didn't call my mom, but he got my dad and he told me to go home and wait for him. I did that. I was maybe eight years old and I tried to do what I was told. I sat in a room and waited until he came home. Then he tied me to a chair. "You don't wanta go to school?" he said. "I'll give you a reason not to wanta go to school." And he shaved off my hair. I don't know why. It wasn't the style like it is now and I just sat there watching as my hair fell off my head in thick tufts.

"So we were thinking maybe you'd like to put a little of your savings into our project . . ." I could read right through this one. He'd lost in some two-bit card game and somebody was going to get him if he didn't come up with a thousand or so.

I am overcome with this desire to pound my father's face, then toss him into the air. I imagine myself twirling him on the tips of my fingers. I am about to pull my arm back and do this when my mom walks in with a look in her eyes like she's breathing fire. She stares at my dad and Marlene. "Whatever he wants, Brian," she says to me, but she never takes her eyes off of them, "don't listen. Whatever he asks for," she says, "say no."

"Ginnie," he says with a half-cocked smile, "I just came to see my boy."

"He's doing fine without you seeing him." My mother is a tiny woman, not one to raise her voice, but she's acting like she's ready to go two or three rounds. "You visit him again, I'll get a court order." She turns to me. "I was driving by. I saw him sitting here. You okay?"

"Yeah, I'm okay."

"Gimme a slice to go," she says to Sue. "Don't listen to a word he says." Leaning against the counter but never taking her eyes off my dad, she takes her slice on its greasy slip of waxed paper. "I'll be home. If you need me, call," and she's gone.

It's not long before they get up to leave. "Now, listen, Brian," my father says. "Are you sure you can't loan your old man a little?"

"I'm sure. You know, Sue and me, we're thinking of getting married." I glance at Sue, whose eyes roll, then smile complacently at my dad. "But the pizza, Dad, it's on me." As they leave, I watch my father's back recede. I take aim at him, as if I've got a dart in my hand. It was the one game he actually taught me how to play. I think

I'll never see him again. Or if I do, it'll be when I need him the least.

I'm thinking of putting out the CLOSED sign, taking Sue out back, laying her across the butcher block table, and having my way, when the O'Sullivans come in. They seem different somehow and it takes me a while to notice Oscar isn't with them. It's just Buddy and Scott and the parents. Mrs. O'Sullivan looks about ten years older and I'm wondering what I should say when she looks up at me. "The usual, Brian," she says as if nothing's wrong. "Just give us the usual."

I make them a Slice of Life. I order the vegetables and pepperoni in a beautiful swirl like a flower unfolding. The jar with the special ingredients is almost empty. Bennie always fills the jar, but I know he keeps a sack in the back, so I go into the storage room and find it. I reach into the large burlap sack and pull out a slip of paper. It reads: parsley, basil, oregano, thyme. I take a fistful of the ingredients in my hands and sniff it. Is this it? I ask myself, looking back at the slip. Could this be all?

I let the O'Sullivans sit there, munching on their crust, as we close up. Sue hardly says a word as she puts the remnants of her choppings into Ziploc bags—mushrooms, green peppers, sausage—for tomorrow's round. I scrub the counters clean. When they get up to leave, Mr. O'Sullivan comes over and clutches my hand. "Thank you, Brian. You have been very kind."

We lock up late. Some nights after work we bowl a few and some nights we go to a club nearby, but this night I want to take a ride near Pelican Point. "Let's head for the beach," I say. We get in the car and drive. We drive until we spot the moon, resting over the Pacific, round and orange and perfect. I pull into a sandy ditch and for a few moments stare at the sky. Then I cannot resist, I burst into song. "When the moona hits your eyes like a bigga pizza pie, dat's amore . . ."

Sue puts her fingers across my lips. "Shush," she says, "let's just be quiet for a while."

As we sit, I shape my fist into a round, even ball and point it straight at the moon as if I could smash right through the windshield and blot out the light. Sue must know what I'm thinking, because she reaches across and pulls me to her chest. I bury my face against her shoulder at the place where the unicorn must be. She dusts my hair. "You're covered with flour," she laughs, and I let her knead me in her hands like dough.

Spring Break

FAYE MOSKOWITZ

Of course I knew you right away, Laura: the long, straight lemon-yellow hair, raggedy jeans and leather sandals, the T-shirt that announced your latest cause, the same breasts and hips that had cars rear-ending each other on Connecticut Avenue when you were only twelve. And what could you be now? Seventeen, if that. It's been years since you ran away from home to hitchhike across the country, one of those kids who thought she needed to get lost to find herself. After your parents hired the detectives to bring you home, you came back to school a little while, back to my eighth-grade English class, where you wrote poems about unicorns and shimmering butterflies and crystal tears; nothing that could give me a clue as to what you had encountered on that crazy journey.

Not long after your return, you locked yourself in one of the stalls in the school lavatory and wouldn't come out. Do you remember that? When they sent for me as someone who might get through to you, I stood there like an idiot, feeling no more capable of piercing your wall of silence than I could the seamless Formica door that hid you. And why should you talk to me? What language would we use? Who would translate for me the "joints" and "weed" and "nickel bags"? In what dictionary would I find the coupling you discovered at half my age?

Perhaps what we needed to pass back and forth was beyond

speech. No great matter. I waved away the curious glances of the other girls, finally emptied the washroom of all but the two of us. When you persisted in your silence, I thought for a moment of getting down on my belly and crawling under the stall door. In the end, worried as I was, I hadn't the conviction to do it. Whatever you were considering in that makeshift privacy you had created, I fiercely believed I had no right to violate it. So I leaned against a washbasin and said, "Laura, please come out." And finally, why you never said, you did open the door and let me put my arm around your unyielding shoulders.

You sat there in my office and spoke in initials. You said D and C, IUD, never the other word that dropped like a scrim between us. I tried to be calm; I smiled the way teachers do today at all sorts of secrets. I smiled for fear my horror would drive you away from me, would constitute one more betrayal for you in a world where foundations rock so soon. Small ironies pervaded the room like chalk dust; your would-be counselor felt she knew less of life than you did. In fact, I coveted your composure, respected you for having the decency to tremble a little now that it was done. What could it have been like for you to have people poking around inside you?

You sat there, your hair a dim shadow on the rose-magenta silk I had hung the fall before when school began. Outside, the spring snow fell perversely on tight round buds. Make a tiny snowball and push it with the palm of your hand, soft, soft over the ground. Now it gathers more snow to itself, and soon the ball is heavy and hard to push. Two hands and all your body to push until the great round icy thing strips the ground to bare black earth and still you push and still it gathers . . .

For weeks the teachers' lounge talked of nothing but you (in the end I had to tell the secret). At faculty meetings, you topped the agenda. What were we to do with you? We felt tongue-tied around you, as if what you had experienced so early set you apart from all of us. We didn't know how to connect to you, Baby-Woman. Some of us were almost ashamed of how being female had betrayed you. Some of us, deep down, blamed your precocious beauty for what had happened as though you could have cut off those breasts or hidden them in dresses shaped like tents. In all that chatter, we couldn't find the words to comfort you . . . or ourselves.

Pale and pulled into yourself, you came to school, your homework done in a round hand, tiny hearts over the *i*'s and at the ends of sentences. I remember the lunches you would bring in an English tin box printed all in flowers: thin slices of roast beef, bloody and rare, with a small container of hollandaise; huge strawberries, out of season; artichokes you plucked, leaf by leaf, and drew through your sharp little teeth.

Then you stopped coming again. Your father emptied your locker of the papers you had never taken home, gym shorts and shoes, an umbrella, a small teddy bear in a University of Michigan T-shirt. He looked down at the floor, your father, a little man dressed in a blue work shirt and jeans, a silver-and-turquoise belt buckle glittering like a winking eye. He said, "I've given up on her." "You can't say that," I told him. "People don't write off thirteen-year-olds. "I'm used up," he said. "I haven't anything left."

Last week you were waiting in my office when I came out of class, an infant slung on your hip as casually as if it were a bookbag. Your familiar half-smile, worldly and sardonic, now struck me as triumphant too. But what was the battle and what price the victory; you, still little more than a child yourself with a baby of your own, your life on hold for years, if not forever.

Oh, I've kept track of you all this time. I knew about the psychiatric ward. (It was one way to keep you in your place.) And we all saw the "Style" piece in the *Post* on the children's advocate who finally managed to free you. I'd heard your former classmates, seniors now, gossiping about the group house way out in Virginia where you had gone to live when you dropped out of boarding school. Still I was surprised to see you after so long, sitting in my swivel chair with the bemused look of a hippie madonna. Once again your ripeness overwhelmed me, your face and limbs without flaw as if they had been poured from a pitcher.

Outside my small office, piercing bells marked off the school day; teachers passed, bent on errands; lockers slammed. Did all of this strike you with nostalgia? Probably not. You've always been a loner, not unlike myself, but unlike the way I was, too beautiful, too physically precocious for the other girls, too daunting for an adolescent boy to do anything but dream or lie about.

There were so many questions I wanted to ask you, things I had been pondering for so long. When you went cross-country that time, the truck driver who picked you up: what was it like to sit beside him, high up in the cab, sliding around on that leather seat? Did you put your hand on his long, blue-jeaned thigh to steady yourself; did you rest your head against his shoulder and sleep? How did the world look to you, glancing down on the tops of dusty automobiles, staring into windows of other trucks at hungry drivers who would eat you up with their startled eyes?

For a long time after you first came back to my class, I imagined truck stops all over America, places where waitresses with their first names embroidered over their hearts shoveled out eggs and sausages and stacks of toast limp with melted butter, poured refills into heavy china cups. And you there, eating and laughing, your truck driver throwing back his thin shoulders, preening, his gray life made golden by your presence and the envy of the other men.

Was there even one waitress, an older woman perhaps, in a soiled uniform, sweat crescents under her armpits, who spirited you into the ladies' room on some pretext or other to say, "Honey, who is this guy? Do you want me to call someone for you? Do you need some help?" Like as not, the waitresses pursed their lips in disapproval, and mentally stacking tips against debts, found themselves short. Like as not, they thought, I've got troubles enough of my own —and put you out of their heads. That's the way it is, Laura. As for me, I never knew my place with you, not mother or sister, no closer to your parents' world than I was to yours.

Once I dreamed it more simply. I thought I might find a few students like the junior high school girl I was myself, someone whose fingers would tremble when she picked up a new book, who judged its heft by how many hours of pleasure it could give before it had to end. And for a while, you were that girl. Do you recall the rainy night of the seventh-grade school party when we stood in the entryway surrounded by a sea of opened black umbrellas? "Look," you said, your eyes growing wise with the wonder of connection, "It's just like the funeral scene in *Our Town.*" I loved you that moment with an ardor as fierce as anything I have experienced since. But I couldn't save you then as I cannot save you now, or get you out of my head either, on this trip to France, spring break.

I see you everywhere I go, Laura. Sometimes your hair hangs loose, the sun imprisoned in it. Sometimes you capture your hair in a brightly colored scarf, and I can almost feel the heft of it, struggling to escape. French girls are so lovely, swaggering in belted trench coats and deftly knotted silken scarves. I observe them eagerly as if by studying every line I can somehow refashion my own look and shape it to a new design. I study, but it is not enough. I want to stroke the supple boots clinging to curving legs. What is the lesson of rich leather handbags riding sidesaddle on magnificent shoulders?

I know my trouble. People are always telling me to "loosen up" or "wing it." I see the looks at school when my colleagues find me making lesson plans long after the workday should be over. I don't know how they get by. I have to be prepared or I might run out of things to do, and then the kids would run wild, howling and throwing wads of paper and sauntering around the room as if I weren't there at all. You see, much as I love teaching, it's maintaining order I consider my greatest success . . . or necessity, maybe. Groups of kids standing around without purpose frighten me. They're the same all over the world, it seems. Nothing to do with culture. I've seen them here in France, gangs, just like the kids in our school, like the kids in Georgetown, clustering on a street corner, laughing, laughing, as if for the moment they were in on some monumental joke only they can understand.

As if my life were not complicated enough, I find the language difficult here, my college French hardly adequate to avoid constant misinterpretation. The newspaper had banner headlines yesterday: REAGAN BLESSÉ. I thought the Pope had come for a visit to the States. So like me to go for the easy meaning. It was hours before I realized the word *blessé* meant the President had been wounded, and then I couldn't keep myself from running to the American Embassy to find out in English what was happening. I suppose that's what made me think of you again. In the end, what can anybody do about anything, so far from home?

In the market, fish lash their tarnished silver tails in galvanized tubs where housewives reach for them, sleeves rolled up on arms as thick as rolling pins. Close by stand wooden buckets of discarded entrails. Hit him over the head, for God's sake. Put him out of his misery. I'd get sick cleaning him, running water over his slickness, shucking the rainbows from his skin. MAMA PUTS HIM IN THE PAN. BABY EATS HIM LIKE A MAN. How does one eat this flopping flesh that won't die even though its brains and guts are gone? You, fish, stiffening in my hand: I only know that I am shaken by your flopping and your adamant refusal to give up your fishy ghost.

I don't sleep well, Laura; I haven't for years. Whenever I lie down, I'm forced to endure endless reruns of my days stretching back as far as my mind can see. Traveling makes it worse, of course, my present clock on foreign time, my memory clock insisting on its own standard. For days now my clock's been stopped at your last visit. Over and over the scene replays itself in slow motion. You reach into your pants pocket and pull out a tiny drawstring bag and a packet of papers the size of a matchbook. You peel off one of the tissues and shake something into it from the pouch. Your baby crawls around on my office floor, where I fear she will swallow lost paper clips or poke her eye out with a ballpoint pen, but you seem not to have these fears. You expertly roll the paper into a cylinder, lick it, twist it at one end. In a moment, a pungent scent fills my office. Laura, I could have lost my job, yet I said nothing. Was that what you wanted from me? What sort of test was this? Did I pass or fail? We shared a common language for such a little while, and now one of us has forgotten how to speak it.

So, Laura, how shall I respond? Up the street, that girl is naked under her sweater: gray cashmere, the color of just before a storm. She will keep coming toward me, her breasts, heavy triangles suspended from invisible wires, the nipples keeping the wool one flicker away from the rest of the rounded flesh. In that space, that fraction between flesh and wool, I have lost myself. That distance is my destruction. She, you, the two of you pull me from pole to pole. You suck my marrow as autumn draws the green out of an arching branch.

Animal Rights

JESS MOWRY

"Animal rights organizers in the Bay Area joined today in voicing support of an activist group claiming responsibility for vandalizing property in Santa Cruz County. The office and adjoining structure of a small business was ransacked, files destroyed, and a bloodlike substance was splashed over wall and floors. According to a spokesperson for the activists, animals, primarily white rabbits, rats, and mice, were being raised on the premises for the purpose of laboratory experimentation. Cages were destroyed and all animals removed. The spokesperson refused to disclose where the animals were taken, saying only 'to a place of refuge and safety.' The spokesperson declined further comment, adding only that 'animals have no one to speak up for them and their welfare should be the concern of every caring human being'. Authorities are still investigating. In local news, last night's drive-by shooting of an East Oakland youth . . ."

The boy stared at the TV screen, not hearing much more than the soothing cadence of the white lady's voice, or seeing anything but shifting colors. Dimly, he remembered his mom telling him something . . . a long time ago . . . about *in one ear and out the other.* That was cool. Nothing stayed inside long enough to hurt.

The boy sat small, deep in the big old couch. It was covered in worn-out red velvet, but enough of the nap remained to feel soft on his body. There were no sharp angles to hurt him. He wore only jeans, faded 501s that were a little too small, so three of the buttons were open. They too were soft against his skin. The open buttons kept them from pinching. That was cool. Nothing hurt, and they were probably better than what he'd been wearing before . . .

Before what?

In one ear and out the other.

The TV voices droned on and the pretty colors shifted. If the boy thought hard enough he might remember that this was the early-morning news. Soon there would be cartoons. He didn't know how long he'd been watching the screen; all night, weeks . . . or years. It didn't matter. He drifted at peace in softness and warmth. If he concentrated he might have remembered more, but nothing hurt, so there was no reason to remember.

The boy was maybe ten, his skin like ebony velvet, with eyes that looked large and lost in a small peaceful face, long-lashed and gentle obsidian. His body was just beginning to take on the puppy look of major growing. He was thin. Small, tight muscles had started to define chest and arms, but now seemed slack and fading as if no longer needed. His hair was bushy and wild, but clean, and scented with lice shampoo. Sometimes he was given a bath. Since when, he couldn't remember, but it didn't matter. Here he was, and nothing hurt.

There were cartoons. The Teenage Mutant Ninja Turtles. Vaguely he recalled it being a cool show that he liked. But now he couldn't remember their names.

The man's voice came from over his shoulder. ''Boy! You got to go?''

The boy considered the words. What did they mean? He half turned his head toward the voice, but then forgot why. It didn't seem important.

''Shit!'' said the voice. Then: ''Irene! Get his ass to the bathroom fore he go an mess himself again!''

The boy didn't like the voice when it sounded that way. Maybe it reminded him of something? The woman came . . . Irene . . . and took his hand. It was a surprise to discover he could stand . . .

that his legs held him up even though he walked on clouds. It was a surprise to find he *could* walk; to see his very own bare feet way down on carpet and then cross faded green linoleum one step at a time. Green like grass. He hadn't walked on much grass in his life. Even the linoleum felt soft. Linoleum grass. A new idea. The woman . . . Irene . . . set him on the toilet. He wondered if that should piss him off. After all, he wasn't a goddamn baby, and boys stood on their own two feet to piss. But that didn't seem to matter to the woman. Maybe she just wanted to be safe? He supposed he should do something, but seemed to have forgotten what it was. He was aware of the woman's hands, soft and warm on his bare shoulders, holding him. Her voice was carelessly gentle. "C'mon, boy, do somethin for Momma fore you go noddin again."

The boy had a name, but couldn't remember it. The woman . . . Irene . . . wasn't really his mother. Maybe he did do something in the toilet because he found he was standing on his own special feet once more, and the woman was buttoning his jeans. All but the top three. She led him back to the couch. There were more cartoons, but he wasn't sure what they were about. The old velvet was soft, but it seemed important to remember his name. Why?

The man's voice: "For chrissake, feed him, Irene! Saturday busy as hell . . . be goddamn barrasin he die on us!" Laughter.

No, Irene wasn't really his mother. But mostly she was kinder than his mother had been. Even the man was kind in his way, though not as gentle-voiced anymore as when he'd picked the boy up in his big new car and brought him here. Wherever *here* was. It didn't matter. Here was a lot better than *there.* Here was warm and soft and nothing hurt.

Except . . .

The boy wasn't sure. Not yet. But he almost remembered.

A spoonful of color appeared under his small snub nose. Lucky Charms. Marshmallow shapes. Pretty. A spoonful of sweetness fed to him. He concentrated on not choking. Milk dribbled down his chin and chest. The woman clucked her tongue gently, the way his mother had done long ago. A soft cloth cleaned him up. Good as new. When had his mother been so kind? A long time before he'd come home from school to find the apartment empty? He was starting to remember. The Lucky Charms were sweet and crunchy, and the marshmallows melted to warm syrupy goo in his mouth. The woman was gentle as she fed him, waiting until he remembered to swallow, sometimes reminding him to. Did she love him? Most times she was kind . . . except when he messed himself like a goddamn baby. Or choked. Or forgot what to do on the toilet. Then she would shake him. Sometimes she'd shake him for no reason he could figure, but she never hit him. Even the man was kind in his way . . . he didn't want him to die.

The cartoons were almost making sense now. If he blinked his eyes and thought mega-hard he could remember things . . . fog drifting through the night streets, following him. Streetlamps haloed, cold, wet, and lonely. He shivered. It hurt to remember.

A knock on the door. Men voices, mostly the man. He had a name . . . a street name . . . but the boy couldn't remember it. Yet. Maybe if he could remember his own it would help? If he concentrated with all his might he could just understand the men's words . . .

"I tellin ya, Jack, be prime product I got here."

"Yeah? An how I know that, man? Could be death in a sandwich. Don't know you from nobody. Your price be the only thing I *know* prime, for a fact!"

The boy looked down at his arm. Sometimes it hurt. Things weren't supposed to hurt. It said on TV that it shouldn't hurt to be a kid. The man voices, rising and falling, reminded him of that.

"Shit, man! You got to take nuthin on faith! Not from me. Come along here an check this out. Right from the bag, see? You watchin?"

The boy stirred. The TV screen blurred. His arm hurt again and he began to remember. His name! Almost, he had it!

Man shapes standing over him. Tenseness in the air. Smells of suspicion. Man voices again. "Yo! Check this out. My own son here! Boy I love. Word up!"

The pain of the needle, sharp in his arm. ''Man laughter. ''Yo! He look like he dyin to you, man? Hell, watch him long's you like.''

More laughter. The voices fading . . . fading like the pain until nothing hurt anymore. All was softness and warmth, and sometimes even a gentle touch.

So why, the boy wondered, was he crying?

The Year of the Parrot

HELEN NORRIS

Scrabbling the floor of his golden cage, fluttering, screeching terrible oaths, the parrot was carried into the house. Cuddles the cat, a rangy, slate-gray, striped beast, who years ago had outgrown his name, ran beside the cage, his whiskers a-twitch, his tail alert, his green eyes narrowed to slits of fire. "Soak yer head!" the bird screamed at him.

"My God, not there!" Norma screamed in turn, as her husband, George, was lowering the cage, skimming the top of the baby grand. "There, out there!"

"The will said . . ."

"I know what it said. The sun porch is close enough. Too damn close! He was there before. We didn't get any flak before."

Robbie, their son, who was five years old, caught Cuddles's tail and held it tight while he watched his father struggle to lift the swaying cage to its hook in the corner of the porch. "Who is it?" said Robbie, climbing onto a chair. "Does he belong to us?"

"You're too young to remember him," said his father. "He was here with us three years ago."

Rob was impressed with how green he was, as if he'd been freshly picked from a yard. There were layers of brilliant red in the wings, unfolding like a lady's fan, as the bird did a dance to keep his balance. His beak was a crackery color and round, like a chunk of bubble gum stuck to his nose. The eye, an emerald, glinting wrath, was ringed with feathers of deepest gold. Rob had never before in all his life seen such a scary, beautiful bird. "Is he ours?" he asked.

"He's ours for a year," his mother said, "and then, thank God, he's somebody else's."

Cuddles had leapt to the chair with Rob and waved a paw at the swaying cage. "Yer dead meat!" the bird squawked at him. He was scudding around his still-rocking cage, dragging his wings and biting the bars. One eye was closed. "Drop yer drawers!" he screeched at Norma. "I'll butter yer buns!"

"Why does he talk like that?" said Robbie.

"Because he's a foulmouthed fowl," she said.

"Does that mean we don't have to be nice to him?"

"No," said his father, "it means we do."

"Zip yer fly!" the bird squalled at George.

"He doesn't look good to me," said Norma. "If he dies on us it's Orin's fault."

With his head cocked, the parrot swept from bar to bar like an old duenna dragging her skirt. A green feather floated through the bars and Cuddles dived. "You see?" said Norma. "He's delivered to us in a dying state."

But George laughed. "He's good for another hundred years."

Robbie was naturally confused. So his father sat down to explain to him in words that a child could understand, but that was pretty hard to do, and he strayed into fields where Robbie got lost, where the grass, so to speak, was above his head. The old bird cocked his head to listen, though he must have heard it a hundred times. In Buddy's house and Orin's house and George's house, and Buddy's and Orin's and George's again, round and round the mulberry bush, told to groups who hugged his cage. He bit their fingers when he could. "Move yer ass!" he would twang at them, and then he would scream a string of oaths and gutter words that made them gasp and titter and laugh.

"You teach him that?" they said to Buddy, Orin, or George.

"No," they were told, "we think he belonged to a pirate once. Or else the pirate belonged to him. A pirate parrot . . . Lost an eye in a fight at sea." Their chuckles produced a rain of remarkable malediction. ''Some of his words are past their prime; still, they will give your hair a perm.''

''What about the children?'' they asked.

''At the end of the day we line them up and wash their ears . . . and their mouths if they've repeated it.''

That was the gravest problem of all: a bevy of cousins growing up with poisoned minds and filthy tongues. They were taken to church and Sunday school for a weekly purification rite, but the old bird had them the rest of the week. ''It's a losing battle,'' Sylvia wailed. She was Orin's wife, with a brood of six. ''What's it all worth if we raise a litter of guttersnipes?'' For one and all, the children thought or looked or said, ''If you let him, then why can't we?''

So they did, and Sylvia cursed the bird. She said she drank because of the bird. The words got better with every drink, till finally she could say them all, a string of them, and they sounded nice. ''Well, it isn't as if they're into drugs. They're into dirty words, that's all.''

George tried to sum it up for Rob. ''Get to the batty old woman,'' Norma said, and left the room. She knew the tale, oh God, she did.

The batty woman was Aunt Agatha. To put it simply, as George once more was trying to do, a lover who died—a captain who had gone down with his ship—had bequeathed her his parrot, Lochinvar. She had nurtured this bird with obsessive care. She had doted on him, as only a maiden lady can dote. Had death not cheated her of the chance, she could scarcely have pampered his master more. She replaced his cage with a gilded one, elegant, snug, commodious, made to order of lightweight steel, since nothing less could contain the bird. He could ravage a wooden cage in a day, spitting the pieces onto the floor. Once in this manner he had escaped and been recovered in a thicket of bamboo down the block, his throat full of curses and wooden chips, his feathers befouled. Freedom had been a total drag . . . Agatha had to be put to bed.

After that, she pampered him all the more. His crackers were buttered with caviar. Jasmine laced the water he drank. His seeds were soaked in a vitamin brew sweetened lightly with lavender honey. His nuts must be macadamias, with toasted almonds once a week. His fruits were papaya and mango and a wild grape imported from Spain. Fresh leaves or grass must floor his cage . . .

Norma was back in the room again. "This is a child you're talking to, and this is the speech you give to friends. You never give them the money part. You imply it's all for love of your aunt."

"The money part is degrading," said George. "As for Rob . . . he often robs his piggy bank. That makes him a man of finance, I guess." So George gave him the money part: Before she died, their Aunt Agatha provided for her darling bird and to some degree for the kin she would leave. She willed him all her considerable wealth in the following outrageous way: He was to reside with each of her nephews or their heirs for a year at a time for as long as he lived. At the end of each year his host would be paid, presumably interest from the estate, the sum of twenty-five thousand dollars as reimbursement for Lochinvar's care. Provided, of course, that the bird was in excellent health at the time and that he had dwelt throughout the year in that part of the house where the family lived. The terms of the trust were precise as to that. He was, it was stated, a sociable bird, accustomed to human society, and must be embraced as a family member. The trustee, one Ellsworth Peckins, a banker friend and confidant—she had fed him supper each Sunday for years—she appointed to inspect the living arrangements for Lochinvar and determine his state at the end of the year before the check should be released. The bird must be fed his accustomed food and given to drink his accustomed brew. And if he should die, the entire estate, after a generous burial sum, would go to a home for aging birds. No more yearly windfalls that handily funded those camps for the children, those months at the shore, that easily become necessities. Brother Buddy had been out of work for a year and now, alas, was totally dependent on the bird.

Between the two, the aunt and her confederate Peckins, they had devised an ingenious system of checks and balances, with each brother kept up to the mark by the others, for as Lochinvar waxed all stood to gain, and as he waned all stood to lose. Even Peckins himself was factored in. His tidy payment for handling the trust lent ardor to all his inspection trips. Could a plan to ensure the comfort of a bird, his health and long life, be tighter than this?

When at length they complained to Peckins about the unreasonable nature of the trust, the coercion of it, the coarseness of it, he assured them firmly that it was he who had gently led her away from a plan to leave at her death the entire sum to a bird retreat called Lochinvar House in which Himself would reign supreme. But news of it hardly assuaged their wrath. "Why couldn't she just have left it to us?"

Peckins smiled. "And what would the robin do then, poor thing?"

George struck his pipe against his palm. "Your robin was raised in a brothel, I'd say. How did Aunt Agatha stand his filth?"

Peckins smiled again. "Well, happily she was hard of hearing."

"This bird would curdle the ears of the dead."

"I know, I know. But your aunt was truly an innocent. I don't think she understood at all . . . They weren't exactly birds of a feather." Peckins fancied himself a wit.

"He's so damn nouveau riche," said George.

At times the bird would whimper and wheedle, "Aggie . . . Aggie . . ." in a purling voice like a pigeon in heat.

"You suppose he's missing her?" Norma asked.

"Not him," said George. "He was after her money."

And so they all, three families of them, were stretched on the rack, their spirits torn between wishing him well and wishing him ill. All, that is, except Cuddles and Rob. For Cuddles totally wished him ill. And Robbie liked him more and more. He sympathized with his being caged. For Robbie was one to chafe at strictures: Don't do that and don't go there . . . Go to bed when we tell you to . . . He admired the way the bird got by with words Rob wasn't allowed to say. Whenever feathers fell out of the cage, as more and more they were doing now, Robbie shooed Cuddles and picked them up. He stored them all in a Band-Aid box and kept them safely under his bed. At night he would tickle his nose with them and dream that Lochinvar spoke to him, which he never had, not even once. If being little was all it was, why would he talk to Cuddles, then? The feathers were green and yellow and red. Some of them smelled of caviar and some of the jasmine in the drink and some had a lavender-honey scent. And because he snapped them up as they fell, no one noticed the bird had gone into a fearful molt and indeed was declining under their eyes.

They only observed that his humor was worse. "Drop yer pants!" he would squawk at guests. "Bloody hag!" the reprehensible bird would scream. At times he flew into a fearsome rage, banging his little golden swing, biting his bars, tossing with vengeance his carpet of leaves, littering the porch with crackers and nuts, yelling out in his throaty voice: "Slit yer gullet! Rip yer belly! Scuttle the ship!" His pirate blood welled up in him. Battle language tore his throat. What centuries were stored in him! Almost as fierce were his brothel days. When he was struck with a seizure of them, Robbie was sent to play in the yard. "Nasty old thing!" his mother would say. Robbie sat in the swing and swung and rehearsed the words in a singing voice.

So extreme were the moods of the bird, they began to suspect him of drifting into a manic-depression. A sane Lochinvar was trial enough, but an unhinged parrot was too damn much. They were coming a little unhinged themselves, what with the arrogance of his abuse. Once it was something to be ignored; now it eroded their self-esteem.

Of course, it is told, a parrot knows nothing of what he says. He only mimics the sounds he hears. But you couldn't sell that to Robbie's clan. There was too much pernicious malice in him. When the Reverend Mr. Evinrood called, he would ripple at him, "Feelin' horny today?" And then he would utter unspeakable things.

"Pray for us, Reverend," Rob's father would say.

"You bet," the reverend said, and heaved a sigh. "A creature of Satan indeed, I'd say."

They had been favored with Lochinvar and he with them three months and more. And that was about the time it took for them to observe the graying beak, a clouding of the baleful eye, a certain brooding ennui, and fear that their fortunes declined with him. Was it simply a dip in his fluctuant moods? Then Robbie showed them his store of feathers. Oh God! they said, and they called the vet, a heavyset man with hairy ears.

"How old would he be?" he inquired at once.

"We don't know," they whispered. "You tell *us.*"

He shook his head, peering into the cage, and poked Lochinvar with an incautious thumb, which the bird clipped. "Puke yer porridge!" Lochinvar screeched.

"Ow!" the vet said, and sucked his wound. "Prickly, ain't he? Looks old to me. Course, they don't have no rings you can count like a tree."

"What can you do for him?" they said.

"Well, birds ain't exac'ly in my line. I handle anything four legs. My best advice, you git 'im up to the school at Auburn. Them perfessors up there is up on birds. I handle anything four legs." And he bent to Cuddles, who dived under a chair. He straightened and sighed. "It could be just his time to go. It comes to ever'thang that breathes."

Norma shrieked. "George, you better call Buddy and Orin. He didn't look good to me when he came. I told you, didn't I tell you so?" She began to cry as her future grew bleak. Her membership in the country club . . . all the icing down the drain.

"I see you all mighty fond a this bird. I know you given him lotsa love. But ever'thang that breathes, you know . . ."

But George had closed the door on him.

Norma wept. "Did you hear what he said about lots of love. We never gave him a single drop. You suppose he missed Aunt Agatha's love and needed ours for the will to live?" Whereupon she advanced upon the cage and caressed it with a penitent hand. "Lochinvar," she said in a broken voice, "we may not have shown it, but down in our hearts . . ."

Lochinvar raised his head from his ruff and shook it a bit and dropped a feather. "We love you, Lochinvar," she said.

Robbie listened with widened eyes. He knew a lie when he heard a lie.

So did the bird. "Rustle yer bustle," he piped at her. When she didn't stir, "Move yer ass!" he shrieked with rage.

She drew back. She whispered, "He makes it really hard."

"Well, I like him," Robbie said. Everyone listened when Lochinvar spoke, and nobody listened when Robbie did. But Rob didn't care, if Lochinvar would just listen to him. I know he can see me, Robbie thought. Especially when I stand on a chair.

Norma and George went into a slightly hysterical huddle. They decided between them that Orin's and Buddy's respective wives would be too much, too bloody much. Sylvia would drink, and Rita, Buddy's wife, would weep. And both of them would pass the blame. They agreed to seek the wisdom of Peckins.

He came as soon as the bank had closed. He looked at the bird and shook his head. "I never saw him like this before. He looks as if . . ."

"As if . . . ?" they said.

"As if he might soon join Agatha."

They gnashed their teeth. "Then all of it goes to that home for unwed parrots?" said George.

Peckins simply inclined his head.

"Have we no legal recourse?" said George.

"The trust is tight as a drum," said Peckins, almost with triumph, it seemed to them, although he as well stood to lose by it.

Norma whispered, "We ought not to talk before him like this, as if the money was all it was . . . We love you, Lochinvar," she lied. "We're going to make you well again."

With Peckins's consent they rang up the university and made an appointment with Dr. Johns, professor of ornithology. Lochinvar roused when his cage was moved. He protested in the vilest terms, while Cuddles stalked him up to the very door of the car, his eyes like a serpent's, slits of green. "Go suck an egg!" the bird squalled at him. Peckins sat in the back with Rob, the cage between them on the floor. "I never had special rapport," said Peckins, "but I feel that Agatha would want me along.'' And Robbie whispered into the cage, ''I'm your friend . . . I'm your friend.''

Down a hall noisy with cries of birds, into a small antiseptic room, they carried gently his gilded cage and laid it on the concrete floor. Dr. Johns, who was old and frail, with a beaklike nose, donned a leather glove and poked at the bird with a trembling digit. The throat of Lochinvar swelled with a curse, but he did not snap at the glove or move.

The man of science inquired the age. They shook their heads. He nodded his. ''He appears to be very old,'' he said.

''So what is wrong with him?'' they wailed.

''Age,'' he said. ''It afflicts us all.'' He snuffled through his beak of a nose, the only sturdy portion of him. ''There's such a thing as parrot fever. Have you let him have intercourse with others?'' They stared at him. ''Other parrots.''

''We don't know other parrots,'' they sighed.

He pondered this. ''He appears to me to have reached his limit.''

''What can you do for him?'' they implored.

''I can put him out of his misery. If that's what you want. I assume you do.''

They shrank in horror. They stood in silence around the bird. Then Norma ventured: ''What about prayer?''

They stared at her in disbelief. She had been an attender, not a believer. She read her husband's mind at once. ''So what?'' she said. ''I've always believed in the power of prayer . . . Wonderful things get done with prayer.''

Peckins looked away. He had always put his trust in trusts, fiduciaries, that sort of thing.

''We do not pray,'' said the man of science.

Norma stood her ground. ''May we keep him here till we can get someone here who does? I mean . . . he can't stand another trip.''

''We close at five,'' the professor said. As he left the room, he tossed his gauntlet onto the table, by way of a challenge, it seemed to them.

"You got some plan?" said George to his wife.

She heard his sneer. They had pushed her small craft out to sea. "You got one yourself?" she snapped at him. "I'll be glad to hear."

What she grimly did was to find a phone and summon the Reverend Mr. Evinrood. The good man did not believe his ears. He had never prayed for a parrot before. He did not like this particular parrot, who he truly felt was beyond redemption. He could not pray with a whole heart. Besides, he thought, if it ever got out . . . "Our assistant pastor is terribly, terribly good with pets. He understands them better than I."

Mr. Phinny was with the teenage boys on the grounds of the church. More precisely, he was on the ground of the church. By nature of a delicate build, and now on the brink of passing its less than stalwart prime, he found himself unsuited to scrimmage. He was always getting himself banged up and mounting the pulpit with blackened eye. But in the division of holy labor it seemed that Evinrood sliced the pie. "A parrot!" he said. "You're kidding me."

"Go!" said his boss. "They have asked for you." He would ask the Lord to forgive the lie. "And don't change. There isn't time. They're attenders," he added. "Contributors." He was aware of the terms of the trust and looked for a sizable drop in the pledge. If prayer failed. He feared it would.

So it was that Mr. Phinny, clad in a sweatshirt and dirty shorts and sneakers with laces trailing him, reluctant, but glad to be free of scrimmage, arrived to pray for Lochinvar. Having recently answered their church's call, he did not recognize any of them. They seemed, however, to recognize him, though not to be overjoyed at the sight. The two men gravely shook his hand. The woman, he saw, had been shedding tears. She tried to enlist goodwill for the bird. "He knows more words than anybody I've ever known . . . He's probably several centuries old."

Phinny was awed. He walked to the cage and looked down at the bird. Lochinvar's head was hunkered down in his ever so slightly mildewed ruff. His wings encircled him like a shroud. The golden ring that had long encircled the emerald eye was all but gray. The eye was closed.

Mr. Peckins touched the reverend's arm and whispered to him in legal tones, "More is riding on this than perhaps you know."

Phinny wondered if it was a threat or a plea. He recalled with longing the game of scrimmage. He cleared his throat. "May we join hands? . . . Oh, you too," he said, noticing Rob, who was always the last to be noticed of course. But Rob didn't mind, if Lochinvar would just notice him.

They joined hands in a circle about the cage.

"What is his name?" Phinny gently inquired. "I'm sure the Lord has long known it of course."

"Lochinvar," Norma whispered to him.

All except Robbie closed their eyes. There was silence while Phinny primed his pump. At last he prayed: "Lord, we lift to you this day one of your creatures . . . one of your own, this Lochinvar. One who has long dwelt upon your earth." Again he was silent. "We ask you, Lord, we ask you now to restore to health . . . to perfect health . . . this fine, beloved family friend . . . Those who have served you and loved him long ask it now in Jesus' name."

Lochinvar slightly tilted his head till his pale beak rose from the mildewed ruff. His eye was shut. He squawked at Phinny, "Yer fulla crap!"

They dropped their hands and fell back. Phinny was utterly at a loss. He thought hard thoughts of Evinrood. Norma looked for the bird to fly to hell with Agatha's fortune under his wing.

But Robbie fell to his knees by the cage and stroked its bars. He said to the bird, "Fella, I'm your friend."

Lochinvar slowly opened his eye, first the cloud of white, then like the sea breaking through the mist, the old green fire. Just for a moment, then it was gone. In a chill falsetto he shrilled, "Drop dead!"

Lochinvar's words, the first the bird had favored him with, so filled the boy with excitement and awe, the rage of the scorned, a budding sense of outrageous fortune's arrows and slings, and joy at the chance to at last give vent to an indignation enjoyed by the rest, that he sprang to his feet and struck the cage.

"You crazy old bird, drop dead yourself!"

And the old bird did.

A Natural Resemblance

LINDA BARRETT OSBORNE

My grandmother Anna always said that the ideal woman could cook lasagne for twenty-five and still hold down a full-time job. She said it frequently to build my character the year we became housemates in her slim brownstone on Manhattan's Upper West Side.

Angelina, my father's mother, lived there too. Friends since childhood, my grandmothers joined forces in widowhood, sharing the cooking and cleaning, At seventy-four, Anna ran her own dress shop, and Angelina, a year younger, sold jewelry and cosmetics at a Woolworth's where you could still buy goldfish and parakeets and eat grilled cheese and bacon, lettuce, and tomato sandwiches at the L-shaped counter at the back.

I had just graduated from Princeton and was looking for an apartment, although my parents couldn't believe I didn't want to live in my old room on Long Island. "For years we kept it nice," my mother accused her unrepentant prodigal daughter. "You belong with us. And anyway, you don't have enough money for a decent place of your own."

But I longed to be in New York, so I spent three weeks walking through every tiny, dark place that grew there: mushroom caves with closets pretending to be bedrooms; two-dimensional kitchens that were really half a wall. Paint peeled in long strips like potato skins, and hallways smelled of cat, olive oil, and worse. One apartment had a mural of a mermaid amidst conch shells and nets. ''Art,'' said the landlady placidly. ''Of course, you pay more for that.''

Exhausted, I stopped by Anna and Angelina's for tea. I had always loved their block, the way it grew immediately quieter when we turned off Broadway, the elegant line of narrow houses with their bay windows to catch the light. My grandmothers' house had leaves and scrollwork carved into stone and a finely cut cornice. Inside, the staircases and moldings were oak and the plaster swirled with vines and flowers. Each room had a fireplace and built-in bookshelves, and the bedrooms all had dressing rooms with hand-painted porcelain sinks and marble counters. Anna had inherited the house from her Uncle Guido, who made his fortune as a butcher and wanted a house full of marble to remind him of Italy.

''You wouldn't believe the prices of the rooms I've seen today,'' I said to them, sitting at the kitchen table, tracing the swirly patterns on the Formica I had traced as a child. ''And there's nothing like this place. I love this house.''

''Good,'' said Anna, cutting a giant wedge of cheesecake. ''You should live here with us.''

''You're kidding,'' I said, knocking tea onto the table.

''It's a good idea, baby,'' said Angelina. ''You could have the whole top floor. Your own bedroom. It's pretty up there. Lots of sun.''

''Thanks, but I want my own place. My own place,'' I said again, loudly. ''No, thanks,'' I gestured to Anna, ''I don't want any more to eat.''

''Would we bother you?'' Anna handed me the cheesecake. ''You'd be on the top floor. We never go up there anymore. At our age, it's hard to climb the stairs.''

At their age they were both working, agile as lizards, the envy of every senior citizen in New York. Anna had even attacked a mugger three years before, belting him from behind with a shopping bag full of Italian pastry. He'd fled, and the astonished victim, an English professor at Columbia, could only light his pipe and murmur over and over, ''Well done!''

''If you lived with us, you could save money,'' Anna purred. ''You could have your own nice apartment in a year.''

''A year. My God.'' I tried to imagine it. TV every evening, the latest cure for cancer to talk about. They would make me eat seven hundred pieces of cheesecake and I'd gain three hundred pounds.

''It's out of the question,'' I said. ''Thanks anyway.''

I moved in the following week.

''You're going to live with them?'' my mother screamed, as if I'd thrown in my lot with drug dealers.

''It's your mother. I thought you'd be pleased.''

''The food isn't good enough here? We don't leave you alone?''

''I told you, I just want to be in the city.''

''The city! I don't understand any of you. Here it's quiet and safe. We worked so hard to get out of the city.''

They had. It was a ballad of my childhood, how my father, an engineer, saved a little money, bought property just after the war, and managed to erect a house on it within eight years. He took well to suburban living, puttering in the garden, seeding and weeding his infant lawn, setting out his hammock to watch the first stars appear at night.

My mother too thrived in her paradise of burgeoning shopping centers and subdivisions. She bought white wrought-iron lawn furniture topped by a giant, flowered umbrella, where she could linger over coffee on summer mornings with her friends. When she went back to work as a secretary, it delighted her to drive to the office in her own car and never have to take a dirty bus or subway again.

''You could commute,'' my mother tried one more time. ''You could look for a job on Long Island.''

''I don't want to waste two hours a day packed like a sardine, and I'd rather work in New York. Besides, I'm too old to live with my parents.''

''So you're going to live with your grandparents,'' she said, and then: ''Why should I be surprised? You're just like them. You know everything, and you're stubborn.''

I took over the top floor of the brownstone, breaking my

mother's heart. I hung my jeans in the walk-in closet, my Matisse prints above the fireplace. I filled the cases with my books.

Angelina had been right, my room was saturated with light. What she didn't tell me was that it only came in the morning, when the sun would insist its way in, spilling over the bed like melted butter. It hit the pillow first, moving toward the foot like a curious, desultory lover. There was no sleeping late in that room. Shades didn't help. The rays seemed to bend around their edges, setting the walls and floor on fire.

I wondered how long Anna had planned to get me into that room. Anna, the early riser, up before 6 A.M., running enough water to quench Mount Vesuvius into her bath. Anna, who never took showers, because nothing is healthy if you stand up to do it. That's a scientific fact, she said. There was Anna, secretly hoping to get me into that prism of a room. "She sleeps too late," she would tell Angelina. "It's not good for her health." And Angelina would nod in agreement, knowing that Anna was right, because in this world, God knows, *nothing is good for your health.*

So I would wake up with the sun, letting my bare feet hit the warmed floorboards. For a while I planned to read through those extra minutes, moving peacefully into the day. But Anna, who had miraculously learned to climb the stairs, could hear my shallow breathing behind the door, sniffed out the turning pages. She would knock on some pretext: "Your pantyhose, Laura, there's still time to rinse them out if you hang them by the radiator." I'd close my book and pad out to the bathroom, pushing my way through jungle vines of underwear.

I had never seen underwear so spacious as Anna and Angelina's. The word "panty" was too small to contain those billowing, silky shorts. Next to them, my bikinis looked like doll clothes.

There were always notes in the bathroom too, fastened to the light switch with Scotch tape: "Towels in hamper," or "Bring Kay $10," or my favorite, "Angelina, DON'T FORGET LUNCH!" The frayed edges of old tapes were everywhere, and I would stand there in a morning reverie, scraping them off with my nails.

Anna taped notes downstairs too, over doorknobs, on lampshades, scrawled in her turn-of-the-century script. "Buy margarine," a scrap in the living room might read; "Do laundry" on the back door. I could never figure out how the notes got where they did. It was as if Anna's brain couldn't rest until she'd got her thoughts on paper, and after that it didn't matter where they lay. Old notes stayed up, sometimes two or three months, fossils to chart the history of our daily survival. Angelina sometimes did it too. The kitchen was a symphony of themes and responses on torn napkins.

"Cook dinner," I found myself writing three weeks after I'd moved in. I taped it to a burner, and Anna said, "What's this, baby?" as she put water on for coffee.

"I want to make something special for you tonight to celebrate my arrival."

"Should I pick up some fresh pasta from Fontana's?"

"I'm planning this myself," I said. "Just be at the dining-room table at six-thirty. You don't need to do a thing."

"The dining room?" said Angelina. "But you have to carry everything up from the kitchen. We always eat down here."

"The dining room," I said again. "Six-thirty. Trust me on this."

When I carried up the meal on a huge chrome tray they were both sitting, apparently obedient, at the table. "Cloth napkins!" Anna said to Angelina, fingering the linen. "It's extra to wash and you have to iron them."

"I'll wash them. I'll iron them," I said, setting down a platter and a basket of eight-grain bread. I poured white wine into glasses and sat at my place.

"There," I said. "Salmon salad."

They both looked at me.

"Do you want me to serve?" When no one answered, I began putting a portion on each plate.

Anna rummaged around with her fork. "We're having lettuce for supper?"

"This must be the antipasto," Angelina said suddenly.

"No, it's the whole meal. You each get a hard-boiled egg. And all that salmon. Go ahead, take some bread."

They each took a piece. "We usually eat . . . ," Anna started.

I held up a hand. "I know you buy rye sometimes."

"Without the seeds," said Angelina.

"This has rye flour in it, and lots of other things. Just try it."

Angelina took a bite. "It's hard to chew."

"It has texture." I started to rise. "If you want, I'll go down and get your bread."

"Sit," Anna said. "This is your special meal for us. We'll eat it." She picked at the greens on her plate, knocking over a chunk of salmon. She held up a dark leaf on the edge of her fork. "What's this?"

"It's spinach."

"You didn't cook it?"

"It's healthy that way," I said, reaching for my glass of wine. "It keeps all the vitamins when you eat it raw."

Angelina focused on her plate, carefully cutting a tomato wedge. Anna gulped her wine and poured more from the bottle. We ate in surprising silence. I could hear Angelina chewing patiently on the lettuce and the bread. I was the only one to take seconds.

"I'll get dessert," I said, "and start the coffee." I stacked the dishes onto the tray.

"We'll do that, baby," said Anna.

"Whoever doesn't cook does the dishes," Angelina said.

"That's okay. Tonight I'll do everything." I started toward the stairs.

"You can't carry that by yourself. It's too heavy." Anna rose.

"No, it's not," I said, knocking into the stairwell. I puffed downstairs and dropped the tray with a thud onto the counter. While I waited for the coffee I drank another glass of wine. Then I shoved everything on the tray again and clumped back upstairs.

They stopped talking when I entered, smiling as if I'd come onstage at a dancing-school recital. "It's strawberry shortcake," I said.

"Beautiful, baby," Anna said.

"What bakery did you get it from?" asked Angelina.

"I made it myself."

"Of course she did, Angelina," said Anna. "Does that look like cake from a bakery?"

"It looks that good at Romano's."

"Romano's, sure, but that's in Brooklyn. Would she go to Brooklyn for a cake?"

"If they make the best cakes."

"Would anybody like some?" I said, serving.

"Delicious," said Anna.

"As good as Romano's," said Angelina.

"Better." Anna lopped off a large piece with her fork. "Just think, Angelina, our granddaughter can make a cake like this."

I smiled, grown-up Laura, who could cut her own meat now and didn't need to sit on two telephone books to reach the table. "It's only fruit and cream," I said.

"But the cake part is so light. Not everybody can cook so good these days, baby. It will help you find a husband."

"That's ridiculous," I said.

"It's true."

"I don't mean . . . First of all, why would I go out and look for a husband, and second of all, why should the fact that I cook matter?"

"Should he pick you because you can't cook?" Angelina sounded surprised.

"He shouldn't pick me at all. That's not how it works."

They looked at each other. "Tell us," said Anna, "how does it work?"

"You fall in love, you . . . well, anyway, you have things in common, you get along well. It doesn't matter who cooks and cleans. You both should. If a man likes to cook . . ."

"They always leave a mess in the kitchen," said Angelina.

"Your grandfather cooked," said Anna, "until Angelina told him to stop. He wanted to make soufflés. Six pans with egg stuck on them. He wanted to put thyme in the spaghetti sauce. Who wanted to eat it?''

''I think that's great.''

''You didn't have to clean up after him,'' said Angelina.

''Whoever doesn't cook does the dishes,'' I said.

Angelina started to rise.

''No, sit, I'll do them,'' I said. The telephone rang. I ran to answer.

''You didn't call,'' said my mother.

''But I just talked to you last week,'' I said, beginning to feel weary.

''It must take up a lot of time, waiting for a crowded subway, shopping in those tiny grocery stores. Your father and I drove to the beach today. We were there in fifteen minutes.''

''Great,'' I said. ''I cooked dinner for us tonight.''

''They let you?''

When I was growing up, Anna would cook for my mother. She would arrive on Sundays with half the meal packed into shopping bags, kicking at the door with her foot to announce she was there. She dusted too, and even did the laundry. ''Ma, it's my home,'' my mother would sigh, but Anna would say, ''Let me. You work. You need help,'' forgetting that she worked too and didn't.

It made my mother anxious. She and my father had been waiting years to take over. They wanted to be the family adults, the wise ones, but as long as my grandmothers remained healthy and strong and independent, they were still, somehow, children. All their lives, they'd been told what to do, without anyone to tell. They wanted to show that faint condescension of the middle-aged toward the elderly; instead, every solicitation was met by argument and, worse, action which ignored them. ''I know best,'' said Anna. ''I'm your mother.'' What could my mother do?

''So what's it like living there?'' asked my mother, curiosity and anxiety fighting in her voice.

''Great. We watched a special on 'Cancer: The Champion Killer' last night.''

''We saw that too. Who would have thought that sun is bad for you? But what's it like?'' she pressed. ''Who does the housework?''

''We share,'' I said. ''Look, Mom, I'm a big girl now. I'm independent too. *They* know I can take care of myself.'' For a minute I almost believed it.

''Sure,'' said my mother. ''You wait . . .''

''Mom!''

''Let me talk to your grandmothers.''

''Hold on, I'll get them,'' I said, but when I looked in the dining room, nobody was sitting there.

I found them in the kitchen, doing the dishes.

Two Girls

JAYNE ANNE PHILLIPS

No one but her mother called her Catharine. Like Catharine Winthrop of Connecticut, Catharine Briarley was destined to attend a good Eastern boarding school and then go on to Barnard, but Catharine Briarley existed nowhere on earth. If she did exist, she would be dangerous and vengeful, a desperado implemented to avenge Catharine Winthrop, who likewise did not exist in Gaither, West Virginia. Cap wanted to be stalwart. She wanted to learn to curse as her father cursed, voice held in check, the flat, buttery Georgia inflection and the words burned in, branded on the flesh of their intended. *You want I should send her off to some horse-infested snoot school, pay to get her bedded bucked and fucked by some married faculty shit who digs for urns in Turkey and runs home to give schoolgirls the clap?* Then her mother's voice, her funny, broken tone, defeated, choked with rage: *You ignorant jube. You like it that she spends her time with kids whose fathers crawl around in that mine of yours. One of these days she'll marry some grease monkey from the Texaco and then you'll be satisfied, write her a big check when she hasn't got a dime and be the hero.* Her father's lilt of laughter. *Big check? Why she won't need any big check. She'll have that famous trust fund your daddy will invent any day, she can write me a check, she can marry the fucking janitor out at Consol Coal and fly him to some ritz penthouse. Let her do anything but don't let her be you because you are done for, you have been done.* His disappointed, self-mocking chuckle. *Many times, many many times. And remember, should you conde-*

scend to play golf in Gaither, you'd better be playing with somebody's wife. This is not Westchester or New Haven, your checkered career is over.

Their fights taught Cap the only version she knew of her mother's history. Here Catharine had no friends who picked her up in sports cars; she had only Juanita. Juanita was the maid who wore no uniform because there were no maid's uniforms in Gaither, whose husband dropped her off in the pickup every morning and came back for her at night, who sat peeling potatoes while Cap did her homework at the same kitchen table. Juanita tightened her lips while words floated down from the ceiling, she clicked her tongue and watched the kitchen clock. She crossed herself. Cap's mother said Juanita was a gypsy from over around Dago Hill and she was the only one who'd answered the ad, but she was punctual and she didn't steal. *What the hell would she want that you've got,* Henry laughed. If they broke a glass quarreling while they drank cocktails, Juanita cleaned it up before she left. At night, when Henry went to Catharine's room, Juanita wasn't there and didn't hear them. Cap, alone in the dark, heard muffled sounds she thought were more fighting until she was old enough to discern the difference.

They'd lived in Gaither five years. That first summer, Catharine stayed in Connecticut. Henry and Cap lived out of suitcases, their clothes laundered but never ironed, the big rooms of the Victorian house emptying off each other like a series of deserted squares. Cap lay on the cool wooden floor of her room after Henry went to the mine office, knowing all she had to do that day was wash the sticky plates from their morning flapjacks. Cicadas were starting in the summer trees and they lulled her back to sleep with their warbled buzzing; when she woke the light had changed and heightened. She ran from room to room, drawing the blinds and shutting windows to keep the house cool; she ran the narrow back stairs, up and down from attic to basement, whooping. At noon she made sandwiches for herself and the stray cats that lived in the ruined garden of the house; she tied yarn around their necks and called them by the colors: Red, Black, Blue. Hopscotch, solitaire, and card houses, stacks of books she unpacked into an upstairs room and read by turning to a page in the middle. Her mother's old school anthologies she defaced, ripping out paragraphs and crumbling the paper into balls she threw in the empty fireplace; she thought Catharine wasn't coming back.

Finally, she investigated the neighborhood, which seemed as empty as the house. For a couple of blocks on either side, the expansive Queen Annes with walled yards continued. No kids, older doctors and dentists, aged professors from the local college, their aged wives, who stayed indoors out of the heat. Just before Main Street and a downtown of hardware stores, banks, gas stations, ladies' shops, the three restaurants she and her father patronized for supper, was the Baptist church, a yellow-brick edifice with vast windows leaded in fantastic shapes. Here Cap first saw Lenore, sitting on the steps of the church while her mother signed her up for girls' confirmation classes. Lenore lay across the steps as though the steps were not stones, her pale hair in braids, her face so still Cap thought she was asleep and bent over her, looking. When Lenny opened her eyes and stared, her gaze was empty and calm. She was the opposite of Catharine Briarley and belonged where she was, like rain on a window.

In the next few weeks Cap and Lenny sat together in the sanctuary while the minister lectured them about joining God's flock. A stained glass *Jesus and the Children* towered over them, Jesus' robe scarlet against the blue sky of that other world. Cap believed Lenny to be an incarnation of the girl in the massive image, the child whose hand rested on a lamb, whose expectant, forgiven gaze was the essence of glass. Together they were confirmed. Henry, amused, watched from the congregation. Their baptism took place the next morning, privately, in the strange cement pool behind the altar. The pool was an empty rectangular hole perhaps four feet deep, hidden behind a heavy velvet curtain. The girls wore white cotton gowns and were barefoot; the pool was filled with water made aquamarine by chlorine drops. Potted lilies lined the border of the cement. The snowy, waxen flowers seemed drowsy. Cap, sputtering from her own immersion, saw Lenny submerged in the minister's black-robed arms, her hair suddenly swirling in an underwater cloud, her face expressionless. She was the only one who had believed she would float in the act of coming to God, her arms straight in her belled sleeves. When the minister let go and raised his hands to say the words, Lenny, underwater, opened her eyes, gazing upward as though the roof had lifted from the building. Sinking, she looked like a drowned angel. She exhaled a Milky Way of tiny bubbles and Cap found herself suddenly within that liquid crescent—she never remembered deciding to jump in. The water was big, filling her up when she tried to talk. She grabbed the folds of Lenny's gown and dragged her to the surface within it. They stood gasping and Cap was doubly confirmed: it was the first time she had tried to save anything but herself.

Audrey

DAVID SHIELDS

Audrey Baranishyn lived alone in the Haight at a time—1969—when it was still very stylish for eighth-graders to be living alone in the Haight. She was thirteen, a waif, immensely sophisticated, beautiful beyond belief, had tortured ballet toes, Russian ancestors, and a leather purse, but the telling detail about her was that she liked nothing better than blowing Double Bubble at the same time she was inhaling Tareyton 100's. She was an amazing mixture of pink innocence and smoky extinction: one day, she was all light and dance and Communist bloc folklore; the next, she was all gloom and doom and standing with me on the Golden Gate Bridge, looking down.

It was she, of course, who made the first overture. I've never had the courage to want the world. I've always let it come to me, which is a rather negative approach to existence, but the funny thing is: inevitably, it comes. Sooner or later, whether you want it or not, the world comes to you, it comes at you, and in this case it came in the form of someone with a taste for the simultaneity of Tareytons and Double Bubble. She was head cheerleader of the Bayshore Bobbettes and, though she didn't know a jump shot from a running pick, she accepted the post—she told me later—not for the enormous prestige it heaped upon her person but because she was obsessed with the color and shape of my legs in the artificial light of the gymnasium in the afternoon.

All during basketball season, she'd cheer loudly when my name was announced, bring me sticks of grape licorice at halftime, and jump up and down whenever I was shooting a free throw, which caused my free throw percentage to drop a few points, but I didn't care: she looked so happy, jumping up and down and screaming like that. Week after week of buying gum and cigarettes for her at the Safeway, walking her to the bus station, talking on the telephone until midnight, but nothing was ever said, nothing was ever done. Then, two weeks after the eighth-grade basketball season was over, in the extraordinary manner in which junior high school romance is carried out, I was handed a letter by Elaine, the assistant head cheerleader of the Bayshore Bobbettes and Audrey's nearest and dearest friend, which said:

> *Sweet Jeremy: March 27th (Tomorrow!) as I hope u already know is my birthday! I'm gunna be 14! You (of course!) are cordally invited. Pleez! Pleez! don't bring any presents. All I want u to bring is your ID (that's identificashun, dummy!) bracelet and if u don't have one you're rich enough to go get a nice new one! I hope u don't have to ask what the ID bracelet is for, but if u do you'll just have to wait until the party to find out! (Surly u can guess, you're so smart!) Also: I got a big! big! check from welfare tuesday, so I'm renting a motel room in the mountains of Marin that I heard about (special heart-shaped swimming pool) where we're all gunna swim and smoke and drink and lie out in the sun celibrating my 14th! Oh, also: Elaine's brother volluntiered to drive us all out there (he gets a free dip in the pool as pay-mint) so meet tomorrow at Elaine's house (u know where it is, doncha?) at 10 am, sharp. All u gotta bring is your ID bracelet, a beach towl, and some snazzy swim trunks!*
>
> *XXXXX OOOOO*
> *XXXXX OOOOO*
> *Audrey*

March 27 wasn't her fourteenth birthday, and she probably hadn't received a big! big! check from welfare so much as gotten hold of some very high-grade acid and sold it at triple profit. I honestly didn't know why she wanted me to bring an identification bracelet to the party but I purchased a silver chain bracelet with my initials etched on the underside, a couple cartons of cigarettes, an entire bag of chewing gum, and a pair of red swimming trunks with a blue anchor at the crotch. I arrived bright and early the next morning at Elaine's house.

Other than Charles, whom I hadn't seen for a while, I didn't really have any friends, so I couldn't say Audrey ran with a different crowd than I did. They were certainly a switch, though, from the kind of people who showed up at Mother's coffee klatches. Audrey's friends all seemed to have parents who were dead, diseased, or sadistic. They all seemed to have spent a night in jail or a month with Synanon. They all loved, absolutely loved, the Dead. There was a story called "The Dead" which at the time was completely incomprehensible to me. Audrey's friends weren't referring to *Dubliners*. I thought the Dead were maybe an occult group that scavenged shallow graves, looking for immortality. They—Audrey's friends—liked to say that, at thirteen, they had lived and loved and now were ready to die. They'd gone out in the world and found it a waste, whereas I was still trying to build up enough bravery to walk alone through North Beach.

This discrepancy between my innocence and their decadence made me a little uneasy, but they'd say, "That's what Audrey digs about you, man. You're one of the few uncorrupted cats left." I disliked being called a cat—I saw myself, instead, as an infinitely poignant cocker spaniel—and thought Audrey had selected me because she was obsessed with the color of my legs in the artificial light of the gymnasium in the afternoon. I've always prided myself on projecting an image of brooding, masculine depravity, but women always end up saying, "Who are you trying to kid? You're so innocent. You're such a baby." I suppose Audrey was unusual only in being the first to perceive this fact.

None of these hesitations seemed to matter anymore when I was sitting with twelve other people in the back of Elaine's brother's red pickup truck, smelling spilled beer, feeling Audrey's fingers crawl across the floor toward mine.

"I hope you brought the bracelet," Audrey said, rubbing her wrist.

I patted my shirt pocket and nodded.

The motel was something of a disappointment. It wasn't on the edge of a cliff overlooking the bay, as its brochure said it was, but on a dirt road with an unobstructed view of an abandoned filling station. The swimming pool was indeed heart-shaped, but was enclosed by a barbed-wire fence—no obscurity to this motel's symbolism—the gate to which had to be opened for you. The room Audrey had rented was a dusty, dark affair, with gold bedspreads, sliding doors that wouldn't slide, and Venetian blinds that blinded. A color TV hung from the ceiling like a dead turtle. Quite a few of Audrey's pals wanted to watch late-morning cartoons as desperately as my Mission District playmates had, but, as the station announcer insisted on informing us every thirty seconds, we were experiencing difficulty with the audio portion of our program. "Cartoons without sound ain't shit," one of the partygoers observed and everyone agreed, so the television set was turned off.

Apparently, Audrey had told everyone not to bring presents but if they really wanted to bring something, a carton of Tareytons and a six-pack of Double Bubble would be great!, because everyone handed her exactly the same thing. Some people had brought bottles of liquor or water pipes for themselves. While they drank and sucked, Audrey blew smoke rings and popped gum bubbles. I sat at her side on the gold bedspread, reading Double Bubble comics. Someone asked the manager of the motel to unlock the gate to the heart-shaped pool. None of them wanted to swim. They just sat along the edge and watched me tread water. They were extremely impressed with how long I could keep bobbing up and down, but it's nothing, really. I've always been able to stay barely afloat forever. After a while, Audrey grew bored sitting in the sun and watching me swim. It was her party, so when she asked me to bring her the bracelet I jumped out of the pool and ran across the rocky parking lot to the room. When I returned, Audrey was leaning back in the lounge chair, and they were all gathered festively around her.

"Here it is," I said, handing it to her.

"Well?" she said.

" 'Well?' " I said.

"Well?" she said.

"Well, here," I said, taking the bracelet out of her hands and giving it to her again. "Happy Birthday."

"Won't you be so kind as to wrap it around my wrist, sweet Jeremy? For as of this moment you and me are goin' steady."

Most laughed. I thought maybe I'd been brought here as a comic example of pubescent sincerity or that Audrey was sexually slumming—going through initiation rites she'd outgrown when she was nine. But she, if not the rest of them, also seemed deadly serious. Her perfect blue eyes were aching with emotion, with a thirteen-year-old's thirst for romance. Maybe her mock-epic tone was for the amusement of her friends. I knelt down and clasped the chain around her wrist. I didn't know what it meant to be going steady, but I supposed it meant I couldn't see other girls, and I wasn't, so going steady seemed fine.

"It's beautiful. It's so silvery. I've never owned silver before. Never owned JJZ before either," Audrey said, digging her fingers into the carved initials, tugging on my trunks. "To celebrate, I'm gonna go slippin' down the slide, but I don't know how to swim real well, so you catch me when I hit water, okay, sweet Jeremy?"

Everyone else stood off at a distance. I dove in, Audrey climbed the ladder. At the top, she stopped and spat the chewing gum out of her mouth, as if she were doing away with whatever was silly juvenilia. Her legs were spread, her arms were flapping, the straps to her suit were slipping off. She was lying when she said she couldn't swim. She could swim as well as or better than I could. She grabbed my hair, wrapped her legs around me, and pulled me under. The deep end was only six feet, so we went all the way to the bottom. Through air bubbles and chlorinated water, she kissed me. One always wonders what the first kiss will be like; suddenly one is in the midst of it and it doesn't seem to matter anymore what it should or would or might be like. It is. What it is is something entirely different from familial good-night and good-morning kisses. It's a different thing altogether. The shaking of heads, the rubbing of bodies, the touching of tongues—all this seemed excellent enough. But what I really thought was too wonderful for words was that someone finally liked my mouth, someone finally liked me and was concentrating all her admiration on my mouth: on my trepidant lips. I came up for air first. Then, a second later, Audrey rose, looking for all the world like a mermaid in love.

In the way that all people in any deep passion attempt to separate themselves from their society, Audrey said goodbye to her group and, while I didn't bid farewell to my family, I temporarily stopped seeing them as the center of my universe. Audrey sent me ungrammatical love letters in geography class. I wrote poems (very free verse) to her during math. It was eighth-grade romance, spring passion, a flush feeling in the face.

Although Audrey was still smoking too much to be in very good athletic shape, she joined the girls' track team, principally, I think, to look at the color of my legs in the natural light of the playground in the afternoon. Soon enough she'd turned herself into an excellent little sprinter and was running anchor leg for the girls' quarter-mile-relay team. I ran the last hundred and ten yards for the boys' team. Sometimes the boys would race against the girls. I'd receive the baton a second or two before Audrey did, wait for her, run shoulder to shoulder for ninety yards, then let out a little kick at the end. It's always seemed to me that, if you're really fast and know in your own mind how fast you are, from time to time you'll let the other person win. I've never been that fast in anything. I've always had to prove how superior I was. Audrey didn't care, though. She had weirdly low self-esteem and wouldn't have wanted to win.

Besides, once track practice was over, we'd run together around the playground until the last school bus came to take her home. The Bayshore track consisted of nothing more than a painted white circle describing the width of the asphalt field. We'd run round and round the circle, holding hands, me in baggy gray sweats and de rigueur Adidas, and Audrey in absurdly brief briefs, white tennis shoes with pink laces, a San Francisco Giants baseball cap, and sunglasses (''shades, man, to obstruct reality''). There is a particular feeling, when you are young and sweaty and exhausted, that gathers around dusk and macadam and has much to do with a delusion of immortality—with the pervasive sense that the world is dying but you are indestructible. There's no feeling the physical world produces which is quite so fine, but you're only supposed to get it when you're alone and, even then, only once or twice a year. I was getting the feeling every day: every afternoon, at dusk, on the paved track with Audrey.

She didn't say anything about cement or everlasting life, and at the time I wasn't one to ruin paradise by conversing about it. ''Running like this, with you, sweet Jeremy, it almost makes me want to quit smoking,'' Audrey said. The pavement was starting to give her shin splints, though. One Saturday morning she called and said we were going running in Muir Woods. Muir Woods was like the High Sierras in that just its name sent shivers down my spine: it was a formal artifact independent from assault. We took a bus across the bay, then hitchhiked through the mountains to the forest. While other people were taking guided tours of the trees, looking at labels in Latin, feeding chocolate bars to chipmunks, counting year rings and exclaiming, Audrey and I ran deeper and deeper, higher and higher into the woods, back where the trail narrowed, vegetation rioted, and big trees were kings.

Audrey had brought a backpack full of snacks. When we'd run far enough that we could no longer hear the troops below, we stopped and she spread a tablecloth across a patch of pebbles and crabgrass, offering apples, processed cheese, Ritz crackers, and a bottle of Ripple. The entire gesture—the white tablecloth, the prepared lunch, the Saturday-morning excursion to a local landmark—was so uncharacteristically and hopefully domestic of her that I passed into a state of such profound happiness nothing could perturb me. I lay back, looking at timber, tiny bugs, and bluebirds, with cheese and crackers in my mouth and Audrey's head in my lap.

That head, into which so few thoughts entered, was, in such an idyllic setting, receiving more data than it knew what to do with, and Audrey finally blurted out: ''Damn! Sometimes, you know, I wish I had parents. Some people seem like they have parents. Other people seem like they don't. You do."

"Do what?" I said. I was studying a tree twig and didn't want to talk.

"You heard me. Have parents. You seem like you have parents."

"Yes," I said, "I have parents."

"Don't play dumb, Jeremy. I'm talking seriously for once. Sometimes I wish I hadn't grown up—if that's what you want to call it!—in an orphanage. Sometimes I get tired of filling out forms and telling people I live with my aunt. Sometimes I wish I had a home to, you know, go home to."

I couldn't believe anyone was so innocent she actually believed that houses were great hearths of banked fires, that families were healthy groups offering comfort and reassurance. I pulled her hair back, kissed her somewhat awkwardly on the nape of the neck, and said, "You can always come home to me."

It was a sentimental thing to say. It was meant as nothing more than metaphorical consolation. But maybe she never had anyone tell her that before. Tears came to her eyes and she fairly attacked me with kisses. She kept saying she loved me and banging my head against the ground. I couldn't tell whether she was hysterical or just very happy. I thought it best, in either case, to let her do what she wanted to do and not interfere. She seemed to have been through all the motions before, while I had no idea exactly what my responsibilities were. She licked my ears, unbuttoned my shirt, tugged at my trousers, and I just lay there. I wasn't only afraid of serious arousal. I was incapable of it. I don't know about other boys at twelve and a half, but I was still prepubescent. I was perfectly content to run and clasp hands and kiss on the lips.

Audrey, bored, rolled off me, took solace in a Ritz cracker, and said, "What's the problem?"

"Nothing."

"Then why did you stop?"

"Stop?"

"Don't you want to go all the way, man?"

"No," I said, "no, Audrey, not here, not yet. Maybe soon. Indoors, somewhere, at night, in a week or two. Do you mind?"

She waited three long weeks for me to grow up, during which time I consulted numerous anatomy texts and even visited an East Bay medicine man who, in a *Berkeley Barb* classified advertisement, promised Organ Increase. At the end of three weeks was the eighth-grade graduation dance. It was tradition for couples who had yet to sacramentalize their unity to do so on mattresses along the side of a hill that overlooked the gymnasium. Audrey wasn't waiting any longer.

She came dressed in a black evening gown she'd borrowed from Elaine; stockings, which I'd never seen her wear before; and high heels, in which she was slightly taller than I was. With my hair combed across my forehead and my shirttail flapping, I must have looked like her younger brother or eldest son. Everyone, absolutely everyone, including my basketball coach, invited Audrey to dance, but that night she had eyes only for me and said no to every last one of them. We danced every dance—the fast ones, at which she said I looked like a skittering jackrabbit, as well as the slow ones, during which I smelled the miscegenation of the sweat on her back with the perfume behind her ears. Whenever the jukebox broke down, I'd buy plastic cups of orangeade and we'd go kiss in dark corners.

As the dance progressed, there were fewer and fewer people in the gym and almost no couples. Audrey's hints that we ought to take a walk in the dark or get a breath of fresh air became increasingly persistent and obvious. I finally agreed to leave. Walking along the base of that hill was like coming into a war zone: hearing bodies collide, great screams of pain and expectation. It terrified me. When Audrey took my hand and suggested we—as it was called—climb the mountain, I panicked and ran. At night it always seems like you're running faster than you ever have in the daytime, and I felt like I was flying. I ran all the way home. I didn't look back once.

I dreamt about international hand-to-hand combat and the next morning got what was coming to me—a letter from Audrey, delivered by Elaine with knowing condescension.

Jeremy: I am writing this lettter at three oc'lock in the morning in my dingey little apartmint the lectricity the gas the heat none of them paid for and none of them probably ever will. Goddam you, anyways! I have given you 4 hole months of my life, and what do I get out of it, a lousy crushed Dixie cup of orangeaid! Why did you run away from the hill like a scittering jackrabbit? Scared, huh? Afraid? Mama told you not to? Well, I've had enough of Little Boy Blue and his goody-goodiness all the time. I just can't take it any more. Inclose pleez find your ID bracelet (slitely scrached a bit on the back—sorry!—twenny minutes ago got mad and took my penknife to it!) Maybe we can still be friends kinda like Elaine and Michael, and I know I'll always value your advice on things, and your buying me all that gum and cigarettes (musta cost you a fortune!) and the nice way you talk and all the running we did together waiting for my bus to come and my birthday party at the motel (First kiss is always best!) and, most especilly, sweet Jeremy, your legs in the gym's flooresent lights right around quarter a four in the afternoon. But I'm sorry! All the lovey-dovey handholding and kissing is fine for awhile, but finilly I want someone who's willing to climb the mountain with me at least once in awhile, doncha know? I'm sorry, Jeremy, you just aren't giving me enough action. I need someone a little older or at least a little more experienced. It was just too embearassing to be alone at midnight at the bottom of the hill at the graduation dance. Maybe like I say we can still be friends, and I do still love you but only like friends.

Luv:

Audrey

P.S. Maybe we can do some running together this summer!

Yes, maybe we could still be friends. Maybe we could do some running together this summer. Maybe the Golden Gate Bridge could collapse. It was eleven o'clock (''oc'lock'': I loved that) on a Saturday morning in May. I sat in a chair in the living room and read the letter six or seven more times, to savor all the misspellings but also to make sure I hadn't misinterpreted its overall message, then staggered down the stairs to my bedroom, where I drew the curtains, killed the lights, took out a black-and-white photograph of Audrey, crawled under the covers, and made my first prolonged attempt at self-abuse. It took nearly forever. Twenty minutes later I was still squirming on the sheets, holding the snapshot in one hand and my barely increased organ in the other, shaking the latter like a pen that wouldn't work. I created blood blisters around the rim, producing fluid that was neither as yellow as urine nor as white as semen, and I finally quit when I'd reached not so much orgasm as utter anguish.

We've all heard that the essence of eros is its incommunicability. The terror that lives at the heart of love is silence, etc. We've all heard that a hundred times and I daresay we've all heard wrong. What's valuable about love is that you at last get to talk to someone. You at last get to be heard and the words hardly matter anymore, only the reassurance of their sound—unless, of course, you've run away from the mountain of mattresses or talk with a catch.

A Portrait of an Acrobat

MONA SIMPSON

It was an ordinary Friday afternoon. The air was moist and almost white, dull in a protecting way. When the wind blew the gray clouds into banks that broke, the sky showed a tender blue.

His office was on the ground floor of a white building once meant to look a little bit Greek. The Music and Art Building. They taught languages there too. The outside stone walls were dirty now.

I went to the girls' bathroom before. I zipped my jacket up to the collar. I looked like any other college kid, more or less.

I'd told him most of it already, three Fridays ago, and now I sort of went in every week at the end of the day.

Last night had been a bad night. Memories I hadn't known before had come. I'd gone on my bike to Janine's room. It was an inopportune moment. She had a guy there and they were sitting on her bed with their shirts off. She sent him away.

Professor Ludwig was extremely thin. He looked the way I wished a man to. His face was like a bird's. He had high clear bones and then hollows and his jaw was so you could see the two balls. He had thick wavy black hair with five threads of gray. His ankles stuck out amazingly thin. He always wore pants with a slight cuff. He had been in Auschwitz as a boy and the Friday afternoon I saw him he was only thirty five. This is how long ago that was.

I went in and sat on the chair. There was a chair for me and that was where I always sat. His chair that he sat on was broken. From inside, the building seemed like a stone cage with holes cut out. There was a slight hill and students walking close by. I could have reached out the open window and touched one. In the distance, I saw the campanile.

"I remembered really violent things," I said, "like weird torture." I wrinkled my nose. That was a little bit put on. I still wanted to seem young too, along with the other. I lay my two hands on a part of his desk and looked at them while I spoke. I would pull the fingers of my right hand up with the left.

"I remembered them last night and still it was like watching a movie, I feel like it's happening to some other girl and I feel sorry for her but I'm glad it's not me."

He faced me. "What kinds of torture?"

I noticed the doorknob. It was brass, old. I always didn't want to be using too much of his time. This wasn't for class really. I knew that. He was my History of Music teacher.

"Oh, lots of things. Like he put glass in me."

"Ouch," Professor Ludwig said. "Didn't your parents know when that happened? You didn't have to go to the hospital? Blood."

"I remember blood but I don't remember it hurting."

"It must have hurt."

I nodded. "And once he put his fist."

There was some noise at the door. It was someone else, another student, the door opened a wedge, she had huge long hair, some kind of floating skirt.

I rose to go and looked for my purse at my shoes. I felt gloomy and awkward. Big.

"I've got someone here," he said. "Could you come back Monday?"

"Oh sure," she said. Her voice was low and stony but her feet made whispering noises in Chinese slippers.

"Sit back down," he said.

That pleased me like something in my chest, spreading. I put my hands on his desk again. "Maybe it's good to tell you because you're not, you're not Janine." Janine was my best friend. She saved me everything. "I remembered all these things last night that I'd rather not even remember and I went over to her room and she really worried about me, she said she thought I might break down, she thought I was hysterical. I don't think I was hysterical, it was just the first time I cried about it.

"And he burned me with matches."

"On your skin?" Professor Ludwig touched the center of his palm.

"Well, on the inside of my thighs. I have a scar here on my waist. I never knew where it came from and now I think I know. I used to feel magic with pain. I thought I couldn't feel it. I used to show my brother, I'd stick pins in my hands and I wouldn't hurt. But it must have hurt. I must have felt something. I ate pins."

When I said that, after, I didn't know if he would believe me. It was true but so much of my life was hard to believe. The rest was really easy, like everyone else. I watched outside. The break of sky had ended. Drifts of deep gray fog banked the distance, admitting no real light, but shedding a faint softness, something mute and battening. Berkeley was like that. I loved the weather. I never missed the sun. The cool fog was like a mother's hand on my forehead. And what was left, the scatter of just popped cherry blossoms on a branch still mostly green, a waxy magnolia, beginning to brown in a line around the edges, all seemed to hold the light like a closed fist and so the white pink blossoms glowed in the dull smaller world.

A girl with a thick braid rolled her red bicycle slowly. It was wide-wheeled and old, dented.

My eyes sketched behind Professor Ludwig at the bookshelves that were full of things like owl feathers, a map of the world, a violin, bones, butterflies, and an old globe. His little office was like that, like an elementary school classroom. He had a record player and tiny speakers. Sometimes he would play me an opera.

But he was looking at me, steady. It was easy to tell him this. He was so different from anyone I knew. In Kansas, where I came from, we had no Jews.

Some people you told them—they would look at you a different way. I knew. A girl in my dorm had been raped. Already this had happened and we were not even twenty. People looked at her—she was a pretty girl, tiny, weak-seeming—and the idea of it happening to her played over them. Some guys, even nice guys, said it was hard not to do that. They said it was a little bit a turn-on.

People looked at her different. I knew. I did it too. Myself.

But when he talked to me like this I could tell he wasn't imagining my cousin doing these things to me. He was feeling them being done to him.

"I think you have to remember it all," he said.

Our conversation went slowly in that little room. We were quiet a long time before I answered and then it wasn't much of an answer.

"I'm not sure I want to remember."

"It's better if you do," he said. He was certain. Sometimes he said things like he knew they were absolutely true. I didn't think then of his experience. I just thought he was older. My life had made me selfish. I was possessed. I had a quiet way but I was finding my own path through the trees. Anyone else was only something to help me.

Once standing up he had told Janine and me that the horror was not Auschwitz for him, it was Birkenau where he lost his mother. And father, he said. First it was mother. We saw a movie with ferny birch trees planted in a line. That was Birkenau now. I was a kid in Auschwitz, he said. He shrugged. Sometimes it was even fun. Crazy life, he said, apologizing.

That day when he explained, his sorrow was already old. It was a used thing, not in his words. It was nothing alive. Janine asked more. She was most ways older than me. Janine was more like him. She was Jewish and I was nothing. I had thin hair and freckles and just American pale skin. Whenever I thought that, I minded but I just exhaled. I had worse things to worry about than if I was his favorite. I needed him even if I wasn't. We had heard he was a kind of hero, tricking the guards, stealing food under his cap. We had heard that he had been an acrobat. Janine asked. No, he had said, not me.

"Yeah," I said. "It's sort of this thing that's over here and I never even thought about but then it changes my whole childhood. Like last night I remembered being really strange when I was a child and staying in my room a lot and going into closets like for hours. I remembered trying to kill myself when I was eleven.''

''How did you do that?''

''I took aspirin. Then, Janine called my parents last night and I talked to them too. I wanted to find out if it really happened or if I just imagined it and they said it really happened, they just never mentioned it again because they thought I didn't want to.''

''These things you remember, after a while, they'll just become one of the things that happened to you in your life.''

''I feel pretty far behind.''

''But a life is so big, Candy.'' That was my given name.

''Yeah.''

''How's the guy? Are you still seeing the fellow?'' Two Fridays ago I told him how it started. This guy following me around saying I love you, Candy, I love you like a beggar follows you asking for money. And I started and that's when I remembered things. Once before, a guy in high school had liked me. We'd kissed and after the first time I hit him hard all over his face.

''Janine really likes him,'' I said. ''I don't know, I feel so bad. I get really repulsed by him sometimes. I never understood before why I never had any interest in anybody that way. I'd always liked guys but they were really high up like on billboards almost, you know what I mean? They never wanted me.''

''Whizzing by on bikes, driving trucks, trapezes, sure.''

It was our little chance to laugh. He seemed to have two smiles; one which meant satisfied anger and the other, a rueful one, that said: you and I understand and no one else will ever know, will they? No. No one else will ever know.

''Well, this can't be easy for you now with this fellow,'' he said. ''It wouldn't be with anybody.''

''I'm still really embarrassed to be seen with him in public. And all these other people, they're couples and they eat together in the cafeteria. I feel so strange. You can't really talk about it, like if somebody comes up to you and says you look depressed, you can't say, well, my father just died.''

''No.'' He swiveled his chair. As long as I'd known him that chair was broken. It was a regular wooden office chair with a coil spring but the spring was shot and when he leaned back, his arms crossed behind his head, he went back too far, so he looked like he would fall. I knew he wouldn't fall.

"A lot of the kids around you are going to have an easier time with love. You're not going to have that. Maybe later you will but just not now. You won't have that with anybody."

That was true. I felt that sinking, all the high pretty boys dissolving like a pill stuck in your windpipe when it finally begins to go. I was sorry—really sorry—but at the same time I could almost see a way to learn to live with it.

Certain bad things you know right away are true and when someone says them it's almost a relief because you already knew but were working so hard not to. Like the boy in high school I'd hit his face after we'd kissed, he told me I wasn't pretty but he loved me because I tried so hard. To be pretty? I said. That fell away like a mask dropping from the balcony down onto the dark lawn. I had tried then to be pretty. I wore a kind of light blue eye shadow. No everything, he said, you just try so hard.

Professor Ludwig's feet crossed on his desk. He was still a young man but he wore formal shoes, the kind with little holes punched in the leather. They were battered up.

"You're not going to get that now. But your talent—that they don't have. The rest of these kids, they're in awe of you for that."

That may have been part a lie but I believed it. Not too many kids were in awe of me. I wasn't good-looking and that's most of what people were in awe of. Also, I was always losing things, dropping letters in the hall, all over campus. There was always someone coming up to me in the cafeteria and saying, Excuse me, are you Candy Brown . . . ?

They knew I was a mess. But when he said that it was true too. Some people envied me. That was right. I played the organ. My cousin had taught me. The same cousin that did everything else. That was what he had done for a living. He lived with my grandmother and played twice a week at a small church on their own road.

Outside it was a shade the sky got before dark. It was cold out but just spring. The campus lanterns were flickering on in a stutter against the sky.

Most people who walked by now had on buttoned-up jackets or army coats.

That was the same day I saw a plump smooth owl, egg-shaped, perching heavily on the pitch top of a fragile bush. I knew it would not fall.

''The guy sounds good,'' he said.

I didn't want to leave yet. I was supposed to go meet the fellow at his job. He worked the Wednesday/Friday-night shift for security. I kind of dreaded it but it was nice to have somewhere I was supposed to be going.

''Yeah, he's very nice. But some of the things he says make me guilty. I don't want to use someone like that. You know.''

''Go ahead with it,'' he said. ''Go on and do it.''

''Yeah,'' I said. ''I know. I think so too. And I don't think that's what it is.''

''No,'' he said.

Then after I was outside again and I saw Mr. Ludwig in his office. He looked dense and dark bent over his desk writing. I stared inside the one open window, the small room cluttered and precious with its toys. It looked like it would all go away.

His head lifted up and he glanced outside a minute before he saw me. Then he did. His face broke into an uneven straight-line smile, like a twig snapped, one end longer than the other. I was bent down in a slant unlocking my bicycle. I knew at that moment he thought I was pretty.

To Leonard Michaels, my teacher, and to my students, Jen Goebel, Jeannette Montalvo, and Claudia Smith.

El Radio

GARY SOTO

At seven-fifteen in the evening, Patricia Ruiz's mother dabbed lipstick on her small, shapely mouth. Her father worked a red tie around his neck, swallowing twice so that his Adam's apple rode up and down like an elevator. At seven twenty-two, both were standing at the mirror in the bathroom, her mother rubbing Passion-scented lotion on her wrists and her father spraying Obsession in the cove of his neck.

They were in a rush to go to the opera, a recent interest Patricia couldn't understand. Only a year ago they were listening every Friday night to "The Slow-Low Show" of oldies-but-goodies, hosted by *El Tigre*. Now it was opera on Friday nights, and a new Lexus in the driveway, a sleek machine that replaced their '74 Monte Carlo.

"Lock all the doors, *mi'ja,*" Patricia's mother said, swishing in her chiffon dress. To Patricia, her mother looked like a talking flower, for she was slim as a flower and a bouquet of wonderful smells rose up from her.

Her father came into the living room plucking lint from the sleeve of his jacket. Patricia thought her father was handsome: his trim mustache, the silver at his temples, his romantically sad-looking eyes. Her girlfriends said he resembled Richard Gere, especially when he was in a stylish suit, as he was now.

"Pat, I rented you a movie," her father said, pointing vaguely at the cassette on the coffee table. "We'll be home by ten-thirty, eleven at the latest."

From the couch, a *Seventeen* in her lap, Patricia watched her parents get ready for the evening. She thought they were cute, like a boyfriend and girlfriend brimming with puppy love.

"I'll be okay," she said. She got up from the couch and kissed them. Their delicious smells were pleasantly overwhelming.

As her parents hurried out the front door, Patricia hurried to the telephone in the kitchen. Her best friend, Melinda, who lived two blocks away, was waiting for her call.

"They're gone," she announced. "Come on over."

Patricia hung up and took down a can of frozen orange juice from the freezer. While she was mixing the juice, spanking the clods of frozen orange pulp with a paddlelike spoon until they broke apart, she snapped her fingers and said, "It's party time!" She remembered that "The Slow-Low Show" of oldies-but-goodies was on the air. She turned on the small radio on the windowsill and the stereo in the living room. *El Tigre,* the host of the program, was sending out the message, "Now this one goes out to Slinky from Mystery Girl in Tulare. And this goes to Johnny Y in Corcoran from *La Baby Tears,* who says, 'I'll be waiting for you.' And we got special love coming from Yolanda to her old man, Raul, who says, 'Baby, I'm the real thing.' Yes, *gente,* the world turns with plenty of slow-low romance."

While *El Tigre* put on the record, "Let's Get It On," Patricia went to the kitchen to make popcorn. She got a bottle of vegetable oil from the cupboard and a pot from the oven. The oven's squeaky door grated on her nerves when it was opened or closed. She was pouring in a handful of kernels when Melinda pounded on the back door.

"Hey, *Ruca,*" Melinda greeted her when Patricia unlatched the door. Melinda was a chubby classmate in eighth grade at Kings Canyon Junior High. She was wearing a short black dress and her lipstick was brownish red against a pale, pancaked face. Her eyelashes were dark and sticky with mascara.

"*Ruca,* yourself, *esa,*" Patricia greeted, shaking the pot over the burner and its flower of bluish flames. The kernels were exploding into white popcorn.

Melinda turned up the radio and screamed, "*Ay,* my favorite." "Ninety-Six" was playing, and Melinda, standing at the counter, was pretending to play the keyboard. She lip-synched the words and bobbed her head to the beat. When the song ended, Melinda poured herself a glass of orange juice and asked her friend, "Patty, you ever count how many tears you cried?"

Patricia shook her head and started giggling.

"One time, when my mom wouldn't let me go to the Valentine's dance—the one last year when the homeboys from Sanger showed up—I cried exactly ninety-six tears. Just like the song."

"Get serious," Patricia said, her eyes glinting in disbelief. She poured the popcorn into a bowl, with just a pinch of salt because she heard a spoonful of salt was worse for your complexion than nine Milky Way candy bars devoured in an hour. "How can you count your tears?"

"I used my fingers."

"No way."

"*De veras,*" Melinda argued. She clicked her fingernails against the counter, and the sound resembled the *click-click* of a poodle's nails on a linoleum floor.

The two of them took the popcorn and orange juice into the living room and cuddled up on the couch, careful not to spill. On the radio, *El Tigre* was whispering, "This one goes out from Marta to *El Güero.* And we got a late bulletin from Enrique to Patricia. Message is—"

"Hey, Patty, some guy's got eyes for you," Melinda said. Her eyes were shiny with excitement. She jumped up and boosted the volume of the stereo. "The message is," *El Tigre* continued, " 'don't get fooled by plastic love.' "

"I like that," Melinda said.

"*Chale.* No way," Patricia said, trying to laugh it off. She got up and turned down the volume. "I don't know no Enrique."

"Enrique de la Madrid!" Melinda screamed. "Danny's brother."

''That little squirt? The *vato* just lost his baby teeth last week.''

The girls laughed and started dancing separately to Mary Wells's song, ''My Guy.'' They continued dancing, fingers snapping and bodies waving in slow motion when the song ended and was followed by Aretha Franklin's ''I Heard It Through the Grapevine.''

When that song faded to a thumping bass followed by a scratchy silence, they sat down on the couch, legs folded underneath them. There was a glow of happiness about them, a shine in their eyes. Patricia took a single popcorn and threw it in Melinda's mouth. Melinda threw a single popcorn at Patricia's mouth. It hit her in the eye, and they laughed and threw handfuls of popcorn at each other. They liked hanging out together. They liked that they could dance wildly and lip-synch nonsense lyrics without feeling stupid.

They became quiet when *El Tigre* cleared his voice and whispered, ''From Fowler, we celebrate the first but not last anniversary of Susie and Manny. From us, *su familia,* steady love for that eternal couple. And check it out, real serious commotion from Softy, who says to his Lorena in Dinuba, 'Let's get back together.' ''

When ''Angel Baby'' came on, the girls eased into the couch and nursed their orange juice and slowly chewed their popcorn. Their feelings were smoky. They synched the words, certain that the singer must have had a deep relationship. Patricia figured that the singer's boyfriend must have found another girl, and then lost that girl and joined the Army.

Melinda looked at Patricia, who looked at Melinda. Melinda asked, ''Anyone ever call you Angel Baby?''

Patricia sat up and, giggling, said, ''*Cállate,* Melinda, you're ruinin' the song.'' She thought for a second about Melinda's question. ''No, no one's ever called me Angel Baby. But my dad calls me Sweetie.''

''My dad calls me *La* Pumpkin.''

''*Órale.* Your *papi*'s got it right,'' Patricia laughed. She bounced off the couch and, heading to the kitchen, asked, ''You want more orange juice?''

''*Simón, esa,*'' Melinda said.

While Patricia was in the kitchen, Melinda spent her time at the mirror on the far wall, where Patricia's baby pictures hung, wrapped in the dust of years. She dabbed her lips with lipstick and picked up a picture. She looked at her friend and had to admit that she was a cute little thing.

When Jr. Walker and the All-Stars' "Shotgun" began its soulful blare, Melinda put down the picture and started chugging to the song, elbows churning at her side, singing, "You're a lousy, no-good, stinkin' Shot-gunnnnnnnn."

"Go, brown girl, go!" Patricia yelled when she came into the living room. She put down the glasses of orange juice and chugged along with Melinda, elbows flapping at her side like the wings of a wet chicken. They laughed and felt happy, and couldn't think of a better time. When the song ended, Patricia felt her cheek with the back of her hand. She was hot but feeling great. She took a drink of orange juice.

"Yeah, we're gonna have to come up with a name for you, *ruca,*" Melinda said. She sized Patricia up, and, stroking her chin, said, "How 'bout *La Flaca?*"

"*Y tu, La* Pumpkin!" Patricia chided. She ran her hands down her hips. Yeah, I am skinny, she told herself, but at least I'm not a fat *mamacita!*

"*La Flaca!*"

"*La* Pumpkin!"

"La Flaca!"

"La Pumpkin!"

The girls laughed at their nicknames and threw popcorn at each other. Melinda then suggested that they call *El Tigre* and dedicate a song.

"*A quién?*" Patricia asked.

"Enrique de la Madrid," teased Melinda as she jumped over the couch and headed for the telephone in the hallway.

"*Chale!*" Patricia screamed, her heart pounding from the fear and delight. "I don't like that squirt."

"But he got eyes for you."

"You mean *you.*"

"*Pues no.* You mean *you!*"

Patricia pulled on Melinda's arm and Melinda pushed Patricia. Suddenly they were on the floor wrestling, both laughing and calling the other by her nickname. In the background, *El Tigre* was whispering, "Now stay cool, *y* stay in school."

When Melinda reached for the telephone, the receiver fell off the hook and corkscrewed on its cord. Even though her mouth was inches away and she had yet to dial the radio station, she was yelling, "*Esta ruca, se llama la Flaca de* Kings Canyon Junior High, wants to dedicate a song to her sleepy boyfriend. She wants—"

Patricia put her hand over Melinda's mouth and felt the smear of lipstick working into her palm. Melinda pulled Patricia's hair, lightly, and Patricia pulled on Melinda, not so lightly. They struggled and laughed, and finally Melinda said, "Okay, okay, you win."

They both sat up, breathing hard but feeling good. After catching her breath, Patricia said, "I'll call *El Tigre* and have him do a *dedica* to my parents.

"*Que idea!*"

Patricia dialed "El Radio," and immediately she got *El Tigre,* who said in a low, low-riding voice, "*Qué pasa? Cómo te llamas, esa?*"

Without thinking, Patricia said, "*La Flaca y mi carnala La* Pumpkin *del barrio de* South Fresno."

"*Y tu escuela?*"

"Roosevelt High," Patricia lied. She didn't want *El Tigre* to know that he was rapping with a junior high kid.

"And what oldie-but-goodie do you want me to spin for you? *Y tu dedica?*"

"I wanna hear 'Oh, Donna,' by Ritchie Valens." Patricia moved the telephone to her other ear, giving her time to think about the dedication. "And I . . . I want to dedicate the song to my parents, Jerry and Sylvia, I do love you, from your only but eternal daughter, Patricia."

"*Pues,* I'll get it on in a sec. Stay cool, *ruca,* and keep up the grades."

Patricia hung up, heart pounding. She had never been so nervous. She put the telephone back on the table.

"You did good. 'Oh, Donna' is my next favorite," Melinda said. Melinda got up slowly from the floor and went to the mirror to tease her hair back into shape. She looked down at her hand and made a face. "*Ay,* Patty, you broke one of my fingernails."

Patricia felt her cheek. She was hot from wrestling and talking with *El Tigre.* The only other famous personality she had spoken to was Ronald McDonald when he came down in a helicopter at the McDonald's on Kings Canyon Boulevard. And Ronald was nothing like *El Tigre;* he only gave away french fries, not oldies-but-goodies.

"You ever been on TV?" Patricia asked. She was high about her voice carrying over all of Fresno on "The Slow-Low Show."

"Nah," Melinda said. She had her compact out and was retouching her face. "I was in the newspaper once."

"You were?"

"Yeah, it was when they reopened the pool at Roosevelt. I was first in line." She closed the compact and brought out her mascara. "The paper was hard up."

On the radio, the Supremes' "I Hear a Symphony" was playing, a song which prompted Melinda to ask, "So your dad and mom are at the symphony?"

"Opera," Patricia corrected.

"They like that stuff?"

"*Quién sabe?* I think they want to try something they don't know about."

"Shoot, if I had their car, I'd be cruisin' Blackstone," Melinda said. She began to fumble in her purse for her lipstick.

"But you don't have a license," Patricia said.

"*Pues,* I'll just put on some more makeup, and who can tell?"

"But you don't know how to drive."

"It's easy. Just put the stick on 'D,' and press the *cosita.*"

"Yeah, but what happened when your brother took out your mom's car?"

"You comparin' me to my brother? The guy *es un tonto.*" Melinda took a fingernail file from her purse and began to whittle down her broken fingernail. ''Yeah, your dad's Lexus is sharp, but so was his Monte Carlo.''

''Yeah, I don't know why he traded it in,'' Patricia reflected.

At that moment there was the jingling of keys at the front door. Melinda gave Patricia a frightened look. Patricia's eyes flashed to the spilled popcorn and the blaring stereo, then to the clock on the end table. It was only 9:35.

''It's either the cops or my parents,'' Patricia said.

''Same thing,'' Melinda said, as she started to rush to the kitchen in hopes of making it to the back door.

But it was too late. The door opened with a sigh and the two girls were staring at Patricia's shocked parents. Her father took the key from the door, and her mother looked around the room trying to assess the damage.

''What's been going on?'' her mother snapped as she walked toward Patricia. For a moment, Patricia thought she was going to pinch her but she only stomped into the kitchen. ''Are there any boys here?'' she asked. Her voice was edged with anger.

''No, just me and Melinda.''

Her mother sniffed the air for boys and cigarettes. She saw the popcorn spewed over the rug.

''I spilled the bowl, Mrs. Ruiz,'' Melinda volunteered as she and Patricia scrambled to pick up the popcorn. ''I tripped.''

''I can't leave you alone! Can't I trust you?''

''Mom, we were just listening to *El Tigre*.''

Patricia's father was quiet and withdrawn. He undid his tie and turned down the stereo. He threw himself into his easy chair, feet up on the hassock.

''What's wrong?'' Patricia asked her father. He seemed unusually quiet.

He turned his sad eyes to his daughter. ''The car broke down. It's brand-new.''

''Broke down!'' Patricia shouted.

''Yes, *broke down*,'' her mother repeated. Turning to Melinda, she asked, ''Does your mother know where you are?''

"Ah, sort of," Melinda lied, her face turned away from Patricia's mother. She hated lying to grown-ups, especially parents with bad tempers.

Patricia's mother gave Melinda a doubtful glare and muttered, "*mentirosas,* both of you." She wiped away a few loose kernels of popcorn from the couch and sat down, her high heels dropping off her feet like heavy petals from a branch.

"You mean you didn't get to the opera?" Patricia asked. Before her mother or father could answer, a quick-thinking Melinda raced to the stereo and turned up the volume. *El Tigre,* in his Slow-Low low-riding voice, was whispering, "I'm coming at you at nine thirty-nine, and I hope you're kicking back in the heart of *Aztlán.*"

"Yes, and I might be kicking these low-class *cholas* in the behind," her mother spoke to the radio. Patricia could see that her mother was softening and that she and Melinda were out of danger.

"We got *una dedica," El Tigre* continued, "from Larry M. to Shy Girl in West Fresno, who says, 'I lost a good thing.' To Gina of Los Banos, 'Happy Birthday,' from her father and mother. And from *La Flaca* to her parents Jerry and Sylvia, I do love you, from your only but eternal daughter. *La Flaca* has asked for "Oh, Donna," *y pues,* why not?"

"That's me, Mom. *La Flaca!"* Patricia yelled.

"You?" her mother asked, giving her daughter a questioning look.

"Yeah. I'm *La Flaca* and Melinda's *La* Pumpkin."

"My dad calls me *La* Pumpkin." Melinda grinned.

Patricia's father laughed. He laughed long and hard until a single tear rolled from one of his eyes. "Did you hear these *cholas? La Flaca y La* Pumpkin." He got up and boosted the volume of the radio, which was playing "Oh, Donna." He asked his daughter playfully, "How'd you know my first girlfriend was named Donna?"

Patricia's mother slapped his arm and said, "*Ay, hombre.* Now look at you with a broken-down Lexus."

"Dad, you should have kept the Monte Carlo," Patricia said, feeling truly out of danger.

"Yeah, you're right." He smiled wearily.

''Come on, Dad, let's dance,'' Patricia suggested.

''Let's party down!'' Melinda yelled. She chugged off to the kitchen, lip-synching the words to ''Oh, Donna.''

''The heck with the opera,'' he said after a moment of hesitation. ''It's better with *El Tigre.*'' He took his daughter's hands in his and they danced, one-two, one-two, while her mother snapped her fingers to the beat. In the kitchen Melinda stood at the stove making a new batch of popcorn.

Uncle Dick

PAUL THEROUX

When people say of someone, ''You'll either love him or hate him,'' I always have the feeling I'll hate him. Then I remember my Uncle Dick and I know better.

Uncle Dick seldom spoke to us except to tease or criticize, but once he told me that his mother had never picked him up when he cried in his crib. She simply let him lie there and scream—didn't touch him, didn't talk to him, didn't feed him until a specific minute on the clock. He must have been forty-something when he confided this, and he looked at me and said, ''Imagine.''

He was unshaven and his whiskers were grayer than they should have been. He was always clawing his hair. I never saw him sit down at his table to eat a meal. He stood up, looking out the kitchen window, forking tuna fish out of an open can, then he threw the can away and wiped his hands on his shirt. He drank out of bottles—even milk bottles, even milk cartons that had spouts that missed his lips. He put his mouth under the faucet. He hated the way other people ate—sitting down, taking their time. Just a small amount of sitting down made him jump up and rage. ''We're wasting time! I've got so much to do!'' His house needed painting, he said; his grass had to be cut. He needed something at the hardware store—and it might be a hinge that he would fasten by banging screws through the holes as though they were nails, he was so impatient to get the thing hung. And the way he used a hammer made you think of a murderer.

I went one hundred and forty miles with him in his old Ford, on a winter day. He owned a pony then, and his blue jeans were stiff with pony shit. The car windows were shut tight and his heater was on. "I never got carsick when I was your age," he said, as I held my face miserably in my hands. "It's his fault that I'm late," he said to the salesman when we got to the shop, which was outside Bridgeport. It looked like another hardware store or a junk shop, but he came out with a book. He let me glance at it—gold-stamped leather and tissuey pages. He put it into a brown paper bag and I never saw it again. He kept such treasures in a trunk in his attic, or in drawers. If he opened a drawer and you looked in you would see glints of gold, daggers, chains, dented goblets, silver plates, carvings; and then he shut it and complained. "I have nothing," he said. "No wife, no money, no children, nothing."

You saw him with a woman one week and the next week if you asked him about that woman he would shriek at you. It was always possible to tell, when he was on the telephone, whether he was talking to a woman or a man. If his voice was normal it was a man.

His closets were full of fine clothes but the clothes he wore were torn. He wore everything until it was in tatters and then he threw it away—wore his shoes until they were cracked and broken, wore his sweaters until they were frayed and pilled, and I have already mentioned his pony trousers. I never saw him in clean clothes, and while from a distance in these torn things he looked like a boy, up close he looked like a tramp, and he smelled.

"You're wasting water!" he screamed at me one time when I was letting the water run from his faucet.

Was that it? That he felt that by not washing he was saving water? Certainly he was frugal. He ate alone, he slept alone in a narrow bed, and if you asked him whether he had seen a particular movie he would say, "Six bucks! I'm not paying six bucks to see a movie. I wouldn't give them the satisfaction."

They and *them* were words he frequently used. "You know what they're doing to the interstate? They're widening it!" "They always say 'Happy Holidays' and never 'Merry Christmas' at this time of year. I hate that!'' ''They're building another supermarket!''

He was the sort of person who, if you didn't see him for a while, you might think had killed himself or gone to Alaska, and then when you saw him again you realized that he'd probably never die, nor would he ever go anywhere at all.

When he did go outside his house strange things happened—people drove more slowly and always in front of his car and he yelled at them, his spit flecking his windshield; and red lights came on suddenly and made him stop and curse some more; and the sky grew cloudier. The sun dimmed, dusk came, it rained, the wind came up, leaves were beaten from the trees and Uncle Dick would say, ''I left my windows open!'' When he was out, the world stopped being simple. It filled with obstacles, and my uncle tripped or banged his head or caught his finger in the slamming door or spilled his coffee—and he raged. Just being with him could make you very tired.

His silences were worse than his shouts. Sometimes he stared and said nothing, and you wanted to run. When he was silent his face was darker, his movements much slower, his clothes dirtier and more rumpled. He would not linger—he fell silent and a moment later he was gone. He would stay away for months or more. One entire year we did not see him, though we saw his car flash past. He reappeared complaining about the price of paper—so many dollars for a ream, and after he told me what a ream was I wondered why he needed all that paper. He made no mention of what he had done in the year that he had vanished. And then his real reason for showing up after all that time came out. ''I need a hand moving a ladder.''

It was a big ladder, splashed with paint, and carrying it through his cellar I saw a number of shadowy objects, some I couldn't make out, but others I clearly recognized—a spinning wheel, a cider press, a musket, a brass telescope, a copper basin, a thunder jug, an ornate spittoon, a marble-topped table, a walking stick with a bird's beak as a handle, a toothy jointed pair of shark's jaws, a Chinese lantern, and something that looked very much like a human skull, the color of old meerschaum. Just as he kept treasures—daggers, chains, silver coins—in trunks and in drawers, he kept larger objects here in his cellar. It was all hidden, but why?

"That looks like part of a skeleton," I said, because I was too timid to admit that I saw a human skull resting on the top of a windup victrola.

Instead of replying he began to rant.

"Everyone's got a big American flag flapping in front of his store or his gas station or whatever," he said. "Ever notice that? I've got a theory that they're meant to attract attention. It's not patriotism—it's a kind of advertising."

But I was glancing back at the spittoon and the skull and the musket, and I lost control of the ladder.

"Why don't you drop the ladder? Why don't you hit something with it, like the doorframe? Chip some paint off—why not? Come on, make it hard for me. I like it! I want to spend the rest of the afternoon fixing that door you just scratched—"

He stopped when he saw that I was crying, but after we put the ladder against the house he simply climbed it and slung a bucket of paint on a hook and began working white paint onto the eaves with a stiff brush. I knew that it was time for me to go and that I would not see him for a long time.

Perhaps he went away. If he was planning to travel a long distance he rose at four in the morning in order to beat the traffic and he set off in the dark. He had always been an early riser. But that also meant that he was tired by evening. He was usually in bed by eight or so, which was why he never went to dinners or to parties. *I'm tired!* he shouted if you called him after six-thirty or seven. But he also said that he never slept through the night, and sometimes at odd hours his big house would be in darkness, except for the blue flicker of the television upstairs by his bed.

He yelled at the television too.

We were watching a program once and an elderly man came on smiling and talking about politics.

Uncle Dick smiled and said, "That's Wilson Shockley. He hates me."

It was rare to see Uncle Dick smile, but it was *He hates me* that made me stare at him.

He was sitting in a battered chair, wearing a thrift-shop T-shirt and torn jeans and mud-caked shoes. His baseball hat was on backwards, the fits-all-sizes adjustable band against his forehead. There were green stains all over him, the smears of a whole day's grass cutting, and small green clippings clung to his clothes and his arms. And this Wilson Shockley, looking like a college professor, was smiling in a television studio almost two thousand miles away in another time zone in Chicago. What was the connection?

"I wrote him a letter," Uncle Dick said. "I set him straight."

Eventually it came out, because he was proud of it. He had written letters to the governor (about the state of the roads), the Pope (because of his stand on abortion), the Prime Minister of Canada (acid rain), and not the President of the United States but his wife, the First Lady, because of something she said, a careless remark about Princess Diana of Great Britain—about her eating habits, I think. And there were more letters—to movie actors and famous sportsmen and millionaires—especially millionaires. He had, he said, sent detailed letters of advice to football coaches and city planners. He scolded celebrities. *You have all the qualities of a dog except fidelity,* went one of his letters, so he said. He was proud of them, and proudest of all when he got a reply, no matter how baffled or hurt it was. A nasty reply excited him into writing another stinging letter, and he would keep it up until he had the last word.

His letters all said, more or less, *I'm watching you.* When he was sitting in front of a television he imagined that these people were looking back at him—specifically him: they knew he was watching him.

But that mention of letter writing had made me pause because I had always assumed that Uncle Dick was a handyman or the blackest of the family sheep. And it can be rather alarming when someone you consider to be eccentric says they have written something. It seems a reckless confession, it suggests they are insane, and in Uncle Dick it was like one of the many things he said to shock people.

" 'I think my private parts are beautiful,' " he said once. " 'I have black tarry bowel movements. Answer true or false.' Those are two of the questions I was asked on an exam once at graduate school."

The shocking thing was that I hadn't realized he had been to graduate school.

"I originally wanted to go to West Point," Uncle Dick said. "Did you know that in 1957 you could be refused entry to West Point for"—and here he made a horrible face—" 'excessive ugliness?' "

He could get angry in seconds if you said the wrong word.

"People who say 'preppy' are preppies," he snarled. "People who use the word 'yuppy' are yuppies."

He screamed at the word *hopefully,* but he smiled at *wing nuts,* or *pebble dash,* or *griddle iron,* or *grout.* He laughed when he heard someone like an old carpenter look up at his house and say, "The cheeks of that dormer are out of whack," and once when I said "shitsy" he wrote it down.

I said, "Why did you do that, Uncle?"

He said, "I didn't do anything. I didn't write anything. What are you talking about?"

I hadn't even said what he'd done, but there was the pen in his pocket, and the little notebook. He saw me looking.

"That's my wallet," he said. "I use it as a wallet. Don't you know that it's rude to stare? A gentleman never stares."

He was wearing a stretched Red Sox T-shirt, a ski hat with a bobble on top, a pair of army pants with big deep pockets at thigh level, and string instead of laces in his broken shoes.

People thought he was half Indian—he had that look, dark and unpredictable, as though he would fly into a fit of sudden anger or else stalk away. He didn't look like anyone else in the family. Uncle Dick's appearance convinced me that a person's disposition gives them certain features and changes them physically for life. He was big and shaggy and fierce, and if he was invited for lunch he probably wouldn't come, but if he did he would show up late in his ragged clothes, stinking of his stables, and his expression and the look in his eyes challenged you to make a comment. *I dare you to mention my clothes.*

If you did he would not say anything, though he would hesitate, as though pronouncing a curse on you, and wiggles of steam would start from his body. Next he would vanish and someone would say *Where's Dick?* and somone else would say *He was here just a minute ago.* Eventually you would get a letter—a horrible corrosive letter, one of his worst—and no one would see him for months.

But when you saw him he might be wearing Mickey Mouse ears and singing, "My name is Annette Funicello," or else doing the bunny hop across Route 28, down by the mini-golf, to make the traffic stop and to amuse the person he was with, probably a woman giggling with bewilderment.

He did not drink alcohol. He stopped smoking through sheer willpower and then he gained, he said, twenty-five pounds. He cried when his cat MacMorris died. He was always to be avoided when the Boston Celtics lost a game.

A lunch party he was invited to might result in much worse than his disappearance. What if there was someone present he instinctively disliked, such as one of the celebrities or millionaires to whom he aimed his poison pen letters? What if it was someone to do with books? He seemed to develop an instant hatred for anyone who wrote or published or sold books, and his hostility could be baffling. It often took the form of fooling questions, and the people didn't know whether they were being mocked. Maybe Uncle Dick was just being friendly, they thought. But I knew better.

"Spell 'minuscule,' " he would say to these book people, and most of them thought the word began m-i-n-i-. Or he would chant at them, "Harry Martinson! Odysseus Elytis! Rudolf Eucken! Karl Gjellerup! Verner von Heidenstam!"—and sometimes more names; and when he had the attention of the whole room he would say, "Who are they?"

No one ever knew until Uncle Dick laughingly told the book people that these men had won the Nobel Prize for Literature.

With other party guests he took a different line. If they talked about art he changed the subject and complained about the high price of kitty litter, or said he had never missed a single episode of *Dallas,* or wasn't it time we espoused a keener interest in the future of the Kurds?

"I didn't hear your poem," he said, tottering like a bear and with his cheeks blown out, and facing the man who had just recited the poem, "because I was eating crackers and I like to hear them crunching in my ears as I chew."

When his glasses broke he mended them with Scotch tape that gradually grew yellower and more brittle. He squirted the wrong type of oil on his shoes, but boasted about how cheap it was, and then his shoes caught fire from a match someone had thrown. He bought two-gallon jars of mayonnaise that said "For Restaurants and Institutions." One Christmas he gave my forty-three-year-old aunt a baby doll and told her it was very valuable. That same year he gave me a pair of nutcrackers. They were rusty but Uncle Dick said, "Made in Germany. The finest nutcrackers are made in Germany."

For three years Uncle Dick wore nothing but black clothes and —someone said—a cape. But I never saw the cape. He was expert at table tennis, pool, basketball, and chess. He claimed to know the obscure rules of various card games. He was unbeatable at tic-tac-toe. He said he had once eaten kangaroo meat, smoke-dried, on the Gulf of Carpentaria, in Australia. You would have to marvel at this because if you doubted it he would go silent and vanish again.

He could not swim and once, out quahogging, he stepped in a hole and almost drowned. He was afraid of spiders and loud noises —thunder in particular—and said he was disgusted by the sight of people's feet. He hated high winds and after a few days of it he would climb onto his roof and fire his shotgun into the gusts. Ice cream he said was his weakness. He would drive fifteen miles to a place that sold frozen pudding flavor ("Howard Hughes was addicted to chocolate chip," he said, "which is another difference between us"). He had a fondness also for pumpkins, lobsters, and pistachios ("It means 'grinning' in Farsi, as you know"). He could eat great quantities of dog biscuits.

He had a habit of leaving notes for you—stuck in the window or shoved under the door or squeezed beneath the windshield wiper.

The messages said *I totally disagree with you* or *Do not make any attempt to communicate with me* or *I will be unavailable until November.* The simple message was hurtful enough, and then you realized that in order for him to get the message to you in this way he had had to sneak to your house in the darkness, sometime between two o'clock and five o'clock that morning.

I'm busy! I've got a million things to do! he would shriek just before he left us.

He had no wife, he had no children, he had no job, he lived alone, he never traveled. We could not imagine what he was busy doing. *Don't ask* was a family caution.

On one occasion Uncle Dick began to reminisce, to an Irishman, about Dublin. He named specific streets, and pubs where he had drunk pints of ale, and churches where he had prayed. He lamented that it was all gone—replaced by cheapness and fakery. Afterward it gave me a pang to recall the look on the Irishman's face as he listened. But some years later I discovered that Uncle Dick had never been to Ireland, nor had he been to Australia.

He said he could speak Swahili, but since no one else knew how there was no way of verifying it. "Conversational Latin" was how he described another language he knew.

He liked telling the story of how he had had an appointment with a billionaire ("There are only thirty-six of them in the whole world"). This was to have taken place at the Ritz-Carlton in Boston, but Uncle Dick had been turned away by the doorman for not wearing a tie—he was wearing a war surplus sailor suit and rubbers. The billionaire had to meet him at the Shamrock Luncheonette.

He had once been bitten on the thigh by a rat, he said. "This was in Mombasa. Oh, years ago."

He owned a pair of wooden skis, a wooden tennis racket, a leather hat, a manual typewriter, clamp-on roller skates, and a bike with no gears. I never saw him use any of them.

After he stopped visiting us, Uncle Dick was seen playing with the children who regularly came to his house. He gave them candy, he showed them his Japanese sword, he taught them how to do the bunny hop, he played tag with them, he encouraged them to tell him about their fears and hopes. At Halloween he put on a mask and led them around the neighborhood. He was Santa Claus at Christmas, he was the Easter Bunny, and on the Fourth of July he let off fireworks in his orchard. While small children boldly went upstairs and demanded candy, we hung back—too afraid to approach, afraid he would angrily send us home. We stood at the margins of his yard and saw him playing—running, screeching, his gray hair twisted, his shirttails flying. "You can't catch me!"

People saw him at the playground, the beach, the schoolyard, the swings.

I was at college then. One weekend, returning from Boston, I bumped into Uncle Dick at the post office. I never knew what sort of welcome I would get from him and so I gave him the most tentative greeting. He surprised me by saying how glad he was to see me.

"Want to see something? Huh? Something really amazing?"

He was breathless, he was flying. His shirt was on inside out, he was wearing striped pants and high-top sneakers. He hurried me to his house and pulled out a drawer—one of his treasure drawers. He took out a toy rifle—an air rifle, but an old one. "It's a BB gun—the original. I had that very model when I was ten years old. See the Red Ryder insignia on the stock? Listen, it's in perfect working order."

He aimed it and went *pah! pah! pah!*

"I've been looking for one of these for years."

There was more in the drawer. A green plastic water pistol. A pack of bubble gum wrapped in colored waxed paper and containing two baseball cards. A Sky King ring, with a secret compartment. A copy of *Tales from the Crypt* comic book. A hat—but no ordinary hat. He put it on.

"We used to call this a beanie," Uncle Dick said. There was a propeller on top. He spun the propeller with his finger and said in a small boy's stuttering, quavering voice, "I got an idea! Let's go down to Billy's house and play marbles. Hey, I got my bag of aggies. These are good shooters." He swung a little clinking bag out of the drawer. ''This one's a pisser. Hey, what's wrong, don't you want to come?''

He took me by the arm. The propeller on his beanie was still slowly turning. Was he defying me to make a remark?

I nervously clutched the books I had brought home for the weekend, for the paper I had to write.

''Malinowski makes the point,'' Uncle Dick said—but how had he seen the small printed name on the spine of that book?—''that in the Trobriand Islands, the relationship between a woman's brother and her son is stronger than between the boy and his father. In other words, the uncle and nephew—because there is a definite proof of a blood relationship and there is always an element of doubt about the true paternity of a child. And similarly, in *Beowulf* you see the same affinity—the uncle and nephew usually fighting together in battle.''

As he spoke the propeller on his beanie still spun.

''Am I keeping you?''

The propeller stopped as he stared at me.

He's a wicked enemy, people used to say; but he can be much worse as a friend.

We saw less and less of him. He stopped phoning. He didn't even call us when he wanted to move a ladder or push his car. Instead, we heard stories about him. His name would come up, and someone in the room would say softly *I once got a letter from him* and would turn pale and serious. You wouldn't want to know any more.

Or someone would tell how Uncle Dick had been terribly ill, and had spent a month in the hospital. We would feel ashamed that we had not known; but then the stories would come out—how he had insisted on wearing his bobble hat while being X-rayed; how he had accused someone of stealing his old pocket watch; how he had run up an enormous phone bill by making repeated calls to London, England; how he had begged his nurse to marry him and then refused when he had discovered that she had been recently divorced; and how, when he was discharged, the television set in his room was missing, along with a gallon jar (''For Institutional Use'') of aspirin.

Another story began circulating that he had been seeing a psychiatrist for some time, that he had told this man of how his mother, my grandmother, had never picked him up when he had cried in his crib. And that was not all. There were childhood humiliations, episodes of loneliness and rejection and total isolation, stories of his imaginary friend "Larrance" who was sometimes a boy and sometimes a girl, his nightmares and his rituals about opening jars and crossing streets. In this story about Uncle Dick and the psychiatrist, the analysis went on for about a year, and then after listening to so many of these sad strange tales, the psychiatrist became depressed, canceled the remainder of the sessions, and killed himself.

Uncle Dick vanished so completely we thought that he had died. Then even the stories stopped. There was no word of him. We got on with our lives, feeling steadier and more certain now that he was gone.

He was not dead. How silly of us not to have realized what he had been doing all this time.

When Uncle Dick's novel was published it was praised for its humanity, its luminous subtlety, its sense of fun, its quiet wisdom. It was, everyone agreed, a masterpiece of sanity and elegance.

A Rule of Travel

JAMES THOMAS

We live in a world of coincidence. How else do lovers ever meet—but through a lucky accident of time and place? Yes, a world of coincidence, and also of premonition. You are thinking, for instance, of someone you have not seen for some time when the phone rings. You knew it would. You know who it is.

The two people in this story have not yet met, but they have thought of one another often. *Envisioned* one another. Dreamed. She, an attractive woman known for her unusual fortitude, of a man who can not only appreciate her strength, love her for it, but make use of it. For she would be used—fairly. He, a man recognized for his highly creative mind and sensitive nature, of a woman courageous enough to encourage him in his bold ideas. With such a woman he would fashion a new kind of life.

When they do meet—and they will because this is nothing if it is not a love story—they have both perceived, imagined, yes, had a premonition, that a bell will ring. They don't know why, but they know it will.

As always in such affairs, the paths of the two converging lives could be traced far back from the point where they actually cross. Taken back to birth, it would be found that he was born two years earlier than she, but under the same sign, and the one sign known to be particularly compatible with itself. Taken back just eighteen months, they would both be found extricating themselves from intentionally childless marriages at which they had worked hard, yet failed. And both divorces, when final, are curiously amiable.

She practices law in New Orleans. Civil rights is her underpaid passion. He is a struggling postmodernist architect in Chicago, just beginning to get the attention he needs. And after the requisite months of postdivorce depression both have decided to swallow the expense and take a three-week vacation—to go somewhere, alone and unencumbered except for that impossible dream of meeting someone new, someone right. Therefore somewhere civilized yet exotic.

Greece. And no package tour, but an independent and spontaneous exploration of that exalted island nation.

They book their reservations within an hour of one another, have chosen the same airline and departure times for their flights from New York to Athens and back. And they would be sitting next to each other on the flight out except that he has generously given up his window seat, at the check-in counter while transferring at JFK, to a skinny teenaged girl, also traveling alone, who so wanted one.

They *do* see each other, in that anxious and furtive business of glancing around the cabin before takeoff—for even now they are only a few seats and an aisle away in the large aircraft—but they are both too intelligent to have put specific faces on their dreams, and do not expect to recognize one another based on mere appearance.

At the airport in Athens his baggage is stacked on top of hers when it is hauled from the plane to the terminal building, but then separated when carelessly tossed to the conveyer belt. And while she takes a taxi to the hotel booked by her travel agent, the same hotel he has chosen on the recommendation of a friend, he takes a bus for the adventure of it. Their rooms are on the same floor, but at opposite ends, and by the time he arrives she is already undressed and in bed, resting from the long flight, sleeping, dreaming.

On their second day in the city they both take walking tours, and it is hardly a surprise that she is climbing down the steps of the Acropolis just as he is climbing up. The surprise is in the wind, which has come up suddenly from the south and which keeps everyone's head down, and their eyes averted.

They go to different travel agencies in the Plaka that afternoon but choose remarkably similar itineraries for a tour of the islands; and on the big boat which sails from the port of Piraeus the next morning her face does seem vaguely familiar to him although almost everyone's face soon goes white with the heaving sea. When they disembark at their first island five hours later no one is looking at anyone else.

The storm, thankfully, is over before sunset—and the rest of their vacation will be under beautiful Aegean skies, blue and brilliant by day, star-studded at night, designer skies, designed for romance.

Although they do not always take the same boats on the same days between the islands—for there are many boats in the popular month of August—they are together without knowing it on Mykonos and Paros and Ios and Santorini, on Crete and on Rhodes.

On Santorini she has a three-night affair with a flamboyant expatriate Irish painter, frivolous by definition but satisfying since she is the one defining it, and even if no fulfillment of her premonition.

On his boat to Crete he meets a bright college girl from Cincinnati with whom he explores the fabled ruins of Minoan palaces for several hot days, and while she is clearly too young for him he is nonetheless deeply saddened for her when she confesses to a boyfriend back home, whom she fears she has betrayed, and collapses in a bed of tears.

Rhodes is a long last stop for each of them. The Island of Roses. By now Greece seems familiar with its sage-shot geology rising out of the sea, the rocky sound of its language, the sun-darkened faces of other tourists who keep reappearing on similar cobblestoned streets. Here the premonition of meeting is strongest for them both. For five days they walk and take motorbikes and ride horses over the island, and at night, in hotels across the street from one another, they restlessly try to sleep off the weariness of vigorous travel.

On their next-to-last day she notices someone reading a copy of the *International Herald Tribune* in a taverna they have both chosen for dinner. She hasn't read any news these past three weeks, and would ask him if she could see the paper when he has finished, until she notices that the principal news on the front page—which hides his face—is of a disaster at sea about which she would rather know nothing.

On the short flight back to the mainland she is in the front of the plane, he in the back. Neither of them is ready to go home, and it is difficult for them to accept that their vacation is nearly over, even after they have changed planes in Athens and are in the air again, bound for New York. By coincidence, they are sitting next to each other.

Who can explain why they don't speak, beyond the usual civilities, until they are more than halfway across the Atlantic? The attraction is there, they are touching shoulders.

It takes a fatefully spilled drink, hers on him, a gin and tonic, to do it. They look at each other, open their mouths to speak, and long before the flight attendant appears with a damp towel they have both glanced at their watches to see how long they will be together.

Three hours go quickly when there is so much to review, to communicate, to share. They do the best they can. They lurch through the past, hover over the present, and have broached the future, in a frank discussion of how they are both glad not to have had children before now but hope to share that experience with someone soon, when a bell rings.

The significance of it, the imperfect timing, is easier to read than the sign above their heads which advises them to fasten their seatbelts. In a few minutes they land.

There is an hour and a half before her connecting flight, but customs is busy and frustratingly slow. They are barely in line together. They manage to exchange addresses and phone numbers, but their only kiss, in a crowd of two hundred at an anonymous boarding gate, is more the afterthought of old friends than the promise of new lovers.

Still, she is thinking of him a few months later when the phone rings. He has been invited to address a symposium on neoclassicism in New Orleans. He could fly in early or even stay over a weekend, will she be there? By unfortunate coincidence, she has to tell him, that's the one week she has agreed to go river-rafting down the Colorado with a friend, and one of her strengths is that she always honors her commitments.

In the back of his mind he has expected just such a complication, and he will continue to think of her off and on for a year, but the streak of pride which runs through his sensitive nature will prevent him from calling her again—a sadness since she would call him, as she told him on the phone she would, were her purse with credit cards, cash, and her address book not stolen at a restaurant in the French Quarter a week after her river trip. And even then she tries, but his name is a common one and the directory assistance operator is no matchmaker.

We live in a world of coincidence and premonition, and this is nothing if it is not a love story. We live, we love, and above all we dream. What is there, after all, in your own uninvented future that is not possible?

The Icehouse

MARK VINZ

''I saw him go in,'' she says. ''Told me he was walking over to the crossroads to get a paper, but I knew better. He's out in that icehouse again. That's one crazy little Irishman who'll be in deep trouble one of these days.''

Such has been her threat for the few winters that I can remember and many others I can imagine. ''Well, you better go out and check on him,'' she says, filling her coffee cup one more time. ''It's for sure I'm not going to.''

So I struggle into my heavy coat and overshoes, called back twice from the porch—once for a hat and once for a scarf. It's only about a hundred yards from the house to my grandfather's ice-fishing shack, though you'd think it was miles. She forgets how warm it gets inside—if she's ever *been* inside. When I open the door I'm nearly knocked down by the hot, moist air, the overpowering stench of kerosene, cigar smoke, and whiskey. Mostly whiskey.

''Don't let the wind in, boy,'' the old man says, perched with his five-pointed spear on his favorite chair next to the three-by-four-foot hole in the ice. ''Secret is to keep the spear tips in the water,'' he says—the first lesson for all who enter here. ''Don't want to break the water when you let go the spear. Won't get no fish that way.''

Inside, the eight-by-ten-foot house is filled with eerie light rising through the ice. Even when it's getting dark outside, it stays light in the icehouse.

"So, what's the old woman doing this morning?" he asks. "Drinking coffee, I bet. And fussing. Listen, boy," he says, drawing me close to his brown and broken teeth, "promise me you'll never marry a Swede."

I promise him I won't. I promise too that I won't get too close to the hole, and if I sit like a good fellow and just watch the water with him for a while, then he'll let me throw the heavy spear.

"Not *throw* it," he says. "Drop it, push it down." Up from the hole he drags a small walleye, lets me pull it free of the barbed tines and fling it outside into the snow. It's illegal to spear anything but northern pike, but my grandfather spears whatever swims under his hole in the ice.

I, on the other hand, have never speared anything, not even the sunfish poking around the minnow decoy. Soon enough I tire of staring into the hole, even if I can see a few little fish moving across the weeds on the green and glowing bottom ten feet below us. "Just like an aquarium," he says, and cuts me a slice of apple with his fillet knife. It tastes of fish and tobacco, but I gobble it down, and two more slices and a piece of stale beef jerky so spicy it makes my eyes water. And then we sit and watch some more, until he says, "Go and tell that old woman I won't be in till dark."

I can hear him laughing, even halfway back to the house, and underneath the words of my grandmother, who still wonders after nearly twenty years why she ever agreed to move to a house on a lake when she could have stayed in town with friends and stores. "At least," she says, "it's only in the winter that we really lose him. Can you believe it? That old fool sits on the porch all summer and never wets a line."

"Don't care about fishing from boats," he says. "Why should I go out in a boat anyway? Never learned to swim."

"Never learned to do a lot of things," she says.

"Sit on the porch and listen to *her,*" he says. "Listen to her Swede crabbing all day long."

"What'll we do with him come summer?" she says. "Five years since the railroad retired him and it keeps getting worse."

"What we need," he says, "is a good blizzard."

In the last blizzard, two years ago, the windchill dropped to eighty below and in the blinding white you couldn't see twenty feet from the porch of the house on shore. He found the icehouse anyway, over the drifts on his hands and knees, and then he stayed out there for two days and two nights, listening to the wind howling all around him. When my grandmother finally called for help and the sheriff's man got across the drifts with his snowmobile, he had to *drag* the old man back to the meal she'd been keeping warm for him.

"Would've served him right," she says, "if he'd fallen into that hole and never come up again." That's what she worries about most. She tries to hide his whiskey and his money but he always seems to find a way to get both.

"The saddest day of the year" is what he calls the one in late February when icehouses have to come off the lake. Once, in a season of early thaw, the old man refused to do anything, until his icehouse had sunk a foot or more into the slush, where it refroze. It took two cursing friends with pickaxes most of an afternoon to free it and drag it to shore.

"Sometimes I think we should just tether him to the wall," she says, "like your mother used to do when you were a toddler."

"She'd like that," he says. "The only tethering I'll do is stretch a rope between the porch and this icehouse." That way, if there's another blizzard he won't have a bit of trouble getting out here.

"Keep company with yourself," she says. "You don't have any friends left."

"Died off." He grins. "Crabbed to death by old women."

"Tell me a story," I say, fighting off sleep in the heavy heat and smells of the icehouse.

"You tell *me* one," he says. "You're the storyteller. I'm just a fisherman.

"And a railroad man."

"Brakeman," he says. "All the way to Seattle and back." He takes a long pull from his bottle, and then there's a fish, a big northern, ten or twelve pounds for sure, being dragged up twisting and flopping at the end of his spear. I didn't even see it until he pulled it from the hole.

"I'm getting tired of all this fish," is what she says.

"This is the way you set the decoy," he says, dangling the artificial minnow into the water.

"And then they'll slam it?" I say.

"You bet," he says. "They slam it and you slam them. That's the way she works, all right."

He teeters closer to the hole and I grab his leg. "Go tell the old woman I'm going to stay the night," he says. "Not much time left out here before thaw."

"That's the last straw," she says.

When the sheriff's man arrives on his snowmobile from across the lake, we can't find my grandfather anywhere. The little kerosene heater is going strong inside the icehouse, but the old man isn't there.

"Maybe he went for a walk," the sheriff's man says.

"He won't walk," my grandmother says, "not when he could be sitting."

It's then that we both know what they'll find a few weeks later when the ice finally goes out and they can get a boat in the water to start their dragging.

"We came across him out by the point," the sheriff's man tells us. And then, maybe he says it to make my grandmother feel better, but as I watch her face I know his words are having the opposite effect. "If I didn't know better," he tells us, "I'd swear that old man was smiling. Down there in twenty feet of water, with that spear still in his hands."

"I knew we should have tied that old fool to the wall," my grandmother says, biting at her lower lip.

"That's a pretty good ending," the old man says to me, "but I'm disappointed you gave that old woman the last word in the matter." Then he grins and shows me again how to set the decoy and hold the spear, and together we sit and stare into the glowing green water beneath us.

Almost Browne

The Twice-Told Tribal Trickster

GERALD VIZENOR

THE ABSOLUTE TRUTH

Almost Browne was born on the White Earth Indian Reservation in Minnesota. Well, he was *almost* born there; that much is the absolute truth about his birth. Almost, you see, is a cross-blood and he was born on the road; his father is tribal and his mother is blond.

Hare Browne and Marthie Jean Peterson met on the dock at Sugar Bush Lake. He worked for the conservation department on the reservation, and she was there on vacation with her parents. Marthie Jean trusted her heart and proposed in the back of a boat; Hare was silent, but they were married last year at the end of the wild-rice season.

Hare and Marthie had been in the cities over the weekend with her relatives. The men told stories about fish farms, construction, the weather, and automobiles, and the women prepared five meals that were eaten in front of the television set in the amusement room.

Marthie loved fish sticks and baloney, but most of all she loved to eat orange Jell-O with mayonnaise; she had just finished a second bowl when she felt the first birth pain.

"Hare, your son is almost here," she whispered in his ear. Marthie did not want her parents to know about the pain; naturally, they would never have allowed her to return to the reservation in labor.

Marthie never forgot anything; even as a child she could recite the state capitals. She remembered birthdates and Presidents but that afternoon she packed two baloney sandwiches and forgot her purse. She was on the road in labor with no checkbook, no money, no proof of identity. She was in love and trusted her heart.

The leaves had turned earlier than usual that autumn, and the silent crows bounced on the cold black road a few miles this side of the reservation border. Ahead, the red sumac burned on the curve.

Hare was worried that the crows would not move in time, so he slowed down and honked the horn. The crows circled a dead squirrel. He honked again but the crows were too wise to be threatened. Then the engine wheezed, lurched three times, and died on the curve.

Almost earned his nickname in the back seat of that seventeen-year-old hatchback; he was born on the road, almost on the reservation. His father pushed the car around the curve, past the crows and red sumac, about a half mile to a small town. There, closer to the reservation border, he borrowed two gallons of gas from the station manager and hurried to the hospital on the White Earth Reservation.

The hatchback thundered over the unpaved government road; a wild bloom of brown dust covered the birch on the shoulders; the dust shrouded the red arrow to the resort at Sugar Bush Lake. The hospital was located at the end of the road near the federal water tower.

Wolfie Wight, the reservation medical doctor, opened the hatchback and reached into the dust. Her enormous head, wide grin, and hard pink hands, frightened the mixed-blood infant in the back seat.

Almost was covered with dust, darker at birth than he has ever been since then. Wolfie laughed when the child turned white in his first bath; he was weighed, and measured, and a tribal nurse listened to his heartbeat. Later, the doctor raised her enormous black fountain pen over the birth certificate and asked the parents, "Where was your child born?"

"White Earth," shouted the father.

"Hatchback?" The doctor smiled.

"White Earth," he answered, uncertain of his rights.

"Hatchback near the reservation?"

"White Earth," said the father a third time.

"Almost White Earth," said the doctor.

"White Earth," he repeated, determined that the birth of his son would be recorded on the reservation. He was born so close to the border, and he never touched the earth outside the reservation.

"Indeed, Almost Browne," said the doctor, and printed that name on the birth certificate. Wolfie recorded the place of birth as "Hatchback at White Earth" and signed the certificate with a flourish. "One more trail-born mixed-blood with a new name," she told the nurse. The nurse was silent; she resisted medical humor about tribal people.

Almost was born to be a tribal trickster. He learned to walk and talk in the wild brush; he listened to birds, water, lightning, the crack of thunder and ice, the turn of seasons, and he moved with animals in dreams, but he was more at home on cracked polyvinyl chloride in the back seats of cars, a natural outcome of his birth in a used hatchback.

Almost told a blond anthropologist one summer that he was born in the bottom of a boat and learned how to read in limousines; she was amused and recorded his stories in narrow blue notebooks. They sat in the back seat of an abandoned car.

"I grew up with mongrels," he told the anthropologist. "We lived in seven cars, dead ones, behind the house. One car, the brown one, that was my observatory. That's where I made the summer star charts."

"Indian constellations?" asked the anthropologist.

"Yes, the stars that moved in the sunroof," he explained. "I marked the stars on cards, the bright ones that came into the sunroof got names."

"What were the names?" asked the anthropologist.

"The sunroof stars."

"The names of the constellations?"

"We had nicknames," he answered.

"What were the names?"

"The sunroof charts were like cartoon pictures."

"What names?"

"Moths are on one chart."

"What are the other names?"

"Mosquitoes, White Lies, Pure Gumption, Private Jones."

"Those are constellations?"

"The sunroof charts are named after my dogs," he said, and called the mongrels into the back seat. White Lies licked the blond hair on the arms of the anthropologist.

Almost learned how to read from books that had been burned in a fire at the reservation library. The books were burned on the sides. He read the center of the pages and imagined the stories from the words that were burned.

Almost had one close friend; his nickname was Drain. They were so close that some people thought they must be brothers. The two were born on the same day near the same town on the reservation border. Drain lived on a farm, the fifth son of white immigrants.

Drain was a reservation consumer, because he believed the stories he heard about the tribe. He became what he heard, and when the old men told him to shout, he shouted; he learned to shout at shadows and thunderstorms.

Almost told stories that made the tribe seem more real; he imagined a trickster world of chance and transformation. Drain listened and consumed the adventures. The two were inseparable; one, the mixed-blood trickster, the other a white consumer. Together, the reservation became their paradise in stories.

Almost never attended school; well, he almost never attended. He lived on the border between two school districts, one white and the other tribal. When he wanted to use the machines in school, the microscopes, lathes, and laboratories, he would attend classes, but not more than two or three times a month. Each school thought he attended the other, and besides, no one cared that much where he lived or what he learned on the reservation.

Almost learned four natural deals about life from his grandmother; he learned to see the wild world as a deal between memories and tribal stories. The first deal, she told him, was chance, things just happen and that becomes the deal with animals and their languages; words were pictures in the second natural deal; the third deal, she said, was to eat from the real world, not from the pictures on menus; and the last deal she told him was how to liberate his mind with trickster stories.

"In natural deals," he explained to his best friend, "we act, bargain, agree, deliver, and remember that birds never eat monarchs in our stories."

"What monarchs?" asked Drain.

"The milkweed butterflies."

"So, what's the deal?"

"We're the deal in our stories."

"Some deal," moaned Drain.

"The deal is that whites are fleas and the tribes are the best dealers," said Almost. "Indians are the tricksters, we are the rabbits, and when we get excited, our ears heat up and the white fleas breed."

Almost converted a reservation station wagon into a bookmobile; he sold books from a rack that unfolded out of the back. The books, however, were not what most people expected, not even in trickster stories, and he needed a loan to expand his business.

"We're almost a bookstore," said Almost.

"Blank books?" shouted Wolfie. "You can't sell books on a reservation, people don't read here, not even blank ones."

"Some of them are burned," said Almost.

"You're crazy, blank and burned books," said the doctor, "but you do have gumption, that much is worth a loan." She polished her black pen on the sleeve of her white coat and signed a check to the mixed-blood.

ALMOST THE WHOLE TRUTH

Almost is my name, my real name, believe that or not, because my father ran out of money and then out of gas on the way back. I was born in the back seat of a beat-up reservation car, almost white, almost on the reservation, and almost a real person.

White Jaws, the government doctor who got her cold hands on my birth certificate, gave me my name. Imagine, if we had run out of gas ten miles earlier, near a white hospital, my name might be Robert, or how about Truman? Instead, White Jaws made me Almost.

Listen, there must be something to learn in public schools, but not by me. My imagination stopped at the double doors, being inside a school was like a drain on my brain. So, my chance to learn came in bad nature and white books. Not picture nature in a dozen bird names, but road kills, white pine in eagle nests, fleas in rabbit ears, the last green flies in late autumn, and moths that whisper, whisper at the mirror. Nature voices, crows in the poplars, not plastic bird mobiles over a baby crib. So, nature was my big book, imagination was my teacher.

Classrooms were nothing more than parking lots to me, places to park a mind rather than drive a mind wild in the glorious woods, through the dangerous present in the winter when the whole real world struggles to survive. For me, double doors and desks are the end of imagination, the end of animals, the end of nature, and the end of the tribes. I might never have entered the book business if I had been forced to attend a white school.

The truth is, I almost got into the book business before my time. A blond anthropology student started a library on the reservation and she put me in charge of finding and sorting books. I found hundreds of books that summer. What a great time, books were like chance meetings, but the whole thing burned down before I almost learned how to read. The anthropologist told me not to use my finger on the page but we never practiced in any real books. She talked and talked and then when the building burned down she drove back home to the city. People always come here with some other place in mind on the reservation.

Drain, he's my best friend, said it was a good thing the library burned because most of the stuff in there was worthless digest books that nobody wanted to read in the first place. Drain is a white farm kid who lives on the other side of the road, on the white side of the road, outside the reservation. He learned how to read in another language before he went to school.

I actually taught myself how to read with almost whole books, and that's the truth. I'd read with my finger first, word for word out loud right down to the burned parts and then I'd picture the rest, or imagine the rest of the words on the page. The words became more real in my imagination. From the words in pictures I turned back to the words on the center of the page. Finally, I could imagine the words and read the whole page, printed or burned.

Listen, there are words almost everywhere. I realized that in a chance moment. Words are in the air, in our blood, words were always there, way before my burned book collection in the back seat of a car. Words are in snow, trees, leaves, wind, birds, beaver, the sound of ice cracking, words are in fish and mongrels, where they've been since we came to this place with the animals. My winter breath is a word, we are words, real words, and the mongrels are their own words. Words are mixed-bloods too, almost whole right down to the cold printed page burned on the sides.

Drain never thought about real words because he found them in books, nowhere else. He taught me how to read better and I showed him how to see real words where we lived, and the words that were burned on the pages of my books. Words burned but never dead. It was my idea to open a bookstore with blank books, a mobile bookstore.

Dr. Wolfie gave us a loan, so we packed up and drove to the city, where we started our blank-book business near the university. Drain somehow knew the city like the back of his hand. I told him that was the same as finding words in animals. Everything was almost perfect; we were making good money on the street and going to parties with college students, but then the university police arrested us for false advertising, fraud, and trading on the campus without a permit. The car wasn't registered, and we didn't have a license. I think that was the real problem.

Drain played Indian because the judge said he would drop the charges if we went straight back to the reservation where we belonged and learned a useful trade.

"Almost Browne, that's my real name," I told the judge. "I was almost born in the city." The judge never even smiled. These men who rule words from behind double doors and polished benches miss the best words in the language, they miss the real words. They never hear the real words in court, not even the burned words. No one would ever bring real words to court.

Drain was bold and determined in the city. He drove right onto campus, opened the back of the station wagon, unfolded our book rack, and we were in business. That's how it happened, but the judge was not even listening. Wait, we played a shaman drum tape on a small recorder perched on the top of the car. The tape was old, the sound crackled like a pine fire, we told the judge.

Professor Monte Franzgomery was always there, every day. He would dance a little to the music, and he helped us sell blank books to college students. "Listen to that music," he shouted at the students. "That's real music, ethnic authenticity at the very threshold of civilization." That old professor shouted that we were real too, but we were never sure about him because he talked too much. We knew we were on the threshold of something big when we sold our whole stock out in a week, more than a hundred blank books in a week.

Monte said our blank books made more sense to him than anything he had ever read. This guy was really cracked. Our books were blank except on one page there was an original tribal pictomyth painted by me in green ink, a different pictomyth on a different page in every blank book. Yes, pictomyths, stories that are imagined about a picture, about memories. So, even our blank books had a story. I think those college students were tired of books filled with words behind double doors that never pictured anything. Our blank books said everything, whatever you could imagine in a picture. One pictomyth was almost worth a good story in those days.

Well, we were almost on our way to a fortune at the university when the police burned our blank books. Not really, but a ban on the sale of blank books is almost as bad as burning a book with print.

So, now we're back on the reservation in the mail-order business, a sovereign tribal blank-book business in an abandoned car. Our business has been brisk, almost as good as it was at the university; better yet, there's no overhead in the back seat of a station wagon on the reservation. Listen, last week the best edition of our blank books was adopted in a cinema class at the University of California in Santa Cruz. Blank books are real popular on the coast.

Monte promised that he would use our blank books in his seminar on romantic literature. He told a newspaper reporter, when we were arrested the second time, that the pictomyths were a "spontaneous overflow of powerful feelings."

Drain said we should autograph our blank books, a different signature on each book. I told him the pictomyths were enough. No, he said, the consumer wants something new, something different from time to time. The stories in the pictomyths are what's new, I told him. He was right, and we agreed. I made pictures and he signed the books. He even signed the names of tribal leaders, Presidents, and famous authors.

Later, we published oversized blank books, and a small miniature edition of blank books. Drain bought a new car, we did almost everything with blank books. We even started a blank-book library on the reservation, but that's another story for another time.

The Prayer Lady

SYLVIA WATANABE

In late summer, when the spirits of the dead returned to eat with the living and to walk under the sky again, the villagers in the Japanese plantation camp put food out for the hungry ghosts and celebrated their coming with dance. On the last night of the *bon* festival, as time drew near for the lantern procession to light the spirits down to the sea, the retired head priest woke from a dream of falling water and called his wife to dress him in his white silk laying-out kimono. It was nearly time for their boy, Kitaro, to come for him, he said.

Okusan hurried into the living room, where her husband lay upon the couch, ensconced among stacks of dog-eared journals and rolls of rice paper covered with Chinese characters. As she stood trying to catch the drips from the spoon she'd been using to stir the red bean soup, now getting ruined on the stove, she stifled the impulse to inquire if their dead son had been informed of this plan. Instead, she said, "Wouldn't you feel better if you had something to eat?"

"I would feel just fine if other people didn't stand around making unnecessary observations," Sensei snapped. "Now hurry, woman, we mustn't keep Kitaro waiting."

Okusan looked closely at his face for new symptoms of the falling-down sickness. She wasn't sure exactly what she was looking for; three different medical specialists had been unable to name the first attack, which had come on suddenly during a meeting of the temple elders a few months before. Her husband had been the only one among that gathering to oppose the new head priest's latest revenue-making scheme of importing a rock star from Japan to appear at the following year's *bon* festival. "I built this temple with my own hands before you were even a smile in your papa's sleep," he had begun to object when, as he later told it, the room had suddenly turned very light, and then darkness had covered him over like a wave.

The fit had passed quickly, but it had left him paralyzed in both legs. Word had spread through the village that the old priest had finally been defeated by progress. For Okusan, who did not put much store in progress, and especially not in medical science, her husband's fit had been an almost magical event—like all the sudden things that happened in a person's life. She wished that her mother, who had been well versed in traditional lore, were alive to advise her. One cure, Okusan recalled, required little more than a change of name to restore a person's health—a treatment which the old man had predictably resisted. He had not proved any more cooperative in her more recent attempts to seek out other, more suitable methods.

"Ugh, chives," Sensei grimaced as his wife bent over him. Each week, she smelled of the most recent curative she'd heard about on the "People Speak" radio show. Though she was afflicted with rheumatism, she wasn't averse to trying out remedies for liver spots, heartburn, memory loss, or any of the other ailments people called in about. There had been the period when she'd been consuming a bulb of garlic every day; that had been worse than the chives. But he had liked the lemon grass. He closed his eyes, as if to shut out the memory of that clean, tart scent.

"Old man, why are you in such a hurry to leave me?" Okusan knelt beside the couch. How thin he'd become; he'd had no appetite for days. Despite her earlier annoyance, she had no doubt he possessed the determination to die out of sheer cantankerousness, and she did not know how to stop him from doing it.

"Let's call the Prayer Lady," she found herself saying. "It can't hurt to try.'' Then, taking her husband's silence as a sign of encouragement, she hurried on. ''Didn't Nobu Kobayashi, the fish vendor, go to the Prayer Lady for that heart condition that the doctors swore would kill him inside a year, and here he is, fifteen years later, even better than new? And what about Minerva Tanaka? She would have died for sure after that bad fall if the Prayer Lady hadn't gone to the hospital every day and prayed and prayed. And remember, oh remember, that time last year when Little Grandma Mukai sprained her hip?''

Sensei remembered. Among the villagers, it was rumored that the Prayer Lady could heal people just by touching them with her hands. As the story went, she had acquired her special powers one rainy summer afternoon when she was carrying out the trash. A sudden gust of wind had blown the torn page from a sutra book across a neighbor's yard into her hand, and as she held the page, the full meaning of the text had filled her mind in an infusion of light. From that moment on, she had possessed a special connection with the Dharma that gave her the power to heal with her touch. For years, Sensei had regarded her as a less-than-creditable rival for the loyalty of his congregation. Who knows, he thought, if it hadn't been for that old fake carrying on her services down the road, church attendance might have been higher. And if attendance had been higher, he might have had better luck in convincing his superiors to appoint a more like-minded successor to his post. The image of the barely pubescent rock star with the ducktail hairdo flooded his consciousness.

''Hmph,'' he said.

Okusan pressed ahead. ''So many people say such good things, such encouraging things about the Prayer Lady.''

''Stop calling her that,'' Sensei cried. ''That old crank! That garbage can Buddha! You'll kill me with your silly notions before Kitaro even arrives.'' His wizened face had drawn taut, and his eyes were bright. ''Are you going to help me get ready or aren't you?''

Momentarily chastened, Okusan left to assemble the change of clothes her husband required. From the carved wooden chest in their bedroom, she collected a pair of straw sandals, a yellowing silk robe, and a brocade sash decorated with gold and silver cranes. Through the open window, she could see the ring of lights encircling the temple yard, and the festival-goers congregated on benches around the musicians' platform and in groups along the beach where the lantern ceremony was to take place. "Hot noodles! Hot dogs! Genuine good-luck charms!" She could hear the cries of the hawkers plying their trade among the crowd.

She turned to examine the framed snapshot of their son on the nightstand next to the bed. The picture had been taken the day he had been drowned, nearly eighteen years before. By the time her husband and she had gotten the news, it had been too late even to call the Prayer Lady. Suddenly, Okusan knew what she had to do. She gathered up her husband's things and started down the hall. Though he called to her, she didn't stop as she passed the entrance to the living room, but went straight to the kitchen and picked up the phone.

"It's about time," Sensei said when his wife reappeared a few minutes later.

"The soup was burning," she explained. "Are you sure you wouldn't care for some?"

Outside, the last tour bus rattled in from the resort across the bay. The doors hissed open, spilling out a stream of tourist voices that flowed away across the parking lot, in the direction of the festivities. Sensei said, "That would be Tanji in his papa's truck, bringing our boy home to us." Tanji had been a friend of Kitaro's. They had both died in the same fishing accident.

Okusan sighed. Old man, even if you live through this, you'll drive everyone away with your crazy talk, and that'll be the same as being dead, she thought. Across the temple yard, the drums began to beat and the bamboo flute sang out an invitation to the dance. *"Arya sa, korya sa,"* the singers chanted. Inside their darkened living room, Okusan wrapped her husband in funeral silk the color of old photographs.

The dream seemed painted there, behind his eyes. Always the same dream. The sea. The boy. Brown limbs flashing against the white sand. Hands reaching up to release the kite into the bright sky, like a prayer. "Oh, look!" Sensei could hear his son cry out, as the luminous shape soared overhead. Kitaro had been the last of his children, the only one not buried in the sandy earth of the temple graveyard.

Sensei had built the temple with the labor of his hands—hauling stone, mixing mortar, and sawing wood until he'd thought he'd never stand straight again. But as he'd raised walls and hammered roof beams, his body had grown taut and brown. His faith had become strong. And long after he'd finished with the mortising, shingling, and painting, the structure had continued to shape what he'd become. Through its doors, he'd entered the life of the community. He'd presided over weddings, births, and funerals, and mourned his stillborn children there. In the dream he'd dreamed within those walls, even the loss of Kitaro had been made bearable by the embrace of ritual which had bound the living and the dead, and made time whole.

Now, as the old man went back into that dream, Okusan finished dressing him. "There," she said, propping him into a sitting position, with a book of sutras on his lap and his legs stretched out. "How handsome you look." The reflection from the reading lamp behind him glowed upon his smooth, bald scalp.

Okusan went to the window and peeked through the blinds. "Is Kitaro out there?" her husband called. "What do you see?"

The dancers were circling the musicians' tower, the sleeves of their summer kimonos fluttering in the night breeze. Before she could answer, the sound of footsteps crossed the porch and someone knocked at the screen door. "Good evening," a cheerful voice called out. The door pulled open, and the Prayer Lady was standing on the stoop, with the light from the festival lanterns burning in the darkness behind her. She was dressed in a plain cotton shift, printed with tiny star-shaped flowers, and her white hair was neatly pulled back into a bun. She carried a bag of strawberry guavas and a bunch of golden chrysanthemums in her hands. "Hello, Okusan," she said, passing the flowers and fruit along, but her attention was focused on the old priest installed in his funeral clothes upon the couch. When she spoke, her voice was solemn. "If I'd known it was this serious, I'd have come sooner to pay my respects."

Sensei glared at his wife.

"I'll go and get some tea," Okusan said, and hastily removed herself.

The Prayer Lady hadn't taken her eyes off the old priest. She nodded approvingly. "I see you've dropped a couple of pounds. A person who wasn't informed of your condition might even say that it suited you."

"Um," Sensei grunted.

"In fact, if I didn't know Okusan better, I'd be tempted to think she was prone to exaggeration. You're holding up remarkably well," the Prayer Lady said.

"Um," Sensei grunted again.

"But I see it depresses you to talk about it." She went from window to window, pulling up the blinds. The night filled the room. The music soared. "Ah, but it's splendid out, isn't it? Smell that sea air."

"I heard you were in a retirement home," Sensei hissed.

The Prayer Lady settled into an easy chair facing him. "The things people say. You wouldn't believe what I've heard about *you*—that you've finally gone and lost your grip, and that it was the best thing that happened when the new priest took over."

Sensei glowered. "A point of view that you could appreciate, I'm sure."

The Prayer Lady shrugged. "I've never claimed to know what's best." She leaned toward him confidentially. "I do know, however, that it takes a lot more than missing a few dinners to starve yourself to death."

The old priest had pushed aside his cushions and was sitting upright. His face was flushed. "Oi!" he yelled for his wife.

"In fact," the Prayer Lady continued, "didn't Gandhi once go on a hunger strike that lasted an entire year? But I expect he wasn't surrounded by all this temptation." She gestured toward the coffee table between them, piled high with baskets of fruit, plates of sweets, and other get-well offerings brought by members of the congregation.

"Omae!" Sensei yelled louder.

"This is quite a spread," she observed, helping herself to a sliver of Haru Hanabusa's tofu pie. She opened a greeting card, attached to a dish of pink and white rice cakes, and read aloud, "With best wishes for your speedy recovery, from Emiko McAllister."

"Get out!" Sensei was shaking with rage. "Get out, get out!"

The Prayer Lady remained unruffled. She wiped the crumbs from her mouth, then said, "I'd keep that pie refrigerated if I were you." She picked up her handbag and went to the door. Just as she was about to let herself out, she turned and faced the priest again. "Oh, Sensei," she said; it was the first time she had used the term of respect. "Neither of us could have held back what is happening."

He looked up, surprised by the gentleness in her voice, but she was already gone.

"What's all the fuss?" Okusan asked, carrying in a lacquered tray laden with tea things.

The old man didn't answer. After sitting still for a very long time, he laboriously swung one leg and then the other onto the floor and got to his feet. He waved aside his wife's offer of help and unsteadily made his way across the living room and out the front door. The night was alive with stars and the sound and smell of the sea. Okusan watched from the porch steps as he slowly crossed the temple yard and followed the procession of lights down to the bay. *"Arya sa, koryaa sa,"* the singers chanted. "It has been so. It shall always be." The lanterns glowed on the dark water, as the words faded, and there was only the hiss of the waves on the sand.

Newborn Thrown in Trash and Dies

JOHN EDGAR WIDEMAN

They say you see your whole life pass in review the instant before you die. How would *they* know. If you die after the instant replay, you aren't around to tell anybody anything. So much for they and what they say. So much for the wish to be a movie star for once in your life, because I think that's what people are hoping, what people are pretending when they say you see your life that way at the end. Death doesn't turn your life into a five-star production. The end is the end. And what you know at the end goes down the tube with you. I can speak to you now only because I haven't reached bottom yet. I'm on my way, faster than I want to be traveling and my journey won't take long, but I'm just beginning the countdown to zero. Zero's where I started also, so I know a little bit about zero. Know what they say isn't necessarily so. In fact the opposite's true. You begin and right in the eye of that instant storm your life plays itself out for you in advance. That's the theater of your fate, there's where you're granted a preview, the coming attractions of everything that must happen to you. Your life rolled into a ball so dense, so super heavy it would drag the universe down to hell if this tiny, tiny lump of whatever didn't dissipate as quickly as it formed. Quicker. The weight of it is what you recall some infinitesimal fraction of when you stumble and crawl through your worst days on earth.

Knowledge of what's coming gone as quickly as it flashes forth.

Quicker. Faster. Gone before it gets here, so to speak. Any other way and nobody would stick around to play out the cards they're dealt. No future in it. You begin forgetting before the zero's entirely wiped off the clock face, before the next digit materializes. What they say is assbackwards, a saying by the way, assbackwards itself. Whether or not you're treated to a summary at the end, you get the whole thing handed to you, neatly packaged as you begin. Then you forget it. Or try to forget. Live your life as if it hasn't happened before, as if the tape has not been pre-punched full of holes, the die cast.

I remember because I won't receive much of a life. A measure of justice in the world, after all. I receive a compensatory bonus. Since the time between my wake-up call and curfew is so cruelly brief, the speeded-up preview of what will come to pass, my life, my portion, my destiny, my, my, my career, slowed down just enough to let me peek. Not slow enough for me to steal much, but I know some of what it contains, its finality, the groaning, fatal weight of it around my neck.

Call it a trade-off. A stand-off. Intensity for duration. I won't get much and this devastating flash isn't much either, but I get it. Zingo.

But the future remains mysterious. Room in the flash for my life and everybody else's, too much for everyone alive now or who has ever been alive to understand, even if we all put our heads together and became one gigantic brain, a brain lots smarter than the sum of each of our smarts, an intelligence as great as the one that guides ants, whales, or birds, because they're smarter, they figure things out not one by one, each individual locked in the cell of its head, its mortality, but collectively, doing what the group needs to do to survive, relate to the planet. If we were smarter even than birds and bees, we'd still have only a clue about what's inside the first flash of being. I know it happened and that I receive help from it. Scattered help. Sometimes I catch on. Sometimes I don't. But stuff from it's being pumped out always. I know things I have no business knowing. Things I haven't been around long enough to learn myself. For instance, many languages. A vast palette of feelings. The names of unseen things. Nostalgia for a darkness I've never experienced, a darkness another sense I can't account for assures me I will enter again. Large matters. Small ones. Naked as I am I'm dressed so to speak for my trip. Down these ten swift flights to oblivion.

Floor Ten: Nothing under the sun, they say, is new. This time they're right. They never stop talking, so percentages guarantee they'll be correct sometimes. Especially since they speak out of both sides of their mouths at once: *Birds of a feather flock together. Opposites attract.* Like the billion billion monkeys at typewriters who sooner or later will bang out this story I think is uniquely mine. Somebody else, a Russian, I believe, with a long, strange-sounding name, has already written about his life speeding past as he topples slow motion from a window high up in a tall apartment building. But it was in another country. And alas, the Russian's dead.

Floor Nine: In this building they shoot craps. One of many forms of gambling proliferating here. Very little new wealth enters this cluster of buildings that are like high-rise covered wagons circled against the urban night, so what's here is cycled and recycled by games of chance, by murder and other violent forms of exchange. Kids do it. Adults. Birds and bees. The law here is the same one ruling the jungle, they say. They say this is a jungle of the urban asphalt concrete variety. Since I've never been to Africa or the Amazon I can't agree or disagree. But you know what I think about what they say.

Seven come eleven. Snake eyes. Boxcars. Fever in the funkhouse searching for a five. Talk to me, baby. Talk. Talk. Please. Please. Please.

They cry and sing and curse and pray all night long over these games. On one knee they chant magic formulas to summon luck. They forget luck is rigged. Some of the men carry a game called three-card monte downtown. They cheat tourists who are stupid enough to trust in luck. Showmen with quick hands shuffling cards to a blur, fast feet carrying them away from busy intersections when cops come to break up their scam or hit on them for a cut. Flimflam artists, con men who daily use luck as bait and hook, down on their knees in a circle of other men who also should know better, trying to sweet-talk luck into their beds. Luck is the card you wish for, the card somebody else holds. You learn luck by its absence. Luck is what separates you from what you want. Luck is always turning its back and you lose.

Like other potions and powders they sell and consume here, luck creates dependency. In their rooms people sit and wait for a hit. A yearning unto death for more, more, more till the little life they've been allotted dies in a basket on the doorstep where they abandoned it.

The Floor of Facts: Seventeen stories in this building. The address is 2950 West 23rd Street. My mother is nineteen years old. The trash chute down which I was dropped is forty-five feet from the door of the apartment my mother was visiting. I was born and will die Monday, August 12, 1991. The small door in the yellow cinder-block wall is maroon. I won't know till the last second why my mother pushes it open. In 1990 nine discarded babies were discovered in New York City's garbage. As of August this year seven have been found. 911 is the number to call if you find a baby in the trash. Ernesto Mendez, 44, a Housing Authority caretaker, will notice my head, shoulders, and curly hair in a black plastic bag he slashes open near the square entrance of the trash compactor on the ground floor of this brown-brick public housing project called the Gerald J. Carey Gardens. Gardens are green places where seeds are planted, tended, nurtured. The headline above my story reads "Newborn Thrown in Trash and Dies." The headline will remind some readers of a similar story with a happy ending that appeared in March. A baby rescued and surviving after she was dropped down a trash chute by her twelve-year-old mother. The reporter, a Mr. George James, who recorded many of the above facts, introduced my unhappy story in the "Metropolitan" section of the *New York Times* on Wednesday, August 14, with this paragraph: "A young Brooklyn woman gave birth on Monday afternoon in a stairwell in a Coney Island housing project and then dropped the infant down a trash chute into a compactor 10 stories below, the police said yesterday." And that's about it. What's fit to print. My tale in a nutshell followed by a relation of facts obtained by interview and reading official documents. Trouble is I could not be reached for comment. No one's fault. Certainly no negligence on the reporter's part. He gave me sufficient notoriety. Many readers must have shaken their heads in dismay or sighed or blurted Jesus Christ, did you see this, handing the "Metro" section across the breakfast table or passing it to somebody at work. As grateful as I am to have my story made public you should be able to understand why I feel cheated, why the newspaper account is not enough, why I want my voice to be part of the record. The awful silence is not truly broken until we speak for ourselves. One chance to speak was snatched away. Then I didn't cry out as I plunged through the darkness. I didn't know any better. Too busy thinking to myself, *This is how it is, this is how it is, how it is* . . . accustoming myself to what it seemed life brings, what life is. Spinning, tumbling, a breathless rush, terror, exhilaration, and wonder, wondering is this it, am I doing it right? I didn't know any better. The floors, the other lives packed into this building were going on their merry way as I flew past them in the darkness of my tunnel. No one waved. No one warned me. Said hello or goodbye. And of course I was too busy flailing, trying to catch my breath, trying to stop shivering in the sudden, icy air, welcoming almost the thick, pungent draft rushing up at me as if another pair of thighs were opening below to replace the ones from which I'd been ripped.

In the quiet dark of my passage I did not cry out. Now I will not be still.

A Floor of Questions. Why?

A Floor of Opinions. I believe the floor of fact should have been the ground floor, the foundation, the solid start, the place where all else is firmly rooted. I believe there should be room on the floor of fact for what I believe, for this opinion and others I could not venture before arriving here. I believe some facts are unnecessary and that unnecessary borders on untrue. I believe facts sometimes speak for themselves but never speak for us. They are never anyone's voice and voices are what we must learn to listen to if we wish ever to be heard. I believe my mother did not hate me. I believe somewhere I have a father, who if he is reading this and listening carefully will recognize me as his daughter and be ashamed, heart-broken. I must believe these things. What else do I have? Who has made my acquaintance or noticed or cared for or forgotten me? How could anyone be aware of what hurtles by faster than light, blackly, in a dark space beyond the walls of the rooms they live in, beyond the doors they lock, shades they draw when they have rooms and the rooms have windows and the windows have shades and the people believe they possess something worth concealing?

In my opinion my death will serve no purpose. The streetlamps will pop on. Someone will be run over by an expensive car in a narrow street and the driver will hear a bump but consider it of no consequence. Junkies will leak out the side doors of this gigantic mound, nodding, buzzing, greeting their kind with hippy-dip vocalizations full of despair and irony and stylized to embrace the very best that's being sung, played, and said around them. A young woman will open a dresser drawer and wonder whose baby that is sleeping peaceful on a bed of dish towels, T-shirts, a man's ribbed sweat socks. She will feel something slither through the mud of her belly and splash into the sluggish river that meanders through her. She hasn't eaten for days, so that isn't it. Was it a deadly disease? Or worse, some new life she must account for? She opens and shuts the baby's drawer, pushes and pulls, opens and shuts.

I believe all floors are not equally interesting. Less reason to notice some than others. Equality would become boring, predictable. Though we may slight some and rattle on about others, that does not change the fact that each floor exists and the life on it is real, whether we pause to notice or not. As I gather speed and weight during my plunge, each floor adds its share. When I hit bottom I will bear witness to the truth of each one.

Floor of Wishes. I will miss Christmas. They say no one likes being born on Christmas. You lose your birthday, they say. A celebration already on December 25 and nice things happen to everyone on that day anyway, you give and receive presents, people greet you smiling and wish you peace and goodwill. The world is decorated. Colored bulbs draped twinkling in windows and trees, doorways hung with wild berries beneath which you may kiss a handsome stranger. Music everywhere. Even wars truced for twenty-four hours and troops served home-cooked meals, almost. Instead of at least two special days a year, if your birthday falls on Christmas, you lose one. Since my portion's less than a day, less than those insects called ephemera receive, born one morning, dead the next, and I can't squeeze a complete life cycle as they do into the time allotted, I wish today were Christmas. Once would be enough. If it's as special as they say. And in some matters we yearn to trust them. Need to trust something, someone, so we listen, wish what they say were true. The holiday of Christmas seems to be the best time to be on earth, to be a child and awaken with your eyes full of dreams and expectations and believe for a while at least that all good things are possible—peace, goodwill, love, merriment, the raven-maned rocking horse you want to ride forever. No conflict of interest for me. I wouldn't lose a birthday to Christmas. Rather than this smoggy heat I wish I could see snow. The city, this building snug under a blanket of fresh snow. No footprints of men running, men on their knees, men bleeding. No women forced out into halls and streets, away from their children. I wish this city, this tower were stranded in a gentle snowstorm and Christmas would happen day after day and the bright fires in every hearth never go out, and the carols ring true chorus after chorus, and the gifts given and received precipitate endless joys. The world trapped in Christmas for a day dancing on forever. I wish I could transform the ten flights of my falling into those twelve days in the Christmas song. *On the first day of Christmas my true love said to me . . .* angels, a partridge in a pear tree, ten maids a-milking, five gold rings, two turtledoves. I wish those would be the sights greeting me instead of darkness, the icy winter heart of this August afternoon I have been pitched without a kiss through a maroon door.

Floor of Power. El Presidente inhabits this floor. Some say he owns the whole building. He believes he owns it, collects rent, treats the building and its occupants with contempt. He is a bold-faced man. Cheeks slotted nose to chin like a puppet's. Cold, slitty eyes. Chicken lips. This floor is entirely white. A floury, cracked white some say used to gleam. El Presidente is white also. Except for the pink dome of his forehead. Once, long ago, his flesh was pink head to toe. Then he painted himself white to match the white floor of power. Paint ran out just after the brushstroke that permanently sealed the closed bulbs of his eyes. Since El Presidente is cheap and mean he refused to order more paint. Since El Presidente is vain and arrogant he pretended to look at his unfinished self in the mirror and proclaimed he liked what he saw, the coat of cakey white, the raw, pink dome pulsing like a bruise.

El Presidente often performs on TV. We can watch him jog, golf, fish, travel, lie, preen, mutilate the language. But these activities are not his job; his job is keeping things in the building as they are, squatting on the floor of power like a broken generator or broken furnace or broken heart, occupying the space where one that works should be.

Floor of Regrets. One thing bothers me a lot. I regret not knowing what is on the floors above the one where I began my fall. I hope it's better up there. Real gardens perhaps or even a kind of heaven for the occupants lucky enough to live above the floors I've seen. Would one of you please mount the stairs, climb slowly up from floor ten, examine carefully, one soft, warm night, the topmost floors, and sing me a lullaby of what I missed.

Floor of Love. I'm supposed to be sleeping. I could be sleeping. Early morning and my eyes don't want to open and legs don't want to push me out of bed yet. Two rooms away I can hear Mom in the kitchen. She's fixing breakfast. Daddy first, then I will slump into the kitchen Mom has made bright and smelling good already this morning. Her perkiness, the sizzling bacon, water boiling, wheat bread popping up like jack-in-the-box from the shiny toaster, the Rice Krispies crackling, fried eggs hissing, the FM's sophisticated patter and mincing string trios would wake the dead. And it does. Me and Daddy slide into our places. Hi, Mom. Good morning, Dearheart. The day begins. Smells wonderful. I awaken now to his hand under the covers with me, rubbing the baby fat of my tummy where he's shoved my nightgown up past my panties. He says I shouldn't wear them. Says it ain't healthy to sleep in your drawers. Says no wonder you get those rashes. He rubs and pinches. Little nips. Then the flat of his big hand under the elastic waistband wedges my underwear down. I raise my hips a little bit to help. No reason not to. The whole thing be over with sooner. Don't do no good to try and stop him or slow him down. He said my mama knows. He said go on, fool, and tell her, she'll smack you for talking nasty. He was right. She beat me in the kitchen. Then took me into their room and he stripped me butt naked and beat me again while she watched. So I kinda hump up, wiggle, and my underwear's down below my knees, his hand's on its way back up to where I don't even understand how to grow hairs yet.

The Floor That Stands for All the Other Floors Missed or Still to Come. My stepbrother Tommy was playing in the schoolyard and they shot him dead. Bang. Bang. Gang banging and poor Tommy caught a cap in his chest. People been in and out the apartment all day. Sorry. Sorry. Everybody's so sorry. Some brought cakes, pies, macaroni casseroles, lunch meat, liquor. Two Ebony Cobras laid a joint on Tommy's older brother, who hadn't risen from the kitchen chair he's straddling, head down, nodding, till his boys bop through the door. They know who hit Tommy. They know tomorrow what they must do. Today one of those everybody in the family and friends in dark clothes funeral days, the mothers, sisters, aunts, grandmothers weepy, the men motherfucking everybody from God on down. You can't see me among the mourners. My time is different from this time. You can't understand my time. Or name it. Or share it. Tommy is beginning to remember me. To join me where I am falling unseen through your veins and arteries down down to where the heart stops, the square opening through which trash passes to the compactor.

The Golden Darters

ELIZABETH WINTHROP

I was twelve years old when my father started tying flies. It was an odd habit for a man who had just undergone a serious operation on his upper back, but, as he remarked to my mother one night, at least it gave him a world over which he had some control.

The family grew used to seeing him hunched down close to his tying vise, hackle pliers in one hand, thread bobbin in the other. We began to bandy about strange phrases—foxy quills, bodkins, peacock hurl. Father's corner of the living room was off limits to the maid with the voracious and destructive vacuum cleaner. Who knew what precious bit of calf's tail or rabbit fur would be sucked away never to be seen again.

Because of my father's illness, we had gone up to our summer cottage on the lake in New Hampshire a month early. None of my gang of friends ever came till the end of July, so in the beginning of that summer I hung around home watching my father as he fussed with the flies. I was the only child he allowed to stand near him while he worked. "Your brothers bounce," he muttered one day as he clamped the vise onto the curve of a model-perfect hook. "You can stay and watch if you don't bounce."

So I took great care not to bounce or lean or even breathe too noisily on him while he performed his delicate maneuvers, holding back hackle with one hand as he pulled off the final flourish of a whip finish with the other. I had never been so close to my father for so long before, and while he studied his tiny creations, I studied him. I stared at the large pores of his skin, the sleek black hair brushed straight back from the soft dip of his temples, the jaw muscles tightening and slackening. Something in my father seemed always to be ticking. He did not take well to sickness and enforced confinement.

When he leaned over his work, his shirt collar slipped down to reveal the recent scar, a jagged trail of disrupted tissue. The tender pink skin gradually paled and then toughened during those weeks when he took his prescribed afternoon nap, lying on his stomach on our little patch of front lawn. Our house was one of the closest to the lake and it seemed to embarrass my mother to have him stretch himself out on the grass for all the swimmers and boaters to see.

"At least sleep on the porch," she would say. "That's why we set the hammock up there."

"Why shouldn't a man sleep on his own front lawn if he so chooses?" he would reply. "I have to mow the bloody thing. I might as well put it to some use."

And my mother would shrug and give up.

At the table when he was absorbed, he lost all sense of anything but the magnified insect under the light. Often when he pushed his chair back and announced the completion of his latest project to the family, there would be a bit of down or a tuft of dubbing stuck to the edge of his lip. I did not tell him about it but stared, fascinated, wondering how long it would take to blow away. Sometimes it never did and I imagine he discovered the fluff in the bathroom mirror when he went upstairs to bed. Or maybe my mother plucked it off with one of those proprietary gestures of hers that irritated my brothers so much.

In the beginning, Father wasn't very good at the fly-tying. He was a large, thick-boned man with sweeping gestures, a robust laugh, and a sudden terrifying temper. If he had not loved fishing so much, I doubt he would have persevered with the fussy business of the flies. After all, the job required tools normally associated with woman's work. Thread and bobbins, soft slippery feathers, a magnifying glass, and an instruction manual that read like a cookbook. It said things like, ''Cut off a bunch of yellowtail. Hold the tip end with the left hand and stroke out the short hairs.''

But Father must have had a goal in mind. You tie flies because one day, in the not too distant future, you will attach them to a tippet, wade into a stream, and lure a rainbow trout out of his quiet pool.

There was something endearing, almost childish, about his stubborn nightly ritual at the corner table. His head bent under the standing lamp, his fingers trembling slightly, he would whisper encouragement to himself, talk his way through some particularly delicate operation. Once or twice I caught my mother gazing silently across my brothers' heads at him. When our eyes met, she would turn away and busy herself in the kitchen.

Finally, one night, after weeks of allowing me to watch, he told me to take his seat. ''Why, Father?''

''Because it's time for you to try one.''

''That's all right. I like to watch.''

''Nonsense, Emily. You'll do just fine.''

He had stood up. The chair was waiting. Across the room, my mother put down her knitting. Even the boys, embroiled in a noisy game of double solitaire, stopped their wrangling for a moment. They were all waiting to see what I would do. It was my fear of failing him that made me hesitate. I knew that my father put his trust in results, not in the learning process.

''Sit down, Emily.''

I obeyed, my heart pounding. I was a cautious, secretive child, and I could not bear to have people watch me doing things. My piano lesson was the hardest hour in the week. The teacher would sit with a resigned look on her face while my fingers groped across the keys, muddling through a sonata that I had played perfectly just an hour before. The difference was that then nobody had been watching.

''—so we'll start you off with a big hook.'' He had been talking for some time. How much had I missed already?

''Ready?'' he asked.

I nodded.

''All right then, clamp this hook into the vise. You'll be making the golden darter, a streamer. A big flashy fly, the kind that imitates a small fish as it moves underwater.''

Across the room, my brothers had returned to their game but their voices were subdued. I imagined they wanted to hear what was happening to me. My mother had left the room.

''Tilt the magnifying glass so you have a good view of the hook. Right. Now tie on with the bobbin thread.''

It took me three tries to line the thread up properly on the hook, each silken line nesting next to its neighbor. ''We're going to do it right, Emily, no matter how long it takes.''

''It's hard,'' I said quietly.

Slowly I grew used to the tiny tools, to the oddly enlarged view of my fingers through the magnifying glass. They looked as if they didn't belong to me anymore. The feeling in their tips was too small for their large, clumsy movements. Despite my father's repeated warnings, I nicked the floss once against the barbed hook. Luckily it did not give way.

''It's Emily's bedtime,'' my mother called from the kitchen.

''Hush, she's tying in the throat. Don't bother us now.''

I could feel his breath on my neck. The mallard barbules were stubborn, curling into the hook in the wrong direction. Behind me, I sensed my father's fingers twisting in imitation of my own.

''You've almost got it,'' he whispered, his lips barely moving. ''That's right. Keep the thread slack until you're all the way around.''

I must have tightened it too quickly. I lost control of the feathers in my left hand, the clumsier one. First the gold Mylar came unwound and then the yellow floss.

''Damn it all, now look what you've done,'' he roared, and for a second I wondered whether he was talking to me. He sounded as if he were talking to a grown-up. He sounded the way he had just the night before when an antique teacup had slipped through my mother's soapy fingers and shattered against the hard surface of the sink. I sat back slowly, resting my aching spine against the chair for the first time since we'd begun.

"Leave it for now, Gerald," my mother said tentatively from the kitchen. Out of the corner of my eye, I could see her sponging the kitchen counter with small, defiant sweeps of her hand. "She can try again tomorrow."

"What happened?" called a brother. They both started across the room toward us but stopped at a look from my father.

"We'll start again," he said, his voice once more under control. "Best way to learn. Get back on the horse."

With a flick of his hand, he loosened the vise, removed my hook, and threw it into the wastepaper basket.

"From the beginning?" I whispered.

"Of course," he replied. "There's no way to rescue a mess like that."

My mess had taken almost an hour to create.

"Gerald," my mother said again. "Don't you think—"

"How can we possibly work with all these interruptions?" he thundered. I flinched as if he had hit me. "Go on upstairs, all of you. Emily and I will be up when we're done. Go on, for God's sake. Stop staring at us."

At a signal from my mother, the boys backed slowly away and crept up to their room. She followed them. I felt all alone, as trapped under my father's piercing gaze as the hook in the grip of its vise.

We started again. This time my fingers were trembling so much that I ruined three badger hackle feathers, stripping off the useless webbing at the tip. My father did not lose his temper again. His voice dropped to an even, controlled monotone that scared me more than his shouting. After an hour of painstaking labor, we reached the same point with the stubborn mallard feathers curling into the hook. Once, twice, I repinched them under the throat, but each time they slipped away from me. Without a word, my father stood up and leaned over me. With his cheek pressed against my hair, he reached both hands around and took my fingers in his. I longed to surrender the tools to him and slide away off the chair, but we were so close to the end. He captured the curling stem with the thread and trapped it in place with three quick wraps.

"Take your hands away carefully," he said. "I'll do the whip finish. We don't want to risk losing it now."

I did as I was told, sat motionless with his arms around me, my head tilted slightly to the side so he could have the clear view through the magnifying glass. He cemented the head, wiped the excess glue from the eye with a waste feather, and hung my golden darter on the tackle-box handle to dry. When at last he pulled away, I breathlessly slid my body back against the chair. I was still conscious of the havoc my clumsy hands or an unexpected sneeze could wreak on the table, which was cluttered with feathers and bits of fur.

"Now, that's the fly you tied, Emily. Isn't it beautiful?"

I nodded. "Yes, Father."

"Tomorrow, we'll do another one. An olive grouse. Smaller hook but much less complicated body. Look. I'll show you in the book."

As I waited to be released from the chair, I didn't think he meant it. He was just trying to apologize for having lost his temper, I told myself, just trying to pretend that our time together had been wonderful. But the next morning when I came down, late for breakfast, he was waiting for me with the materials for the olive grouse already assembled. He was ready to start in again, to take charge of my clumsy fingers with his voice and talk them through the steps.

That first time was the worst, but I never felt comfortable at the fly-tying table with Father's breath tickling the hair on my neck. I completed the olive grouse, another golden darter to match the first, two muddler minnows, and some others. I don't remember all the names anymore.

Once I hid upstairs, pretending to be immersed in my summer reading books, but he came looking for me.

"Emily," he called. "Come on down. Today we'll start the lead-winged coachman. I've got everything set up for you."

I lay very still and did not answer.

''Gerald,'' I heard my mother say. ''Leave the child alone. You're driving her crazy with those flies.''

''Nonsense,'' he said, and started up the dark, wooden stairs, one heavy step at a time.

I put my book down and rolled slowly off the bed so that by the time he reached the door of my room, I was on my feet, ready to be led back downstairs to the table.

Although we never spoke about it, my mother became oddly insistent that I join her on trips to the library or the general store.

''Are you going out again, Emily?'' my father would call after me. ''I was hoping we'd get some work done on this minnow.''

''I'll be back soon, Father,'' I'd say. ''I promise.''

''Be sure you do,'' he said.

And for a while I did.

Then at the end of July, my old crowd of friends from across the lake began to gather and I slipped away to join them early in the morning before my father got up.

The girls were a gang. When we were all younger, we'd held bicycle relay races on the ring road and played down at the lakeside together under the watchful eyes of our mothers. Every July, we threw ourselves joyfully back into each other's lives. That summer we talked about boys and smoked illicit cigarettes in Randy Kidd's basement and held leg-shaving parties in her bedroom behind a safely locked door. Randy was the ringleader. She was the one who suggested we pierce our ears.

''My parents would die,'' I said. ''They told me I'm not allowed to pierce my ears until I'm seventeen.''

''Your hair's so long, they won't even notice,'' Randy said. ''My sister will do it for us. She pierces all her friends' ears at college.''

In the end, only one girl pulled out. The rest of us sat in a row with the obligatory ice cubes held to our ears waiting for the painful stab of the sterilized needle.

Randy was right. At first my parents didn't notice. Even when my ears became infected, I didn't tell them. All alone in my room, I went through the painful procedure of twisting the gold studs and swabbing the recent wounds with alcohol. Then on the night of the club dance, when I had changed my clothes three times and played with my hair in front of the mirror for hours, I came across the small plastic box with dividers in my top bureau drawer. My father had given it to me so that I could keep my flies in separate compartments, untangled from one another. I poked my finger in and slid one of the golden darters up along its plastic wall. When I held it up, the Mylar thread sparkled in the light like a jewel. I took out the other darter, hammered down the barbs of the two hooks, and slipped them into the raw holes in my earlobes.

Someone's mother drove us all to the dance, and Randy and I pushed through the side door into the ladies' room. I put my hair up in a ponytail so the feathered flies could twist and dangle above my shoulders. I liked the way they made me look—free and different and dangerous even. And they made Randy notice.

"I've never seen earrings like that," Randy said. "Where did you get them?"

"I made them with my father. They're flies. You know, for fishing."

"They're great. Can you make me some?"

I hesitated. "I have some others at home I can give you," I said at last. "They're in a box in my bureau."

"Can you give them to me tomorrow?" she asked.

"Sure," I said with a smile. Randy had never noticed anything I'd worn before. I went out to the dance floor, swinging my ponytail in time to the music.

My mother noticed the earrings as soon as I got home.

"What has gotten into you, Emily? You know you were forbidden to pierce your ears until you were in college. This is appalling."

I didn't answer. My father was sitting in his chair behind the fly-tying table. His back was better by that time, but he still spent most of his waking hours in that chair. It was as if he didn't like to be too far away from his flies, as if something might blow away if he weren't keeping watch.

I saw him look up when my mother started in with me. His hands drifted ever so slowly down to the surface of the table as I came across the room toward him. I leaned over so that he could see my earrings better in the light.

"Everybody loved them, Father. Randy says she wants a pair, too. I'm going to give her the muddler minnows."

"I can't believe you did this, Emily," my mother said in a loud, nervous voice. "It makes you look so cheap."

"They don't make me look cheap, do they, Father?" I swung my head so he could see how they bounced, and my hip accidentally brushed the table. A bit of rabbit fur floated up from its pile and hung in the air for a moment before it settled down on top of the foxy quills.

"For God's sake, Gerald, speak to her," my mother said from her corner.

He stared at me for a long moment as if he didn't know who I was anymore, as if I were a trusted associate who had committed some treacherous and unspeakable act. "That is not the purpose for which the flies were intended," he said.

"Oh, I know that," I said quickly. "But they look good this way, don't they?"

He stood up and considered me in silence for a long time across the top of the table lamp.

"No, they don't," he finally said. "They're hanging upside down."

Then he turned off the light and I couldn't see his face anymore.

Mortals

TOBIAS WOLFF

The metro editor called my name across the newsroom and beckoned to me. When I got to his office he was at his desk, trying to look executive and calm. A man and a woman were there with him, the man nervous on his feet, the woman erect in a chair, sharp-faced and watchful, holding the straps of her bag with both hands. Her suit was the same bluish gray as her hair. There was something soldierly about her. The man was short, doughy, rounded off. The burst vessels in his cheeks gave him a merry look until he smiled.

"I didn't want to make a scene," he said. "We just thought you should know." He looked at his wife.

"You bet I should know," the metro editor said. "This is Mr. Givens," he said to me, "Mr. Francis Givens. Name ring a bell?"

"Vaguely."

"I'll give you a hint. He's not dead."

"Okay," I said. "I've got it."

"Another hint," the metro editor said, as if he hadn't heard me. Then he read aloud, from that morning's paper, the obituary I had written announcing Mr. Givens's death. I'd written a whole slew of obits the day before, over twenty of them, and I didn't remember much of it, but I did remember the part about him working for the IRS for thirty years. I'd had problems with the IRS, so that stuck in my mind. Even in the abstract, and supposedly dead, the guy had managed to rub me the wrong way.

As Givens listened to his obituary he looked from one to the other of us. He wasn't as short as I'd first thought; it was an impression he created by hunching his shoulders and thrusting his neck forward like a turtle. His eyes were soft, restless. He used them like a peasant, in swift measuring glances with his face averted.

He laughed when the metro editor was through. "Well, it's accurate," he said. "I'll give you that."

"Except for one thing," the woman said. She was staring at me.

"I owe you an apology," I told Givens. "Somebody really pulled the wool over my eyes."

"Apology accepted!" Givens said. He rubbed his hands together as if we'd all just signed something. "But I have to admit, it took us aback. What was it Mark Twain said? 'The reports of my death—' "

"So what happened?" the metro editor said to me.

"I wish I knew."

"That's not good enough," the woman said.

"Dolly's pretty upset," Givens said. "That's why we came in."

"You had every right to come in," the metro editor said. "Who called in the notice?" he asked me.

"To tell the truth, I don't remember. I suppose it was somebody from the funeral home."

"You call them back?"

"I don't believe I did, no."

"Check with the family?"

"He most certainly did not," Mrs. Givens said.

"No," I said.

The metro editor took his feet off the desk and looked thoughtfully at the place where they had been. "What do we do before we run an obituary?"

"Check back with the funeral home and the family."

"But you didn't do that."

"No, sir. I guess I didn't."

"Why not?"

I made a helpless gesture with my hands and tried to appear properly stricken, but I had no answer. The truth was, I never followed those procedures. People were dying all the time. I hadn't seen the point in asking their families if they were really dead, or calling funeral parlors back to make sure the funeral parlors had just called me. All this bureaucratic stuff was beneath me, I'd decided, and rendered me absurd in its execution; it didn't seem possible that anyone could find happiness in concocting phony death notices and impersonating undertakers. Now I saw that this was foolish of me, and showed a radical failure of appreciation for the varieties of human pleasure.

But there was more to it than that. Since I was the new guy in metro, I wrote a lot of obituaries. Some days it was all I did, one obituary after another, morning to night. After four months of this duty I was full of the consciousness of death. It soured me. It puffed me up with morbid snobbery, the feeling that I knew a secret nobody else had even begun to suspect. It made me wearily philosophical about the value of faith and passion and painful striving, at a time when my life required all of these. It got me down.

I should have quit, but I didn't want to go back to the jobs I'd been working before a friend fixed me up with this one—waiting on tables, mostly, doing night security in apartment buildings, anything that would leave my days free for writing. I'd lived like this for years, and what did I have to show for it? A few stories in literary journals that nobody read, including me. I began to feel sorry for myself. I had, it seemed, given up everything for my writing—respectability, money, even love—and my writing had proven itself unworthy of the sacrifice. So when this job came up I took it. I hated it and did it badly, but I meant to keep it. Before long I'd move over to police beat. Things would get better.

I was hoping that the metro editor would take his pound of flesh and let me go. But he kept after me with questions, probably showing off for Givens and his wife, letting them see a real newshound at work. In the end I was forced to admit that I hadn't called any other families or funeral homes that day, nor, in actual fact, for a good long time.

Now that he had his answer the metro editor didn't seem to

know what to do with it. It seemed to be more than he'd bargained for. At first he just sat there. Then he said, ''Do you mean to tell me we've been running unconfirmed obituaries?''

''I'm afraid so,'' I said. And as I made this admission I felt a smile on my lips, already there before I could fight it back or dissemble it. It was the rictus of panic, the same smile I'd given my mother when she told me my father had died.

But of course the metro editor didn't know that.

He leaned forward in his chair and gave his head a little shake, the way a horse will, and said, ''Clean out your desk.'' Just like that, just like the movies. Then he blinked several times. I don't think he'd meant to fire me; he seemed surprised by his own words. But he didn't take them back.

Givens looked from one to the other of us. He was panting softly. ''Now hold on here,'' he said. ''Let's not blow this all out of proportion. This isn't something a man should lose his job over.''

''He wouldn't have,'' Mrs. Givens said, ''if he'd done it right.''

Which was a truth beyond argument.

I cleaned out my desk. As I left the building I saw Givens by the newsstand, watching the door. I didn't see his wife. He walked up to me, raised his hands, and said, ''What can I say? I'm at a loss for words.''

''Don't worry about it,'' I told him.

''I sure as heck didn't mean to get you fired. It wasn't even my idea to come in, if you want to know the truth.''

''Forget it. It was my own fault.'' I was carrying a box full of notepads and files, several books. It was heavy. I shifted it under my other arm.

''Look,'' Givens said, ''how about I treat you to lunch? What do you say? It's the least I can do.''

I looked up and down the street.

''Dolly's gone on home,'' he said. ''How about it?''

I didn't especially want to eat lunch with Givens, but I liked the idea of him picking up the check. That was a consideration. And I didn't feel ready to go home yet. What was I going to do there? Sure, I told him, lunch sounded fine. Givens asked me if I knew anyplace reasonable. He was a little short, he said, it being the end of the month. There was a Chinese place next to the paper, but it was always full of reporters; I didn't want to watch them try to conjure up sympathy over my situation, which they would laugh about anyway as soon as I left, not that I blamed them. I suggested Tad's Steak House over by the cable-car turnaround. You could get a six-ounce sirloin, salad, and baked potato for a buck twenty-nine. This was 1974.

"I'm not that short," Givens said. But he didn't argue, and that's where we went.

Givens picked at his food, then pushed the plate away and contemplated mine. When I asked if his steak was okay he nodded. He said he didn't have much appetite.

"So," I said, "who do you think called it in?"

His head was bent. He looked up at me from under his eyebrows. "Boy, you've got me there. It's a mystery."

"Think it could have been someone you worked with?"

"Nah." He shook a toothpick out of the dispenser. His hands were plump and pale.

"It had to be somebody who knows you. You have friends, right?"

"Sure."

"Maybe you had an argument, something like that. Somebody's mad at you."

He had his mouth covered with one hand while he worked the toothpick with the other. He said, "How do you figure that?"

"Well, it's a pretty rough piece of business, calling in a death notice on someone. Pretty threatening. I'd sure feel threatened, if it was me."

Givens inspected the toothpick, then dropped it in the ashtray. "I hadn't thought of it like that," he said. "Maybe you're right."

I could see he didn't believe it for a second—didn't understand what had happened. The words of death had been pronounced on him, and now his life would be lived in relation to those words, in failing opposition to them, until they overpowered him and became true. Someone had put a contract out on Givens, with words as the torpedoes. Or so it appeared to me. I was full of such ideas. I thought this was a detective story, and that I was the detective.

"You're sure it isn't one of your friends?" I said. "It could be a little thing. You played cards, landed some big ones, then folded early before he had a chance to recoup. I know that always pisses me off."

"I don't play cards," Givens said. He was enjoying this. He leaned back, waiting for my next move. There was an assumption of authority in his regard of me.

"How about your wife? Any problems in that department?"

"Nope. Not that I know of."

"Everything smooth as silk, huh?"

He shrugged. "Same as ever."

"How come you call her Dolly? That wasn't the name in the obit."

"No reason. I've always called her that. Everybody does."

"I don't feature her as a Dolly," I said. "She's way too serious. Ask no quarter, give no quarter."

He didn't answer. He was watching me.

"Let's say Dolly gets mad at you, really mad . . . She wants to send you a message—something outside normal channels."

"Not a chance." Givens said this without bristling. He didn't try to convince me, so I figured he was probably right.

"You're survived by a daughter, right? What's her name again?"

"Tina," he said, with some tenderness.

"That's it, Tina. How are things with Tina?"

"We've had our problems. But I can guarantee you, it wasn't her."

"Well, hell's bells," I said. "Somebody did it."

I finished my steak, watching the show outside: winos, evangelists, businessmen, whores, outpatients crying to heaven, fake hippies selling oregano to tourists in white shoes. Pure theater, even down to the smell of popcorn billowing out of Woolworth's. Richard Brautigan often came here. Tall and owlish, he stooped to his food and ate slowly, ruminating over every bite, his eyes on the street. Some funny things happened here, and some appalling things. Brautigan watched it all and never stopped eating.

I told Givens that he was sitting at the same table where Richard Brautigan sometimes sat.

"Sorry?"

"Richard Brautigan."

Givens shook his head.

"You're in a hell of a fix," I told him. "Someone's trying to kill you, and you don't know who Richard Brautigan is."

"No one's trying to kill me."

"They want you dead. It's a pretty short step from here to there."

"Nobody wants me dead. Your problem is, you think everything means something."

That was one of my problems, I couldn't deny it.

"Just out of curiosity," he said, "what did you think of it?"

"Think of what?"

"My obituary."

I told him I didn't know what he meant.

He leaned forward and started fooling with the salt and pepper shakers, tapping them together and sliding them around like partners in a square dance. "I mean, did you get any feeling for who I was? The kind of person I am?"

I shook my head.

"Nothing stood out?"

I said no. This was not quite true, but I didn't want to get going on the IRS.

"I see." He nodded. "Maybe you wouldn't mind telling me, what exactly does it take for you to remember someone?"

Were we seeing some temper? I thought so. "Look," I said, "you write obits all day, they sort of blur into each other."

''Yes, but you must remember some of them.''

''Some of them—sure.''

''Which ones?''

''Writers I like. Great baseball players. Movie stars I've been in love with.''

''Celebrities, in other words.''

''Some of them, yes. Not all.''

''You can lead a good life without being a celebrity,'' he said. ''People with big names aren't always big people.''

''That's true,'' I said, but it's sort of a little person's truth.''

''Is that so? And what does that make you?''

I didn't answer. We were definitely seeing some temper.

''If the only thing that impresses you is being big, then you must be a regular midget. At least that's the way I see it.'' He gave me a hard look and gripped the salt and pepper shakers like a tail gunner about to let off a burst.

''That's not the only thing that impresses me.''

''Oh yeah? What else, then?''

I let the question settle for a while. ''Moral distinction,'' I said.

He repeated the words. They sounded pompous.

''You know what I mean,'' I said.

''Correct me if I'm wrong,'' he said, ''but I have a feeling that's not your department, moral distinction.''

I had no argument to offer.

''And you're obviously not a celebrity.''

''Obviously.''

''So where does that leave you?'' When I didn't answer, he said, ''Think you'd remember your own obituary?''

''Maybe not.''

''No maybe about it! You wouldn't even give it a second thought.''

''Definitely not, then.''

''You wouldn't even give it a second thought. And you'd be wrong. Because you probably have other qualities that would stand out if you were looking closely. Good qualities. Everybody has something. What do you pride yourself on?''

"I'm a survivor," I said. But I didn't think that claim would carry much weight in an obituary.

Givens said, "With me it's loyalty. Loyalty is a very clear pattern in my life. You would have noticed it if you'd had your eyes open. When you read that a man has served his country in time of war, stayed married to the same woman forty-two years, worked at the same job, by God, that should tell you something. That should give you a certain picture."

He stopped to nod at his own words. "And it hasn't always been easy," he said.

I had to laugh, mostly at myself for being such a dim bulb. "It was you," I said. "You did it."

"Did what?"

"Called in the obit."

"Why would I do that?"

"You tell me."

"That would be saying I did it." Givens couldn't help smiling, proud of what a slyboots he was.

I said, "You're out of your ever-loving mind," but I didn't mean it. There was nothing in what he'd done that I couldn't make sense of, even, to some degree, admire. It was quite a stunt. Givens had dreamed up a way of going to his own funeral. He'd tried on his last suit, so to speak, seen himself rouged up and laid out, and listened to his own eulogy. And the best part was, he resurrected afterward. That was the real point, even if he didn't know it, even if he thought he was doing it to throw a scare into Dolly, put his virtues on display . . . whatever. Resurrection was what it was all about, and this tax collector had gotten himself a taste of it. It was biblical.

He'd resumed fooling with the salt and pepper shakers.

"You're a caution, Mr. Givens. You're a definite caution."

"I didn't come here to be insulted," he said. He looked up at me and quickly down again.

"Relax," I told him. "I'm not mad."

He scraped his chair back and stood up. "I've got better things to do than sit here and listen to accusations."

I followed him outside. I wasn't ready to let him go; he had to give me something first, some confirmation. ''Just admit you did it,'' I said.

He turned away and started up Powell.

''Just admit it,'' I said. ''I won't hold it against you.''

He kept walking, head stuck forward in that turtlish way, navigating the crowd. He was slippery and fast. Finally I took his arm and pulled him into a doorway. His muscles bunched under my fingers. It surprised me how strong he was. He almost jerked free but I tightened my grip and we stood there frozen in contention.

''Admit it.''

He shook his head.

''I'll kill you if I have to,'' I told him.

''Let go,'' he said.

''If I kill you, your obituary will be solid news. Then I can get my job back.''

He tried to pull away again but I held him there. His breath came faster and faster. Then he said, almost inaudibly, ''Okay.'' Just that one word.

It was the best I could get out of him. It had to be enough. I let go of his arm and he turned and ducked his head and took his place in the stream of people walking past. I started back to Tad's for my box. Just ahead of me a mime was following a young swell in a three-piece suit, catching to the life his leading man's assurance, the supercilious tilt of his chin, the way his gaze passed over the supporting cast all around him. A woman laughed out loud. The swell looked back and the mime froze. He was still holding his pose as I came by. I slipped him a quarter, hoping he'd let me pass.

Millionaires

AL YOUNG

The bells started ringing while I was sliding into a dance step that took me gliding around the floor in super slo mo, so slow I felt like I'd never catch up with Alison, my TV girlfriend. But while I was jiggling in the shadows like an instant replay, trying my best to figure out why this was happening, the chiming woke me up.

That's when I realized which edge I was on; the edge of the bed. I mean, it was a small sofa bed, really; the same one Elvira, the housekeeper, and my two aunts slept on when they stayed overnight with my grandmother. Slowly I began to focus. It was Sunday, this was Pittsburgh, and the bells were coming at me from the African Methodist Church, Mama's church, a block away; the same church that had built the senior housing complex she lived in. Thanks to a canceled flight connection, there I lay.

As my eyes opened, the first thing I noticed was Mama, sitting there in her wheelchair, staring at me. She was still holding the hundred-dollar bill I'd handed her just before we'd said good night.

''Good morning, son,'' she sang. It had been twenty-five years since my mother and her two sisters had finally convinced Mama that moving up to Pittsburgh wouldn't be the end of the world, and yet my grandmother still had that slow, singsong country lilt in her voice. It wasn't at all fast the way people talk in L.A., where I've been ever since ''Live and Let Love'' broke big, or like New York, where I got my start doing furniture and car commercials, before I started getting parts on soaps. You know how they talk in those big cities. In L.A. it's "Hey, why don't you have your machine talk to my machine and let's do sushi real soon, okay?"

Mama, she's strictly Wismer, Louisiana. And when she talks, she makes me see all those dirt roads and cotton fields and sugarcane and persimmon trees and chicken roosts and pigs and cows and barns and Saturday nights and Sunday mornings I used to be so crazy about when I'd get sent down there from Pittsburgh to spend summers with her and Papa. And from June to early September, when school started back, lasted an eternity; a couple of years, it seemed. That's how Mama spoke. Real slow. She wasn't in any hurry to do anything.

"Child," she was saying, "you must've really been tired. Did you sleep all right?"

"Must have," I said. "I'd completely forgotten where I was. I was having some pretty weird dreams too."

"I know," she said. "You were wiggling around on that little bed so much, I was scared you were gonna fall off and hurt yourself. She let her wheelchair roll back a ways. "Sylvester," she sighed, "I wish you didn't have to fly back to California so soon. Maybe that misconnection was meant to be; it did connect us back up with one another."

"Maybe so," I said.

"Son, I had so much fun sitting up last night, reminiscing and listening at you tell about the kids and y'all's lives, and learning about the television people . . ."

"For me too, Mama. It beats letters and talking on the phone, doesn't it?"

She blinked and, smiling like she used to do when I'd surprise her with a bucket of figs or blackberries I'd picked without being asked, she said, "But I do enjoy getting your little letters, even though my eyesight's done got to the place now where, to read anything, I need both my glasses *and* the biggest magnifying glass Elvira could find me. And I appreciate the money you been sending too."

"Has it come in handy, Mama?"

"Well, there really isn't all that much I need to be buying anymore. The Lord has given me just about everything I could possibly need. I might not be a money millionaire like you," she said. "But, in terms of blessings, I'm a millionaire just the same."

"Yes, Mama, only . . . well, I was thinking maybe you could use some of that money to get some things you *want.*"

She looked at me real funny when I told her that. "You wanna know the truth?" she said, then paused as if she was trying to make up her mind to say what she'd started to say or not. Finally, after smoothing and folding the hundred-dollar bill with her twisted, arthritic fingers, she wheeled in close.

"I don't think I'd ever even seen a fifty- or a hundred-dollar bill, Syl, before you started sending 'em to me. I couldn't of even told you whose picture was on one. I don't see too much of it anyway."

"Huh?" I was startled. "What do you mean, Mama?"

"I mean, your grandfather was right. He used to say, 'It's the folks that's closest in around you that do you the most dirt.' "

"Mama, what are you saying?"

"What I'm saying, Sylvester, is that Elvira—that very Elvira who was all up in your face being sweet and kind—is stealing everything from me, I swear, that isn't hot and nailed down. After I take them Ulysses S. Grants and Ben Franklins out the envelope, I can't ever find 'em again. And I'm pretty slick about where I hide 'em too."

"Aw, Mama," I said, stunned. I'd been taking great pride in sending her those surprise bank notes from time to time. "That I find hard to believe. How could somebody like Elvira, who's been knowing us since Louisiana days, pull something like that?"

"Child, I hate to say it. But I'm telling you what God loves—the truth. All I know is I see the money when it first gets here, then it disappears. Since your mother passed away, the only people that spend any time here are Elvira and your Aunt Minnie and Aunt Jo. I hate to be saying that my own flesh and blood would do me like that too. But you draw your own conclusions."

Sitting up, I felt at once the strange sort of power a fully dressed person can have over someone who hasn't yet showered or shaved. For a moment, I expected Alison or someone from the show to rush onto the set, yelling, ''All right, Syl, that's enough blocking and run-through. We got dress rehearsal right after lunch.''

Mama pointed at the TV and said, ''I still have the picture you sent. Even had it framed. And look where I keep it.''

Even though we'd talked about it the night before, almost from the very minute Elvira, her housekeeper, had let me in the apartment and led me to down the hallway to where Mama was watching ''Amen!'' on TV, I studied that old eight-by-ten glossy, a publicity shot actually, pretending to my grandmother I was seeing it for the first time.

''You look just like Papa,'' I heard her say again. ''Favor him so much I get gooseflesh sometime.'' She moved over to the photo, which she took down, picked up, and stared at before letting it rest in her lap. I could feel, almost smell the sadness spread from her and mix with all the other leftover, stacked-up smells of hot-combed hair, mothballs, Ben-Gay, steam heat, and cooking grease.

''If I had it to do all over again,'' she said, ''I wouldn't of married that worrisome old rascal for nothing in the world. All I ever done was work my life away, having his young-uns and taking care of their young-uns and waiting on him hand and foot.''

Finally I got to my feet. ''Mama,'' I said, ''tell you what. Let me just slip in the bathroom, wash up, and get myself together, then I'll fix us some breakfast.''

''Do you remember,'' she said, still fidgeting with the hundred dollars, ''how to make grits and eggs the way I taught you?''

''If I don't,'' I told her, remembering Little Willie John's record ''All Around the World,'' which had come out the summer she'd taught me to cook a little, the same summer Papa died, ''If I don't remember what you taught me, then grits ain't groceries, eggs ain't poultry, and Mona Lisa was a man.

''Mama,'' I asked at last, now that I had cheered her up, ''what are you doing with that money?''

''That's what I wanted to ask you. I been running out of hiding places. I don't know *what* to do with this.''

She held up the bill, and when I glanced at it again and saw the framed picture, which still lay in her lap, something clicked. Without missing a beat, I said, "The picture, Mama. We can hide the money there. Nobody'll ever know."

Mama gawked first directly at me, and then at the picture of me. "I don't understand, child."

I took the portrait from her and slid the picture out. "There," I said, showing her, "it's as simple as that. You slip the money back here, in between the picture and the backing—*ta-dahhh!* See?"

Her laughter put me at ease but, right in the middle of it, she squinted at me suspiciously. "That's pretty clever, very clever, but . . ."

"But what, Mama?"

"You came up with that awful quick, Syl!"

Mama scooted her wheelchair right up to where she could watch everything I was doing in the kitchen. "You didn't boil enough water for that amount of grits, Syl. And you need to whip up a little sweet milk in your eggs if you want 'em to come out fluffy the way they're supposed to."

"Mama," I said, "while I'm doing this, why don't you find us something on TV to look at while we eat?"

"It's Sunday," she said, "and with you sitting right here, why would I wanna be looking at television?"

"Mama, I want to make this nice breakfast, but I can't. Not while you're staring at me."

I didn't mean to hurt her feelings, but acting's about the only thing I do well under surveillance. In reality, I wondered, did I ever stop acting? There I was bummed out about how stupid I'd been in the first place to be sending Mama cash through the mails. What I should've done was open her an account. At least I was starting to get wise. All the so-called Friday hooks they write into "Live and Let Love" couldn't even come close to matching the kind of left hook real life's got built right into it. And yet, while I stirred and mixed and went in and out of the fridge and Mama's pathologically neat cupboards and drawers, I hummed and whistled and did my best to sound cheerful and busy and up.

In one drawer crammed with kitchen odds and ends, I went rummaging around for a garlic press. That's where I noticed a small pile of balled-up foil packets stuffed into a corner at the rear of the drawer. Thinking I'd do Mama a favor and throw the things away, I plucked one up and opened it. Metamucil. So Mama took a fiber supplement. Quickly I scooped up the rest of the discarded packets, thinking it odd that Mama would have any reason for saving them. No odder maybe than her daughter, my mother, who compulsively hoarded packets of crackers and napkins from restaurants.

But something about these crumpled Metamucil wrappers didn't feel right. I mean, they didn't seem completely empty. Carefully, I ripped one of them apart. And there it was. The little green-and-white ball of paper I found inside had been wadded so tightly I thought it was a set of directions. But when I flattened and smoothed it out on the counter, I got so upset that there was nothing left to do but groan and laugh. I crammed all the tinfoil balls into one pocket, figuring I would deal with this later.

"Son," Mama said as I poured her coffee, "I think that's a wonderful idea. That's just where I'm gonna keep this money—right here in this picture frame. This'll be our secret, okay?" She giggled. "People'll be sitting up here looking at you and Alison and Hardy and them on 'Live and Let Love' and won't even know. You don't think they'd get suspicious, do you?"

"How do you like the eggs?" I asked, almost queasy with boredom by then.

She took her time chewing and said, "First-rate, Sylvester. You get an A-plus on the eggs."

"Mama, I love you," I told her, meaning every word of it. "I think we've got the same guardian angel. Or maybe . . . just *maybe* it might be a guardian devil."

Mama wasn't tickled. "All I know, she said, "is we are both blessed—and the devil ain't got nothing to do with it. Now, tell me, are you gonna fool around on that program and let Hardy steal Alison away from you?"

"Mama, I really don't know."

"What you mean? They got all this worked out in advance, don't they?"

How was I ever going to explain to my grandmother that the producer didn't let us know the long-range story line because she doesn't want it to affect our performance; that she wants us to stay on our toes.

Notes on Contributors

ALAN CHEUSE, the author of two short story collections, three novels, and a memoir, has served as a book commentator for National Public Radio's "All Things Considered" for the past ten years. *The Light Possessed,* a novel, and *The Tennessee Waltz and Other Stories* are his most recent books. A native of New Jersey, he now lives in Washington, D.C., and teaches in the creative writing program at George Mason University in Fairfax, Virginia. He has been the producer/host of "The Sound of Writing" since 1988.

CAROLINE MARSHALL grew up in Minnesota, where she worked as a newspaper reporter, foundation administrator, and poet-in-the-schools before moving to Washington, D.C., where for eight years she served as poet-in-residence at Children's Hospital. She became director of the Syndicated Fiction Project and executive producer of "The Sound of Writing" in 1987. She is the author of *Fugitive Grace,* a collection of poems.

JAMES MICHENER was forty before he decided on writing as a career. By then he had already been an academic, an editor, and a lieutenant commander in the U.S. Navy. It was the latter experience—serving in the Pacific theater during World War II—that prompted him to write *Tales of the South Pacific,* which won the Pulitzer Prize and launched him as a literary force. In the ensuing years he has published thirty-seven more books, most of them monumental best-sellers, virtually all of them invitations to explore unfamiliar cultures. They include *Sayonara, The Bridges at Toko-Ri, Hawaii, Texas,* and *Mexico,* his most recent. Mr. Michener now divides his time between Florida, Texas, and sites for new literary adventures.

JULIA ALVAREZ was born in the Dominican Republic and came to the United States when she was ten years old. The experience of being of two worlds, languages, and ways of making meaning spurred her on to become a writer. Her books include *Homecoming,* a book of poems published in 1984, and *How the Garcia Girls Lost Their Accents,* a novel-in-stories that came out in 1991. She lives in Vermont with her husband, where she teaches at Middlebury College and is at work on a new novel.

RICK BASS was born and raised in Texas, but he has lived and worked in Arkansas, Mississippi, and Utah in the years since. Montana, where he now lives with his wife and daughter, provides much of his work, including *The Watch* (a collection of stories), *The Deer Pasture, Wild to the Heart,* and most recently, *The Ninemile Wolves,* with unforgettable settings. Following the allegiances between friends, family, and landscape, his work often reveals the healing lessons of natural systems.

RICHARD BAUSCH's stories appear regularly in *The Atlantic, Esquire,* and *The New Yorker,* and frequently in *Best American Short Stories* as well. He is the author of five novels, the latest being *Violence,* and two collections of short stories, the most recent of which is *The Fireman's Wife and Other Stories.* His novel *Take Me Back* and his story collection *Spirits* were both nominated for the PEN Faulkner Award for Fiction. In 1993 he received a Lila Wallace-Reader's Digest Award for his body of work. He lives in Virginia and teaches at George Mason University.

ANN BEATTIE is the author of numerous novels and story collections, the most recent of which is *What Was Mine.* She was raised in

Washington, D.C., attended American University, and currently lives in Charlottesville, Virginia.

PINCKNEY BENEDICT lives on his family's dairy farm north of Lewisburg, West Virginia, where he grew up. He came across a number of "nifty" tales about local car accidents while researching junkyards for the title story of his latest collection, *The Wrecking Yard.* His story "Buckeyes" grew out of one he uncovered.

ROBERT OLEN BUTLER served with the U.S. Army in Vietnam as a linguist, an experience that set him off on many of the explorations he has since undertaken in fiction. His stories often give voice to Vietnamese expatriates living in America and have appeared in *The Best American Short Stories* of both 1991 and 1992. Many are collected in *A Good Scent from a Strange Mountain,* his most recent book, for which he won the 1993 Pulitzer Prize for Fiction and which was a nominee for the 1992 PEN/Faulkner Prize. The author of six novels as well, he teaches at McNeese State University in Lake Charles, Louisiana.

JOSEPHINE CARSON lived in Mexico in 1951, where her story "The New Boy," takes place. Depicting a refugee from the Spanish Civil War becoming muse to the artistic growth of a young American painter in a culture alien to both of them, it is the first in a work titled *He Told Me.* Ms. Carson is also the author of three novels, including *Where You Goin', Girl?,* and a nonfiction work about southern black women titled *Silent Voices.* Recently retired from the faculty of Mills College, she lives in San Francisco.

ELENA CASTEDO's fiction and essays examine the intricacies of exterior and interior exile within a clash of cultures. Her novel *Paradise,* which she wrote in English and in Spanish, was nominated for the 1990 National Book Award, for Spain's Cervantes Prize, and was named Book of the Year by Chile's main daily, *El Mercurio,* making it the first novel to be nominated or win major literary awards in both languages. Castedo was born in Barcelona, grew up in Chile, and lives in Cambridge, Massachusetts.

KEN CHOWDER was raised in a small, verdant, and soundless New England town and has subsequently lived for a number of years in various cooperative households in the Far West. His story ''We're in Sally's House'' is based on one of those experiences and is, alas, a true one. The author of three novels, he also writes scripts for documentary films.

SANDRA CISNEROS was born in Chicago, the daughter of a Mexican father and a Mexican-American mother. She has worked as a teacher with high school dropouts, a college recruiter, and a visiting writer in schools across the country. The author of *The House on Mango Street,* which received the American Book Award from the Before Columbus Foundation, *Woman Hollering Creek,* a collection of stories that won both the Lannan and PEN Center West Awards for Fiction, and most recently, *My Wicked Wicked Ways,* she lives in San Antonio, where she is at work on a new novel, *Caramelo.*

DAGOBERTO GILB is a journeyman carpenter who has worked in the trades—at city jobs and side jobs, high rises and custom homes —since 1976. His stories reflect the experiences of working people, and, in particular, those of the too often unacknowledged urban Mexican-American working class. A collection of his short fiction, *The Magic of Blood,* came out in 1993. A native of Los Angeles, he now lives in El Paso, Texas.

RON HANSEN's books include *Desperadoes, The Assassination of Jesse James by the Coward Robert Ford,* and the short story collection *Nebraska,* for which he received an Award in Literature from the American Academy and Institute of Arts and Letters. Hansen directs the creative writing program at the University of California, Santa Cruz, and lives in Palo Alto. His most recent novel is *Mariette in Ecstasy.*

JAMES D. HOUSTON was born in San Francisco and with his wife, Jeanne Wakatsuki Houston, has traveled widely in the regions of the

Pacific. His stories and articles dealing with his cross-cultural experiences on the West Coast and in Hawaii have appeared in the *New York Times, The Michigan Quarterly Review, Manoa,* and elsewhere. He is also the author of five novels and two story collections, most recently *The Men in My Life.* In 1983 he received an American Book Award from the Before Columbus Foundation for his nonfiction work, *Californians: Searching for the Golden State.* He lives in Santa Cruz.

JEANNE WAKATSUKI HOUSTON is the co-author of *Farewell to Manzanar,* a work based on her family's experience in a World War II Japanese internment camp that is now a standard text in schools throughout the United States. She also co-authored the award-winning teleplay that became an NBC World Premiere movie in 1976. "Rock Garden" is one of a number of essays and stories collected in her new book, *Colors,* which explores Asian-American womanhood. A resident of Santa Cruz, she recently returned from Japan, where she was a U.S.–Japan Exchange Fellow.

CLAIRE KEMP, originally from Massachusetts, now lives in Gulfport, Florida, where she works at a beachfront hotel and is involved with Community Care for the Elderly. The small beach towns on Florida's west coast and their unusual mix of inhabitants inspired "Keeping Company." Two of her stories have been published and broadcast via the Syndicated Fiction Project. She is currently at work on a novel.

WILLIAM KITTREDGE, a Westerner both by birth and by inclination, grew up in southeastern Oregon. He is the author of two story collections, *We Are Not in This Together* and *The Van Gogh Field,* and a volume of essays, *Owning It All.* His most recent book, *Hole in the Sky,* is a memoir that describes his experiences as a rancher and the trauma of leaving ranching for another life. He lives in Missoula, Montana, where he teaches at the University of Montana.

BRET LOTT is the author of four novels, most recently *Reed's Beach,* as well as a collection of stories. "The Difference Between

Women and Men'' is the title story of his second collection, which will be published in 1994. He is writer-in-residence at the College of Charleston, South Carolina, and lives with his wife and two children in nearby Mount Pleasant, South Carolina.

CLARENCE MAJOR is the author of seventeen books of fiction and poetry and has, in addition, written or edited five volumes of nonfiction. His most recent novels include *My Amputations,* which won the Western States Book Award; *Such Was the Season,* which was a Literary Guild Selection for 1987; and *Painted Turtle: Woman with Guitar,* named a Notable Book of 1988 by the *New York Times.* A collection of stories, *Fun and Games,* came out in 1990. He lives in Davis, California, where he directs the creative writing program at the University of California and teaches African-American literature.

RICHARD McCANN was raised in Silver Spring, Maryland, and writes often about family life in America's middle-class suburbs. His fiction and poetry have appeared in *The Atlantic, Esquire,* and *Ploughshares,* as well as such anthologies as *Men on Men: Best New Gay Fiction, I Know Some Things: Contemporary Writers on Childhood, Poets for Life: 76 Poets Respond to AIDS,* and *The Penguin Book of Gay Fiction.* He co-directs the creative writing program at the American University in Washington, D.C. His story, ''Fugitive Light, Old Photos,'' is an excerpt of a novel to be published by Pantheon.

MARY MORRIS's vision as a writer has been shaped by the places she has lived or traveled in. Her trips through Latin America and the Soviet Union resulted in the widely admired travel memoirs *Nothing to Declare* and *Wall to Wall: From Beijing to Berlin by Rail,* respectively. She is the author of two collections of stories and three novels too, the most recent being *A Mother's Love.* ''Slice of Life'' evolved out of time spent in Santa Ana, California, in 1987, driving the strips, visiting pizza parlors.

FAYE MOSKOWITZ was born in Detroit, Michigan. The experience of teaching English to seventh- and eighth-graders in Washington,

D.C., for twelve years, however, prompted her writing career. Examining their own lives, her adolescent students taught her to reexamine hers, a process she documented in the personal essays of *And the Bridge Is Love* (1991) and *A Leak in the Heart* (1985) and the stories to be found in *Whoever Finds This, I Love You.* A mother of four and grandmother of two, she now directs the creative writing program at George Washington University.

JESS MOWRY was born in Mississippi, but he was raised in Oakland, California, which provides the setting for much of his work. He attended school there through the eighth grade and began writing in 1988 after buying a used typewriter for ten dollars. His first collection of stories, *Rats in the Trees,* won the Josephine Miles Award in 1990. Since then he has published three novels, the most recent being *Six Out of Seven.*

HELEN NORRIS grew up in rural Alabama, which nourished an imagination hospitable to characters of all sorts, including the feathered hero of her story ''The Year of the Parrot.'' She has published four novels and three collections of stories, the latest being *The Burning Glass.* The title story of her book *The Christmas Wife,* a PEN/Faulkner Award finalist, was produced for television with Jason Robards and Julie Harris. Her stories have garnered four O. Henry Awards and a Pushcart Prize.

LINDA BARRETT OSBORNE was raised in an Italian-American family on Long Island, though she never lived with her grandmothers as did her protagonist in her story ''A Natural Resemblance.'' Her articles and book reviews have appeared in the *New York Times,* the *Washington Post,* the *Detroit News,* and *FAN,* a literary magazine of baseball. She now lives in Washington, D.C., where she produces documentary films.

JAYNE ANNE PHILLIPS lives in Massachusetts, but much of her fiction takes West Virginia, where she was raised, as its setting. She is the author of a novel, *Machine Dreams,* as well as two collections of short stories. Her first, *Black Tickets,* won the Sue Kaufman Prize for First Fiction. Her second, *Fast Lanes,* is her most recent book.

DAVID SHIELDS's stories are collected in *A Handbook for Drowning,* which came out in 1991. Earlier, he completed two novels, *Heroes* (1984) and *Dead Languages* (1989). He lives in Seattle, where he teaches at the University of Washington.

MONA SIMPSON, a former Hodder Fellow at Princeton University, taught for five years in the graduate writing programs of Columbia and New York University, and is currently a Bard Center Fellow at Bard College in upstate New York. Her story "A Portrait of an Acrobat" came from the strange and mimetic experience of becoming a teacher of writing after having been herself an acolyte on the other side of the desk. She is the author of two novels, *Anywhere But Here* and *The Lost Father,* as well as numerous stories. They have appeared in *Granta, The Paris Review, Harper's,* and *Best American Stories.*

GARY SOTO was born and raised in Fresno, California, and presently lives in Berkeley with his wife and daughter. He has written for both adults and children and has produced two films for Spanish-speaking children. His books include *Who Will Know Us?* and *Baseball in April and Other Stories,* both of which were published in 1990. He occasionally teaches at the University of California.

PAUL THEROUX is well known for his adventures in foreign territories and alien cultures. His best-selling books include the nonfiction works *The Great Railway Bazaar* and *Riding the Iron Rooster,* as well as the novel *The Mosquito Coast,* which became a popular movie starring Harrison Ford. Among his many other novels are *Fond and the Indians, The Consul's File, Jungle Lovers,* and most recently *Chicago Loop.* When not traveling, he lives on the coast of Massachusetts.

JAMES THOMAS traveled abroad extensively before he married in 1984, and many of his stories reflect that experience. His story "A

Rule of Travel'' is based on a rule invented by his friend Michael Fogarty, which holds that ''if two single people of the opposite sex meet on an exotic foreign beach, and each has an airline ticket to a different destination the next morning, it is axiomatic that they *will* fall in love.'' He is the co-editor, with Robert Shapard, of the influential *Sudden Fiction* collections, and, with Denise Thomas, of *The Best of the West* series. His own story collection, *Pictures Moving,* came out in 1985. He teaches at Wright State University in Dayton, Ohio.

MARK VINZ has been familiar with both the reality and the mythology of Minnesota winters most of his life—discovering, too, how conducive those frigid days and their attendant rituals can be to indoor sports such as storytelling. His most recent books are *Late Night Calls: Prose Poems and Short Fiction* and *Minnesota Gothic,* a collaboration with the photographer Wayne Gudmundson, which won Milkweed Editions' Seeing Double Award. A native of North Dakota, he now lives in Moorhead, Minnesota, and teaches at Moorhead State University.

GERALD VIZENOR teaches Native American literature at the University of California, Berkeley. He has published more than a dozen works of fiction, poetry, and narrative history, a number of them dealing with his youth in Minnesota. His novel *Griever: An American Monkey King in China* received the American Book Award. *Dead Voices: Natural Agonies in the New World* is his most recent.

SYLVIA WATANABE was born and raised in Hawaii, when almost every neighborhood had its own Prayer Lady, as does the setting of her story ''The Prayer Lady.'' In the linked stories of her first collection, *Talking to the Dead,* she explores how the European and Asian traditions, brought to the islands, have been transformed by their contact with one another and with the indigenous Polynesian culture. The book was a PEN/Faulkner Nominee for Fiction in 1992. She lives in Grand Rapids, where she is at work on a novel.

JOHN EDGAR WIDEMAN grew up in the Homewood section of Pittsburgh, which provides the setting for his trilogy of novels, *Sent for You Yesterday, Hiding Place,* and *Damballah. Philadelphia Fire,* his fictionalized account of the bombing of buildings housing members of a civil rights group, won the PEN/Faulkner Award. After reading the *New York Times* headline that became the title of his story "Newborn Thrown in Trash and Dies," he says he sat down in rage, frustration, and sorrow to speak the unspeakable—what was silenced when a human being was discarded. Wideman was the recipient of a 1993 MacArthur Foundation Award.

ELIZABETH WINTHROP is the author of a novel entitled *In My Mother's House,* which explores the effects of incest on three generations of women. She has published over thirty books for children of all ages and is a founding partner of Editor's Ink, which offers evaluating and editorial services to writers. "The Golden Darters" was selected by Robert Stone as one of *The Best American Short Stories of 1992.* Winthrop lives in New York City.

TOBIAS WOLFF worked for some time as a newspaper reporter and once had the experience of writing an obituary for a man not yet deceased, an experience akin to that of his protagonist in "Mortals." He is the author of a novel, *The Barracks Thief;* two collections of stories, *Back in the World,* and *In the Garden of the North American Martyrs,* which won the PEN/Faulkner Award for Fiction; and most recently a memoir titled *This Boy's Life.* He lives in Syracuse, New York, where he teaches at Syracuse University.

AL YOUNG spent his formative years moving between the rural South of Ocean Springs, Mississippi, where he was born, and the urban Midwest of Detroit, where he grew up. Author of more than a dozen books, including novels, poetry, and essays, he has also written for film and magazines. His most recent books include *Seduction by Light,* a novel, and *Heaven: Collected Poems 1956–1990.* Based in Palo Alto, he now travels widely, giving lectures and readings and performing his work with jazz and blues artists.

Acknowledgments

"Snow" © 1988 by Julia Alvarez. Broadcast Winter 1988. First published in *Warnings: An Anthology on the Nuclear Peril* (Northwest Review Books, 1984). Reprinted in *The Writer's Craft* (Scott, Foresman Co., 1986); *The Village Advocate* (January 3, 1988); the St. Petersburg *Times* (January 16, 1988); *Writing with Confidence: A Modern College Rhetoric* (D. C. Heath & Co., 1989). Reprinted from *How the Garcia Girls Lost Their Accents* (1991) by permission of Susan Bergholz Literary Services, New York.

"The Valley" © 1992 by Rick Bass. Broadcast Fall 1992. First published in *American Short Fiction* (Vol. 2, No. 8, Winter 1992).

"The Knoll" © 1994 by Richard Bausch. Broadcast Winter 1994.

"The Longest Day of the Year," from *What Was Mine* by Ann Beattie. Copyright © 1991 by Ann Beattie. Broadcast Summer 1989. Reprinted by permission of Random House, Inc. and the author.

"Buckeyes" © 1993 by Pinckney Benedict. Broadcast Fall 1993.

"Crickets" © 1989 by Robert Olen Butler. Broadcast Summer 1989. First published in the *Chicago Tribune Magazine* (July 9, 1989) and the Kansas City *Star* (October 1, 1989). From *A Good Scent from a Strange Mountain* by Robert Olen Butler. Copyright ©1992 by Robert Olen Butler. Reprinted by permission of Henry Holt & Company, Inc., and the author.

"The New Boy" © 1989 by Josephine Carson. Broadcast Fall 1989. First published in *American Short Fiction* (Vol. 1, No. 1, Spring 1991). Reprinted by permission of the author.

"The White Bedspread" © 1991 by Elena Castedo. Broadcast Winter 1992. First published in *Iguana Dreams*, Delia Poey and Virgil Suarez, ed. (Harper Perennial, 1992).

''We're in Sally's House'' © 1993 by Ken Chowder. Broadcast Winter 1992. First published in *American Short Fiction* (Vol. 3, No. 10, Summer 1993).

''Divine Providence'' © 1991 by Sandra Cisneros. Broadcast Winter 1992. First published in *New Chicano Writing,* Charles Tatum, ed. (University of Arizona Press, 1992). Reprinted by permission of Susan Bergholz Literary Services, New York.

''Truck'' © 1992 by Dagoberto Gilb. Broadcast Fall 1992. First published in *American Short Fiction* (Vol. 2, No. 7, Fall 1992).

''The Theft'' © 1993 by Ron Hansen. Broadcast Fall 1993. First published in *Witness* (Vol. 7, No. 1, 1993).

''A Family Resemblance'' © 1989 by James Houston. Broadcast Fall 1989. First published in *ZYZZYVA* (Fall 1991). Reprinted by permission of the author.

''Rock Garden'' © 1990 by Jeanne Wakatsuki Houtson. Broadcast summer 1990. Published by permission of the author.

''Keeping Company'' © 1990 by Claire Kemp. Broadcast Fall 1990. First published in the *Chicago Tribune Magazine* (August 26, 1990). Reprinted in *Literature and the Writing Process, 3rd ed.,* Elizabeth McMahan, Susan Day, and Robert Funk, eds. (Macmillan, 1993). Reprinted by permission of the author.

''Looking Glass'' © 1992 by William Kittredge. Broadcast Fall 1992. First published in *American Short Fiction* (Vol 3, No. 11, Fall 1993).

''The Difference Between Women and Men'' © 1991 by Bret Lott. Broadcast Fall 1991.

''Scat'' © 1979 by Clarence Major. Broadcast Fall 1992. First published in *Calling the Wind: Twentieth Century African-American Short Stories* (HarperCollins). Reprinted by permission of Susan Bergholz Literary Services, New York.

''Fugitive Light, Old Photos'' © 1992 by Richard McCann. Broadcast Winter 1992. First published in *American Short Fiction* (Vol. 2, No. 8, Winter 1992). Reprinted by permission of Brandt & Brandt Literary Agents, Inc.

''Slice of Life'' © 1990 by Mary Morris. Broadcast Summer 1990. Published by permission of the author.

''Spring Break'' © 1990 by Faye Moskowitz. Broadcast Fall 1990. Published by permission of the author.

''Animal Rights'' © 1993 by Jess Mowry. Broadcast Fall 1993.

''The Year of the Parrot'' © 1991 by Helen Norris. Broadcast Fall 1991.

''A Natural Resemblance'' © 1988 by Linda Barrett Osborne. Broadcast Summer 1990. First published in the *St. Petersburg Times* (January 30, 1988) and *The Village Avocate* (February 28, 1988). Reprinted by permission of the author.

''Two Girls'' © 1992 by Jayne Anne Phillips. Broadcast Fall 1992. First published in *Witness* (Vol. 6, No. 1, 1992).

''Audrey'' © 1989 by David Shields. Broadcast Summer 1990. First published as a portion of *Dead Languages* (HarperCollins). Reprinted by permission of Donadio and Ashworth, Inc.

"Portrait of an Acrobat" © 1992 by Mona Simpson. Broadcast Winter 1992. First published in *Witness* (Vol 5, No. 1, 1991).

"El Radio" © 1993 by Gary Soto. Broadcast Fall 1993. First printed in *Local News* (1993). Reprinted by permission of Harcourt Brace Jovanovich.

"Uncle Dick" © 1992 by Paul Theroux. Broadcast Winter 1992. Published by permission of the author.

"A Rule of Travel" © 1989 by James Thomas. Broadcast Fall 1989. Published by permission of the author.

"The Icehouse" © 1992 by Mark Vinz. Broadcast Fall 1992.

"Almost Browne" © 1988 by Gerald Vizenor. First published in *Indian Youth of America* (1988). Broadcast Fall 1991. Reprinted from *Landfill Meditation* © 1991 by Gerald Vizenor (Wesleyan University Press) by permission of the University of New England and the author.

"The Prayer Lady" © 1992 by Sylvia Watanabe. Broadcast Fall 1993. First published in *Talking to the Dead* (1992). Reprinted by permission of Doubleday/Anchor Books.

"Newborn Thrown in Trash and Dies," from *Stories* by John Edgar Wideman. Copyright © 1992 by John Edgar Wideman. Broadcast Fall 1992. Reprinted by permission of Pantheon Books, a division of Random House, Inc.

"The Golden Darters" © 1991 by Elizabeth Winthrop. Broadcast Fall 1990. First published in *American Short Fiction* (Vol. 1, No. 4, Winter 1991). Reprinted in *Best American Short Stories 1992* (Houghton Mifflin).

"Mortals © 1990 by Tobias Wolff. Broadcast Fall 1991. Published by permission of the author.

"Millionaires" © 1990 by Al Young. Broadcast Fall 1990. Published by permission of the author.